The Basra Pearls

BY KATE L HART

Victorian Women Voices series
Book 3

Cover by Angel Leya

Jacob Marley
PUBLICATIONS

© 2022 Copyright Katherine Louise Petersen

1-11643164591

Library of Congress Control Number: 2022915984

All rights reserved. No part of this book may be reproduced in any form or by any means without written permission

Books by Kate L. Hart

The Reality Show series

The Reality Show – Book 1

The Whole Package – Book 2

Relevé Book – 3

Voices of Victorian Women series

The Lark – Book 1

High Bred Rose –Book 2

The Basra Pearls –Book 3

Tattered Sik – Book 4

Contents

Chapter One 1

Chapter Two 26

Chapter Three 38

Chapter Four 45

Chapter Five 52

Chapter Six 68

Chapter Seven 79

Chapter Eight 94

Chapter Nine 107

Chapter Ten 113

Chapter Eleven 129

Chapter Twelve 136

Chapter Thirteen 147

Chapter Fourteen 155

Chapter Fifteen 161

Chapter Sixteen 180

Chapter Seventeen 191

Chapter Eighteen 196

Chapter Nineteen 202

Chapter Twenty 209

Chapter Twenty-one 214

Chapter Twenty-two 225

Chapter Twenty-three	236
Chapter Twenty-four	243
Chapter Twenty-five	260
Chapter Twenty-six	270
Chapter Twenty-seven	276
Chapter Twenty-eight	290
Chapter Twenty-nine	298
Chapter Thirty	318
Chapter Thirty-one	335
Chapter Thirty-two	342
Chapter Thirty-three	345
Chapter Thirty-four	354
Chapter Thirty-five	363
Chapter Thirty-six	375
Chapter Thirty-seven	380
Chapter Thirty-eight	387
Chapter Thirty-nine	391
Chapter Forty	398
Chapter Forty-one	406

Chapter One

"Millie! Mr Williams will soon be here," Mother shrilled in a forceful tone. "Clara Bolton has taken ill. This is your chance to charm him."

"I listen to him speak endlessly and he is charmed," I said under my breath, exhausted of her never-ending nag.

"You know what this means to us," she glowered. Her hearing was impeccable when she wished it.

"I will try my best," I said, exasperated. I ducked back into the hydrangea bush where I cut blossoms.

Three months ago, when Mr Titus Williams of the Williams banking family came to stay the summer in our little parish, Mother sacrificed her finest gowns to be refitted into fashionable clothes for me. She bought from the baker the scones Mr Williams liked the most. We would forever eat potatoes and onions because of it. She sacrificed her relationship with her sister – and best friend – when she swore my cousin Frank had not a chance with me and wasn't to come around anymore.

Though Mother would never admit it, shooing away Frank had been the greatest sacrifice. After father died, Frank ensured the transfer of our property into Mother's name and took care she got the income from her little plots of worked land. Father would never have allowed my mother's excess in the pursuit of Mr Williams. Even with Father's kindness still upon our backs, in our pantry, and evident in every comfort of our daily living, Mother did not mince words. She told Frank if her sister would not unite us with her heir, we would find a more advantageous match than a country constable and second son. That is how she sent him off.

Of course, I did not fancy Frank as a lover. He had always been like a big brother to me. Still, I wish I had bravely told him we could never be, instead of my mother's callous brush-off.

I did not ask Mother for any of this sacrifice. She'd done it and now I must win Mr Titus Williams' heart, or we would have a very bleak winter.

"Millie," Mother shouted from the bench where she worked her yarn into a shawl for the cool Autumn air she swore was coming, though it still sweltered in the middle of September.

"Yes, Mother," I said. I tipped myself out of the bush again.

"Get out here this instant!" she scolded. "It is almost his time for calling and I will not have you sit here with twigs in your hair."

Mr Williams often commented that my hair was the color of his coffee after the cream was poured in. Mother took this to heart and for over an hour braided a crown atop my head to make it look as if his coffee were swirling. I could not believe I looked French and sophisticated, as she said. I did not care if her creation snagged.

"What are you doing over there?" she exclaimed again when I did not come right away.

"I've lost my shears and you wished for me to be cutting flowers when he comes," I said pointing to the large bluish-purple balls of petals. "I cannot do it without my shears."

"Walk among the roses. There are a few still in bloom," she snapped. "Just don't lead him down the lane toward the peonies; the bushes there are dreadful." She moved her hand gracefully while she watched.

She suddenly stopped and sat at attention at the sound of his approach. Mr Williams trotted his gig quickly into our sideyard. I stood straight and deserted my shears inside the bush. His eyes looked for me as he drew back on the reins. There was no pleasure, or even… Frank always looked relieved when he saw me. I was fairly certain Mr William's attentions toward me arose simply from boredom.

"Ah here you are," Mother said to him as though it were her he courted. "What a pretty little carriage you've brought. Is it new?"

Mr Williams nodded and his hefty, muscled form jumped from the gig. He looked surly as he hitched his horse to the post. He straightened his cravat, smoothed his sandy hair, and skulked toward us. Frank often told me when someone clenched his jaw and looked about dissatisfied, his agitation had nothing to do with me personally. It was hard to believe as Mr Williams stalked toward me, imposing his sizeable form into our space and frowned at me. He nodded in response to my mother's slathering compliments upon him and his wandering green eyes examined the crumbling bricks on the corner of our house in disgust. His eyes next rested on the scones he enjoyed. Without being invited to, he strode over and took one. Frank would call this disrespect. My mother did not notice, but instead asked, "Would you like some coffee?"

Her eyes glowed as she waited for him to respond. She'd sent off for Ceylon coffee, something Mr Williams swore he could only get in London. He turned abruptly from the scones and motioned to me.

"Come. I wish to take a ride with a pretty lady."

I looked to my mother. Would she allow me to go, unaccompanied, in the open carriage that only held two?

"Just a turn around town I suppose," Mother said, her lips turned up and brown eyes danced as though she was asked to take a jaunt.

He looked away from her.

"Come now, Millie, up you go," she said, her sense of romance overflowing.

I glanced at her, but Mr Williams put a hand at my elbow and boosted me into the gig with little effort. I could not be sure what to do except scramble up. In these little moments of improprieties, I remembered Mr Bolton's letter warning us that Mr Titus Williams was not what he appeared. Mr Williams had countered by saying the letter was sent only to give Miss Clara Bolton his undivided attention. But something was not quite right about the man. Especially at this moment.

Mother swore if he were really bad, Clara's father would not have allowed Mr Williams in their home. Still, I had a foreboding shudder in my stomach as he whipped his horse and we lurched forward. I looked back at Mother, but she waved happily as we left the yard.

"Are you quite all right, Mr Williams?" I asked, feeling a cool breeze play gently across my face.

"Michaelmas approaches and I am meant to choose between you and Miss Bolton," he said as if taunting me.

Mother was not there to bestow her assurances of my charms on him. I said, "I suppose a man does have to consider such things. Will you be glad to go back to school?"

"No, I will miss you exceedingly," he said, but with so little feeling I did not know why he bothered saying it. Despite his declaration, it shocked me when he reached over, took me by the waist, scooting me into him. With no warning, he pushed his lips against mine. I did not know what to do. It hurt a little, and we were on a very public road. When he finally let go of me, my heart pounded, and I wished to cry with fright as I wiped his saliva from my mouth. I tried not to show my repulsion: what if he meant to marry me after all?

When we reached the crossroad into town, he did not turn toward the steeple of the church, but rather he swerved away on a side lane.

"Where are we going?" I asked. Dread bubbled up from my heart.

"Just a quiet drive along a quiet road," he said looking at me. He looked hungry and it frightened me. Instead of kissing me again, he used his whip to pick up the pace of the horse.

"I do not believe this is what Mama had in mind, Sir," I said clutching the side of the carriage and feeling the bile rising up my throat.

"She just wants you to be with me," he said. "That's all your mama cares about."

"I think you take her instructions too liberally," I yelled back as the trees and brush sped by at an alarming rate.

"Nonsense," he said, growing maniacal.

"I think, Sir, it is time for us to turn back. We certainly have gone too far."

"Oh, we are only getting started," he said. The horse veered as he reached out to grab my arm, again pulling me toward him.

"What are you doing?" I cried pushing myself away to the edge of the seat. He glared, dividing his attention between me and the horse.

"You are a smart girl. You'll figure this out," he said smirking. The way he leered at me gave credit to Mr Bolton's declaration that Mr Titus Williams was untrustworthy.

We drove too fast for just under an hour until we came to a lonely wayside inn.

Looking at the inn, I knew I was in trouble. Not just the meddling childish trouble I'd been in before, but real, dangerous trouble. It hit my chest as he slowed. He crawled over the top of me wrapping his strong arms around me, and jumped from the carriage. With a yank, he dragged me down with him.

"What are you doing?" I asked, trying not to cry.

"How else is a man to make a decision?" he said keeping a strong arm on my waist, half carrying, half dragging me toward the door to the inn. He practically kicked the door open so he didn't have to let go of me.

"Ah, is there something I can help you with, Sir?" a man asked, recognizing my capture. He walked toward us, looking at Mr Williams; his eyes didn't meet mine. If I hadn't been taught to read shame so clearly, I would think he didn't notice me hanging there like the man's kill of the day.

"I need the private room we discussed," Mr Williams said, a whole pound transferring to the Inn Keeper's palm.

"Of course, Sir," he said.

"I am tired. Thank you, brother," I said, glaring at Mr Williams. He laughed a little and pushed me toward the stairs. The innkeeper indicated which door was his, and extended a key to Mr Williams as he dragged me. He pulled me up the stairs and through the door. He almost threw me into the room and pulled the door shut behind him. He took out his pocket watch.

"I didn't think it such a long ride," Mr Williams said eyeing his watch and the bed in turn. "I need to… fix a few things. I will have to leave you here for a time."

Trying to placate him, I said, "I can manage the carriage. I will find my own way home." He rolled his eyes and picked up my hand, pulling me toward him. He smelled like scones.

"It will bring me very much joy to know you are here waiting for me."

He kissed my hand, and I felt my stomach roll.

"Maybe I have time for just a little taste," he said putting his hands on my waist and moving them up my ribs with too much familiarity. Instead of repressing my vomit, I wretched, aiming for his chest, encouraging it. I threw my head violently forward so he would step away from me.

"What...?" he took a step back. He reached toward me with the hands that caressed my waist, and I tried forcing more bile up my throat.

"Please!" I cried out. "Just let me go home!"

"Clearly you need time to get used to our arrangement," Mr Williams said backing out of range. I scooted further away from him, but not in the direction of the bed. I continued to wretch.

"If you ever wish to see your mother again, nay, if you wish for another meal, you will gain control over yourself. You must be kind to me so I will be kind enough to offer you my protection."

"Your protection?" I questioned with a tremble in my voice.

"You are mine, and I will have what is mine," he almost shouted. He turned and left the room, slamming the door. I heard the lock turn and couldn't be sure what to do.

A shudder ran through me. I ran to the door, trying to wrench it open, but it would not budge. I was in trouble. The innkeeper took Mr Williams' money. He would not help me. I was alone, in the middle of nowhere. What could I do?

I tried to wedge open the window, but it didn't dislodge. The window was small squares of thick glass, and even if I could break a few of them the wooden frame would keep me from shimmying out… if I were brave enough to jump.

If I cried out, would someone open the door? I listened with my ear at the door for a long time hoping to hear footsteps. No one passed. No one would be traveling this lone road. Especially by carriage when the trains were running. This inn was likely empty until the season began in February.

I felt so weak – such a child. I could not escape. I paced the room knowing he could not be back for at least two hours since we drove for an hour to get here. That was three hours I'd be missing at the very least. My character would be destroyed to be missing such a time.

Would Mother be humble enough to go to Frank if I didn't return? Was Frank even now looking for me? I doubt Mother had that much humility, or perhaps she thought it romantic my being whisked away in this manner.

I remembered the day I found her with a smile on her face, humming, and dancing around the sitting room with a duster. I caught her so off guard that when I made her aware of my presence, she jumped. I asked what she dreamed of. She said it was my wedding.

Frank taught me how to catch a person in a lie; she blushed as her face belied her words. I thought maybe she dreamt up a relationship between herself as a younger woman and Mr Titus Williams. She thought him very handsome. Whatever the fantasy, it was as tangible to her as mist concealing the hills in the distance. Only she did not see how foolish she became climbing the hill to reach the mist. She would not listen when I explained that Mr Williams had no substance to him.

After that day, I stopped trying to argue with her but waited for Mr Williams to break her heart.

Mr Titus Williams was most concerned with beauty and appearance. Clara Bolton, with her reddish-blonde locks and blue eyes, was born with a rare kind of beauty. Not in my wildest imaginings did I believe my mother's efforts to charm Mr Williams would end in me trapped at a lone inn far away from any modicum of help.

My heart rung and my stomach twisted with every minute that passed, throwing me deeper and further into desperation. I couldn't imagine this could be romantic, even to my mother. The near-empty room provided me with nothing I could use to defend myself. I tried several times to lift the washbasin, but I doubted I could get it high enough to even distract Mr Williams, let alone stop him. I had no way out and I could not tolerate being in.

Finally, after excruciating hours, and a million different plans to persuade Mr Williams to let me go, the doorknob rattled. Somehow, a plea that I didn't like him, that I only pretended to for my mother's sake, seemed flimsy and ridiculous. In my heart I knew he did not care. The lock clicked back and the door flung open.

Instead of the large, terrifying form of Titus Williams storming in, a lither man entered with a quick searching step. I shrunk back at his entrance and grabbed the washbasin that I may at least try to throw it at him. Confronted by clear, intelligent blue eyes, eyebrows creased assessing the situation, I let go of the basin and rushed to him sobbing out, "Frank!" I sprang into his protective arms.

"Millie, are you hurt?" he asked, taken back by my sudden warmth.

"Mother sent you to find me?" I asked hopefully, looking up at him.

He did not respond right away. His eyes fell from the relief he first displayed to betrayal and anger. The hope that filled me up at the sight of him now failed me. His disappointment could not be clearer. I took a step away from his condemnation. I wrapped my arms about me. I wanted to weep knowing my eyes weren't likely to remind him of the large brown eyes of a doe ever again. Not after accidentally running away with a mad man. I stepped back from his cold condemnation.

"Your mother sent me to force Mr Titus Williams to marry you," Frank finally answered, but he did not look for the man. His disparaging eyes just watched me.

I knew even if he hated me, Frank would protect me.

"That is why she sent me riding alone with Mr Williams? She is no longer interested in a legitimate connection but hopes for ensnarement. And now she will use you just as Thomas does, forcing her own agenda?"

I dropped my face into my hands and Frank came in close. He put a large warm hand on my neck as I wept. I felt Frank's chest heave against the dark decorative braid Mother spent over an hour forming in my hair. For her to use Frank after she was so cruel to him… she knew he loved me. For her to expect Frank to force another man to marry me proved her cruelty.

"Come now, Millie, we can lose no more time," Frank said shaking me a little.

"What are you going to do?" I asked looking up at him terrified.

"What do you want Millie?"

"I do not want to marry Mr Williams, he is a … there is something not quite right about him. He is cruel and hurtful. … oh, what a mess this is. Now I suppose I have no choice in the matter. I am ruined in reputation if I cannot manage to ensnare him. And say what you will, he does not mean to marry me," I said.

Turning away from Frank I retched again, the bile burning up my throat this time.

"Not so, Millie. Everything can be made right," Frank said kinder.

"How?" I asked turning to him for a miracle.

"Mr Titus Williams is dead," he said.

"What!" I stared at him in complete shock. I could not help the relief that washed over me.

"He was killed earlier in the evening when he broke into the Bolton's home."

"I do not understand," I said.

"From all I can piece together, Titus Williams was challenged to a duel by a soldier who claims Mr Williams killed his love."

"He killed a woman?" I asked, shocked.

"No, not outright. Apparently, Mr Williams ran away with Miss Black and left her at an inn for weeks with nothing. Miss Black starved to death before he could get back to her. Perhaps Mr Williams forgot which inn he left her at," Frank said looking around at the lonely wayside inn.

"Or more likely, she would not put herself under his protection," I said allowing myself to understand what Mr Williams wanted from me since he was dead and could no longer get it.

"Millie, I…" Frank started.

"His price was too dear for her to pay and he would not support her because of it," I said, the tears dripping down my face. I refused to look at him; I felt him condemning me for something I could not control.

"She was very brave then," he said softly.

"Why was he breaking into the Bolton's home?" I asked.

"It is believed he meant to abduct Miss Clara Bolton. He probably meant to bring her here."

"I… what did he leave me here for?" I asked. Frank squinted his eyes at me. Of course, I knew why a mad man would take a young woman to an inn, though as a young woman, I was to pretend not to know.

"I mean, he would have us both here," I said, restating the question.

"I do not know; his actions do not make any sort of pattern. He was a coward. He would not meet the duel. Titus Williams was running away."

"Yes, collecting all of his belongings like I was just a part of his baggage," I said remembering the way he insisted that I was his, and he would accept nothing less.

"I would have seen him hung if he had not been killed."

I looked up surprised. Frank's usually calm blue eyes blazed, and his face turned red. His glare extended to me. Was he accusing me of something? He knew me. He knew my mother. I didn't choose this. I hated all of them. I hated Titus Williams. I hated Frank. I hated every one of them. Especially my mother.

"Can… can you take me home?" I asked trying not to sob again.

"We must go get my mother first," Frank said.

"Excuse me?" I asked.

"We are much closer to my brother's house. My mother must explain that Titus Williams dropped you off with her, because it grew late, and he needed to meet with his father. Remember to keep what you say simple, short. Do not offer more information than necessary."

"You wish for me to lie?" I asked.

"Yes, Millie. Mother must say you came to her, and have been with her all this time. You couldn't face your mother having lost Mr Williams… I don't know… perhaps you begged Mother to advise you. Whatever you can say, Millie, you must say it. If my mother is not with us when we take you home, you came to an inn as an unmarried lady with an unmarried man. If you are with my mother, it was all chaperoned. Do you understand? Mr Clarke and your mother are keeping vigil."

"You are going to…?"

"Fix this. Yes, Millie, for the girl I loved all my life, I am going to fix this last mess. Then I am going to leave you be, and I expect you will finally find your way into Rick Bolton's heart."

"I… I do not mean to…" I did not realize he had guessed the greatest secret of my heart.

He scowled at me.

"Thank you, Frank," I said humbly, knowing nothing I could say would matter.

"Hurry! Put on your bonnet and shawl and come with me," he said. I did as he instructed and followed him. He went to find the innkeeper.

"Ah, I see you found who you were looking for," the innkeeper said to Frank. Turning toward me he asked, "Is your brother not coming back?" eyeing me amused.

"He's dead," I said glowering. The man stopped and looked back at Frank, realizing I was after all protected.

"I was in a hurry before and did not introduce myself," he said. "I am Constable Frank Hadleigh. I suppose you know of me?"

"We don't want trouble here," the innkeeper said, quickly growing penitent, afraid of Frank like many who did not know him personally.

"Yet, I am sure you took trouble's money," Frank snapped.

"They came in and everything was in order... it weren't none of my business. I run a clean ...."

"I need a carriage," Frank said cutting the man off. Frank pulled out a pound and handed it to him. "I also need you to have something of a forgetful evening."

"Yes, Sir," the man said bowing to Frank. Then he nodded to a boy, who ran out into the yard. We followed him. The innkeeper was glad to see us go.

Frank helped me climb into the gig he rented – the very carriage I rode to the inn with Mr Williams. We said nothing as we drove. I tried not to cry but I couldn't help it. It made me sad that Frank knew what I'd done. I thought I could endure almost anyone else knowing, but not Frank.

He hid the carriage in his barn. We walked the mile to his brother's home. He quietly slipped me in a side door. We took the back way up to his mother's private sitting room. He left while I sat and waited.

Finally, my aunt came in. She and my mother were sisters, but Aunt Hadleigh was smaller with light brown hair and eyes like me. Their temperaments were the difference between hot and cold: one sister always insisted on being so close to the fire, the other learned to deal with a chill. Aunt's kind, soft eyes took in my disheveled appearance and cried, "Millie what happened to you?"

"She left her mother's house with Titus Williams hours ago," Frank said.

"What happened?" Aunt asked terrified, helping me take off my bonnet.

"Mr Williams dropped her off here, and she has been here all along mother. She has lost Mr Williams to Miss Clara

Bolton and did not dare tell her mother. She came to you for advice."

Aunt looked hard at Frank, then at me.

"Her mother is keeping vigil with Mr Clarke," Frank hinted.

"I am so glad she sought out my advice, but it is about time we get her home. Her mother must be worried sick."

I blushed deeply as my aunt put her arms around me and let me cry into her shoulder.

"What really happened?" she whispered as if the walls had ears.

"Mother insisted I ride with him," I sobbed, my body convulsing. "He abandoned me at an inn. From all I can gather, he meant to return and ruin me and leave me there so I'd have no other choice but to put myself under his protection. I... I believe I ... I hope I would have let myself starve to death like the other girl." I continued to shake. "I hope I would have been that brave. I did not do anything to compromise myself, I can promise you that."

Aunt held me while I wept. Frank watched me over his mother's shoulder. I looked fiercely at him as though he had imprisoned me instead of rescuing me. I remained silent as they spoke.

"I know my girl, I know," Aunt said, "but we are running out of time. We must get you back before it grows too late. Will the young man collaborate the story?"

"Mr Titus Williams is dead," said Frank. "He was killed breaking into the Bolton's estate. You cannot know that yet. As long as Millie has been here, both of you must be ignorant of his demise...."

"Your brother has been gone all evening. Henrietta is barely returned from her daily sojourn. Neither has seen me; I took my supper in my room. This will work," Aunt said smoothing my hair with pins from her own.

"I… what if … perhaps I could disappear instead," I said quietly. Frank flinched and looked at me, alarmed.

"Perhaps I could go to London where I am unknown. I am not afraid to work in a mill," I said looking from Aunt to Frank.

"No, Millie," Frank said. "Please, no."

"No, you must face your mother," Aunt said taking her handkerchief and dipping it in her cold tea to wipe my face clean.

"Why? It is she who schemed this. She meant for me to entrap him. She thought it all so romantic. I do not want this," I said.

"Face this, darling. Face it," Aunt said. "I promise running away never solved anything."

I glanced at Frank. His opinion always meant more than my own, yet he looked like he could say nothing. I could still read the fear on his face. He no longer condemned me. I suddenly realized he had saved me. Gratitude washed over me.

"Very well, I will pretend if Frank thinks it right," I said.

"You stay here. I'll come around and ring at the front door. Let Thomas and Henrietta discover her," Frank said.

"Yes, that is wise," Aunt said finishing up a few final touches to make me look presentable.

We sat for only a few minutes until the bell rang. A servant came and knocked on the sitting-room door.

"Enter," Aunt called.

"You are wanted in the Drawing Room, and I believe your young charge is wanted as well," the butler said looking at me, relieved.

I followed my aunt down the hall. We entered the pretty drawing-room with a striped sofa and matching armchairs facing the fire. Two extra spoon-backed chairs sat on each side of a window. A secretaire sat against the wall with a small wooden chair under it where Aunt did all her writing.

Frank paced the room, away from Aunt's oldest son, Thomas, and his wife, Henrietta, who sat in front of the fire and must have been fighting. Thomas had his arms crossed annoyed. He looked more like Aunt; he was smaller and shorter than Frank with darker hair and brown eyes instead of Frank's blue. Henrietta's light curls were tight around her indignant heart-shaped face, but her top hair was askew after relieving her curls of the weight of her bonnet. Her light brown eyes glared sideways at me, like she couldn't lower herself to look at me straight on. I stopped in the doorway, feeling extremely unwanted in the tense room.

"What is all the to-do about?" Aunt asked pushing me the rest of the way into the room. "I am trying to entertain."

"Millie, it grows late. Your mother is worried over you," Frank said.

His eyes did not condemn me this time; he still looked alarmed. He could always tell truth from lies, so much so no man in the parish would play cards with him. He knew I had not been bluffing about running away. If I could manage it somehow, I would go.

Thomas and Henrietta, clearly tangled in their own fight, watched our performance with little interest. I had been sneaking over since my mother forbade it, and they knew nothing of my disappearance with Titus Williams.

"Oh dear," Aunt said turning to the butler. "Millie's outer things are in my sitting room and will you get my bonnet please."

The man nodded, happy to comply.

"I mean to accompany you home, Millie. I can only hope my sister is in a forgiving mood."

"I doubt it very much," Thomas said tilting his head and looking at me with pity. It was not hard to look scared as I nodded in agreement.

"Thomas, please have the carriage brought around. We must go back properly," Aunt said. Henrietta turned her pretty face enough to frown at me, but Thomas nodded to a footman.

"The carriage hasn't even been put away, Sir," the man said with a bow. I dipped to Thomas and his lady and walked out of the room to await the carriage. Aunt came up behind me and put a strong arm on my shoulders. I listened as the sounds of the carriage came to the front door. I rarely rode in the beautiful new carriage, and cringed entering it. Frank rode behind on his tired horse.

Four years previous, my father and Uncle died in a carriage accident that made my mother and her sister both widows. My mother never said it out loud, but she blamed my uncle for not maintaining his carriage properly. It wasn't his fault, though. They were descending a steep hill and the horses spooked. An axle broke. The driver was able to jump from his seat before the carriage rolled down the steepest part. Both my uncle and father were gone by the time the driver made it down to help them.

I climbed into the fancy new carriage, the one that replaced the fallen one, wishing my father weren't gone. He would have protected me. As we drove, we agreed upon what needed to be said, preferably before Mr Titus William's death was announced. Yet I quaked when the carriage pulled up the front drive of my mother's house.

"Be brave, dear," Aunt said over my shoulder.

I nodded, watching Frank dismount his horse. He looked disheveled and annoyed. I charged forward, away from him and his disappointment.

The front door of the house was open before my aunt and I even walked up the steps. I did not look up. The shadow of my mother's plump figure kept me from the light.

"What is this?" she demanded.

"I am come home mother," I said. Behind her, the rector held his Bible to his chest, but I could not address him with respect before mother grabbed my arm.

"Where is Mr Williams?"

"How would I know that? He let me off at Aunt's house many hours ago," I said pulling away. I pushed past her into the house and handed my bonnet to our one servant.

"What?" she asked following me.

"It was all in the note Aunt sent; will you force me to say it?"

I stopped. I turned at the sound of a distinct footfall. Rick Bolton, of all people, came out of the drawing-room to the rector. Rick Bolton's eyes were drawn in concern. Was that concern for me? He was not the sort to wear his heart on his sleeve like Frank. He nodded hello to me, his face relieved. It gave me something tangible by way of emotional support. I stammered and could not look away.

"Hello, Sir," I said with a nod of my head.

"Please come sit down," Rick said politely, "I think there has been some mistake."

I glanced at Frank self-consciously. He watched me interact with Rick. I could feel his disapproval when I stepped in close, as Rick lightly touched my arm to guide me into the sitting room.

"Miss Fielding."

I heard the rector coming in behind me.

"Yes, I am sorry. How do you do, Sir," I said finally, bowing to the man.

"You can guess why I am standing vigil with your mother."

"I cannot, Sir," I said looking confused.

"From what I understand Mr Titus Williams has imposed upon you," he said coming in near, forcing Rick to retreat.

"He has, and I demand the young man be made to marry her," Mother said.

"There are a few impediments to that," Rick said now standing closer to my mother.

"I cannot see that he imposed on me," I snapped, fueled by an anger I could not even place. "Mr Williams, at your say so, Mother, took me for a ride in his gig. His purpose was to tell me he had chosen to propose marriage to Miss Clara Bolton. We spoke on the matter for a time, then he realized we had driven too far. He had an appointment to keep... something about his father. We were awfully close to Aunt Hadleigh's home, so I asked him to take me there... I knew how disappointed you would be and I... I feared to tell you."

"I sent you a message, Minnie," Aunt said calmly to her sister.

"I did not receive any message, Rachel," Mother said, agitated. She frowned at her sister, and Aunt gave her a look that must have meant something, for mother flinched.

Aunt continued, "Oh dear. Thomas was out at the time. I will see what went wrong."

"A servant could not be spared from Henrietta's trips about the county, no doubt," Mother snapped.

"It is true. If Henrietta had not been gone, I could have brought her home sooner. Henrietta has just returned from her sister's so we could use the carriage. I explained it all in the note," Aunt said, giving Mother that look again. "Isn't it better to know she was safe with me managing her heartache?"

I turned white and swallowed when Aunt mentioned my disappointment. Certainly, I did not wish for Rick Bolton of all people to hear about my heartache. I could not fathom why my eyes went to Frank first.

Rick was more obtuse than Frank. One saw nothing, the other saw everything. Rick's hair, like shiny copper, was impeccable. Frank's light toffee brown locks fell on his forehead, askew from riding so hard. Frank was four years Rick's senior, yet he looked young next to him. Rick, only slightly shorter than Frank, was very muscular. Frank was strong, but with long muscles that propelled him forward. Rick always kept himself immaculate, but then Frank had become disheveled saving me. He came for me. Rick didn't. I would have died of starvation waiting for Rick Bolton to be my hero. Finally, when Aunt managed to quell Mother's tongue, I set forth to clear my name.

"It is settled, Mother. Mr Williams will marry Clara," I lied quietly, knowing I was not convincing; the rector must see my soul burning from the inside out.

"I cannot see how Miss Bolton deserves Mr Williams' affections. With all he has done to court Millie, I demand you force him to marry her," Mother said, seething. She glared at the rector and then Frank, certain someone should be able to do the deed.

"I am sorry Ma'am," Rick said loudly. "Mr Williams was caught breaking into our house today. He was shot . . . to death."

"What!" Mother cried. She sat hard on the sofa. She looked to Aunt and something of understanding crossed her face.

"Yes, and his desertion of your daughter is a gift," said Rick. "You would not wish him for a son. My father would never consent for the morally bankrupt man to marry Clara if he were still living. Especially considering Mr Williams was already married."

"What?" Mother stammered.

This time I sat down hard.

"His wife is here from Scotland where she resides with their son."

"How dare he... how dare he come here and court my daughter as if …."

"We tried to warn you Ma'am, but it is no matter now since he died."

"He spent every day at your house," she insisted.

"Yes, it was all done in pretense so my father might monitor his interactions with my sister. We meant to get the law involved when we had proof enough of his deeds. It was a delicate situation; wouldn't you say, Frank?"

Rick looked at Frank with such respect. Frank, caught looking like the jealous boy he was, squinted his large almond-shaped, sapphire eyes at Rick and said:

"There was nothing the law could do if he lived unless he actually married Millie and then it would be bigamy. The first marriage would have to be proved, and I doubt anyone, not even the supposed wife, could entrap such a man as Mr Williams," Frank said more to my mother.

"I…" Mother blushed. Having pushed Frank out of our lives she certainly had no one of sense to rely on – she did not consider me in that category. My mother looked so befuddled. She didn't know what to do next. Rick, strong and manly, put my mother in her place.

"It is time to accept that the man is gone. Millie is better off. She will start over," Rick said. Did he... what did he mean by starting over? Would he court me? What had Frank meant, that I may try for Rick at last? Did he know something about Rick that would give me hope? Rick was the very picture of perfection to me.

I glanced up at Rick from where I sat. He would not even look at me. My heart dropped. He knew. He must have known all. He would never consider me now. I was destined to die alone with only a long-ago memory of being kissed by the man I loved. The timid kiss of children Rick and I once shared, and the horrible, smashed mouth of Titus Williams on mine was the most pathetic beginning and end to romance I would ever have.

"Well, it does seem we have found our way out of trouble, doesn't it?" Mother said, seeing her conquest dead, no marriage of fortune could be had. She already snubbed Rick Bolton several times in the pursuit of Titus Williams. Rick stood cold and aloof with his arms crossed to her.

Mother could only retrench. Despite all she said about him being unworthy, she turned to Frank, put a hand on his arm, and for the first time since Mr Williams entered the county, she smiled upon him and said: "Frank, I... we owe you a debt. Thank you so much for bringing Millie. Mr Clarke, I raised the alarm in error. Please forgive me, Sir."

"One cannot be too careful," replied the rector. "You are a good mother to your fatherless girl, and I am only too pleased to stand in his place in these times when one is so desperately needed. I thank the good Father the situation was not so hopeless as it seemed," he said bowing. Then I could not help but think perhaps the rector could not see a person's soul burning when he or she lied to him.

"Thank you, Sir," she said, the telltale blush upon her face as she turned to her sister. "Rachel, you will want to get to the bottom of your servant issues. Your household has not run smoothly since Henrietta came, but I will say no more; you know my opinion of that matter. I am glad no harm has come to my girl."

I could see her disappointment had quickly turned.

"Miss Fielding," Rick said to me.

"Yes," I said, the color on my face rising as I turned to him. He was not warm to me in any way that would indicate affection. Would this be a final goodbye upon his lips? Would he give me something to remember his love over the lonely years to come?

"My Aunt Myra and Clara are hoping you will take tea with them very soon." He bobbed his head.

"Oh," I said confused and let down. Is there no gallant parting he could give me? Some crumb to hold me over in the years I would spend yearning for him?

"I am needed at home," Rick said, turning from me.

I suppose not. He had no hint of disappointment in leaving me or even revulsion in my person. Rather disinterestedly, he seemed to have somewhere else to be. He never noticed me long enough to be disappointed in our parting anymore.

He'd noticed me often enough in our youth. He had kissed me in his orchard when I was fourteen and I swore he'd always have my heart. He was not so committed. He went back to school and I faded into the background of his vision. He took leave of the rector and Frank. He did not notice Mother, who whispered at Aunt. He turned without looking back and left.

The woman in me wanted to rage, but I considered my own heart. I was not disappointed in him, but rather the fickle, flimsy emotion love turned out to be. After I remembered the way Mr Titus Williams claimed me as his, I didn't know if I would ever be tempted to marry, anyway. Marriage felt horrible and scary.

Shortly after, Frank took his mother home and the rector followed. I looked at my mother to see if she would ask what really happened. She said, "You will have to get yourself ready for bed. I need Liza to help me. I am exhausted."

And she left nodding to our servant to follow her. I walked slowly up to my room, starved, but certain mother had consumed the other two scones Mr Williams left. I could not look at the cooked potatoes and onions in the pantry. I'd rather starve. Once alone, I bolted the door and windows not even tempted to crack them to get a breeze like I usually did.

Chapter Two

I stayed home all of Saturday, the result being Sunday at church was a most trying experience. Instead of seeking out one of her sisters, Henrietta spent Saturday in town with Thomas to hear the gossip. She did not hesitate to spread some of her own, claiming to never have seen me in the house until that most convenient moment when I was found. She did not mention she had been out until nearly that moment herself, and would have had no opportunity to see me before.

Henrietta's real purpose was to punish Mother with a scandal. Mother had done the same to her just before her wedding day, telling all she was the abandoning sort, as she had left a man in favor of Thomas. Many sent her pots of blooming Jilting Jessie on her wedding day as a gift. Henrietta now returned the favor to Mother.

As a result, in church, I sat low in my pew trying not to look at the faces of my town shunning me. Only Clara Bolton approached me after the services and, in her innocence, believed I had not run away with Titus Williams. She and her father were the only ones to speak to Mother and me. Clara's aunt Myra may have, but she and Rick went to Titus Williams' funeral, of all things.

The handsome young widower, Mr Evans, who had paid me a few pretty compliments of late, glanced at me a few times. His face was full of judgment, and I could not stop the hot tears from falling as I quickly exited the chapel.

People acted as if I were tricking them. I tried not to judge them, or feel angry. Because, in fact, I was.

But what had I done wrong? I tried to get Mr Williams to take me home. I did not ask him to… had I done something to...? My mind ran round and round the subject until I could not say what happened. If I told everyone in my village exactly what happened, would they shun me still, or the memory of him?

To make matters worse, as we walked home, Mother mourned how I'd gotten poor Mr Williams killed. I tried to tell her what happened, but she did not wish to hear it. Instead, she chose to believe I'd been with Aunt instead of on the edge of something tawdry. She had the audacity to be irritated with me, implying that if I'd encouraged Mr Williams more, he would never have left me to go find Clara. She did not act as if she put me in a terrible situation; that I eked through only by chance, and the young man's death.

I could not imagine the rest of my life, alone with my mother, while she lamented the death of Titus Williams.

Thankfully, Aunt took pity on us and invited us for scriptures and tea so we did not have to be alone together. My mother, with no other choice, accepted. She rarely went to Aunt's house since Thomas offered for Henrietta. For some reason, she thought Thomas ought to have offered for me. It was the same reasoning she used when convinced Mr Williams loved me. It was my fault, for not being pretty enough, or Henrietta's when she was too pretty and mother had to be disappointed. Mother was not kind when she was disappointed.

Father smoothed things over in his way at the time of their marriage, but after he passed, the standoffishness between the current Mrs Hadleigh and mother grew gnarled and thick, something that could never be smoothed. Usually, Henrietta, offended by the insinuation Mother often made that I was better for Thomas, ignored me.

Not this evening. She sat in her striped armchair like a queen reigning over us – Mother, Aunt, and I on the sofa.

"You know Millie, Poppy does not remember hearing the bell the other evening when you were here instead of with the Williams boy," Henrietta said tilting her innocent face at an angle in accusation. Thomas glared at his wife. He thought it best to admonish me via the scriptures. His reading had been vaguely about familial obligations.

Frank and mother both started, but I was quicker, trying to give the truth.

"I used the side door. I suppose there have been a few times I have come without Poppy knowing."

"Yes," Thomas said looking relieved. "In fact, a fortnight ago, I went in to get mother and there was Millie hiding out in her rooms."

"I would suspect Millie has been here more often than yourself in the last few weeks, Henrietta," Mother snapped.

"If Frank had not rung the bell," I said, ignoring Mother, "your maid likely would not have known when I left, though it was rather late for one of my visits."

"Yes…and it would have been a pity as you would not have such an innocent excuse as you do," Henrietta said.

"What exactly are you implying?" Mother asked, glowering. Henrietta said nothing. She had no qualms about calling Aunt a liar, but she rarely confronted Mother head on. Mother had the perfect blend of a nasty tongue and a simpering manner that spread gossip like the plague. She, being an established member of the neighborhood and also a widow with no son, was heard, but could not be retaliated against without the person being labeled cruel and unchristian.

Henrietta had only been here for five years and did nothing to engrain herself into the neighborhood. Instead, she left for one of her many sister's houses most days. That is why people took Mother at her word.

"I am always glad of Millie's company," Aunt said, patting my hand, hoping to soothe the situation.

"Yes," Mother said. "Considering you have no one else. We do not ever see you out and about these days. Thomas, some people wonder if you are keeping your mother captive in this house."

"That is not true," Henrietta answered. "She dined with Frank three times last week."

"And yet due to a conflict with her carriage – the new carriage that her jointure paid for – she refused at least two invitations in the last fortnight."

How Mother could mention the new carriage without flinching astounded me. I glanced at Frank where he sat on a spoon-backed chair pulled up to the fire, and found him watching me. Catching my eye, he raised his eyebrows. I could see he meant to make me his friend again. I smiled for him, forgetting any implication he had made. It was the way of our friendship.

Aunt said nothing. She could have claimed it of no real inconvenience, and defended Henrietta to Mother as she usually did. When she did not, Henrietta snapped:

"She is not in the season of her life to need the carriage."

But perhaps she did need her carriage because Aunt called it for us that evening in a way that was meant to remind Henrietta it was hers. I had to wonder if Henrietta even noticed she called Aunt a liar to all her friends.

Aunt noticed.

As a child, I was told by Father of the great London fire. He said a gust of wind swirled up and the hungry flames could not be stopped and like an enormous red-hot tongue devoured anything in its path. The rumors of my lost virtue spread just as quickly. I wished to hide, but mother forced me out and about. She insisted my head held high was the only way to squelch the rumors. I tried to admit it wasn't entirely falsehood, but mother wouldn't hear it.

Mother tried, like those who uselessly trenched against the London inferno, to douse the unquenchable flames. When we went into town to buy potatoes, mother mentioned we read scriptures on Sunday evenings with Aunt. Mrs Smith, the grocer's wife, laughed a little and said something snidely about it being too late now. I had given her daughter a kitten for their barn just the year before. She did look a little ashamed when I bit my lip and my face turned downcast.

After another frosty church service, mother insisted we go to Thomas' house, and sit in front of Henrietta so they could not accuse me as I'd done nothing wrong. Mother had walked into town every day on purpose to run into, and be exceedingly kind to, Mrs Evans so she would invite us to dine with her well-off widower son. Mrs Evans would not take the hint. She invited Henrietta and Thomas instead, and now, the latter read from the scriptures as a rector would.

Henrietta sat very haughtily as he read from the scriptures about moral impurity. Thomas moved about in the scriptures as if he had written down many he wished to read; indeed, there were tabs all through the New Testament. Since he was no scholar, he must have found a tutor.

When he read about learning to control the passions of the body, I shivered. I could not be sure what he accused me of. I remembered the terrible smashing kiss Mr Williams forced on me, and never wished to be kissed again. I could not force my arms around my body tightly enough.

Frank fidgeted with agitation, glaring at Thomas as he read. Mother saw Frank's agitation. After exhausting every other single man in town, her sudden kindness to Frank was humiliating. I glanced at him, hoping he would wink at me, roll his eyes, anything to indicate we were enduring this misery together.

Startled, I found him openly staring at me, only this time he was very serious. I tried to question him without words, and I could see something was brewing inside him. Instead of clearing my confusion, he turned and interrupting his brother's reading he said:

"I think that is enough for tonight."

Thomas flinched and trailed off. His concentration had been intense, and he still had many tabs to get through.

"I…" Thomas looked at his brother and realized Frank was angry with his sudden scholarly perusal of the Bible.

"Perhaps, Brother, you ought to read in James next week. I especially like the passage about a person bridling his tongue," Frank said, his cold stare as much for Henrietta as Thomas.

Strangely, I found because Frank was mad for me, not at me, I could fold my arms and pretend to be indignant. I was not. I was just relieved. The squeezing in my chest eased. As long as Frank, who knew all, didn't think I did wrong, I could endure the slander.

"Oh, I do not… I will think on it," Thomas said. That is when I realized Thomas did something. He must have entered into the gossip, or something like, because he looked ashamed—not just guilty, but brewing shame. Unable to look at his brother, Thomas glanced hurriedly at his wife for support. She nodded a little in the negative and folded her arms sternly.

"Yes, I heard you could not get enough of a certain subject at dinner the other night," Aunt Rachel said. "I heard Henrietta even gave testimony to her unfounded opinions as if they were true facts." She seethed on my behalf. I did not care what was said if my loyal friends were still willing to defend me.

"I am allowed to say what I like," Henrietta defended.

"Even if those words injure the innocent?" Frank asked.

"I suppose we will have to see what the Bible says about it sometime," Thomas said glancing at his mother. He must not have realized how angry she was.

I leaned forward and glanced as well.

Aunt's usually gentle eyes were burning, and her jaw set. I suppose I should have looked at her, despite the inconvenient distance. Mother sat between us on the sofa as Thomas read. Her rigid posture told me I should not worry about what Thomas and Henrietta thought. I could only guess what Henrietta said was repeated back to Aunt. Frank broke the tense silence and said: "Well, hopefully, you research those verses before I leave."

I sat up and forgot everything else.

"You are leaving?" I asked Frank.

Thomas said: "What can you mean?"

"I am no longer required to play the role of constable," Frank said. Thomas balked. I fought the tears as my heart dropped into my stomach.

"Frank, we have been over this. You cannot leave the parish unprotected. It is your duty to keep peace here. Our family has always done it."

"You are magistrate. It is your job. You can establish anyone to act as parish constable," Frank said, looking at his brother coldly.

"Who can enforce the law like you?" Thomas asked, but he squinted as he realized perhaps embracing his sudden popularity brought on by the gossip his wife spread may have been a misstep.

"I am educated to do more than stay in this little parish farming until I must intimidate anyone who dares cross you," Frank said.

"You do not know your place," Henrietta snapped, "Your brother indulged you going to school—"

"My father sent me to school. I earned a fellowship in the law. I worked my way through, and instead of arguing in the top courts of London, I settle petty disputes. There is little I can accomplish here. Sadly, I cannot cut out the tongues of those who slander." Frank fixed his gaze on his sister-in-law.

Was Frank leaving because he could not stand by and listen to me trodden down? I would rather endure all the slander in the world than have him leave. And yet, I could not open my mouth to beg him to stay. I betrayed him. There was nothing left for him here. He always meant to go back to London after his father died. Finally, Thomas said more quietly than his wife: "As magistrate, it is our family's duty... you must fulfil your role as—"

"You can only appoint me to the position of constable if you stay magistrate. I have heard talk among the other landowners. If you continue to exploit the water, they are going to overthrow you and appoint someone else, anyway."

"They would not dare," Thomas said.

"Mr Bolton is acquainted with the Marquess of Dorset. He could depose you easily enough," Frank said.

"Mr Bolton has a lake to draw from and does not care for petty arguments about water, even over this hot summer. You are my younger brother. It is your duty to uphold the family name. I will not support you going to town."

"I do not need your permission, nor support," Frank said.

"It would break mother's heart, not to mention I know you would never leave Millie," Thomas said glancing at me.

"Millie is … she," Frank grew red, and I wondered how long Thomas used me to keep his brother in line.

"Do not let me hold you back. I know it is your dream. Go, Frank," I said choking over my words, unable to contain my tears.

Frank analyzed me. He looked surprised at my words.

"You do not wish me to leave?" he asked as if that was what I really said.

"I would not hold you back, Frank, not for anything." This time I looked at my hands, hiding my face, so he could not read my despair so easily.

"Take her with you, then," Mother said. My head snapped up.

"What?" Thomas and I said together.

"I will give you her hand."

"Frank is too good for her now," Henrietta snapped with a laugh.

"You know nothing of the matter," Frank said glaring at her. "The way you see people as better and worse is ridiculous. Even if she ran away with Mr Williams to the end of the earth, she would always be my ideal, my Millie. And if you cared for our family and not just about getting revenge for your wedding day, and gaining popularity, you would be ashamed of yourself for destroying her reputation when she did nothing to destroy her actual innocence."

Henrietta started to answer, but Mother was quicker, "Frank, you may marry her if you will set yourself up in London and make her a lady. We all know you have the ability. We have all seen you use this divine gift of yours for sniffing out facts from the clues you find. Promise to make her a lady, and I will give you her."

"Mother," I stammered. My face felt on fire.

"She doesn't wish to," Frank said looking at me, and I thought he only said it to hear me respond.

"I...I don't know what..."

He watched me stammer. I didn't know what I wanted; except he could not leave me. I could endure anything else.

"What does she have after Henrietta has spread such nastiness about her?" Mother said, glowering.

"Millie," Frank said. I forced myself to look back at him. He said, "I think I may be brave enough to go if you come with me."

I watched him. He knew I did not love him in the way he loved me. But to leave this place.

"What will become of you, if I leave, Mother?" I asked her.

"You would really come?" Frank asked, analyzing me.

"If I thought Mother was taken care of," I said smiling at him with a little shrug as I always did when we were about to make mischief. Frank was a much better companion than anyone else.

"I will move in with my sister," Aunt said. "My jointure can be set up in an account for me. I will let the two of you have your privacy," she continued.

Henrietta had often bemoaned living with her husband's mother, but did not mind all of the household expenses coming out of the widow's jointure. Henrietta's pin money would not stretch so far when she had to use it for the household.

"You cannot allow this outrage!" Henrietta caught her breath and cried at her husband. Thomas looked at Frank. I could see Frank's hope as easily as he could. Thomas looked to his mother, but she watched Frank, hoping for him.

"Thomas, if you appointed a police constable. Gave up some of the water rights, I believe you will be able to continue on as magistrate," Frank said, less angry and with something of an imploring in his voice.

"I have heard the grumblings," Thomas admitted. "Perhaps an act of goodwill, like giving up the constabulary, possibly to the Baxter boy who has been helping you on occasion."

"Exactly," Frank said, but I noticed Thomas didn't mention giving up any of his water rights.

Thomas looked to be thinking. Henrietta began working on Aunt.

"How can we be sure you will be well with your sister? I do worry she will… strong-arm you into misusing your funds."

"I would do no such thing," Mother snapped, "though I do think you may want to have a few repairs done. The chimney smokes something horribly."

"See, it is already beginning," Henrietta sighed.

I barely heard their back and forth from this point on. I looked at Frank. He glanced at me uncertainly. How would it be if he were my husband? I could not imagine we would ever have the romantic love I'd always dreamt of when thinking about Rick Bolton. Beyond that silliness, there were very few people I liked better than Frank. Sharing a life of adventure was better than growing older and poorer with no opportunity at occupation and little to live on once my mother passed. I smiled at Frank shrugging a little, hoping he didn't want to kiss me too soon.

"It will be an adventure," he said to me as if he could read minds and no one else could hear.

"I have always wanted to see London," I said.

"Yes," Henrietta said, livid, her red face turning on me. "In London, there will be plenty to take care of Frank's husbandly needs since you cannot be trusted to do so."

My jaw dropped.

"You are no lady," Mother snapped.

"Frank will be very lucky in his choice of helpmate if Millie will have him," Thomas said angrily, his eyes on fire. Aunt looked at him with pity. I couldn't help wondering if his anger was more to do with Henrietta leaving every morning and only returning after tea.

"Will you need a tenant to work your land, Frank?" Thomas asked, but he frowned at his wife. I could not understand anything happening, but Thomas did not look like he would fight Frank's departure.

"I have already thought of that. I know of a few tenant farmers from Dodgson's that could use a bit more land. They have been rotating the crops on young master Dodgson's instructions, and wouldn't mind some more land to work," Frank said.

I listened trying to talk calmly of others' affairs. My future strangely gave me a hope I'd never realized I'd been lacking. I glanced up at Frank and caught his eye. Certain I blushed ridiculously, I looked down at my hands

Chapter Three

The next Sunday the banns were to be posted by the parish clerk. I hoped I would receive congratulations, and be prayed over, at least by my friends in our little parish. Mother made sure the whole village already knew of Frank's proposal and how much he wished to marry me. She did this, I supposed, so no one would openly forbid the banns.

Though I waited, the rector did not do his due diligence, crying it over the pulpit so anyone may object. The rector preached about marriage the whole of the service, as was his tradition on the first and third Sundays when he posted the banns for any of his parishioners.

Despite his severe sermon on marriage, no one remembered us. The Marquess of Dorset was in attendance, and the way he jealously guarded Miss Myra Bolton from the attentions of the young widower, Mr Evans, told a story even more interesting than mine.

Overcome by my own littleness, I felt low. My tears fell before I could catch them. In my state of despondency, I couldn't be sure I should be allowed to marry Frank. Is that why the rector did not declare our intentions?

Rick Bolton was there, returned from the funeral. I tried to force myself not to look at him out of loyalty to Frank. Finally, after the struggle grew silly, I allowed myself one little peek. One last little glimpse of romance – the kind of love epic poems were based on. The sweet longing that once curled my insides into squirming was gone.

I felt nothing. Once, as a child, I was terribly ill. The doctor ran his sharp box across my arm until blood dribbled. Then he suctioned the blood into his cups. I felt so weak after he broke the seal and bound my wound. This heaviness that held my body down felt much like it. Was something inside me bleeding only I couldn't see the gushing wound?

I turned away determined to do my best by Frank, but unsure I could do anything for anyone.

Few people acknowledged me these days. In humiliation, but also relief, I slipped out of the chapel alone while my mother went to see what happened. She would ride home in Aunt's carriage while I walked.

It was a lovely autumn day. Michaelmas was at hand, the goose had been killed, and September was almost at a close. It was that time of year when a cool breeze snuffed out the summer heat. Weeds and grasses glowed gold in the low-lying sun and the rich scent of earth turned under the plow made ready for the next round of oats or wheat. The seeds would lie dormant as the autumn cooled further into frozen winter. When the tender greens sprouted in the spring, I would not be there to see it. Who would remember me then?

As I walked toward our house on the edge of town, I heard my name called. Frank came running toward me. He moved with ease, his long legs carried him quickly and his hair fell to his forehead. I like the way he moved with swift purpose. He was not clunky or bulky like the giant figure in my nightmares. I could do worse than Frank as husband.

"Hello, Frank. You look concerned," I said, turning to walk with him.

"A little chastened though I can't say what I've done wrong. Mr Clarke has an extremely strict idea of marriage."

"You do not suppose he did not wish to read the banns—"

"He forgot," Frank said. "Something else was going on that had nothing to do with us. I think the Marquess of

Dorset being in attendance distracted him. He asked me to apologize to you. He will read them out next week."

"You do not think he gives heed to Henrietta's testimony against me?" I asked.

"No, no. From all I have heard he has defended you, being there himself when you came home with Mother. I truly believe he was preoccupied. When I approached him just now, he was very embarrassed he forgot," he said.

"Well, nothing can be done now," I said knowing mother would be livid, but what could one do about an honest mistake?

"Can I see you home?" Frank asked, taking my hand.

"Please," I said taking a deep breath. He grinned and brought my hand to his lips. Out of habit, I pulled my hand away. I elbowed him, ducking my head embarrassed, as he knew I would. It was his favorite game to play. It started as the innocent fun of a sixteen-year-old boy teasing his ten-year-old cousin when he came home for breaks from school.

I do not know when his kiss changed from innocent affection to adoration. I noticed the first time after he returned home from school for good. I turned seventeen and he was a man of twenty-two. Our father's death brought him home, and he paused his education to become a barrister to be his older brother's parish constable.

At the time I had already given my heart to Rick Bolton, but it was Frank who sat and consoled me over my father's death. It was Frank who took up the legal proceedings of our land which we could not, securing my mother the income my father spent his life building up.

I wish I had not fallen so deeply in love with Rick Bolton. It left no room for Frank. I thought myself so romantic at the time, but now it felt a little more pathetic than heroic to be in love with someone I could never have.

Frank's warmth brought me comfort. I reached out and took his hand again. We always walked this way for as long as I could remember. Other women expected a man to offer her his arm, but Frank always gave me his hand.

"On our adventure, may I call you Mrs Frank Hadleigh?" he asked his grin lopsided and his eyes teasing me.

"If I may call you Mr Millie Fielding," I said realizing many people would refer to me as Mrs Frank Hadleigh in the future. I was not ashamed of the name. I'd never tell Frank, but I was proud of him and how he could see the solutions to problems like a puzzle. He could see who was lying simply by the way they told their stories, or how they held themselves. I often joked his eyesight was better than the rest of ours. I couldn't be sure how he did it, but he couldn't undo it. He had to see or it consumed him.

His grandfather had the gift of observation just as Frank did. Frank went to Cambridge at fifteen and quickly progressed in his degree. By twenty he had not only completed his bachelor's degree but had shown such promise in the law he was admitted at Middle Temple, an Inn of Court. He spent another two years studying to become a barrister. Before he could apprentice, his father died.

"Frank, are you very excited to go back to London?" I asked.

"I am excited to take you to London with me. There is so much to see and do," he said. "You will be of so much more use in London."

"Of use?" I asked, confused.

"I have a friend who's written me several times for advice. He's a barrister, and he needs help with a case. He has sent me a train ticket to come to London. I will assist him, and I hope you will be my assistant."

I grinned. Frank knew I wanted to be of use. My father always gave me things to do, and since his death, I lacked purpose. Mother thought useless and ladylike were the same thing and it vexed me to no end.

"Thank you," I said.

"Don't thank me yet. My friend, Mr Jasper Shaw, needs help with a high-profile case. He wants me in an investigative position just now. The solicitor isn't able to do much. Everyone is too afraid of a titled lady involved. If I do well for him and get onto the Middle Temple grounds for a few days, I may renew important friendships that will lead to a pupillage."

"Can Mr Shaw give you a pupillage?" I asked.

"He is not long in the profession, and I do not think it wise. He is flighty. He only became a barrister because his family insisted.... It is a way they can funnel money to him. I know the law better than he. You will understand when you meet him. I have many contacts and seeing them face to face, I will find a pupillage, I am sure."

"I have no doubt. It will be an adventure," I said happily.

"It's another two or three years before I can start really making money, but I will take care of you, Millie."

"You always have, Frank, and I'll be worth it to you. I'll earn my keep… I swear I will," I said earnestly, worried he might regret me.

"Millie," he said squinting down at me, "I love your company. We will be happy together if nothing else."

I saw him grin and I squinted up at him.

"You have a secret," I said.

"Nothing dark, just fun," he said and squeezed my hand.

"Very well," I said feeling better, not so heavy. I wasn't a burden to Frank. I would not die without ever experiencing life after all. I was almost happy until I heard a scuffling sound behind us. I turned to see Mrs Thorne, a middle-aged woman who usually rode home from church in a wagon, which would indicate she followed us on purpose.

Leader of the local chapter of the lady's charitable society, she scurried toward us, arms swinging to catch us; this was not going to be pleasant. Frank saw it too because he curled my hand upward until he held me into his side as support. Instead of pulling away, I held tighter.

"I saw the clerk posted the banns," said Mrs Thorne. "Will you allow Frank to clean up your mess, Millie?"

"What mess?" Frank asked when I would not answer. Should I be allowed to marry Frank?

"There is a virtuous woman who deserves him more than you."

"I prefer Millie," Frank said seeing me struggle with her truths.

"Yes, we all know, which is why everyone has agreed not to forbid the banns. I suppose this is the only way Minnie would give Millie to you after all. But Millie, you ought to know you do not deserve him."

Knowing she did not require a response to her blatant accusations I said nothing. The only other choice was to lie. I thought it best not to defend myself.

"Come, Millie, let me walk you home. Excuse us, ma'am," Frank said tugging on my cradled arm.

"I do require more of an arm to my door than she," Mrs Thorne snapped. "Considering I walked on purpose to give you such good news."

"But..." Frank started, and I nudged him. He looked at me, and I implored him not to make more trouble.

"Very well Mrs Thorne. You may have my other arm," he said.

"There's a good boy," she said clutching his arm, "you deserve so much more than a patched-up arrangement, but I suppose you are a fool to love."

I glanced up at Frank to see him wink at me before he said, "Well that I am, Ma'am. That I am."

Mrs Throne proceeded to tell him about her husband when they were young lovers. He swore he'd have her no matter what. She'd guarded her virtue as expected, and so they had no impediment and no fear of the banns. It isn't fair for one person to dally about, while the other is faithful. And so, she chastised me.

Frank defended me against her, squeezing my hand when she grew harshest, which made me more certain she was right. I'd never appreciated Frank's love to deserve it. Oh, how I hated my stubborn heart for loving Rick Bolton.

Chapter Four

The hot flame of my scandal burned out when the Marquess of Dorset whisked Miss Myra Bolton away, causing a fresh to-do for everyone to speak of. Our neighbors began acknowledging us when they saw Frank and I walk about. With him at my side, and his devotion to me apparent, even the harshest critics gestured in resignation.

Aunt never wavered in her acceptance of me as a daughter. Her popularity among the neighbors brought an invitation to a night of cards, with only the ladies, of course.

Mrs Thorne set up her tables in her dining room. It was a good-sized room that held a hodge-podge of tables and chairs. The hostess played with her back to the wall at a head table so she might see the other three tables with her eagle eyes. Two of the other tables were for cards, and the third was for refreshments.

I always played at the table with the younger girls. It was expected I would teach them the rules and when to bet or let the hand go. When I arrived, I paused, wondering if I was allowed to be company to young girls. It was only a slight head nod from Mrs Thorne toward their table that told me the tides had turned in my favor.

Henrietta arrived early and found a seat among Mrs Thorne and the prominent ladies of the neighborhood.

"I have heard, when Millie marries Frank," Mrs Thorne said, ignoring Henrietta and focusing on Aunt, "you mean to remove to Minnie's home."

"Yes," Aunt said placing a card down.

"I suppose it is so you will not be called a liar in your own home," Mrs Thorne said but looked at Henrietta.

"I mean to keep my sister company and leave the young ones to themselves," Aunt said quietly.

Henrietta flustered as she realized her time on the throne passed without building any solid foundation in the neighborhood.

Mother, who hovered around the refreshment table, waited to the end of the round, and then said loudly to Henrietta, "I believe you are in my seat."

She stood and nodded, moving to the refreshment table. I suspected by the morrow Henrietta would ask to borrow the carriage so she might run off to her sister's. I was sick to death of it all.

"Please excuse me. I need to take a turn about the room," I said bowing politely to the young women I played with. They all bowed back, and I heard one say, "I am sorry I ever gave ear to hear anything against her."

I walked over to Henrietta. I felt it my duty to stop the feud between her and Mother before I left for London. It is what Father would have done. I approached the refreshment table and smiled at her. I asked: "Did not one of your sisters call you Etta?"

Henrietta looked at me with a squint. She glanced at Mother – her curls all set around her smug face sitting in her throne at the table – and I could see she was trying to decide if I was going to trick her.

"Yes, they all do," she said.

"May I then, since we will be sisters soon?" I asked. I saw Mother flinch, and Aunt looked up at me in surprise indicating they both heard. Most of the room went quiet to hear what I would say to her. Most thought I would lash out, no doubt.

"I ... I suppose you may," she said.

"And you must call me Millie," I said.

"That is your name, is it not," she said looking at me from the side, not with the glare she usually used, but with curiosity.

"Well, my mother is Willamina, but she has always been called Minnie. My papa loved her so much that he insisted I also be Willamina, but I went by Millie to distinguish us."

"I did not know that," she said, glancing at Mother.

"Yes, my husband doted on me," Mother said fondly.

"More than doted; yours was a love story, Minnie," said a lady from her table.

"I remember when old Silas walked all the way to Dorchester to get you ... was it candy or something?" asked a woman from the other table over.

"It was a box of brandy balls," Mother said wistfully. I saw her look and realized she had been very lonely since my father died.

"Frank said that Thomas went all the way to London to get you a fine lace veil for your wedding," I said to Henrietta. She blushed to glance at me again, unsure if I was about to strike.

"Yes, he did," she said glancing from me to Mother.

"I have always noticed how much Thomas adores you," I said.

"I... I..." Henrietta did not know what to say.

Aunt, seeing I was trying to endear Henrietta to the neighborhood, or at the very least call a truce between her and Mother, smiled and said, "He came home from the ball over in Sherborne where he met you and I swear he was flying a little."

Henrietta blushed, and the group agreed Thomas had been smitten. Mother, not at all pleased with her friends showing Henrietta warmth, wound up to strike her down. She took such a deep inhale that the latter cringed.

"Mother," I interrupted, "you mentioned since Henrietta, and I will soon be sisters we should plan the wedding breakfast together. Perhaps this warm air invites us to enjoy a picnic since the harvest has been so good."

Mother looked at me and squinted. She could see I meant to embrace Henrietta. She glanced at Aunt, who said, "What a wonderful idea Minnie. I would love to assist in any way I can."

"My sister has the recipe for a lovely pastry that wears well in the outdoors," Henrietta said tentatively.

"Perfect," I said. Others in the room started to say what they could contribute and before long it appeared the whole parish would be coming, though a week before I could have sworn it wouldn't be so. Mrs Clarke, the rector's wife, offered the churchyard as a venue.

Henrietta took a main role in planning, raving over things that must be served. I smiled as she was embraced by Mrs Clarke. The rector's wife only came to our neighborhood seven years previous. She was always consigned to the lower table. She sat with Henrietta and gave many ideas about what should be served. They put their heads together and arranged every detail by the end of the evening.

Mrs Thorne even smiled at me a few times as I worked with the younger girls. I could only suppose she struggled being the leader of the charitable society while her oldest friends were at odds with the magistrate's wife. It must be a hard place for her to navigate socially. In one night, Henrietta forgot all about the seat she felt she ought to play at, and Mother saw the value of one with such a head for entertaining and stayed civil.

I felt better, satisfied about leaving. I felt close to my father and missed him a little less. I did not mind climbing into the carriage so much. Mrs Clarke, who lived closer to Henrietta, offered to take her home in her carriage as they were not finished speaking. It was just the three of us that loaded in at the end of a rather pleasant evening.

"That was very kind of you to help Henrietta," Aunt said.

"Almost too kind, considering how she used you so ill," Mother said.

"I do not know about that, but she will be my sister soon, and I do mean to make peace with her," I insisted to my mother in the way I had seen Aunt do.

"Well, I suppose we must take the higher road," Mother agreed. I did not bother to explain to her that after growing so dirty on the lower road for five years, there was little point in pretending we had always been on the high road. It was one of those little mist-filled images Mother often painted of herself whilst ignoring the solid hill of past behaviors. She would get angry if I pointed it out to her, so I did not.

"I do not think you will ever be anything to her when compared to her real sisters," Mother said.

"I would like to try; I am rather envious of you and Aunt being such good friends. I cannot see why Henrietta and I may not be something to each other."

Aunt grinned at me. Mother shrugged.

My wedding to Frank was a quiet affair. We went to the church Monday morning, four weeks after the banns were posted. It was then the middle of October. Mother insisted I wear the pretty white linen dress decorated in needlepoint pink flowers. She conveniently forgot she ordered it to impress Mr Williams. I covered it in a shawl because of the chill.

I meant to kiss Frank after he became my husband. He did not give me a chance. He leaned in quickly to peck my cheek. I felt let down. He'd given the same to me many times before, and I thought he would… I thought perhaps on our wedding day he would give me a little more affection.

Frank put a beautiful gold ring with little flowers etched into it on my finger and I forgot my disappointment.

"It is beautiful Frank, thank you," I cooed.

Frank smiled at me shyly, and he looked so sweet that I grinned.

The wedding breakfast, moved inside the town hall because it had grown chilly, was a lovely affair. Henrietta brought new recipes that were an instant hit. Mrs Thorne complimented her, and Mother tried to be kind. I knew I had done right by my father and I could leave home in peace.

After breakfast, we only lingered at the carriage door for a moment. My farewell to my mother was discouraging. She patted me with little affection, and could not hide the relief in her eyes at my leaving. She was not sorry to be done with me and even gave me a little push to the carriage after she murmured farewell.

She often looked upon me with disappointment since Mr Williams died, but I thought perhaps she could find some affection for the end of my childhood. I climbed into the carriage first, and by the time Frank climbed in, Mother was already speaking to Aunt of an engagement they had later in the week.

"What is the matter?" Frank asked. I nodded and sat back angry and hurt.

"I am ready for our next adventure," I said resting up against him, hoping to feel just a little warmth. Though I never deserved it, he always gave it. I leaned my head against him, realizing he was my husband and I would always have him. This thought brought me joy.

Chapter Five

We disembarked the train at Nine Elms Station in London. People climbed all over me, like a steady stream of ants on a hill, brushing and bumping, rushed and busy; they knew where to go and what to do. While chaos erupted all around me it took everything in me not to cling to Frank like a child.

We hired a wagon from an opportune fellow. The sort who waited with his outrageous fees for country bumpkins. It turned out especially discouraging considering our inn was around the corner from the station.

The gritty brick building we stayed in never grew quiet. I sat for a time in our sparse room and listened to the noise of the train and the people I could hear but not see.

"I am sorry this isn't the most desirable situation," Frank said. "I hope it will not be long until we can be established in an apartment in Middle Temple. I will see to Jasper as quickly as possible. He does not write concisely but needs help with a case. All I could discern is we must stop an indictment before it goes to Grand Jury in one week. After I finish with that, I will find a suitable learned master for a pupillage."

"It is all well, Frank," I said looking around the small room, trying to keep up my spirits. A mirror over a table with a few toiletries sat on the outside wall nearest the window. Next to it in the corner, our trunks had been set by a changing screen, indicating a family, just coming to the city, would likely have one room for all of them. Crammed against the inside far wall was a small metal bed. I could not be certain how that would work but knew it must.

"I will go find us something to eat if you would like to get settled," Frank said, embarrassed. He glanced at the bed several times, and I could see he had noticed its small size. We had been traveling all day and were both exhausted. I just wanted to go to sleep. While Frank was out, I took the pins out of my hair and let it hang. I changed into my white nightgown. I watched the ring on my finger for a while. I hadn't known if Frank would get me one, but I loved it, so dainty and lovely.

Frank came in with supper and stopped. He stared at me.

"I think... I think we will have to be used to each other in our night things eventually," I said.

"No...yes... I mean, of course," he said, and he looked adorable. His whole face blushed and it made me smile.

"It is late, but I found a vendor selling these meat pies. If this will do for tonight, I will get you a big breakfast," he said looking at me, then looking away.

I nodded and took the pie with low expectations.

"This good," I said after a few bites.

"Is it?" he asked. I'd eaten nothing but potatoes and onions all summer to fund Mother's quest. The meat pie was very superior to beans. Frank took a bite and looked at me. He took another bite, and I could see he did not care for the pie at all. He only ate half of his and offered me the rest. I ate it but almost fell asleep by the time I came to the end.

"Millie, why don't you take the bed, and I'll make myself a little nest on the floor," Frank said in deference as he looked over the scant bedding.

"No, you must not sleep on the floor. I checked the bed for bugs while you were gone, and found none, but I have seen a few rats. I could not sleep listening to them scurry over you," I said.

Frank grimaced but conceded. I lay down and he went behind the screen to change into his nightshirt. My eyes felt too heavy to keep open, so I curled up on one side of the bed and rested. I barely registered Frank shift in beside me, but I readjusted to feel his warmth as the night had grown very chilly and there was no fire in the room.

I felt his body relax into my back and I fell asleep immediately.

The next morning, I woke to find Frank leaning upon his arm watching me.

"Did you not sleep well?" I asked sitting up.

"I…I don't know," he said.

"How can you not know?" I asked.

"It was a very good night," he said but didn't add the word sleep. I laughed unsure what he meant and got up.

"What will today hold?" I asked trying not to look at his long bare legs as he pulled on his trousers.

"Well, I think first thing we should go see Jasper. I would like you to stay with me. I… I know you will think I am overprotective, but the London streets are not like walking alone in the country."

"Very well, Frank," I said moving behind the screen to dress. I wrapped my corset around me, wishing Mother hadn't done the laces so tightly, as I could barely hook the eyes in. I did not want to ask Frank for help like a child.

The top of my traveling dress was easy enough to manage; it draped into a V-shape; the hard part was mostly the hooks I could not reach on the skirt. I twisted like a dog after its tail, but in the end, I could not reach the hooks in the back.

"Frank," I said peeking around the screen.

"Yes, Millie," he said.

"I...I can't hook the back. Would you mind?" I asked.

He came toward me, and the grin on his face told me he would like very much to help me. Humiliation disappeared into amusement at his delight.

"Here?" he asked bending over me. I pulled my hair over my shoulder so he could see.

"Yes," I said, pointing and turning.

"Just relax, Millie. I can do it," he said.

I stood still and he worked quickly.

"Your hair smells very good," he said.

"Mother washed and perfumed it yesterday before the wedding," I said but regretted it. I sounded like a child, letting my mother wash my hair for me. Frank didn't notice but took another deep inhale.

"Until I can get you a maid, I don't mind helping," he said leaning over my shoulder and grinning.

"Thank you, Frank. That is very kind," I said. His smile grew bigger. He looked sincerely happy in a way I'd never seen before.

When we left the room Frank turned the key in the lock and hesitated to be sure the door was firm. Aside from the satchel he always carried across his body, everything we owned was in that little room. We entered the large main dining room and it smelled like fried pork, and something rotten. Frank ordered a large breakfast, and he was famished. He ate more than his share and I gave him off my plate as I was accustomed to going with less and the rotten smell turned my stomach.

After breakfast, we walked a few streets. The city stunk, like rotting, wet mold. Thankfully, it was chilly, and the air did not permeate strongly but it still stunk. I could not imagine what the stench would be in the heat of the summer, not to mention the flies.

    We went to another inn and waited, then loaded onto the largest horse-drawn carriage I'd ever seen. It resembled the closed train car we rode to London, except two huge draft horses pulled it. The body of the cart held seven people sitting on benches with their backs to the sides of the carriage, and there was still ample space on a bench for us. The omnibus pulled away with a lurch and we were on our way.

    We pulled through Lambert to the Waterloo Bridge. Once across, we drove into the bustle of the city. We were let off at the outer edge of the city. I could not believe the enormity of the buildings and people in London. People rushed past each other without a greeting or even acknowledging each other.

    We walked between huge pillars to a large brick gatehouse. We were admitted and entered a little lane that seemed to be cut away from the extreme height of the buildings. The tight path made me feel as if the buildings could shift and come down on me at any time.

    Relief swept over me as I stepped into a lovely, and compared to the bustle of the city, quiet courtyard surrounded by many large rows of buildings. The courtyard was well cared for. Frank took me toward a central area with large, distinguished trees adorned with fiery yellow-orange leaves preparing to float to the ground. The gardens in the distance had a blockade of autumn trees, that I supposed must look out over the river Thames. It was the loveliest sight I'd seen since entering London.

    "I remember walking through this courtyard when I was very first admitted to Middle Temple," Frank said, pointing our direction westward. "I had just finished at Cambridge. I thought I would go home and be a parish constable for the rest of my life. In my last year, I had a professor, who was also a solicitor, drawing up a will. There was a very important family fighting over a deceased man's property. My professor asked us if legally a will is the same as a trust or rather a fee tail, and which superseded, and what must be spelled out in order for a person to inherit."

"Are they not all the same?" I asked.

"No, a trust, in its very name, implies that another, trusted third party, holds the wealth and property in an estate, and use of the estate is granted to the heir for their lifetime only. They cannot give it away, nor can any other have access to the estate except the owner. They ought not be called owners but rather life tenants because they only get their share from the estate during their lifetime. In that way, the property and wealth continue to trickle down the line."

"Like the Dodgson's property," I pointed out. "Even though the wealth is gone, the land cannot be sold to help the family because it is entailed."

"Yes, exactly, but then a will deals with the unentailed wealth a person creates during their own life and may be given to whomever they choose. It must be what they personally own outside the estate – what they have bought or earned during their lifetime," Frank said.

"Like Bolton Lodge was bought by Baron Bolton to go fishing, and he gave it to his second son upon his death because it was not entailed," I said.

"Yes, exactly," Frank said, "In the case we studied, there was a blurred line between the two as the man's only heir died before himself."

"What happened?" I asked.

"Eventually the family would end up at Chancery Court. It focuses only on estate cases. It is vastly different from criminal courts. I researched and wrote an essay that was read aloud to many important people, judges and lawmakers, in lectures. Some of the guidelines I put forth were used in the Wills Act three years ago, though I was not credited," he said.

"Frank, that is something to be very proud of," I said.

"Thank you, Millie. I was honored by the Chancellor His Grace Duke of Wellington. He read the essay and wrote a letter on my behalf to recommend me to the senior bencher here at Middle Temple stating he would sponsor my education. One day I was going to be constable, the next I would become a barrister."

"You never told me that circumstance," I said.

"I thought everyone knew ... my father was immensely proud. He paid for my membership and made a to-do about me getting recommended."

"I remember that, but did not know you had been recommended by the chancellor himself."

"Yes," Frank said. He looked a little embarrassed.

"You often mentioned how content you were with your education. You were happy here, were you not?"

"I was. I studied hard. I came to the table with many of the Master Benchers in Middle Temple to discuss the law and England. Two Learned Masters, whom I very much respected, often went back and forth saying I could do my pupillage with them. It was very flattering."

"But then your father died," I said, realizing for the first time all he gave up by coming home.

"Yes," he said, "I went home thinking I would come back much sooner, but Thomas had such a time taking over as magistrate. It has been four years, and one of the learned masters has been made a member of the Queen's Counsel. The other is an MP."

"Does that mean they cannot mentor you?" I asked.

"It is not likely. Thankfully, membership to the Inns of Court is for a lifetime. After I help Jasper, I will find a master."

"And you can help him – he who is already a barrister," I said.

"I will try for a few days, but I will also go to a few of the formal dinners meant for the students to debate with those who have already gone to the bar. I hope to renew old acquaintances and find someone who can help me. There is no fast rule for how one gets a pupillage. It is based as much on merit as bribery. I think now that I am back on the temple grounds, I will be able to find a few old friends and eventually pick up where I left off," Frank said.

"You have studied hard, even these last four years. Everything will work out as it should," I said. Frank smiled and pulled me toward a curious stone structure that spouted water into the air, like a whale with a blowhole would.

"That is the fountain. I sit near it at times to think. If I close my eyes the sound reminds me of the creek behind my brother's house."

"It is lovely," I said.

"That is the Hall where the suppers are held," he said pointing to a large gothic building with such amorous stained-glass windows it could have been a cathedral.

We walked away from the gardens down a long lane of buildings. Finally, near the end of the row, Frank turned into a brick building that looked the same as all the others.

We entered an arched doorway. The building seemed all passageways. We went to the end of the passageway and Frank knocked on a door. A young man who acted as clerk, probably about my age, welcomed us. He asked if he could know our legal matter that he might advise us whether it was right for his magistrate.

"I am Mr Frank Hadleigh. I am here to see Mr Jasper Shaw," he said authoritatively.

"Yes, Sir," the clerk said and walked us through his workspace and into a moderately sized study called chambers. I could have guessed the young man to be in trouble. The desk full of paperwork, the wall full of empty bookshelves, and large armchairs near the desk stacked high with books indicated chaos.

Before the clerk could announce us, another man came bursting through a side door. This young man looked Frank's six and twenty years. Though I didn't know much about fashion, I could see he was well put together. He was handsome with a strong jawline, gingerbread-colored curls that reached the tops of his ears, and eyes to match. If my heart were not fully occupied, I might have felt an attraction to him.

"Frank, you are here, and just in time. I ..." he stopped, and the two men bowed to each other. Jasper then looked at his clerk, "Get us some tea, please."

"Very good, Sir," he said nodding to me. His nod drew the barrister's eye. His interest diverted from Frank to me as he took a few steps in my direction. Frank also saw and said:

"Jasper, this is my wife, Mrs Millie ... ur Hadleigh."

I dipped politely.

"It is very nice to meet you, Sir," I said.

"No, the pleasure is all mine," Jasper said bowing over my hand. He was not shy and looked at me with appreciation.

"Please. Sit down," he said but turned to find nowhere to sit except a small side table with two small chairs.

"This is a very decent situation your father has gotten you into," Frank said looking around.

"My eldest brother is taking over many of my father's responsibilities. If I could get it into some kind of order. . . I swear Mr Clarkson does not know what he is about," Jasper said.

"Mr Clarkson is meant to bolster your business, not straighten your chambers," Frank said looking over the disorder.

"Whilst he is in my employ, he should do whatever I need," Jasper said.

"I am good at keeping things together. I often did so for my father. Would you like me to help?" I asked, hoping to be useful while they spoke of the case Jasper worked on.

"Yes, please. I am afraid my clerk is being paid to spy on me. Since I started this case, he creeps about. Be sure not to say anything important in front of him."

"Very well. Before he returns, you tell Frank about it and I shall see if I can make use of your shelves," I said, thinking him paranoid.

I opened the desk drawers to try and discern what method was used. It appeared he had none. But then if Frank was right, and it wasn't the clerk's job to keep order, perhaps nobody was doing it all. I set to work. Straightening, stacking and binding the pages in bundles according to his clients. I put all the pages into the drawers alphabetically by last names of his clients. Then I put all the books back on the shelves where they belonged. While I worked, Jasper said, "I am glad you've come, Frank."

"What is this case you need help with?" Frank asked.

"I suppose you have heard Lord Beornmund has died under suspicious circumstances?" Jasper asked.

"I read he is missing," Frank said.

"A young man was caught burying his signet ring."

"I had not heard that," Frank said.

"No, it has been a very quiet affair because the body has not been found. Only the ring."

"Which is proof of a robbery only, and we must prove in court the thief killed the Lord? That should not be hard; a Lord always trumps a commoner," Frank said.

"That is rather the problem. We are hired by the solicitor of the thief's father to keep his neck out of the noose, I'm afraid."

"Ah, a defense case. This is… unexpected. That does complicate the matter. A Lord always trumps a commoner," Frank said.

Jasper nodded and replied, "I suppose earlier this year you must have read about Lord William Russell's murder trial?"

Frank nodded.

"His man, Courvoisier, was hung last July just for having a locket in his possession," Jasper said.

"There was a dead body in that case, and the servant confessed," Frank said.

"He confessed only after he'd been sentenced to hang. He was convicted of murder on the grounds of theft alone. Initially, all they had was the locket. That is nothing to a signet ring," Jasper said.

"Your man will have defense, which is something," Frank said, as the practice was not often done.

"Courvoisier had a defense barrister; he still hung," Jasper said, "The only reason my client, Mr Cecil Chapman, sits at Newgate waiting, instead of being hung, is because the family believes the rest of Lord Beornmund will show up."

"I thought a date was set for the Grand Jury," Frank said.

"Yes, the Beornmund family waited almost four months after Lord Beornmund disappeared, and there is still no body."

"Have they found something new?" Frank asked.

"I do not know. They must have. Why else would the indictment be introduced now?"

"Is there proof that Mr Chapman did it, or motive?" Frank asked.

"The investigation brought in some hounds that uncovered a little finger of a left hand in the park where a neighbor, a man in the public works, swears in an affidavit that Cecil Chapman was digging. The ring fit, though the finger was too degraded for identification by the family, even in a rendering."

"Still a missing finger is not a mortal blow," Frank pointed out, only less confidently.

"And of course, there is no coroner's inquest because there is no body. Now, the Clerks at Old Bailey have sent the charge of murder, by way of a grand jury, of all things. It is all done by Lady Beornmund's solicitor, Mr Archer. A gamble on his part, but he must be confident to make the charge without a body. He must have found some evidence to sway the Grand Jury."

"Other than the little finger," Frank asked.

"Yes, they found the finger months ago."

"You believe the prisoner will be indicted and sent to trial for murder from this unknown evidence?" Frank clarified.

"I do not know why else Mr Archer would move now," Jasper said.

"I do not understand how such an indictment can be made without proof of a death," Frank said.

"This thing is moving forward without hands it would seem. But Michaelmas came and the courts were filled, and they had no charge. It seems they will wait no longer for Lord Beornmund's body to be found," Jasper said.

"If the grand jury confirms the charge, it will not matter what evidence there is at trial," Frank said, thinking.

"You see my dilemma. The Duke of Sussex attended the trial of Lord William Russell's murder. I would not be shocked if he returned for Lord Beornmund's trial if the case is found. The second Lord to die at a commoner's hand within a year is something."

"You think they will try to make an example of your client?" Frank asked.

"Of course. Forty thousand people came to witness the hanging of Lord Russell's valet. The Chartists are gathering signatures as if they can collect enough for the commoners to be listened to. They organize riots in the belief that every man deserves the vote. Clearly, those of us working so hard to earn it should not bother."

"Courting the right Miss is hardly work," Frank teased.

"Come now, this is serious. Every man of wealth and position will push to see Mr Chapman hung just to show the commoners what will come down upon them if they step out of line."

"I do not understand," I interrupted. Jasper looked at me and glanced at Frank. He was surprised I would interrupt him, or need to understand. Frank smiled at me and said:

"The death of a nobleman, the murder, will be the perfect opportunity for those in power to make an example of a commoner," Frank said.

"Against your case, since you are taking the defense," I clarified.

"Yes." Jasper began explaining and I thought maybe he liked his voice very well. "Many will count on the court to come down hard on the death and dismemberment of a Lord, especially as it is the second one in six months."

"But with no body, they cannot even prove the lord is dead," I said.

"It does not seem to matter," Jasper said.

"It is all politics," Frank explained. "There is a group who put out a charter, we call them Chartists, demanding certain rights to all men, whether they own land or not. Though no one will say it out loud, I believe the nobles are terrified of the commoners rising up and coming after them as the French did. They beheaded a king less than fifty years ago, Millie. The example they can make of Jasper's client will be important."

"Oh," I said, feeling my heart sink. Frank was getting involved in an unwinnable situation, and I could not believe that would put him in a good position to gain a pupillage. Almost as if he knew what he'd done to Frank, Jasper admitted, chagrined:

"To make matters worse, the prisoner, Mr Chapman, confessed to burying the finger, but isn't willing to defend himself beyond that."

"Why?" Frank asked.

"Not sure. The solicitor was vague. I suppose it has something to do with Mr Chapman's father. He owns a very exclusive shop in town and has made enough to set up his daughter into better circles. She is expected to marry well, thus elevating the whole family. His priority is to keep his business completely separate from his son's crime. He isn't invested in our success. I believe he only allowed his solicitor to hire me because it was expected of him, but he mentioned three times I'm young and have only argued a few cases. He doesn't expect much," Jasper said.

"He has put you in a poor position," Frank agreed.

"Yes, to have a client hung for killing a nobleman isn't good business. I'd like to find some success in the trial if it goes that far. I will likely get some positive attention from the papers, if I can at least…there must be something," he said searching Frank to find a silver lining.

"I shall hope for the reappearance of the Lord alive, after having been on the continent," I said.

Jasper paused his pacing and smiled at me behind his desk. I tried to smile, but Jasper clearly had a father or older brother willing to support him in another career if this one did not take. Frank and I put everything into this opportunity and having one's name associated with the defense and hanging of a nobleman's killer did not bode well.

"This is where you come in, Frank. You know I can only argue the case according to the dictates of the law. I have no investigation. The Bow Street Runners are disbanded, and everything is in madness. I need you to… well, work your magic, Frank. I will see to it you are well compensated," Jasper said.

"Very well. I can talk to the prisoner, and see what he is about. I suppose I must talk to the father to see if Cecil Chapman is capable of murder. Perhaps find a character witness or two to testify; it could keep him from hanging since there is no body," Frank said.

"The father won't put himself forward as a character witness because he doesn't want people to know it is his son," Jasper said.

"Chapman is a common enough name I suppose," Frank said, "but once the papers get ahold of it, everything about Mr Chapman will be exposed. I will speak to him."

"Take Millie." Turning to me, Jasper said in his warm and inviting way, "May I call you Millie?"

I nodded in assent, and he finished, "And I give you leave to call me Jasper."

I glanced at Frank. He did not appear comfortable with this, but Jasper had already started talking again, so I committed never to address him directly if possible.

"You will be better off with Millie when you go to talk to the father. He mostly sells finery. He is much friendlier to the women of his establishment. His shop is over in the Royal Opera Arcade," Jasper said writing down the instructions, "I'll also have Mr Clarkson write the Lord Mayor and get you a permit to visit the prisoner at Newport."

He left to get his clerk and I looked to Frank.

"If he had mentioned it is a defense case, and the prosecutor was an Earl's family would you have come?" I asked.

"I knew it had to be bad for him to ask for help. I may have hesitated on your behalf if I'd known how bad. Are you sorry we came?" he asked.

"Not at," I said as bravely as possible.

"Is this enough of an adventure for you, Millie?" Frank asked.

I said nothing, for fear he would hear the tremble in my voice, but I managed to glance at him sideways with a smile. He laughed at me, but his laugh wasn't as confident as usual. I spent the rest of that day organizing the chambers that were in sad disarray. Frank researched the law on missing persons, presumed dead without a body, and whatever else he could think. I cannot say what Jasper did. He had one week before the grand jury would hear the charges and determine whether or not to put the young man on trial. He paced a lot.

Chapter Six

We went the next day to St. James before the fashionable people would be out. I could not be more shocked at what we found. An elegant, covered passageway lined with arches led to the shop. Shops along the passageway had enormous windows, almost as large as those in a greenhouse. It was done so the windows could be looked through.

Inside the windows, an ornately decorated shop held the finest of silks and satins. Shelves were brought forward instead of being entirely behind the counter. One could walk among them to inspect boxes of hats, gloves, and stockings. Spools of fabric and fasteners hung everywhere. The eye could not stop moving. I could not imagine how much the toiletries in this shop must cost.

"Frank we cannot pretend to shop in there. They will never believe we belong," I whispered, pulling my eyes from the windows.

"Shall we say you are looking to be a shopwoman?" Frank teased with a little laugh in his voice.

"I could, you know. I could work here perhaps," I said turning to Frank. "I am a fair seamstress."

"They work the shopwomen to the bone. The seamstresses are worked harder. I would rather you not subject yourself to such a punishment. Have a little faith in me, my girl," Frank said growing serious and looking a little sad.

"No Frank, no," I said adamantly taking his hand. "It is not lack of faith in you but rather…I do not wish to be a burden. I desire to help you, that is the only reason for me to volunteer. There is no one in the world so capable as you, Frank."

I hated it when he grew so serious. He searched me in a way that probed my insides.

"You believe that?" he finally asked.

"Of course, I do," I said. He smiled at me softly, pushing the curls on my forehead back and I could feel his love for me flowing from him and wrapping around me. My face lit on fire, and my heart thrummed too quickly.

"I will take care of you, Millie," he said dropping his hand to reach out and play with my fingers.

"But how will I do the same for you?" I asked taking his hand.

"You do just by being you," Frank said.

I threw his hand at him. I crossed my arms saying, "Very well, I will be a fine lady, make as much trouble as possible, and bemoan every slight inconvenience I am asked to endure."

I pushed him toward the door. I didn't stop long enough to feel the heartbreak of being useless. He took my arm and stopped me.

"You are not your mother," he said quietly in my ear, so a passerby did not hear.

"I… I did not mean to…" I stammered.

"And your father, he loved that she needed him. She was never an inconvenience to him. He needed her. He needed her just as I need you, just the way you are. You know that, do you not?" Frank asked. I swallowed hard looking at the ground. I did not know any such thing. I blinked not to cry, but I could not be sure where the emotion even came from.

"Can we speak of this another time?" I asked. We had a rule since our fathers died to defer discussions we did not feel capable of speaking about.

"Come then, let us go find you an extremely expensive trinket," Frank said as he walked me into the beautiful shop. The shopwoman behind the counter wore a simple but clean blue dress. She was exceptionally pretty and had a very elegant air about her. I had to wonder if this was the daughter meant to marry well.

"Good day. May I help you?" she asked coming toward us, eyeing me in my plain country gown and Frank in his coat that had not been fitted correctly.

"We are…" I started, wondering which character I could play.

"We are from the office of Mr Jasper Shaw, Barrister at Law. We need to ask a few questions," Frank said. I realized a moment too late we were not playing one of our games and I should not have spoken. I watched to see if I embarrassed Frank, but he showed nothing.

"You are trying to help Cecil?" she whispered, looking carefully over her shoulder.

"Yes," Frank said.

"Let me find Mr Chapman," she said and quickly scurried to the back room. She returned followed by a well-built man with dark waxed facial hair, and dressed impeccably, as fine as Mr Williams had ever dressed.

"Yes?" he asked sternly.

"Forgive my interruption, Sir. I have to ask a few questions. Master Shaw is preparing your son's plea for the grand jury and hopes to defend him."

"I do not think it is of use," Mr Chapman said looking away.

"And yet, you support him financially at this time with a defense barrister," Frank said.

"I supported him into an apprenticeship. Must not have been enough if he's stealing and pawning Lord's rings. Now, I make him comfortable until he leaves this country and never returns."

I did not need Frank to tell me this man was angry at his son for bringing dishonor to his establishment.

"You do not mention murder," Frank said.

The man looked at Frank hard and long.

"No Sir. He was a bit of a thief, but I never knew him to be violent," he said. Disgust and disappointment etched his face.

"But you will not give his character to the jury if it comes to it?" Frank asked. The man leaned in, and though only his attendant was in the shop to hear he said:

"Cecil made his choice. I will not jeopardize this place, our standing, everything to tell all of England my son is a thief," Mr Chapman said.

"I see," Frank said undeterred. "Did he know the Lord Beornmund?"

"Not that I can tell. Ask him. Perhaps before he is transported," Mr Chapman said. We all jumped a little when the door was thrown open. Before Frank could inform the man that if his son was charged with murdering a Lord, he would be hung, not transported, a young woman entered the shop dressed in an ornate pink day gown.

Her calling out, "Papa, Papa," was the only thing that made her the shopkeeper's daughter, and not that of a gentleman. She glided toward us with strange dancing steps, that I supposed she thought elegant.

Miss Chapman was pretty enough covered in frills. She would attract a husband who cared what her portion would be. Compared to the shopwoman I'd mistaken her for, she was not overly beautiful. The shopwoman outshined her even in her plain blue tunic.

The frills upon the daughter's head turned only for a moment to the shopwoman. The shopwoman folded her arms, glared, and then looked away. There was something in their ignoring each other that denoted a squabble between them. One had everything money could buy, but perhaps she knew all the frosting in the world did not change the bland flavor of the cake, which likely annoyed her.

Why would the shopwoman be angry?

When the daughter reached us, she looked me up and down, and did not bother acknowledging us any other way. Instead, she began to tell her father about an invitation she had received for a private assembly in two weeks. This miss, with a huge turquoise feather and realistic silk flowers fixed to her crepe bonnet, was her father's pride.

"I suppose you can see your way out," Mr Chapman said to us coldly. Then turning to his daughter, he said, "Come, darling, you may tell me more in the back." Taking his daughter's arm, he escorted her back to where he had come from. He paused, and with the glance every shopkeeper has perfected, invited us to leave. Frank shifted as if we would go. The father turned his back on us and I could see he had already done the same to his son.

Instead of leaving, Frank nudged me toward the curly haired shopwoman with beautiful features that forced me to study at her face. She was not much older than I, so I moved over to her. As I approached her, I realized she may cry. Frank nudged me to go to her. I looked at Frank confused. I wondered if he changed his mind about me trying to find work.

"This is so beautiful," I said fingering the fringe of a bonnet but still feeling awkward despite my pretense.

"It is...there is a ... a more affordable one like it at the shops a few streets over. They copy everything we do with more... reasonably priced materials," she said quietly.

"Thank you," I said grinning at her. She blinked and shook her head like she knew she couldn't cry, but the tears tugged at her.

"You do not think Cecil did this?" I asked, much more easily, seeing she wanted to tell me.

"He wouldn't hurt a fly... that's not to say... he was a bit on the mischievous side," she whispered, her face growing into a sad smile remembering.

"What sorts of trouble did he get into?" I asked, feeling Frank creeping in behind me to hear.

"Oh, Elenore told me of little things, like he'd take brass and sell it so he could go betting over holiday. His father doesn't believe in giving money for little expenses so Cecil would get creative with how he found money. Eleanor can have anything she wants. And Cecil ... well, it is not fair. He has not the flair for society like she does. That's not to say...he's grown up in the last few years at the water pumps. He never stops talking about it. He hasn't thieved in years, not since school, and he never took from anyone but his father. I'm sure of it," she said.

"What is that?" Frank asked.

"Thieving?" she asked, confused.

"No, the water pumps."

"He's an apprentice to an engineer out in Chelsea. He isn't a boy anymore; he is a man now. It isn't fair. I think Mr Chapman intends on transporting Cecil without the trial if he can," she said.

"Does his father believe that?" Frank asked.

"What?" she asked blinking back tears.

"That he'll be transported?"

"You think he will stay in London?" she asked perking up.

"No," Frank said. "He'll be hung. It won't be a hushed-up matter either. This establishment will be run through the mud."

"Hung," she whispered, and I took her arm because I thought she might fall.

"Yes," Frank said watching her to see why she was so misinformed.

"But Mr Chapman is sure he'll be transported, not hung, and no one will know."

"How would it stay hushed up?" I asked.

"If this goes to trial it will be highly recorded in the papers. Everything about Cecil will be known. The shop will be mentioned," Frank said. She shook her head as if it couldn't be true.

"It will serve them right if anything happens to Cecil... I cannot believe Elenore will let her brother be accused so she can –" The attendant stopped because a well-dressed woman with a footman came into the shop.

"Would you swear to all you have told us in affidavit if it saved his life?" Frank asked. She glanced at the back door then the front, and only nodded in the affirmative.

She plastered a smile on her face and turned toward the well-dressed woman who did not browse, but instead walked quickly toward us.

"Would you go with him to Australia if he were transported?" I asked. She stopped moving and turned to look at me like I was mad, but I thought I detected some affection. She turned from us, her blush enhancing her pretty features. She politely addressed her customer. The elaborate looking woman walked into our space, and I realized with embarrassment she may have overheard me. She certainly would have heard the shopwoman if she had answered, which she did not.

I stepped away from the attendant to let her work, and took hold of the bonnet I had admired, but did not see it at all. It sounded very romantic to run away to the wilds with a forbidden love. For a traitorous moment, I pictured Rick Bolton building me a little hut on the edge of the wilderness. For some reason, the image fell flat. Perhaps because even in my dream he would not look at me with adoration.

I set down the ridiculously extravagant bonnet, and my breath caught in my chest. The sight of my mother dancing with the duster pricked my memory. Was my daydream about Rick Bolton as absurd as hers about Mr Williams? Was I as bad as her? But then, I had never believed I would marry Rick, I just… My tragic love story enraptured me.

"I think we best browse closer to the door," Frank said breaking my thoughts. He took my arm and we walked slowly. It was then I remembered I was supposed to be observing so I could tell Frank what I saw. Would I dream away my time while real life happened around me?

I turned back to the scene before me.

Miss Eleanor Chapman came bustling into the room calling loudly, "Mrs Ellis, it has been too long."

The large woman with a puff of silver hair under her bonnet, and a long ringlet over her broad shoulder bristled and nodded, but backed toward us. The gentlewoman seemed the sort to put such a Miss in her place, but instead said, "Yes, I was honored by your company at Mrs Talbot's party. It is usually so… exclusive. You are very lucky to be invited." She glanced at us suspiciously. There was some kind of a warning in her tone. Miss Chapman did not notice but glowed with pride, almost as brightly as her father who came in behind her to see what his daughter's exclamations were about.

"That is odd," I said leaning over.

"What?" Frank asked picking up the glove as if to examine it.

"Her boots," I said under my breath. The lady, Mrs Ellis, stood to the side of a shelf that caught her crimson dress when she backed away from Miss Chapman, pulling it slightly to the side so I could see her ankle-length boots. She wore the height of fashion, tight sleeves, and a pointed waist with heavy velvet skirts, but her boots showed signs of wear. The leather looked creased in the extreme, the scuffs could not be buffed out, and the leather over the heels wore upward. Just then Mr Chapman paused in his bowing. He noticed Frank and me lingering.

Frank quickly pulled me from the shop before the man's drop in expression could turn angry. Halfway down the street Frank stopped behind a vendor's cart and bought me a meat pie. I ate and he looked deep in thought. Absentmindedly he handed a coin to a small boy nearby selling bundles of purple blossoms, perhaps the last pansies before the chill at the end of October ruined them for the winter.

"Thank you, Frank," I said taking the flowers.

"It isn't as romantic as being chained together on a transport boat that smells like rotting human flesh until we are worked to death in Sydney, but I suppose it'll do," he teased as if he knew exactly what I had been thinking before. I laughed and brought the blossoms to my face. They smelled much nicer than anything else on the streets of London. Perhaps I would not like a transport ship after all.

"What did you see?" I asked.

"Why wouldn't a father put forth his best foot to save his son?"

"Because he's embarrassed. He has not accepted the gravity of the situation," I guessed.

"Yes, but even if for his business, and his daughter's sake, there should be some fight to keep his name clean. It's more than that. He seemed almost afraid or resigned... I can't put my finger on it," Frank said.

"The assistant truly believed Cecil will only be transported. The father must believe the same," I said. Even I could see that wasn't likely.

"It hasn't been publicized enough now, but eventually the House of Lords will demand Cecil is hung. I don't think it can be avoided. If he is charged with murder, he will be convicted and hung simply as an example."

"Yes, but if the father believes his son will be quietly shipped away, instead of publicly executed, it may explain his reluctance to get involved... I don't know, Frank. Clearly, he favors his daughter."

"Yes," Frank said. "And she seems to be thriving, socially climbing despite her brother supposedly murdering a Lord."

"Oh, wait!" I said realizing a moment too late what I noticed, and I grabbed Frank's arm to stop him.

"What is it, Millie?" he asked.

"The lady, the one shopping – Mrs Ellis," I said.

"Yes," Frank said.

"She... I don't know...she watched us. When she came in, she watched us talk to the shopwoman. She looked...concerned. She came to us too quickly. She did not browse the tables as a person would. I could not stop my eyes from moving about the shop, but she came to us without stopping like she meant to overhear our conversation," I said.

"Yes, and when she told the young lady how lucky she was…" Frank started.

"Yes, it sounded like she personally handed her that luck and she could take it away," I said grabbing his hand as we walked forward. Frank paused to smile at me. It was a strange sort of dreamy smile. The way he looked at me, it was almost like he couldn't believe we were alone in London together. Was I his fantasy?

"Frank," I said, taken back.

"Uh, yes, very well. I think we ought to see if Mrs Ellis is associated with Lord Beornmund."

"Yes," I agreed. With a happy smile, I put the flowers to my face again enjoyed their scent.

Chapter Seven

"Jasper," Frank said walking into his chambers an hour later. "I need to speak to Lady Beornmund."

"Why don't I get you a meeting with the queen while I'm at it," Jasper answered, writing something.

"Millie may like to take a tea at the new palace," Frank said dryly.

"I will see if her solicitor, Mr Archer, will meet with you. That is the best I can do, Frank," Jasper said, focused on the paperwork in front of him.

"I suppose you cannot ask the police to reopen the investigation?" Frank asked.

"There is no one at Scotland Yard to do the deed." He added sulkily, "what's more, the prosecutors will share none of the evidence they've collected. I must wait until it is shown to the jury at trial. How can one prepare a defense under such circumstances?"

"We must talk to Lady Beornmund and hear for ourselves what she's saying," Frank said.

"I'll send a note around to her solicitor, Mr Archer, if you think it that important," Jasper said, seeing how impatient Frank was.

"Millie, what is this system you've used to organize my papers?" Jasper said, smiling at me and pulling a piece of paper toward him.

"I bundled together your clients in the drawers." Then, pointing, I said, "Over there are the… they are called nominate reports, I believe. Frank has shown me them a few times. They are done by the barrister's last name, alphabetically. The books, the binding calls them law reports, they are numbered so that was easy enough."

"These books," Frank said taking one from the shelf, "are all of the most important nominate reports, bound together and published. This collection is very new and valuable in our trade as they are up to date."

Frank smelled one of the books. He valued it, though it wasn't a fine book. A large collection of them were covered in paper board in brown cloth with gold lettering.

"They were a gift from my father, bought by my brother when I went to the bar. I wished for a carriage. He thought these more useful," Jasper said disgruntled but shifted and said, "Millie you have straightened this office, and I thank you. You are much better than Mr Clarkson. I did not understand where anything went before. Now it is so easy to find things."

"I am glad to help," I said, but regretted it. Mr Clarkson entered at that moment, and he glared at me a little whilst pretending to ignore me.

Mr Clarkson handed Jasper his wax that was on a side table with the other writing things. They were so fine and little used, that when I had been organizing, I thought them some sort of office decoration, perhaps antiques. Why would anyone put the instruments of their work at such an inconvenient distance? Perhaps Jasper was right when he said Mr Clarkson was spying on him or trying to thwart him. I thought I may mention this to Frank.

"Millie looks famished. Mr Clarkson. After you express this, can you fix her a cup of tea, please?" Jasper said handing him the note. Mr Clarkson only bowed a little and nodded. He walked away with the note clutched in his grasp. Before he could reach the door, Frank said, "Millie, perhaps we should go find a proper meal. Mr Clarkson must see to his duties."

I nodded, unsure what was happening, but I could feel an added tension in the room. I looked over at Jasper. He watched me. I nodded politely, but walked to Frank, taking the arm he offered.

We left and walked to the Hall to take a meal. I grew very fond of the great building. The ceiling danced in patterns of dark wooden arches, carved into points that looked as though they could drip down upon us. When we finally walked back to Jasper's chambers, he met us at the door.

I sat Frank down on a wooden chair by the table and took his comb. I had longed many times to make him presentable, and he did not mind me putting his hair in place. He played with my skirt as I did it and I thought he liked me combing his hair.

"Something more is going on than your case," Frank said while I worked.

"Why do you say that?" Jasper asked.

"We are next to nobodies, and yet the very day we visit a shop, we have an audience with Lady Beornmund and her solicitor Mr Archer. Something is not right."

"Yes, I do believe Mrs Ellis was trying to hear into our conversation," I said to Frank.

"Ah, they are cousins, she and Lady Beornmund," Jasper said, looking at me with admiration.

"Good observation Millie," Frank said tugging at my skirt in a way that made me blush.

"Do you see? Frank sees. I swear spirits from the other side whisper to him," Jasper said.

"No, not like Frank. I'm not naturally like this. He's taught me tricks to observing people. He's done so since I was very young. It helped me…"

I drifted off. I did not wish to explain why Frank had to help me understand my mother.

"Well, I would be very much gratified if you explain it all to me some time, but now we must go," Jasper said taking my arm as I handed Frank back his comb. He walked me out of the building with Frank following close behind. I glanced back at Frank a few times. He had a nice forehead and looked handsome without his hair flopping over it.

"Here you are, Sir." Mr Clarkson met us at the gate to Middle Temple with a strange-looking carriage. The driver sat up on the back seat behind the passenger seating. It reminded me a little of the carriage Mr Williams ran away with me in and made me uncomfortable.

"What is this?" Frank asked.

"It is a new method of transport; they call it a Hansom Cab. It moves faster than a hackney, and is likely the only way we will make it by the appointed hour," Jasper said.

"It will only hold two," Frank said.

"I will stay here with Mr Clarkson," I said.

"Not at all. We will squeeze. You must act as my assistant," Jasper said, handing me up. Frank brushed him aside and came in next to me.

Once seated, the reins snapped against horseflesh and we flew through London. The driver did not wait for other carriages on the road but drove around them with little effort. I thought I may scream at a few points but held it in. I sat sideway clutching Frank, who kept an arm in front of me so I didn't fall out.

We made it to the center of London before I thought it possible. At our speed, a massive replica of the Pantheon grew quickly up out of the street as we drove on.

"What is that?" I asked loudly in awe.

"It is the Old Lady of Threadneedle Street," Jasper yelled over Frank, then admonished his friend, "Have you shown Millie nothing of our city?"

"It is the Bank of London. It keeps England financed," Frank said in my ear.

We went to a building near the bank and the Hansom cab let us off. We were met at the great outer gates by an extremely proficient clerk in wire-rim glasses. He ushered us down an extensive arching lane lined with many doors labeled with names and professions.

The clerk ushered us into the outer room that was decorated almost as if it were a sitting room. The polished sheen of the wooden tea cart, the fire blazing in the hand-carved hearth, and the softly padded seats said something about the clientele who came to use this solicitor's services.

A large imposing man with his extra girth packed into a very tight waistcoat, or perhaps even a corset under his tight-fitting jacket, met us in this receiving area. His face was tinged in red, and his hair was cropped short. He introduced himself as Lady Beornmund's solicitor, Mr Archer. Jasper introduced himself, barrister at law, and us as his associates, Mr and Mrs Hadleigh. He said no more despite Mr Archer paused waiting for him to explain us. When Jasper did not Mr Archer stared down at us and said:

"Be warned, Mr Shaw. This audience is our favor to you, and if you do not show courtesy to her ladyship and her daughter, you will be sent out."

Mr Archer led us into the inner space where two women in vastly different stages of life cozied into large chairs near the fire. The older lady was dressed in dark blue satin, like she was in mourning. Her person was small, and a trim of lace swamped her thin, boney hands. Despite her size, she had a presence that was somehow substantial. Her face was naturally pointed, and her lips looked a purplish color like she was cold despite her nearness to a stoked blaze.

The younger woman, very pretty with no need of extravagance, stood to hand her mother a handkerchief. The movement caught Mr Archer's attention and he paused to watch her. She glanced up, and upon noticing us she rubbed her mother's shoulder, then sat back down. She moved elegantly, comfortable with the motions of her body. She looked nothing like her mother, with soft features and perfect coloring. She wore a cream jacket cinched to show her small waist flowering up to an ample top and down to a full skirt. The way she smiled in support of her mother indicated a peaceful soul. She acutely contrasted with the solicitor who sweated like it was the middle of summer instead of the first frost coming on.

"Lady Lilian Beornmund, and her daughter, Lady Charlotte Beornmund," Mr Archer introduced.

Jasper and Frank bowed and, when invited, sat across from the ladies. On the way over Frank asked me to pretend to be attending them so I stood in the background, certain I was not supposed to be there. I took out a little notebook from my false pocket to take notes so I did not look so peculiar.

"My Lady, may I start by thanking you immensely for coming today," Jasper said tipping his handsome face forward, his charm falling over her and her daughter. After a few of his excessive flatteries fell to the floor before he could catch them, I noticed the lady relax. She seemed to think Jasper would cow to her. And I believe he would.

She did not know Frank.

After Jasper cleared the way, he said, "This is my associate, Mr Frank Hadleigh. He is helping me prepare for the grand Jury and official indictment. May he address you, My Lady?"

"Have you opened the investigation again?" she asked delicately. "The charge is still... murder?"

I examined her. She seemed almost afraid of the word or perhaps the charge. Mr Archer tried to step in to explain, but Lady Beornmund waved him off. She seemed frustrated with him, and I had to wonder if this sudden push to trial was all the solicitors' doing and she did not like it.

"The charge is not for me to decide, My Lady. Nothing the like," Jasper said. "You must have been told that since there is no body, there was no coroner's inquest made. The clerks at Old Bailey made the charge of Murder. Now it must be presented to a grand jury to find if there is enough evidence to go to trial. They will hear the facts and then decide if a charge can be made. We just need to be sure we have all the facts straight before next week."

"Very well," she said looking at me and then Frank with mistrust.

"Ma'am on the night of Thursday, July the 9th, your husband went missing. Is that correct?" Frank asked.

"Yes," she said flatly looking at her solicitor. She must have wondered why she must confirm what we already knew.

"Did you see your husband on the night in question?" Frank asked.

"Yes, at tea," the lady responded stiffly, grabbing for her daughter's hand, but she was too far to reach, "I took my exercise in the morning. I went to walk the gardens. I then came home and changed my clothes for visiting. My Lord, he is often gone to... his... he is a member at many clubs and... I don't see him until teatime."

"Do you remember who you visited that day?" Frank asked.

"Company was scarce at the time, almost the same as it is now. My acquaintances are few in London until the season starts. I visited Mrs Talbot who sent me a bottle of spices from the continent. I visited Mrs Lockwood and her daughter to return their visit. Lastly, I visited Mrs Ellis."

Her face fell into a frown when she mentioned Mrs Ellis. Frank saw it and asked:

"Why?"

"Excuse me?" she asked.

"Well, you had reasons for visiting the others; why Mrs Ellis?"

"I...she is my cousin, and a very... a friend. I visit her a few times a week," she said, but her scowl grew.

Frank nodded. I wrote down that the friendship seemed tense. A friend who appeared to be spying for her – perhaps she did not like it.

"Thank you. Please continue," Frank said.

"Yes. Well, after that I had a few items I needed. I wanted to choose them myself so I did not send my maid but went to the shops to buy them. It was a very warm day and my head began to hurt. I had asked My Lord for over a month if we were to go to our country estate soon, as I was growing weary of the heat, but he... well, he had reasons for staying in London."

"What reason?" Frank asked, and the woman frowned. He aggravated her on purpose so she would not be so careful with her words.

"Just business," she answered.

"What came after the shops?" he asked.

"I went to my room. I had a headache." Again she frowned at Frank.

"Was that before or after the tea you spent with Lord Beornmund?" Frank asked.

"Oh, yes, it was after tea," the Lady said. Her face colored and she turned to say something to her daughter. The younger woman, probably just entering her twenties, perhaps older, appeared agitated. Frank pretended to write something down, but I saw him glance over the paper at the two women interacting. Frank then went to the other side of the room where we had come in. Jasper and I followed.

"What is it?" Jasper asked.

"She's lying," Frank said quietly to Jasper.

"Why do you say that?" Jasper asked.

"That is very detailed. Mr Chapman was arrested a month after her husband disappeared, yet she recollects everything she did that day? Also, look at her hand when she speaks to her daughter. It rests. Ask her one more time if she saw her husband leave on the night in question. She clenches. She is not telling us the truth. I would guess either she did not see him that night, or they fought, and she does not want to give us particulars on their conversation."

"I'll trust you. I'm not asking that woman anything else. However, it does help Cecil's case if she did not see him in the evening," Jasper said.

"We must prove what she is lying about. I need to try and throw her off. Then tomorrow we will find a witness to prove she lied under oath in the affidavit. It will destroy their evidence," Frank said.

"She is very influential and has many friends in the right places. We must proceed very carefully," Jasper said.

"I'll do it," I said. They both looked at me. Frank just nodded. I walked over with my head in my notebook. Not even looking at the women I said:

"My Lady, I do apologize, I just need to make sure I got everything correct."

"Yes," she said condescendingly.

"You went to bed after tea?" I asked.

"Uh... yes," she said.

"Why so early?" I asked as if ticking off my list. This is how I got information out of my mother when she wasn't forthcoming.

"It...I had to. No, no first I was out shopping," she said repeating her activity earlier in the day.

"Oh, no. I have all that, I need you to tell me about teatime again."

"I'm getting to it," she snapped.

"Excuse me," I said politely, pulling back. Pretending to help her find her place, I said, "You went shopping, and visited. Then at teatime, where was the Lord Beornmund?"

"I... I went shopping. I came home because of the spooked horse and mud on my dress. My maid changed me..."

"Yes. Can you move to teatime," I said curtly.

"She had a headache at tea and went to bed early," her daughter snapped at me.

"Oh, were you present?" I asked innocently.

"No, I was on holiday with a friend," the daughter answered glancing at her mother.

"Excuse me, My Lady, I must have it in her words," I said bowing in what I hoped was respect, but also to draw the distraction out long enough that the Lady would be tripped up again.

"Now, My Lady," I said examining my notes, "It was before teatime your husband left, or he was not home already?" I asked mixing up my words, so she had to think about what I said versus what I meant.

"Claude was gone," she said quietly.

"You said he joined you for tea," Frank said watching her.

"Oh yes, I… I remember, he was home for tea," she said looking at the ground as if there was something there that could help her.

"Then you went to bed early with a headache," I said looking at my notepad.

"Yes," she said looking to her solicitor to see if that was right. Mr Archer looked livid.

"You do not know when your husband left?" Frank asked quickly.

"No…or…perhaps he…" she stammered; this time Mr Archer made to interfere.

"Thank you, My Lady," I cut off, moving to Frank, and away from the large angry man.

"Just one more question," Frank said. "In the investigation, it was learned that the Lord of Beornmund's manservant disappeared a fortnight before himself."

"Yes, that is correct," Lady Beornmund said relaxing.

"Was he replaced?" Frank asked.

"No, Father seemed to think he would be back," Lady Charlotte said.

"You have not heard from the manservant, a Mr Otis Blunt, in the months since Lord Beornmund's disappearance?" Frank asked.

"No," Lady Beornmund said, realizing for the first time it was odd he never returned.

"Who cared for Lord Beornmund's fingernails in his man's absence?" Frank asked.

"It...I haven't any idea," Lady Beornmund said, but she looked at Frank like she understood that the manservant would identify the finger, even when she could not.

"I think perhaps my maid did from time to time. She is very reliable. She would... but she is no longer with us," Lady Charlotte said looking at her mother who flinched.

"Why did she leave your service?" Frank asked.

"She stole from my daughter," Lady Beornmund said, and she looked upset.

"Did you have the police investigate?" Frank asked.

"No, nor shall I. I will not have them poking about. Neither will I have a trusted member of my house taking trinkets. The trustees have been informed, and they will find the only item of value taken. There is not an auction house in all of England that would dare sell it. The matter has been dealt with," Lady Beornmund snapped, and her irritation was real. Someone she trusted, maybe even liked, stole from her. There was something sad in her eyes, a faraway look of something she mourned, and I dared not ask what was stolen. It was her honest, unguarded reaction, and it appeared to me to be the only true unguarded moment of the whole interview.

"Thank you for your time, My Lady," Frank said bowing to her.

"Do you mean to find someone who can identify the finger?" she asked.

"I think it would be best. It seems to me the handling of this case has not been to find the truth, but rather a solution," Frank said candidly. Lady Beornmund nodded in agreement and did not look angry. She looked thoughtful now.

"You will, as a personal favor, keep me apprised of what you find," she said.

"Yes, My Lady, and a good day to you," Frank said with another quick bow. He then turned and walked toward the outer room. I followed behind finishing up my notes so I did not have to look at the solicitor.

"Well done," Frank said taking my arm. I chanced a look back. The mother, daughter and Mr Archer all watched us despite the pretty and very proper farewell Jasper was giving.

Jasper finished bowing over the daughter long enough to remember Lady Beornmund. Finally, he moved backward to us. We all left the office quickly, before they could see we had just poked a major hole in their timeline. Without a body their murder charge was in trouble. Walking toward the outer door of the building, Jasper said:

"That could help us."

"Yes," Frank said with a smile.

"Why?" I asked confused.

"If Lord Beornmund was not present at teatime, then his disappearance could have happened during the day. Cecil Chapman would have been apprenticing all day, and not alone walking home from a public house after taking a meal," Frank said.

"Let's speak to the housekeeper and the butler again," Jasper said.

"None of the lower servants have been talked to," Frank pointed out, "Someone must be able to contradict the others. Not to mention we ought to try and piece together Lord Beornmund's last days to see when exactly he could not be found. If we can prove exactly when Mr Archer lost him, we may have a chance of getting Cecil off."

"Yes, that is good, Frank. I may be able to keep Cecil from being hung after all," Jasper said as if he'd done anything.

"Do you believe he is innocent of killing Lord Beornmund?" I asked.

"I… I don't know," Jasper said holding the door open for me. "I am paid to argue for him, not judge him."

"Oh," I said wondering how he could detach so easily.

"Do you think he killed the Lord?" Jasper asked me, proving he was growing to value my opinion as much as Frank's.

"No. Even his father, who is angry with him, doesn't think he did it. I feel certain he didn't kill the gentleman but had a bit of bad luck finding his finger and signet ring," I said.

Frank looked thoughtful and said, "I suppose we must hear what he has to say."

"The prisoner?" Jasper asked.

"Yes," Frank said.

"According to his solicitor he won't say much, but I've sent the note around. Hopefully, you can get in before the Grand Jury convenes," Jasper said cheerfully.

"It will not change the witness who saw him bury the finger," Frank said trying to temper Jasper's excitement.

"Oh, let him have a moment to feel the good fortune," I said to Frank. Jasper grinned a little and nodded at me. I thought for just a moment he glanced at my figure, appreciating what he saw. I looked to Frank who stepped in front of me, taking my hand.

"We'll part ways here," Frank snapped.

Jasper nodded and quickly moved away from us toward the road. It would appear he was looking for a mode of transportation.

"You did well in there," Frank said taking my arm as we walked to where we could catch an omnibus over the bridge. We stayed over the water, as Jasper called it, with disappointment. I did not mind. London was like a fan, and it took about the same amount of time to get back to the base of the fan, where we lodged, from anywhere in the city.

"I just dealt with her as you said I should my mother. Lady Beornmund was much easier to read. I have started to think perhaps my mother blurred the lines between her dream world and the real world until she told me lies, but believed them herself," I said.

"Perhaps the saddest sort of lie is the one we hold inside us, and cling to as our life. The one that we must convince ourselves is true to keep going," Frank said.

"You mean for me to feel compassion for my mother—she who could not even muster a goodbye for me when we parted," I said.

"You are able to see all sides of a thing, and it makes you kind. You do for everyone; it is your way," Frank said looking at me with admiration.

"Perhaps for now, but when I have been in London a little longer, I shall know whom to be intimidated by, and whom I should step all over," I said with a laugh, looking away from Frank's probe.

"I hope you never get so closely acquainted with the city," Frank said as he helped me onto an omnibus.

Chapter Eight

We had a cozy evening supposing what happened to Lord Beornmund. After only a few days of being married, we did not even pause climbing into bed together. It was growing colder at night, and I relied on his back against mine to keep warm or I could not sleep; the room was so drafty.

The next morning was Sunday and knowing all we needed done in such a short time, it was hard to keep the day quietly. I was allowed a bath by the innkeeper, which was a relief. Then we went to church in an imposing cathedral with pointed arched windows and a fine prospect of the river.

Monday morning, we returned to Jasper's chambers. The grand jury would convene in three days, and we still had not gotten a permit to interview the prisoner. The tension in the air grew as the desperation of the situation crackled like grease on fire.

Frank looked through the investigation for a scrap of information. Jasper, who had lost all hope of avoiding a trial, spent most of his spare time studying the law dealing with murder trials. Frank had a particularly good memory and often paused in studying how to keep Jasper's client from trial, to help when Jasper was not certain on some point. Frank kept explaining to Jasper that avoiding the trial had to be their priority for the time being. Jasper was certain we could not convince Cecil to explain himself, even if we managed to visit him before the Grand Jury. In his mind, there was no hope of avoiding the trial. Frank stopped trying to convince Jasper of anything, and instead studied maps. Finally, mid-morning, Frank tired of looking at the maps. He took up the notes of the investigation again. After a short time, he said, "I found her."

"Who?" I asked.

"Lady Charlotte's lady maid who was accused of stealing and relieved of her position. I knew I'd seen an interview with a former servant. She's the daughter of Mrs Ellis's butler," Frank said.

"She gave no useful information. She was let go before the lord disappeared," Jasper said.

"I'm going to talk to her to see if she knows why the Beornmund estate keeps misplacing people," Frank said.

"A thief maid?" Jasper asked.

"Servants know everything. And she no longer relies on the family for a living," I said.

"She's given her statement. It was of no use," he said looking back at his desk. I glanced over to see he read something entitled, *Fashionable Faux Pas* in the paper, and was not looking at the books Frank suggested to him earlier.

Frank rifled through the investigation.

"I need this," he said, taking the rendering of the severed finger.

"Very well," Jasper said standing and stretching.

"She's found work as a laundress at another great house," Frank said.

"That is quite a fall from status,. Her wages would have been cut in half. But then I suppose it is better than being hung," Jasper said. He examined his cluttered desk and glanced at me.

"Come, Millie, let's go talk to her," Frank said.

"Millie can stay here. She is in no one's way, and she can help me with some straightening I need done. Mr Clarkson is useless."

Without re-explaining Mr Clarkson's job to Jasper, Frank said, "I like to take her. Millie is very good at getting people to talk. I doubt the witness will open up to me. What do you wish to do, Millie?"

Frank watched me. I smiled at him.

"She would much rather be here than tramping about the streets of London," Jasper encouraged.

"I would rather talk to the witness," I said bowing to Jasper. "Please excuse me, Sir."

He laughed, "Very well, my dear. I suppose the city has not lost her charms for you yet."

Just then Mr Clarkson entered with a note.

"Ah, you have permission to enter Newgate tomorrow; that was fast," Jasper said, surprised, looking at Mr Clarkson who seemed to suddenly have become proficient.

"That will be opportune. Hurry, Millie, we must find the lady's maid today," Frank said.

"I charge you both to return here and tell me what you've learned. Tomorrow, I suppose you will also need to experience Newgate, Millie," Jasper said, waving the note.

"I…I would be interested in…" I stammered looking at Frank.

"You will not be forbidden. It is a public place. Many women are incarcerated there. Not to mention those who go to watch the hangings," Frank said.

"I do not think I would like to see someone hanged," I said quietly.

"There are no hangings tomorrow. Now we must go. I'd like to know for sure Cecil is innocent before we meet with him. If I can get enough information to get him to talk, we may have some footing," Frank said to Jasper.

It took us hours to locate the thief maid. We got nowhere entering the servant's door at the townhouse of a knight and his lady she put down as her employment when questioned. Frank finally bribed a young man mucking the stables to learn it was laundry day, and the maid we searched out was likely at the washboard. With no one to give us permission, all of them preoccupied playing their part, we snuck behind the row of townhouses.

It looked as though most of the household linens hung in neat rows to dry. Just past the rows, a woman of thirty stood near the huge copper pot, trying to stoke the fire hotter. The steaming pot had yet to come to a boil and the red-faced woman worked to submerge her whites while getting the pot back up to heat. Her strength made her almost unfeminine. Her rolled sleeves revealed muscled forearms, her damp dress clung to her rounded shoulders. This woman worked hard. Would someone so capable need to steal? She stood in a cloud of steam. She pushed her damp hair out of her face to spare a glance for Frank and me as we approached.

"Miss Sarah Smith, former maid to Lady Charlotte Beornmund, daughter of the Lord Beornmund?"

"Whose askin'?"

"I am apprentice to Mr Jasper Shaw Barrister at Law in defense of Mr Cecil Chapman," he said.

"I weren't aware murder's got defense," she said.

"They do when they can afford it," Frank said.

"I got nothing to say to you," she said. Her forearms bulged as she pushed her mistresses' underthings down into the huge copper pot. Steam billowed out and we all stepped back.

"In truth, any testimony you give would mean little as you are a thief," Frank taunted.

"Hush your mouth," the woman said glancing around to be sure no one heard him.

"Did you steal those baubles?" I asked thinking it wouldn't be worth it, as her job before couldn't be as laborious as using the washboard on her madam's clothes.

"No. It was never proved. The Master is badly in debt to his place for gamblin' and I don't know what else."

"Lord Beornmund is in debt?" Frank asked squinting whether from the steam, or trying to understand her I could not tell.

"Must be. The Lord Beornmund should have money but he don't. I overheard him talk to the old Lady about retrenching. Only the second son, who has been made in Her Majesty's navy, has any money. He sneaks some to his sister when his lordship don't find it. Master'd sniff out money like a bloodhound. I think he let me go because they couldn't pay me. Not because they actually suspected me, or the master would have seen me to the gallows for sure."

"Lady Beornmund believes something was stolen," I said.

"Yes, things went missing, but not by me. I was let go on suspicion because they didn't want to know who really stole 'em," she whispered looking around again.

"Who did it?" Frank asked.

"I...I shouldn't say," she said growing uncomfortable.

"You need not be loyal to them. They let you go on an unconfirmed suspicion," I said.

"No, I ... the young Miss was my charge since she was fourteen years. I... I had just entered service as a lady's maid and she... anyhow, she had nothing to do with any of it, poor dear. I would not spread tales about for her sake," she said.

"We are trying to keep an innocent young man from hanging. You must be willing to save a life," I said.

She stirred her pot with the wet wooden washing bat for a moment. Then it turned out she did not mind so much because she told us the whole history of the family.

As far as I could understand, six years previous Lord Beornmund took a mistress. He settled her in Chelsea because he liked riding his horse about the country, and that was the closest he could get in London. About three years previous, it became clear he went deeply into debt somehow – the way these men do, didn't explain much to me.

Lady Beornmund got her pin money, as it was determined by the estate, but the eldest son, the Viscount Beornmund, was entirely dependent on Lord Beornmund for his funds. When his father sunk in debt, the Viscount sunk with him. He lost a great deal of his allowance. The second son, a captain in Her Majesty's navy, was the only one with funds. He wrote his sister from every port he set in at, and sent her a few pounds. She wished for his return sorely, though he hadn't been home in two years.

In response to his diminished circumstances, the Viscount married an old family friend. The daughter of the Duke of Leicester was perhaps an incurable nincompoop, but she came with an unholy portion settled upon her. The Viscount had expected a large increase in his allowance when he married. It was only fair, as his father, Lord Beornmund, received four percent of the estate, and his portion would have increased significantly after his son's marriage.

Much to his son's surprise, Lord Beornmund bought an expensive rare stallion and did nothing for his son and new daughter. His son raged for days at the unfairness of it and all the servants learned far too much about the family estate.

The Viscount and his new wife were butter on bacon, which had something to do with her wearing diamonds during the day, and him with a boot collection. A year previous, just after his marriage, when the Viscount got nothing extra from his father, his sister, Lady Charlotte, began to misplace her pretty trinkets.

    Most of what she lost were gifts from her many suitors, the prominent suitor being a baron from her part of the country. He looked for Lady Charlotte to wear a pin he bought her, but she couldn't find it. She thought she lost it in her travels. Her mother sent her about the country with friends often after the Viscountess, a silly sort of woman, came full-time to their family. Lady Charlotte wrote the housekeeper of her last stay looking for the pin, but no one could find it. The baron understood, and Lady Charlotte was careful not to lose the gifts he gave her. She was not able to keep all of her pretty things safe, though.

    "Can you tell me specific things that could be identified?" Frank finally asked cutting off her gushing stream of unwilling gossip.

    "It has nothing to do with Lord Beornmund's disappearing, but I can if you like," she said.

    "Please," I said as Frank sounded weary.

    "Well, Lady Charlotte misplaced her set of bronze combs shaped like butterflies, opals set in them. They was not her best combs. Opals are not so fashionable, but she were born in October. She need not fear wearing 'em," she smiled. Then she admitted, "She enjoyed the way it made her friends squirm. The only thing she suffered over was a little moonstone bracelet. She meant to take it to the seaside in June but forgot. When we returned to town in July, she could not find it. She wondered if perhaps she did take it after all and misplace it at the inn. I packed her trunk myself, and I told her twice she forgot it. They was in her dressing table, then they was gone. I swear I…"

I did a little sketch and showed her while she still spoke. She nodded.

"How did you finally get blamed?" Frank asked, cutting her off.

"I... you isn't here to turn me in?" she asked suspiciously.

"I do not believe you stole a thing," Frank said clearly.

"Very well," she said wiping her brow and leaning against the bat. "Three days before he went missing, the master came looking for his heirloom pearls. It were a set of rarely used genuine pearls given as a special gift to the family a couple of generations back. My miss was presented in 'em, and they was beautiful. Shiny as can even be imagined, almost blue or silver, so beautiful, especially on Lady Charlotte. I can't say when the pearls went missing, but those was rare, and worth at least a hundred pounds, probably more."

"Three days before he disappeared, Lord Beornmund was home at night," Frank repeated trying to understand her.

"Yes, spent most of his time in Chelsea with his kept lady. Lady Charlotte was to stay with a cousin the next day and it seemed the Lord came to see her. He fancied her more than the boys," she said.

"By this time, a Mr Blunt, Lord Beornmund's manservant, was not to be found," Frank said.

"Yes Sir, but when Lady Beornmund asked if he needed her to search out another, he swore his man would be back," she said.

"Why did he accuse you of stealing the pearls? How did he know they were missing?" I asked growing weary and wishing to focus on her.

"Lord Beornmund wanted them for some reason," she said.

"Three days before he went missing, he came home doting on his daughter and asked for the family heirloom," Frank recapped for her after she pulled something delicate from her wash to test it.

"Lady Charlotte went herself to get them. She kept them locked in her chest with her other jewelry and treasures."

"Lord Beornmund never took the pearls back after she was presented?" Frank asked.

"She had them even before she was presented. Her Papa couldn't give 'em to her – they belong to the estate. He... I guess you'd call it . . . lent them to her. They were Lord Beornmund's mother's favorite gems. She wore the pearls in a portrait. The headdress is silk strung in pearls, the necklace is three strands clipped with a golden clasp and drop earrings."

"And you have no idea when they disappeared?" I asked.

In her colorful way, she explained Lady Charlotte preferred ribbons on her throat. When she wished to dress up, she pinned a garnet brooch to the ribbon. She was the opposite of butter on bacon, which I took to mean she did not wear diamonds during the day.

"If Lady Charlotte rarely wore the pearls, then the thief thought he could pawn them, and get them back before anyone noticed they were gone," Frank said.

"If it were her brother, he must have been in a bad way to take 'em. To think he could pawn, turn his luck, then get 'em back before anyone noticed... brazen as the day is long. That fob-heavy fool of a Viscount couldn't be so skilamalink to lose 'em."

"The Viscount was angry about his wife's portion being taken up by the trustees, though. Maybe he thought he deserved them," Frank said.

"He spoke much of his disappointment for weeks after his marriage."

"Did he blame his father?" Frank asked.

"He supposed Lord Beornmund could have increased his allowance. Instead, he bought a stallion," she said. "But I've never known the Earl and his heir to be on good terms. It was worse after his marriage."

"The master dismissed you for the crime without amassing any proof," I reminded.

"He knew I didn't do it. He were mad as hops when neither me nor Lady Charlotte could get our hands on the set. He looked around like he was trying to decide who betrayed him. He yelled a lot."

"Lady Beornmund didn't implicate her son?" I asked.

"It's hard for a mamma to see her little man as a thief. I think Lady Beornmund hoped it was me. Lady Charlotte never confided in her she'd been missing her fine things. Lady Beornmund never heard of lost items until that night. Then it was easier if it were me that took 'em."

"Lord Beornmund didn't suppose it was his missing Valet," Frank asked.

"I...he raged at his son first," she said.

"He didn't accuse you right away then," Frank said, nodding like that made more sense.

"No. Not until my poor young lady, who cried and cried, swearing she had locked them in her box and pointed me out and said even I couldn't have gotten to 'em. The master dove on me like a dog breaking the neck of the pheasant. I'm outta my position after ten years at his daughter's side. If he believed I took the pearls, I'd be on the gallows. He couldn't start an investigation in case it led to his son. Likely he couldn't afford my wages no more, and it made him feel better to ruin someone."

She stopped talking and noticed her water finally boiled. Her laundry got a thrashing. She pushed and pulled her laundry through the boiling water with a vigor that denoted anger.

I could see this line of questioning hurt her. Hoping to ease her pain I said,

"Lady Charlotte mentioned you when we spoke to her. She sounded fond of you. She said you were responsible at times for paring her father's fingernails and may be able to help us identify the finger. She trusts you still."

The woman nodded and struggled not to cry.

"Is this Lord Beornmund's finger?" Frank asked taking out the rendering from his satchel and showing it to her.

"I...It don't look like it, the ring fit much looser than that. It is stuck on there, and don't even go down to the base of the finger where he wore it. His fingers were longer, but it could just be a poor rendering."

"The ring was put on the finger after it had been buried for some time," I pointed out.

"The finger may a been bloated in death. I can't be sure, but when he was livin' it don't look like that."

We all saw the movement, but she flinched.

"I need you off now," she said. A woman stomped toward us but disappeared behind rows of hung laundry caught billowing in the wind.

"Thank you," I said. Frank and I ran quickly back to the front of the row of houses before the wind died down. I took Frank's hand and he pulled me along. When we slowed,

I kept ahold of Frank's hand, and we walked to catch our breath.

"Dumped out of her position because the Viscount is greedy," I said.

"I am not so certain the Viscount did it. He would have to be very brazen to sell a family heirloom that he knew could be identified through a picture. I still think the mistress must have something to do with it," Frank said.

"They were at the family house. I doubt she was invited there," I pointed out.

"Yes, but the Valet went back and forth between houses, then disappeared only weeks before the Lord himself."

"That is true," I said. "The valet could have run away with them, then the mistress killed the Lord."

"Yes," Frank agreed. "We can't be sure, but it is a more likely scenario than an employed young man with a bright future suddenly deciding to kill a Lord."

"Especially when two people have verified it is not in his nature," I reminded.

"Either way, it was unkind of the thief to get the poor woman fired and doing the laundry," Frank said.

"I don't know that Miss Sarah Smith is to be pitied for having employment," I said. "She is free, employed. She is making her way in this world. I do not think her situation so bad. Often times I thought I would rather work than do nothing, waiting for…"

"Waiting for Mr Williams to come over. You would rather be a washerwoman than married to Titus Williams?" he asked looking at me with disbelief.

"I would," I answered. "But Frank, I…I am very happy married to you."

I looked up at him nervously. He was examining me.

"You are afraid, though," he said.

"I… I would not like for you to take a mistress," I said feeling something thick in the back of my throat, trying to make me cry.

"I could not afford it, clearly," he teased.

I glanced up at him. He was pushing me on. Why would he taunt me at a time like this? I glared at him. He stopped walking and tightened his grip on my hand.

"I will not go a wandering, my girl," he said seriously and leaned in to kiss my temple.

I smiled again and nodded, content. Frank's word meant something.

"We are on an adventure," I said.

"Yes, we are," Frank said turning and we started to walk again.

"What now?" I asked.

"We trace his last days. The maid saw him three days before he disappeared. Let us see when his most constant companion saw him last."

"Who is that?"

"If he was 'always about on his horse, his pad groom was behind him' like Miss Smith said."

"Yes, but he's an underservant. Why would he bother speaking to him?" I asked flippantly.

Frank laughed.

Chapter Nine

We doubted the pad groom held his place near Chelsea with the Mistress, who likely only kept a team with a curricle. Lord Beornmund had been gone four months. We could not be sure the pad groom kept his employment at all, but if he did, he would be with the stallion. Under the cloak of dusk that day, when the family was most likely to be out, we went to Mayfair, to the parts where the servants stayed. The back lanes, hidden so as not to cause offense, took us to the stables. We found the coachman in the coach house.

Frank approached him and said, "My master's thoroughbred needs a Sire. I am told there may be an opportunity here. Not a draught horse, something special. I would speak to Viscount Beornmund's Pad Groom to vouch for the spirit of the animal."

The coachman scowled at us. The riding horses were not his area. He nodded toward the stable.

"Why did you tell him a pretense?" I asked catching up to Frank.

"It can't be much worse than bribing the boy who helped us find the lady's maid. We haven't time left to be stonewalled by those loyal to the Beornmund family. Besides, it was a good bet the horse would be a worthy sire, and the coachman can probably believe the Viscount would be getting ready to breed his father's horse for ready money. It is the only thing he can do to get his hands on funds until his father is proclaimed dead," Frank shrugged.

The stables were neatly kept and smelled better than most of the streets of London. The sweetness of fresh hay made me a little homesick. We passed teams of horses and

The Basra Pearls

went back to a stall where an Arabian stallion shifted from dark brown to sweaty black as it threw its legs forward, rearing and neighing. He was angry at a young man trying to calm the poor creature.

"He needs working," Frank said walking up to the young man in his early twenties who looked to be talking to the horse.

"I… I have, My Lord would ride him for hours at a time. He should not be left in the stable so long," he said.

"Can you not ride him?" I asked. The magnificent beast should be running free in the countryside somewhere.

"My duties are no longer dictated by Lord Beornmund, but his son, and he does not ride far, nor long. Now that twilight settles, I must take him out to get him calm for the night," the pad groom said.

"I need to know about the night Lord Beornmund disappeared," Frank asked.

"I was not with him that night," he said.

"When did the two of you last ride?" Frank asked.

"A few days before the coachman said he disappeared. We rode out to Camden Town," he said.

"What did you do out there?" Frank asked.

"He visited a man in a shop, then we rode back," he said.

"What shop could the Earl of Beornmund need to visit in Camden Town?" Frank asked.

"It was an apothecary," he said.

"Do you know what he bought?" Frank asked.

"No, Sir. I care for his horse when he goes into the shops," he said.

"Was he ailing?" Frank asked.

"No Sir, I've never seen an older man so fit. I could barely keep up with him. We raced on our way back."

"Where did you go after that?" Frank said.

"He had dinner at his club, then I accompanied him home."

"To the family home? Was he at tea with his family most nights?" Frank asked.

"No, he stayed mostly in Chelsea," he said.

"When did he last come to the family home here in Mayfair?" Frank asked.

"He came to his family the night before we went to Camden Town, and it had been a great while before that. He and his son did not get on," he said nodding in the direction of the great house.

"He came here three days before disappearing, then to Camden Town two days before, then what?" Frank asked.

"I do not know. The next morning, I waited with his horse ready. He never came," he said.

"Is that normal?" Frank asked.

The man, having calmed the horse, fidgeted, and looked at Frank.

"No Sir. He rode every morning," he said. Frank paused hoping the Pad Groom would just keep up with his work and talk to us like the maid had, but he did not seem inclined to gossip. He rubbed between the horse's ears and the beast dropped his head down. The groom opened the stallion's mouth to push the bit up past his teeth. He pulled the bridle up and opened the stall. I stepped back. The horse, at least fifteen hands, huffed through his nostrils and tossed his head.

"He could have been missing two days before it was reported," I said, to hurry Frank up and backing further when the young man made to maneuver around me to get to the horse tack.

"I do not know," he said, and I could see he would not lie, but neither would he suppose nor give opinion on the matter.

"What did you do during the two days?" Frank asked. "Did he have his horse, or did you?"

"I ...I worked Turk," he said nodding to the horse, that rammed the groom's arm impatiently with his muzzle.

"And now what are your duties?" Frank asked.

"I have always kept all the horses. Lord Beornmund trusts...trusted only me with Turk. I also keep the two horses at rented stables in Chelsea for Miss Keppel," he said smoothing his hand over the horse's back and throwing the padding on.

"Did Lord Beornmund send messages during the two days he did not ride his horse?"

"No Sir... I... I... on the second day I happened to see Miss Keppel. I asked if Lord Beornmund was ill, and she said she had not seen him, but suspected he left for the country at last with the family. I told her I had seen Lady Beornmund the day before when I came to the house. The Viscount's horse needed shoeing. She said only that Lady Charlotte needed her horse sent to her in the country. I arranged a rider before I left for the farrier. You see, they were still in town."

"Was Miss Keppel surprised?" I asked.

"She... she cried and asked if My Lord were with his lady," he said. "I told her I did not see him, and he did not take his horse. He did not go far without Turk. Miss Keppel was very confused and sent a note to him at his family's house by me."

"Did you see him respond?" Frank asked.

"No sir, I was told to wait for a response by Miss Keppel. I told her ladyship so, and since Lady Beornmund had not seen her Lord, she took the letter and read it. She responded to it herself," the Pad Groom said.

"When was this?" Frank asked.

"About tea-time on the second day," the Pad Groom said.

"Wait. You are sure it was teatime, on Thursday, July the ninth, the day he was reported missing?" Frank asked. Irritated the groom said:

"I'm not sure the exact day."

"But you must know when the horses are shod," Frank said.

"Yes," the young man looked up like he must tell the truth no matter what he was instructed. Without checking he said, "it was Wednesday, July the eighth I had the horse shod. Second Wednesday of every month. It is checked."

"The next day you went to deliver a note at teatime."

"The tea-things were laid out. I was shown into the room."

"You did not just leave the note?" I asked.

"It was not like My Lord to miss a day's ride – let alone two."

"You were concerned," Frank said.

"He…he wasn't quite himself for a few weeks before."

"You swear you did not see Lord Beornmund?" Frank asked. "Not for two days, especially not when the message was sent to him at teatime?"

"I did not see Lord Beornmund," the young man said, then, having done his duty, turned to lift a saddle over the horse's back atop the padding.

"Did Lady Beornmund seem worried when she responded to the note Miss Keppel sent?" Frank asked.

"Upon reading the note, she looked as though she needed to lie down," he said gritting his teeth tightening the saddle, jamming his knee into the horse's gut.

"She did respond to the note," Frank said.

"As I said." The young man glared, pulling the horse forward. I backed further out of the way. The anxious horse stomped and pawed and tossed his head. Frank tried again to ask the groom more, but he would not acknowledge us while fighting the stallion out of the stable.

We left.

"Their timing of Lord Beornmund's disappearance cannot stand," I said.

"Yes, but the defense does not get a say with the Grand Jury. I wish I knew the witnesses whose testimonies have been collected. It is them I must get to recant. It is clear why the pad groom is not a witness; he is unwilling to lie."

"He is an under servant. I doubt they asked him," I said.

"Which was very unwise," Frank said.

"You still have a day," I said biting my lip.

"Yes, one day," Frank said nodding. Neither of us ate much that evening at tea, though Frank pointed out it was our one-week anniversary, and we ought to celebrate. I tried to match his jovial tone, but my nerves kept me low. Thankfully, Frank came to bed, and I snuggled up into his arm, so I could relax enough to sleep.

Chapter Ten

The next morning Frank and I took the omnibus again. I was growing accustomed to it. It was filled with our sort of people, cleanly kept, though not grand. Professional, just going to their employment every day as we were.

We stopped by Jasper's chambers and picked up the permit admitting us to Newgate Prison. Before we left, Jasper smiled and handed me his handkerchief.

"What is this for?" I asked.

"You will see," he said.

We walked from Middle Temple to Old Bailey Road where Newgate Prison stood. The prison was a huge, eerie building with a sinister feeling of lost dreams and desperation tangibly wafting about the place. I could have sworn spiders crawled over my spine when we came in view of a platform where the square gallows could be erected in a snap. The bell tower stood over the platform in anticipation, ready to ring out telling all to fear justice and live virtue.

We entered the large building and presented our permit to a turnkey. He looked at it, nodded, then asked us to follow him. He took us to the sitting room of an apartment within the prison. There, as if they were old friends, Mr Archer, Lady Beornmund's solicitor, drank porter with the keeper.

"Are you here to question the prisoner as well?" Frank asked looking between the two men.

"I am here in case he confesses," Mr Archer said coldly. He tipped the glass swallowing the last of the dark liquid.

"To what he confesses, I suspect, is rather the question isn't it?" Frank asked, and the man choked on his drink. I took my husband's hand when the man glared at us.

"I'll take 'em," the keeper said motioning for the keys. The turnkey handed them over, and the keeper beckoned us to follow him. We paused to let Mr Archer walk with the man, and we brought up the rear.

After a few turns down passageways, a smell came upon us like that of decay and dampness, mixed with the sour smell of rotten milk and spoiled meat. I felt the jerking at the back of my throat. I held the handkerchief to my nose. It only helped a little.

We walked down a dank, dim passageway made of stone squares and packed with dirt. I felt something crunch under my foot.

"Do not look, Millie," Frank whispered. I scraped my foot along the floor. After the third time, I crunched I could not keep myself from looking. Goo streaked with green slid across the broken stone floor. I scraped it from the under part of my boot.

Even with the handkerchief, I held my breath when I could, and wretched at the back of my throat when I could not. The further we moved on, the more the smell eased. The keeper took us to a section of the prison that was lighter than the passageways we'd been in. An aisle extended before us with many metal doors. The keeper knocked and opened one.

In a small room of length and little width, stood a bed and a desk. Though very tight, it was much more accommodating than I would have thought, considering the smell of the place. Sitting at the desk was a dark-haired young man with large vulnerable eyes who turned when we entered. He must have been in his early twenties.

Frank and Jasper's worry was in vain. No one would hang such an innocent-looking fellow. He stood with a question in his eyes. He was as tall as Frank, but his arms were very muscular. He could probably hurt Lord Beornmund if he chose, but his quiet demeanor and wide, scared eyes did not seem capable, despite his size. I would sooner suspect Mr Archer and his menacing growls.

"I am Mr Hadleigh. I work with Mr Jasper Shaw, your barrister," Frank said. The young man immediately shut down. He leaned away from us and put a hand to his chest. Frank, trying to engage the young man said, "This is a nice room. You are very fortunate."

"My father… continues my allowance. I have bought an easement to give myself a modicum of comfort," Cecil said glancing at me uncomfortably, and even more so at Mr Archer behind me. He barely noticed the keeper who sat on his bed, at home in the place. Cecil, as if in an effort to get away from Frank, stepped back and leaned against his desk.

"I understand you are not telling your story," Frank said, giving up on trying to relax Cecil.

"Sir, I have nothing to tell," he said. He glanced again at me ashamed, and I knew he had something to tell. I do not know what my face showed. But the way he looked at me, and the disgust bubbling in my queasy stomach, I knew I must have been a sight. Frank read his hesitation toward me and while he was off-kilter asked, "You are the apprentice to an engineer?"

"Yes sir," Cecil said. He looked at Frank like he was trying to trick him. Then he looked back at me with the saddest, probing look… did he want me to help him? Or was it absolution he seemed to think I could give him?

"How did you get such an apprenticeship?"

"My father wanted me to have an apprenticeship in engineering, one of the classical professions. The engineer with whom I was apprenticing is the son of a civil engineer who trained him. It is…was a very desirable position," Cecil said, and he looked sad.

"Do you enjoy it?" Frank asked.

Cecil nodded in the affirmative only once, like he must give up the remembrance of enjoying it.

"And how long have you been working at it?"

"Five years. Since I finished school at sixteen, Sir," Cecil said. He flinched as if Frank shocked him, or he just realized how long he had been at it.

"You did not take your meals at the Engineer's residence in the waterworks?"

"Not the evening meal Sir. My father gave me an allowance because Mr Simpson, my master . . . he preferred me off in the evenings. He liked to… in the evenings he designed his…he is …good with steam engines and…it is not a part of the waterworks though, so he gives me the evenings so he can work on his patents," Cecil said.

"Very well, and in the five years you've apprenticed, what have you learned?" Frank asked.

Mr Archer took a step into the room shading us with his huge frame, but it was Cecil's glance he held. The boy looked nervous, he licked his lips, trying to decide what he should say.

"Nothing he can use in here," the jailer said like Frank implied Cecil might escape. Frank watched Cecil to see him relaxed so that he could gauge when he tensed up, but Cecil seemed nothing but tense.

"What part of town do you apprentice?"

"I am…I work at the Chelsea Waterworks, Sir," he said looking back at the solicitor.

"What do you do there during the days?" Frank asked, but his smile grew.

"I... well I manage the pumps, Sir. We have to keep the water clean and moving up to the reservoirs," Cecil said.

"You clean the water for the wealthy areas of the city better than the other districts, do you not?" Frank asked, and I could see he had made it to his point.

"It is a private owned company. Other companies could follow suit if they chose," he said.

"What is this new method to get the wealthy's water clean?" Frank asked.

"Mr Simpson installed a slow sand filter tower, Sir," Cecil said, this time he looked desperately at the solicitor, and his fists clenched.

"How does a filter tower work?" Frank asked.

"It is about two feet of sand and then shell, gravel, and bricks. The water runs through, and the sand catches all the impurities ... well, they are filtered out. It is Mr Simpson's doing; he is my master," he said bouncing a little.

"Do you ever see what is filtered out of the water?" Frank asked.

"I...I don't think..." Cecil looked around blowing air out of his mouth as a whale would a blowhole.

"It is a simple question, either you've looked, or you haven't. Perhaps such a filtration system must be cleaned. Who is there to clean it but the apprentice?" Frank asked.

"Please, Sir," Cecil said looking at Lady Beornmund's solicitor, "Please, may I go back to my book now?"

"First you must tell me some of what you fished out of the filtration system," Frank said.

"This is enough, can't you see you're causing him –"

"I see everything," Frank snapped at the solicitor who did not look so haughty now.

"I do not know what--"

"I am not so complacent as everyone else. I have studied the maps. It is rather disturbing that a severed finger sent down from the closets of Chelsea can be filtered back into the drinking water. That is disturbing. Not the only thing here that is disturbing, but one thing," Frank said looking at Cecil.

"Mr Simpson is... he is working on it," Cecil said.

"And while the issue of disease and human filth is alarming, I suppose we must focus on Lord Beornmund, who is rumored to have spent much of his time in Chelsea. I shall find witnesses if you will not help yourself," Frank said, turning more to Cecil. "Your sister is being introduced into the best of society. She has even dined at Mrs Talbot's exclusive suppers, an admittedly great friend of Lady Beornmund. Mrs Ellis, a cousin of that great lady, now wears the finest of apparel all fashioned from your father's shops. Yet it is curious she cannot replace her boots. Does your father not employ a cordwainer?"

"No, Sir," Cecil said.

"How is it you are sent to prison, and your sister takes one of the greatest social leaps in history?" Frank asked.

"I do not... my sister has always been accepted in circles, that..."

"Nonsense," Frank said glancing at the solicitor who was now very quiet. Cecil looked back to me. I implored, "Your father still gives to you an allowance and believes you will be transported quietly. Nothing makes sense."

"We do not wish to have the thing spread about," Mr Archer said to me, astounded I dare speak in a man's investigation.

Frank laughed. Turning the solicitor's attention to himself he said, "You know what will happen. On the morrow, the prisoner will stand before a grand jury. I suspect you have perfected some story or other that will cement the charge of murder against him. The case will be found, and Mr Chapman will be sent to trial where he will be given one chance to explain himself. He will stay quiet so as not to lie, which in the court's eyes is as good as an admission of guilt. He will do it because of some arrangement his father made with you or Mrs Ellis, I cannot be sure where it was instigated. I can only hope it washes, because she is naive enough to believe she is not killing an innocent man."

"It was not me," Mr Archer said under his breath with great venom.

"I am not afraid of the hangman," Cecil said, growing feisty, his chest puffing out with the truth of his statement.

"Everything about you will be rooted out. The news will spread, the story will be about everywhere. Your sister will not live down this scandal. Your father will lose his shop, and you, Cecil, will hang," Frank said trying to change the brave young man's mind.

"What do you know of it, Sir?" Cecil asked defensively.

"The murder of a nobleman is a case that can make or break careers. No barrister in the country will miss such an opportunity to be a part of your trial," Frank said.

"But my barrister is not known. He has not argued successfully," Cecil said.

"Which means to win a sham case Lady Beornmund's barrister, a Mr Bell, who is very good at his job, will be forced to destroy Mr Shaw's career as well. Not to mention, unless the judge is your uncle, there is no transportation for such a crime as killing a Lord."

With the fight upon his breast Cecil looked at the solicitor, trying to decide if he was trustworthy. Mr Archer, seeing him falter, said quickly:

"Her Ladyship does not wish to be unchristian; she has asked the honorable Sir John Dodson, Queens Advocate who is an old friend, to interfere on Mr Chapman's behalf, recommending transportation. She asked the case be heard in his chambers so it would not be publicized."

"Have you consulted her barrister on the matter?" Frank asked, shocked.

"It is done for the peerage," Mr Archer said avoiding the question. Either he had not thought to run this scheme by the barrister, or he assumed Frank, like Cecil, would not know the complexity of the laws. But even I knew canon law must make way for common law in murder trials.

"You should consult a scholar of the law before making such assurances. I cannot imagine Mr Bell would advise you such a case can be tried in ecclesiastic court. It has not been legal to do so for thirteen years," Frank said.

"If the Queen's Advocate will claim the benefit of Clergy, it will be so. Mr. Bell can have nothing to do with it. This will be done to get him transported instead of hung," the solicitor said forcefully. And he did try to believe it. He flinched and turned red, sweating profusely. It must be hard work to believe he was not going to get an innocent man – nay a boy barely into the world – hung.

Frank ticked his head back and forth proceeding carefully, like he often did when his elders were wrong but would not be convinced of it.

"It would be a break of common law for the Queen's advocate to get involved in a murder case. It has been much debated where the line between clergy and judge should be. If the honorable Sir Dodson interferes in a case at Old Bailey, it will not be a quiet affair I assure you. Mr. Chapman's family will be found out and shunned as soon as the trial is over."

"His sister has already been the belle of many balls. Her standing is already made and can't be taken away," the solicitor said.

"By whom, what balls? There is none now in London," Frank said.

"Not to mention," I followed up, "even at home, in our parish, my sister-by-law gained popularity for a moment. It was stripped off her like a gown after a ball the minute her elevation passed. If I had not intervened, the neighborhood would still shun her and that is only the workings of a country village. You cannot believe they will let the shopkeeper's daughter stay among them after her brother is convicted of murder and she has no advocate?"

Everyone was silent. Frank went in for his final dig:

"It is no time to believe in fairy stories, Cecil. Once the Queens Counsel is involved, all these promises you've been made will be thin air spoken into a wind that has long ago blown away. I promise I am the only one trying to help you. Tomorrow at the very least you must plead Not Guilty if your case is found. Staying silent is the same as admitting guilt, and I can see you do not mean to lie. Saying nothing will be a lie and you will have no chance at trial."

Cecil looked at the solicitor. He looked at me. He was scared but loyal. I could see Frank meant to induce him to defend himself, but this man was a romantic. There was only one to get him to talk. He would not do it to save himself so I said, "A very lovely shopwoman means to give testimony on your behalf. She will do it no matter what path you take. Is it fair to ask her to make such a sacrifice, likely her position with your father and every other good society, if you will not at least try to save yourself?"

"Miss Marianne?"

"Yes. She will fight for you even if you will not fight for yourself. She gave us testimony on your behalf," I said.

"She will condemn herself. She will end in ruin defending the condemned," he said in despair.

"Likely," I said quietly. "It is a fallacy of our society."

"Can you induce her to say nothing? Can she be protected?" Cecil asked.

"I believe that is what you must do," I said gently.

The solicitor could not lie to Cecil and tell him he could guarantee anyone's safety after the trial began. Mr Archer's underestimation of Frank was dissolving into respect, and he stayed silent.

"I … I found the ring in the waterway. It … it was still attached to the finger. Mr Simpson had gone to the country on holiday. It was late, and so I took it home, meaning to turn it into the authorities when the magistrate's office opened in the morning. By chance, my father found it in the parchment I'd carefully put it in to keep it preserved. My father called me a Mudlark for finding it. A disgrace to our family and the apprenticeship he bought me, but I … I didn't mean to find it. It is part of my job to keep the filter going. I had no idea of even trying to pawn it."

"Why did you not turn it in to the authorities?" Frank asked.

"Father forbade me from turning it in. He said we would be ruined. He did not wish to blight our family name. He fears Mr Peel's police force fiercely after a string of shop burglaries a few years previous that were blamed on him, simply because he had a master key. Thankfully, we hired a few men to watch the place, and the culprit was caught in the act of picking the lock or Father would have lost everything. Since then, he has never used the bobbies for anything, even theft in our shop. That is why instead of turning it in, he had me bury the finger, ring, and all in a wooden cigarette box," Cecil said.

"How did it end up pawned?" Frank asked.

"Father asked a few people discreetly about the insignia on the ring – a pelican feeding her young. Mrs Ellis came a couple weeks after it was found. She often offers to be seen in our shop's clothes, and he gifts them to her in hopes she will take an interest in Eleanor. Her estate is all but gone, but her influence remains wide. Father asked if she knew who had such a ring and she recognized it immediately. She said it was her cousin Lord Beornmund's. He had been missing almost a month. When father asked about it, she knew instantly he was involved."

"Did your father fear being implicated again?" Frank asked.

"I...I do not know." Cecil looked from Frank to me. He'd never thought of that. Perhaps that is the reason his father shifted blame so quickly to his son. Perhaps the man did fear the law so badly he thought he had to sacrifice his only son to that far-reaching arm.

"Mrs Ellis said if I pawned the ring, and reburied the finger to be sure the Lord of Beornmund was proclaimed dead, my father's name would never be mentioned. I would be quietly transported, and my sister would be invited to teas and balls... it is all Eleanor has ever wanted."

"Mrs Ellis believes she can arrange that?" I asked astounded, looking from Cecil to Mr Archer, who shrugged as if he knew the whole thing was ludicrous, but perhaps at a certain point, he had a master he did not disobey.

"The witness who watched you bury the finger," Frank said.

"A man who collects my father's duties on his silks. He will often help my father on little matters," Cecil said.

"He was paid then, by whom?" Frank asked.

"That is quite enough," the solicitor stormed seeing himself thrown into a murky area.

"You paid him," Frank said belligerently to Mr Archer.

"You have no right, Sir," the solicitor returned, without denying this.

"Your lady needed a dead husband that she might not wait the seven years it takes for a disappeared man to be proclaimed dead. Her dear friend Mrs Ellis plans for Mr Chapman to take the blame and this ridiculous overly complicated scheme is born. I suppose even now the trustees have given your lady access to her jointure," Frank said.

"Tread very lightly, Sir," Mr Archer said, "or you will learn what you are about, throwing such accusations around."

"That is not my business," Frank said. "Proving Cecil did not kill the man is my business. Proving we have no body will be easier for us than proving there is one. Not to mention there is no cause of death, simply a dismembered finger. For all we know, Lord Beornmund is on holiday and lost a finger in some accident before he left."

"We know the Lord is dead," the solicitor snapped.

"Did the family have the Lord killed?" Frank asked.

"No," the solicitor said, astounded Frank would imply such a thing but they set a young man up to die for finding a finger. What could we expect?

"Where is Lord Beornmund?" Frank asked.

"We do not know. He disappeared. His finger is all we have found of him in months," the solicitor said.

"Well, I think you can let this boy go, anyway," Frank said.

"Certainly not," the solicitor said. "He may very well be lying. He clearly spends much of his time in Chelsea. How do we know he did not kill the Lord and cut off his finger as proof? We have testimony of witnesses that will hold up in court. What proof do you have?"

"Very well. Let us move forward with the grand jury. I believe you will gain a case against Mr Chapman, and it will go to trial. As a sign of good faith, and the promise I gave her ladyship, I will tell you one bit of proof I have."

"Excuse me?" Mr Archer said, surprised.

"Lady Beornmund ought to recant her statement about when she last saw her husband. She does not like to lie. Besides, I would not have her perjure herself to the grand jury, though I fear she's already signed her bill of indictment. I can prove she hasn't any idea when her husband disappeared. The pad groom brought a message to Lord Beornmund at teatime the night she swore she saw him last. He waited for an answer. Lord Beornmund never came. He saw Lady Beornmund answer the note instead. Neither she nor the Mistress had seen him for tea that evening."

Frank continued: "Most interesting fact: The pad groom who was in habit of seeing your Lord every day had not seen him for two days at that point, yet still had care of his prized horse he never went anywhere without. What are the chances the Earl of Beornmund had been gone two days before anyone noticed he was missing?"

The solicitor said nothing, but he looked a little green. Apparently, he had not thought to question the pad groom. But then, as Jasper said, why would you question the under servants?

"Cecil, you may, with confidence say you are not guilty when put on the dock tomorrow. Other than that, hold your peace. We will need no testimony from you at trial. I can see you mean to do right by your sister, but will not perjure yourself. I can respect that," Frank said bowing to him. Cecil closed his tired eyes and the purplish brown bruises from sleepless nights were an intense backdrop to his dark lashes.

Frank turned to the keeper and said, "I suppose you also must hope the charges brought against Mr Cecil Chapman be 'not found' in a day's time. For if not, we will defend him at trial. That will give you very little time to investigate how the ring ended up at the Chelsea Waterworks. You will not wish to look incompetent with no investigation into the matter," Frank said.

The keeper clenched his jaw and glared up at Mr Archer.

Frank finished, "After all, a Lord's death brings the newspapermen. I would track it by the waterways near Lord Beornmund's residence in Chelsea if it were me. Millie, we are finished here."

"Of course," I said, quickly putting my notebook into my pocket and nodding a warm goodbye to Cecil. Frank took my arm and walked me quickly down the aisle while the keeper and the solicitor locked Cecil back up.

"I think you scared that big man," I said as we turned a few halls and stepped back into the concentrated stench.

"I hope so," Frank said nodding seriously, putting a finger against his nose.

"I am sorry I talked in front of them. I know it is not done. Sometimes I just can't help it," I said.

"You're intelligent, and add to the conversation every time you speak. You got Cecil to talk. Why would I wish you to stay quiet?" Frank asked, looking at me a little confused.

"It is not done hereabouts. Women do not interfere in men's business. There are a few wives who help keep their husband's chambers in order, as I am doing for Jasper. But they know to stay firmly in the background. I do not wish to embarrass you," I said.

"I am proud to have you on my arm, Millie. Do not ever think like that. My wish for you is to stun London at every turn with the ponderings of an intelligent woman," Frank said grinning down at me. I leaned my head against his arm trying not to smell the hallway.

"Frank," I asked trying not to wretch.

"Yes,"

"Why did you tell Mr Archer—"

A woman's scream ripped the words from my mouth and echoed through the hallway into my heart. It cut me. It shouldn't have physically hurt me, but I felt agony.

"Is she dying?" I asked, tears springing to my eyes. Such a scream sat on my chest and ate at my stomach.

"No, it happens every so often. I do not know why the women of this prison shriek. Most of the inmates are not kept as comfortably as Cecil," he said.

"That was a very desperate sort of sound," I gasped sadly looking up at Frank, trying not to cry.

"Come dear one, you are too sweet for this place," he said. We walked in silence. The echo of the scream still sounded loudly in my ears; I could not speak over it. Newgate Prison was not a place I wished to revisit.

When we finally breathed the air of the free, I did not feel so constricted by the scream. Every block we walked, surrounded by busy people moving along their way, made me dizzy. I felt alone and swarmed at the same time. I must have swayed because Frank wrapped an arm around my waist to steady me. When we entered the quiet grounds at Middle Temple, I took a deep breath that smelled like wet trees, but mingled with a memory of the smell from the prison. Somehow even the memory of filth made my stomach churn.

We walked silently for a time and I took in the clean woodsy autumn dampness in the air around me as if it scrubbed my lungs clean.

"Sit for a moment, Millie," Frank said guiding me to our bench under a tree near the gentle hum of the water fountain.

The breeze lifted a wet, heavy yellow-orange leaf off an ignited almond tree. The burning leaf, against the blue of the sky, whipped around in the chilly gust. Others held tightly to the branches fighting the inevitable, refusing to die.

After watching several swirling gusts carry away handsful of leaves, I turned to Frank. With a weak hollow voice, I asked, "How did the ring get into the filters?"

"I have no idea, but if the solicitor does, I doubt he'll sleep easy tonight," Frank said with a laugh trying to cheer my sunken spirits.

"Frank," I admonished, nudging him.

"The man, no matter what he tells himself to the contrary, is willing to let Cecil hang, knowing he is innocent. That is the real fallacy here," he said giving me his look, and I could see he meant to engage my soul in outrage. It worked, and I joined in his indignation.

"You are right," I said. "I ... why do I do that? I would forgive the solicitor everything because he works for the right family. He would kill Cecil Chapman to have a murdered Lord so his Lady may have her money. That is the true crime here," I said.

Frank grinned down at me and put an arm around me. His warmth spread through me until my chest did not feel so heavy with the woman's scream, the scream of a person on fire, who finally let go, to be batted about in the wind, and then quietly settle into the earth.

Chapter Eleven

Frank procured me a ticket to Old Bailey for the Grand Jury. Since spectators could not hear the evidence brought against the prisoner, it was not as busy as it would be at the actual trial. I sat in a loft suspended above the proceedings. There were few other women spectating, but many men sat writing. The judge's clerk would read a formal accusation, and the men around me in the gallery would write something if the case seemed interesting.

There was no judge at this stage, just a jury of middlish men – our people. The sort who rode the omnibus with us. The clerks and apprentices, cousins being put forward, and bookkeepers.

After the clerk read out a bundle of indictments, the twenty men who sat in the jury box would then retire to the Grand Jury room. They reviewed testimonies and decided if there was enough evidence to fit a true bill and go to trial or if it should be dismissed.

There was only one murder charge on the docket because most murder cases went through the coroner's inquest jury and then to trial. Because no body had been found for a coroner's jury to examine, they lumped Cecil's murder charge in with the Grand Jury.

The Grand Jury heard mostly indictments for cases of theft. The poor creatures charged had to be brought forward on the dock when the clerk read out their charges. If their charges were found true, they could enter a plea. The hopelessness on the worn faces being accused brought me very low.

The jury listened to groups of charges and went back into their room several times to hear the evidence before it arrived at Cecil's case. Mr Chapman, Cecil's father, joined us in the gallery a quarter of an hour before his son's charges were read.

When Cecil shuffled into the court, the men around me perked up, like a collective group of dogs on the prowl. They came specifically to hear the indictment against him. Cecil wore a mask of bravery, but the way his body turned away from the jury box indicated fear. The crowd around me murmured against Cecil. He stood quietly, head down, waiting to hear his indictment.

"Evil is them that kill in cold blood, but only the daft kill a Lord," said one man in front of me.

The jury eyed Cecil with the same venom. Especially after Mr Bell, Lady Beornmund's barrister, a gentleman of forty or so, dressed handsomely, with a fine figure and nicely kept blond locks, came to the bar.

"The Beornmund's have Bell, poor bloke," someone behind me said. During his education at Middle Temple, Frank told me he met twice with Mr Bell, a bencher. He said the man knew the law better than those making them and could win on his debating skills alone. It disappointed Frank the barrister would participate in Mrs Ellis' underhanded scheme.

The clerk who oversaw the grand jury began.

"The Prisoner, Mr Cecil Chapman, tried for the indictment of Man Slaughter," the clerk said, "Mr Bell, you will represent the victim's family?"

"Sir, but we wish to change the indictment," Mr Bell said.

"Excuse me?" the clerk said, looking up from his docket confused. By the way the men around me reacted, they were as baffled as myself.

"The charge was drawn too quickly. We have not been able to locate any whereabouts of the Lord Beornmund's remains. There is no body. We can only charge Mr Chapman with theft."

"Does your evidence support the change?" the clerk asked puffing out his chest to appear competent to Mr Bell, who clearly intimidated him.

"I can tell you now since you would be the one to draw the charges. There is no need to keep the evidence private since Mr Chapman, who remained silent until yesterday, has provided it himself. Mr Chapman was in possession of the Beornmund family's signet ring, worn always upon Lord Beornmund's left little finger. The finger was severed. The ring attached. Mr Chapman found it in the filter at the Chelsea pumps where he is apprentice. Affeered of being accused and losing his apprenticeship, the boy buried the finger. His father asked around among his elite clientele to find the owner of the ring. One Mrs Ellis recognized the pattern, and informed him that it belonged to the Beornmund family. She notified Scotland Yard, and the young man was taken into Newgate Prison. He has been there since the seventh of August. We cannot be sure it warrants an indictment of theft even," Mr Bell said. I thought he looked relieved to say so.

"They imprisoned the boy three months for finding the finger," a man in front of me hissed.

"Looking for a scapegoat, and it's always falling to the working man," his companion said much louder.

"So much for the end to old corruption," the first said even louder. Then, so the court could hear him, he called, "Can it be wondered at; the young man buried the finger instead of giving it to the bobbies? As soon as he did, he was arrested. No honest working man is safe in London with the… the mutton shunters about."

A few men laughed at the man's barb. I watched Cecil Chapman's father carefully. He heard the men and seemed to agree with them. It must have something to do with his being charged. He sat up straighter, and joined his angry cry with the men.

The clerk glared at the gallery. He looked around slightly vexed, but mostly confused. He avoided Mr Bell's eye, embarrassed he could not keep the courtroom together. The clerk did not know what to do. He was only supposed to keep things running; he didn't draw up charges on the spot. Finally, spying Jasper at the bar, he continued:

"The young man is represented?"

"Yes, Sir," Jasper said.

"Since the evidence is presented, Mr Chapman may come forward."

Cecil shuffled dragging his chains to the front of the dock.

"How does your client plead to the charge of theft if I am to even draw such a charge?" the clerk asked looking to Mr Bell for help. The man looked back patiently letting the clerk decide.

The clerk turned impatiently on Jasper trying to ignore the gallery; they were growing rowdy. Jasper was the only one who looked more confused than the clerk. Completely befuddled, Jasper was not supposed to play a role in the Grand Jury proceedings except to show Cecil would have defense. Jasper glanced at Frank, and I heard a well-dressed man behind me laugh.

"Mr Shaw doesn't know how to win, even when it's handed to him," he said.

Frank, who had been wildly scrawling a note behind Jasper, handed him a scrap of paper, and Jasper read it out.

"We feel there is insufficient evidence to prove a crime has even been committed. Lord Beornmund's disappearance and his severed finger found indicates foul play, but to say Mr Chapman had any part in the foul play is not warranted. As he and his father made every effort to return the ring to the lost party, the indictment of theft cannot be supported."

"Very well. We will not even send the jury back since it seems no one can prove a crime," the clerk prompted the jury, as he had a few times before as to what they should think. "What do you find about this unproved theft?"

A seasoned juror, who did not bother to consult with the other jury members, said, "The case is not found. Furthermore, Mr Chapman's three-month incarceration taking him from his apprenticeship in this way is corruption at its very core and a blatant misuse and overreach of authority."

"Here, here," said the man in front of me.

"The prisoner is to be released immediately," the clerk snapped at the jailor, seeing the whole of the court was against any further proceedings. He ducked his head writing notes on a paper. Cecil's father exclaimed a little and shook hands with the man next to him. Then he got up and made his way down from the gallery.

He reappeared in the courtroom, waiting for his son to be freed of his shackles. He looked nervous to get too close to the jailor, but the court had already moved on to the next case. When free, Cecil was scurried away by his father. I was delighted he came to witness his son's exoneration.

Frank came up to the gallery to take me back to Middle Temple after he had seen Cecil released. The reporters recognized him as the note writer and shook his hand. They plagued him for more information on the Beornmund case, but Frank only said it was a mystery that poor Mr Chapman had nothing to do with. Frank did not stop to talk to them and instead escorted me out of Old Bailey as quickly as possible.

"That was strange," I said when we were away from the reporters.

"Yes, but it is a better representation of what happened," Frank said.

"Mr Chapman looked very happy seeing his son released despite all he said to make us believe he had sworn him off," I said.

"Yes, I was quite surprised he came down acknowledging him as a son again. When it came to it, he values him," Frank said.

"I think it helped Mr Chapman when the reporters who sat near him were appalled at how easily one, out and about, could find himself suspected without reason. Cecil being held at Newgate for so long made them particularly angry."

"Yes, their outrage could be heard on the floor."

"Why didn't Mr Bell present his case at all?" I asked.

"I hoped it would be so. I saw a nobleness in Lady Beornmund when she lied poorly. I would wager she did not like any of this but rather felt bound because her cousin Mrs Ellis already swore in affidavit she recognized the ring, and who knows what else she swore to. They may have still found their case if they presented it to the grand jury, but it would eventually destroy Lady Beornmund's reputation. The papers would have eaten that up."

"I did notice you told the solicitor your evidence before the trial. It was very clever of you to trade her reputation for Cecil's life," I said.

He kissed my hand and grinned. I shoved him for getting so mushy on the street. A peddler woman said, "You batty-fang that un."

We laughed and were very pleased with ourselves the rest of the day.

Chapter Twelve

    The next day's news printed a story about the mystery of the Lord Beornmund's finger, there still being no sign of the Lord. Cecil was only mentioned as the poor bloke who found the finger and was consigned to months of prison for it, crying the peelers would turn London into a police state after all.

    The next morning instead of taking the omnibus over the Waterloo bridge as we usually did, we traversed the Westminster bridge. Frank and I went to see Mr Chapman at his home in St. James. The fine building was not as distinguished as some, but still in a better part of St. James than many families of gentility could claim. Mr Chapman must do well for himself having more money than many of the old families.

    I was not sure why we went, except Frank said he meant to be sure Cecil reconciled with his father. It was meant as a surprise to me as well because Frank kept saying, "Wait and see Millie, wait and see. We will have one entertaining day before we must get down to work."

    He grinned as he reached out for the brass sphinx door knocker that was ostentatious when compared with the plain cast iron ones along the row. The drawing-room was so close to the front door we did not even see past a tight passageway into the rest of the house. The butler showed us into an ostentatious sitting room. Gold-plated frames covered the walls, shaded lamps dripped with crystals, porcelain figurines on stone pedestals stood regally next to rich green and yellow covered settees and a rug. Every inch of the room flourished in flamboyant extravagance like Miss Chapman had. She and the room belonged together.

We stood when Cecil walked into the drawing room. His feelings, as if encouraged by the room, flowed forth in excess as he shook hands with Frank. Frank smiled and nodded uncomfortably at Cecil's overly abundant gratitude.

"I thank you, Sir," Cecil said again and again. His father also came into the room. He did not seem as angry as he had in his shop, but he eyed us distrustfully.

"My solicitor will send payment to your master this afternoon," Mr Chapman said standing near us with his hands behind his back.

"That is all well. I am interested in what Cecil will do now," Frank said glancing at the father.

"There will be shows over the season. He always did well with them," Mr Chapman said looking out the window and hitting his hands together behind him. He gave no indication he was likely to sit, nor offer us a seat.

"I had the impression, Sir, since you have taken up lodgings away from your shop and are training an agent to act in your stead, that you are moving away from the daily running of the place. Having your son run your shows does not help you take on the role of the leisurely gentleman," Frank said.

"I do not think it matters now," Mr Chapman said. "No matter what we do, there is a barrier between us and the Quality."

"I cannot advise you on that; it is not my area. However, the act of giving your son a gentleman's profession has not been wasted. Your son is a gifted engineer," Frank said.

"I do not think Mr Simpson will take him back. He was at the trial yesterday, but would not speak to me," Mr Chapman said.

"I will see to the matter if you give me leave," Frank said.

"You may do what can for him. Perhaps even find him a new master," Mr Chapman said.

"Let us try Mr Simpson first. There was no crime. You have paid the apprenticeship. The law is on your side. Cecil would do best to go on as before. He has done nothing wrong, and since he is found ignoramus there is no reason for him not to go back," Frank said.

"It…I will be let back into my apprenticeship?" Cecil said hopefully.

"We shall see. I mean to do my best for you, Sir. Go put on your outer things; it is a chilly morning," Frank said happily. I could not help myself. I squeezed Frank's arm I still held. Of course, Frank had to be sure Cecil settled back into his life. The idea delighted me. Cecil paused to say to Frank, "I … I do not doubt that you have been a great benefit to me, Sir, for you seem divine, such as a saving angel."

Cecil smiled, he looked very much like his sister when he smiled, but the features being more masculine made his face moderately attractive. After his face filled back out and the dark circles under his eyes faded, he would likely be handsome. He was a warm, vibrant soul, the kind who would sacrifice for the sister he loved.

Miss Marianne and Miss Chapman's feud had been much more significant than one resenting the other's beauty. The former had been angry with Miss Chapman for letting her brother take such a fall. The sister had no choice in the matter as her father thought his loss inevitable, but she had looked guilty. Could she have done more for her brother?

Why would my first thought be that they fought over something trivial when there was a life on the line? Did my mother's silly quibbles about Clara Bolton's beauty and my bland features continue to infect my beliefs that such things were all that mattered to everyone else?

After Cecil left to get his outer things, I thought perhaps Mr Chapman would offer us a seat, but instead, he said:

"I...Mrs Ellis is very persuasive. I should not have... she does not consider anyone but herself. When she convinced me the law would not be on our side considering who was on the other...I gave up. It is not something I should have done. I...thank you... for... thank you," Mr Chapman said nodding to Frank, then turning to look out the window.

"Yes Sir," Frank said politely. As Jasper's client, he repressed all he wished to say to the father. Instead, we stood in the extravagant room in silence.

"I will be at the shop. Come tell me how it goes...Son," Mr Chapman said when Cecil returned.

"Yes, of course, Father," he said, and we followed Cecil out of the room, then onto the street.

"If your father does wish to join the Quality, he needs to learn to invite people to sit," I hinted to Cecil.

"Oh, yes. Sorry. He is so accustomed to standing all day, it does not occur to him," Cecil said with a laugh. "He is not so ornery a fellow. He's just trying to keep things together."

"It is no matter," Frank said clapping Cecil on the back.

Cecil hired a hackney, and we rode out toward the river. The area was very different from London. Our road went along the parks of St. James. The few fashionable people not at country parties walked the streets, ladies with parasols, and gentlemen with canes. All clicked along, wrapped in furs enjoying the sun before the frost settled in. I felt lower simply for being in a hackney, eyed with mild disgust by those riding in new, well-sprung carriages that passed us. Cecil must have noticed because he said, "Father bought Elenore a new curricle last year, but she is out, or we may have taken it."

"This is a very comfortable ride," I said. "We have been used to the omnibus."

"Oh, yes. It is not terribly far to the waterworks. I can walk it in less than an hour. I never learned to ride a horse, but I usually enjoy the walk in the morning and evenings when the streets are quiet," Cecil said.

We drove along the water canal until we were again at the river. This time we were on the westernmost part of the fan of London. There, built on a little inlet, were the tall billowing towers of the Chelsea Water Works. As we alighted the hackney, Cecil paid the man to stay and wait for us. We would be walking if he did not.

We approached the nearest building, and Cecil paused before the door. I thought we might stand there all day but a man with serious dark eyes walked up behind us. I recognized him as the man who laughed in the courtroom when Jasper turned to consult Frank before speaking. The man said, "Mr Chapman, you have made it past your troubles I see."

"Mr Simpson," Cecil said growing pale. "Yes, Sir. I am so sorry, Sir."

"I suppose you wish for your apprenticeship back," he said.

"If it please you, Sir," Cecil said.

"I suppose we will from now on send someone with you when you check the filters," Mr Simpson said.

"I swear, I will never again... ah..."

"You will keep the filters going. In the future, I would have you speak to me about anything you find, not your father," he said with unconcealed agitation, "He is no longer your master. I am."

"Yes, Sir," Cecil said, bowing respectfully.

"Very well. Get your affairs in order and return tomorrow at your usual hour," he said eyeing the waiting hackney.

"Yes, Sir. Thank you, Sir," Cecil said bowing again. Mr Simpson turned to Frank and said, "You did a good job defending him, Sir."

"Excuse me," Cecil said. "Sir, may I present Mr Frank Hadleigh, and his wife, Mrs Millie Hadleigh. Mr James Simpson, engineer of the Chelsea Waterworks."

I curtsied and Cecil asked at the same time, "How did you know it was Mr Hadleigh that defended me?"

"I know the Shaw family well. They are an old family I have been acquainted with for years. I was very unhappy when I learned it would be Mr Jasper Shaw defending you. I went to Old Bailey to see the grand jury indict you if they could. When the Beornmund's barrister, Mr Bell, who is a bulldog, backed down, I knew it was not Mr Jasper Shaw's doing. Especially when Mr Shaw turned to Mr Hadleigh, clearly baffled as to what he should do with the plea," he said with a little laugh.

Frank smiled. It fell when Mr Simpson said, "You are talented clearly; you would do well to find a more… stable sort of apprenticeship."

"Thank you, Sir," Frank said politely, "I do not mean to do my pupillage with Mr Shaw. I was just helping an old schoolfellow."

"That is a relief. And I thank you. Cecil is also talented. He has a head for figuring only someone raised in a shop could and I need some figuring done for a steam pump I am working on. I have been petitioning the Lord Mayor of London for years to redo many of the waterworks. If anyone saw the filters, they would not dare drink the water."

Someone opened the door and called to him. He nodded to us and said, "until tomorrow, Chapman."

"Thank you for a second chance. I swear I will never have need of another, Sir." Cecil bowed yet again, and we left.

"Well, I was not needed after all," Frank said.

"I would never have thought to ask for my apprenticeship back. I do appreciate it, Sir," Cecil said as we walked toward the waiting hackney.

"You are very welcome, Sir. I suppose you would not mind dropping us at a crossroad where we can catch an omnibus," Frank said, taking my hand. Now that Cecil found his path, it was time for Frank to look for his own.

"No, Sir, please. I want to make a gift to your lovely wife. Come, let us go to the shop," Cecil insisted.

"I do not require finery, surely," I said.

"Every woman needs something fine to wear," Cecil insisted.

"It is on our way back to Middle Temple, Millie. You have often looked at bonnets in our travels," Frank said.

I relented and we went with him to his father's shop. I was not feigning reluctance as my mother would have been. I wished Frank had not agreed with Cecil's request to gift me something. I felt… I could not explain it. It is where my mother wanted me, among the Quality, but Westminster was not my place. I was not comfortable there.

We walked in, and the pretty shopwoman, though with a customer, smiled with endearment at Cecil. Cecil forgot us for a moment watching her. That is when Miss Chapman came into the shop.

"Cecil, oh I went to find you, and you were gone. I thought we were to stay together from now on," she said sincerely, gliding over to him with her strange sliding walk.

Cecil hugged her, and together they fit. She was attractive with him, and he was not vulnerable with her. They loved each other.

"Are you twins?" I asked.

"No, I am fourteen months older than he," Miss Chapman said.

"And she will not ever allow me to be grown for it," Cecil said, taking her arm.

The shopwoman finished with her customer. When the shop cleared, she joined our little group in the corner.

"Cecil," she said happily giving him both her hands. He took them and brazenly kissed them. It surprised her, but she smiled, shyly gratified.

"I am very glad to see you, Miss Marianne."

"I am so very glad you have come to no harm," she said.

"What is this?" Mr Chapman asked coming toward us from the back. Letting go of the shopwoman who flinched, startled at her master's voice, Cecil turned to his father happily.

"I am to be at the waterworks at the usual time tomorrow," Cecil said.

"Will you move into the house with Mr Simpson?" Mr Chapman asked.

"No, I think it will be as it was. He prefers his privacy in the evenings," Cecil said.

"Very good, my boy," Mr Chapman said, but he reached out and shook hands with Frank as if he had arranged the whole thing instead of just giving Cecil the courage to see the man about his apprenticeship.

"I suppose you mean to become a famous engineer, tinkering with the steam engines and the like," Miss Chapman said.

"Yes, I do," Cecil said. "Also Father, I have two years left on my apprenticeship. I will likely take a wage within a year, and be able to set up my own household. I would like…may I court Miss Marianne now?"

We all went quiet. Miss Marianne grew red, and her eyes welled with tears, but she took Cecil's arm and looked with hope at her master.

"We… we have made such strides. We are almost free of the stench of servitude," Mr Chapman said looking at the shopwoman. "And she is my most requested attendant. I have never let her out for I cannot afford to lose her. And now I must give her to my own son?"

"Please, Father," Cecil said.

"I have had my moment, Father," Miss Chapman said joining her brother's cause as she should have months ago. "I have felt the loss of my brother. His absence would be greater than any gain I may make in my standing with the Quality. We have friends and acquaintances enough and our own lovely dinner parties are much nicer to attend. Let us live comfortably at our level and not bother with the nobility. What do we need with a society that would have us sacrifice our own flesh to be a part of them?"

Mr. Chapman looked at Miss Marianne and Cecil and slowly nodded his approval to them. "Yes, I suppose you are right," he said. "I can tell you one thing. If she knows what is good for her, Mrs Ellis best not be bold enough to show her face here looking for gifts."

"Ah yes, on that note, I had hoped, Father, we might do something for Mrs Hadleigh," Cecil said looking at me.

"It is not necessary," I said turning bright red.

"Oh, fix the lass up. But nothing recognizable. We have all those ready-made samples you can have pieced together for her," Mr Chapman said. Turning to Frank, he said, "No offense meant Sir, but despite all this high talk, I have my shop's reputation to consider."

"Of course," Frank said bowing politely, but there was a little bit of fiery offense behind his eyes. He tried to hide it, but Frank did not respect Mr Chapman. Miss Chapman and Marianne did and took him at his word. They had the most talented seamstress leave her work and sewed me into a lovely silk and velvet day gown that was almost already sewn. I had never seen a dress that did not start from a bolt of cloth. It was not as ornate as Miss Chapman's, but it suited me. It looked much like what many of the other middlish women wore, and I thought perhaps I would fit in on the omnibus a little better.

When we left the shop Frank told me I looked lovely.

"Thank you," I said, distracted.

"What is it, Millie?" Frank asked.

I looked up at him. There was something I needed to understand. I would not admit why I needed to know; I just did. I asked:

"What did he mean, when he said he did not let Miss Marianne out?"

"In these shops, sometimes it is not only the goods that are for sale. But clearly, he did not allow it," Frank said.

"Because he protected her, or when he said he feared he would lose her, he meant…"

"She would come back to him with child. She could work no more," Frank said.

"Women are to be bought and sold like baubles at a shop, at any man's whim?" I asked sadly.

"It should not be," Frank said.

"Can you wonder why the women in Newgate scream so?" I asked.

Frank took a deep breath.

"No, Millie. I suppose I cannot."

Chapter Thirteen

After leaving the shop we went back to Middle Temple. Frank meant to be paid as soon as Jasper was so his fee would not get swallowed up in Jasper's habits. Jasper received an allowance that paid for his rooms, but he often spoke of his need for just a bit more ready money. Mr Chapman was in his office with his solicitor when we left. We assumed it was to get Jasper paid. Therefore, we went to Jasper's chambers to wait.

At first, I liked looking pretty. I may not have felt any aversion to the strangely pieced-together dress I wore if it had not been for Jasper. When he saw me in my new day dress, he could not stop exclaiming to Frank how fine I looked.

I tried to be civil to him, but eventually, I wished he would not notice me. Later that afternoon, Mr Chapman's solicitor brought Jasper's payment. The man also brought several packages for me since it was not known where else I could be found. I could not decide who was more disgruntled, me, or the solicitor, as he stated twice, he was not a courier.

According to a note, Mr Chapman sent me an additional two dresses he could do nothing with, as he didn't use ready-made in his shop. I began to wish I had not allowed the first dress, let alone more when Jasper expressed a wish to see me in the other dresses as well.

He even encouraged me to open the parcels in his chambers, but I refused and eyed the parcels with irritation. Thankfully, Jasper paid Frank and we made to leave.

"I shall wander about Middle Temple tomorrow visiting some of the benchers looking for a pupillage," Frank said. "We will not likely meet."

"Not so. We have an appointment here at ten tomorrow. I would like to help with that matter since you have done so much for me," Jasper said.

"If you wrote me a letter of character, it would be much appreciated," Frank said stiffly.

"I can do better. You will see. Tomorrow morning at ten sharp," Jasper said slyly. Frank nodded but looked concerned.

I tried not to worry about what Jasper meant by helping Frank as he could barely help himself. Not to mention how uncomfortable he made me. We were trying to leave and he still encouraged me to open my parcels. I would not have kept the dresses, but that evening when I finally did open them a note fell out. It read:

"I am glad I do not have to be transported to be with the man I love. The banns will be posted as soon as he takes a wage. Thank you for saving him, Marianne Smith."

I knew the dresses were from her. There must have been some sacrifice made, either in wages or pride for her to get me the lovely dresses. Then I wanted them. They represent her and me. We were of the lucky few who made it out. But then why is it only by luck and the love of good men a woman could make it out of the sticky mess of maidenhood?

Frank and I went to the theater that night, and I wore a new gown, the color of Frank's eyes. I felt very pretty. Indeed, Frank could not stop looking, but I did not mind his eyes upon me.

The next morning, as was our routine, I went with Frank to Jasper's chambers. When we entered, there was a gentleman in his early forties. He grew large in the midsection and had a rosy face. His acorn brown hair turned white in places and was receding in the extreme. He had an intelligent eye. He sat near Jasper's desk in a wingback chair. His expression turned from annoyed to surprise, and then glee at our entrance. He stood and exclaimed, "Frank, my boy!"

Frank's face split into a smile and he strode quickly to the man. He bowed and took his hand at once.

"Good day to you Sir," Frank said growing relaxed for the first time since Jasper announced he would help him.

"Mr Shaw, you did not say this matter concerned Mr Hadleigh."

"Yes, I thought it would be nice to renew your companionship," Jasper said floundering, then laughing uncomfortably. The wide-eyed look of surprise said he did not know the two were so well-acquainted.

"Well, I suppose your win at grand jury does make more sense. How long have you been in town, Frank?" the man asked.

"Over a week now, Sir," Frank said.

"Mr Shaw, I would like you to go get us some tea and cake please. This is cause for celebration."

Jasper looked at me, almost as if he would like very much to pass the task on, but Frank quickly said, "Sir, may I please make my wife known to you?"

Jasper, still collecting himself, shrugged and left.

"Mrs Millie Hadleigh, this is the learned master, Mr Richard Bethell. He has recently been promoted to Queen's Counsel. I congratulate you, Sir," Frank said bowing.

"Ah, thank you, thank you," he said sitting back down and motioning for Frank to do the same.

He asked all the proper questions about how long we were married and wished us joy when he found it was so recent. Finally, sounding almost hurt, Mr Bethell said, "Frank why you did not come to me for a pupillage?"

"I have not had the chance to even look. I have been so busy with the Grand Jury. I did hope you remembered me.

It has been four years, and I read about you in the papers from time to time. You are coming up in the world, Sir. Does it leave you time to master a pupil?" Frank asked.

"Ah Frank, you are not so easily forgotten. I did mean I would take you in, no matter how long it took you to arrange your personal affairs at home," he said, smiling at me as if I was the cause of the delay. I couldn't be sure I wasn't and looked to the rug unable to stop my blush.

"I have not secured anything of the kind and would be honored to work with you, Sir," Frank said.

"Well, of course, I would take you, but I think perhaps we have landed on a perfect resolution to a problem I have," he said.

"What is that, Sir?" Frank asked.

"We feel perhaps Mr Shaw was sent to the bar too soon. His brother paid out the price of a castle in Scotland to get him a pupillage. I am in the process even now to introduce a bill to standardize education in the law. Something must be done. Young men from wealthy families push their way through to the bar being placed in positions they are entirely unqualified for simply to give them an income."

"I have noticed that myself, Sir," Frank said.

"I had Mr Clarkson watch him," Mr Bethell said bluntly. "I recommended him as clerk to Mr Shaw's older brother on terms of a wage and not a percentage or the man would never make a living.

"When Mr Clarkson told me Mr Shaw took a murder case in the position of defense, I thought this would be the end of him. I had Mr Clarkson investigate who recommended Mr Shaw for such a weighty case and learned it was the barrister whom Mr Shaw bought his pupillage from, a man who knew Mr Shaw would fail," Mr Bethell said.

"Is he related at all to a Mrs Ellis, Lady Beornmund's cousin?" Frank asked.

"You were always a step ahead," Mr Bethell said with a little laugh. "He is the same man who courts Mrs Ellis' youngest daughter."

"She personally put forth a murderer for Lord Beornmund so her cousin could inherit," Frank said.

"I knew something was amiss. I thought Jasper had enough sense to bring it to a bencher. I had no time to intervene myself. I suppose you read in the papers I am placed in the court of Vice-Chancellor Shadwell, who cannot tie a cravat without me, it would seem. Mr Shaw only contacted me now, because he thinks he ought to be appointed to the equity courts, as common law is abysmal. That is his choice of words. He would prefer to take in his wealth while distributing others. I suppose it is all these second sons can do. Mr Clarkson did his best to… well, sabotage him into needing assistance. Instead of coming to the mentors of his temple, he sent for you. At least that is something."

"We have kept in touch," said Frank. "He contacted me about this case as I was ready to come back."

"Well, just in time or that poor boy would have been hung for scavenging. Which brings us back to how you can help me," Mr Bethell said.

"Of course, Sir," Frank said.

"If you did your pupillage under Mr Shaw, and helped him actually earn his silks, I would be happy in a years' time to recommend you to the bar. It would be a fair pupillage as long as you continue to study and become a master at the law."

"I have kept up on my studies over the last four years. I am not so far behind," Frank said.

"Ah, that's my boy," he said, but his expression fell as Jasper opened the door so Mr Clarkson could push a tea tray in. Jasper moved past the tray.

"Yes, now that you two are reacquainted, we must get back to the task at hand. I suppose you remember the essay Mr Hadleigh wrote –"

"We all remember it," Mr Bethell snapped.

"Yes, then you can agree Mr Hadleigh's future ought to be in Chancery Court," Jasper said. I saw Mr Bethell give a slight eye roll before he said, "We have discussed it. Since Mr Hadleigh is already exceptional, I will, on a very provisional term, recommend that you be allowed a pupil as you have requested, Mr Shaw. I will not hear of you charging a fee as your practice is so young. You haven't the training to charge. Together I believe you two may be successful."

"Thank you, Sir," Jasper said looking at me, waiting for my thanks. I stammered. I looked at Frank. I could see he did not know Jasper had made such a request. I tried not to be furious, but for Jasper to be so presumptuous irked me. The way he looked like I should fall at his feet with gratitude was too much to bear. What did Jasper believe he could teach?

Mr Bethell went on and said outright what he meant: his derisive remarks aimed at Jasper amused me in my irritated state. He quizzed Frank and Jasper both on their pleading memorization. Frank recited perfectly; Jasper stumbled.

After some time of renewing the acquaintance, Mr Bethell left. Frank and I went to take a meal away from Jasper so we might discuss this development.

"Jasper would set up your pupillage for you, then behave as if he has done it for anyone but himself. I cannot see how you are to submit to being his pupil," I said angrily.

"It is his way. I suspected he would do something to forward his own position. Jasper kept saying after the grand jury that he was going to help me. I knew when I saw Mr Bethell this morning Jasper had contacted him to request I be his pupil. That is his idea of helping."

"Jasper is arrogant," I snapped.

"Yes, but Millie, I had to get a pupillage. This way I will be useful instead of groveling at some master's feet. Not to mention I thought I may have to appeal to my mother or brother to help pay a pupil master who is competent. Now we will be free of any obligation. It could be worse."

"Are you sorry you cannot have Mr Bethell as your Master?"

Looking over his shoulder, Frank said quietly, "Mr Bethell claims conservatism, but when we would discuss the law at table, he showed himself to be liberal, shifting to almost radically minded. His ideals, such as men should not be jailed for their debt, but allowed to continue to work to pay them off, is very unpopular. Not to mention his views on further limiting the reach of the church: he does not favor ecclesiastical law, but common law. I see his point in a way. Men should go to judges for matters of the law, and clergy for matters of the soul, but the two have been intermingled for centuries. I do not see how they can be untangled."

"I do not know what is right. I've never thought about it before," I admitted.

"I like Mr Bethell very much, and his fervor for England cannot be matched, nor can his wit, but it is best if we stay on popular ground until I can make a name for myself. As Queen's Counsel, Mr Bethell can do whatever he likes, but if my master, I would never have any path but his. With Jasper, I can be very neutral in all my ideals and find my own path when I am made."

"Very well, but I like him," I said.

"He is a fine man, and father," Frank said.

"Yes, he seemed very fond of his many children and their accomplishments, right down to his infant cutting teeth," I said with a little laugh.

Frank laughed too and took my hand. Struck with the image of Frank bouncing a chubby baby on his knee made me smile. He would be a wonderful father. Then I remembered: I would have to be a mother for him to be a father.

Chapter Fourteen

The next day, everything worked together for us. I suspected it was Mr Bethell's doing and not Jasper's. We were given rooms on the grounds in a quiet building removed from the city. It was a sweet little place with a dining room, a sitting room, and a bedroom that came to us at an exceptionally low rate. I felt at home. Not just in the sense we no longer had to stay at the inn, but a feeling of belonging and freedom resided in these rooms.

We could eat in the Hall at a reduced rate, cheaper than going to market. The temple employed washerwomen and maids and we could use them for a few shillings a month, which was encouraged to keep them out of the workhouses. Frank wished to get me a personal maid, but as our clothes were cleaned, our food was cooked, and the rooms were scrubbed, I could not see what I needed a maid for.

A little over a week after the Grand Jury, Frank was explaining to Jasper how to argue another new case when a large looming figure entered the office. Lady Beornmund's solicitor, Mr Archer, grim as ever, walked to a large chair I'd just cleared of Jasper's books and sat down without invitation.

"Can we help you?" Jasper asked, astounded.

"Against my recommendation, My Lady would like to hire your services," Mr Archer said.

"I am well aware Lady Beornmund has several barristers in her immediate family. Mr Bell's repute is well known; how can I help you?" Jasper asked.

"Not you. She would like to engage your investigator's services," Mr Archer said pointing at Frank.

"Nobody knows what happened to Lord Beornmund then," Frank said.

"With the Bow Street Runners disbanded, discreet investigations into such matters have fallen by the wayside. You can imagine it is of utmost importance to the family to find what happened to the Lord, in as quiet a way as possible," Mr Archer said glancing at me as if I were a gossip.

"We can do it," Jasper said. "But such investigations are not done cheaply."

"Compensation will amount in the last quarter of Lord Beornmund's stipend that has accumulated unclaimed. It is bountiful. Discretion is all that matters in this case," Mr Archer said.

"Very well. I will draw up a contract and send it around to your office," Jasper said.

"Have you spoken to the Lord Beornmund's…um other household?" Frank asked.

"We sent someone around. The actress has not seen him. My Lady does not interact with her," Mr Archer said.

"Yes, but it has been four months since Lord Beornmund disappeared. I was surprised she still keeps the place, including a rented stable for her horses. Did he buy the house she lives in?" Frank asked.

"No, he let it. The steward does not take care of the place. We believe Lord Beornmund must have paid it through the year. It is likely the reason he would not leave town this summer."

"If the steward does not pay it, how can you be sure he did not buy the place?" Frank asked.

"I looked into it; it is leased. The actress packed the house. She expects to be displaced soon."

"Neither his wife, the actress, nor it would seem, his groom, had seen him for over two days when the note was sent at teatime. Is that correct?" Frank asked.

"Yes," he almost hissed.

"Why did the…um, the actress wait so long to write?" I asked.

"She thought Lord Beornmund had finally taken his Lady into the country without her. If rumors are to be believed, her relationship with Lord Beornmund was waning. She learned only by chance that her ladyship was still in London. She wrote assuming Lord Beornmund left her. I have seen the note," Mr Archer said.

"We will look into the matter," Jasper said. Mr Archer looked at Jasper, and said haughtily:

"Let it be understood, you will not argue the case if such a thing arises. We are simply using you in an investigative role." The solicitor pulled out a twenty-pound note, straightened it until the swirling print stating it was written on the Bank of England could be read, and handed it over to Jasper, "An advance on your expenses and a down payment for your silence."

"What is the name of your Lord's … dalliance?" Frank asked.

"She was much admired for a few years: Miss Maria Keppel," he said. I handed a notepad to Mr Archer and he wrote down where she resided.

"Also, it is supposed by the way he runs his household that the Lord is in debt. From all my inquiries, I saw no sign of it," Frank said.

"He is not under as badly as he told Lady Beornmund. He keeps his affairs right on the cusp of debt. He draws every farthing of his allotment from the estate, but no man has come asking for money before or after his disappearance. I do not know where it goes," the solicitor admitted.

"Lady Beornmund has nothing but the household pin money, I assume. Is her money exhausted on servants and dinners before the next allotment is due?" Frank asked.

"The London steward pays all that. He never needs more than his allotment. Lady Beornmund gets her pin money. Lord Beornmund has always been very generous to Lady Beornmund. She uses her money to send her daughter to friends, or keep the Viscount from trouble," Mr Archer said.

"Your Lord's share must be a significant amount, enough to do right by all the family, but he cut his heir down to the essentials only," Frank said thinking.

"Which is still ample for a man who has no expenses. The steward pays his club fees directly. His Lordship said it is wasteful to give the Viscount much. He is not wrong," the solicitor said.

"Which means Lord Beornmund would not be likely to overspend his income, and yet it is not to be found," Frank said.

"He never once asked for an advance," Mr Archer said, watching Frank think. When he said nothing else for a few minutes, Mr Archer asked, "Is that all?"

"Yes, I think I have a picture," Frank said. "Have you considered the Earl is not dead, but simply playing possum to get free of some trouble or other?"

"I know only one thing for certain of the man. He would have to be dead or broken not to claim his allotment. He was adamant his money be on time, and in full. It has been ready for him to claim since July 15 and has sat untouched. Considering the boy did find his finger, and the ring is the genuine article, I believe something untoward has happened. You must learn what," Mr Archer said.

"I will. It is a puzzle to be solved. It certainly doesn't make sense," Frank said.

"Well, just between us, young man, common sense is not something of which these people have ever boasted."

I laughed as the solicitor put his hat upon his cropped head, then tipped it to me and Frank. He turned to leave and said, "Keep me abreast of any progress you make and only me. If you need to speak to any member of the family, I will set up the interviews."

"Yes Sir, I have found him as far as three days before he was reported disappeared. I think Miss Keppel must have seen him last. I will start with her," Frank said.

He nodded, then turned, and we all watched him leave.

"You don't investigate. It will cost something to do," Frank said putting his hand out for the twenty-pound note. "If I am doing this, I will take half of the fee as well."

"Of course, of course. Look, Frank," Jasper said handing him the money, "he's right about one thing. There is a gap in Scotland Yard since they've done away with the Bow Street Runners. There is an opportunity here. With your skills, and my knowing many of the right people, we could fill a niche. The people will not hear of the government investigating. But us, me being of the Quality, and you being so clever, we can investigate quietly, find the truth, and argue in court all in the same breath. Think of the money to be made."

Frank and I laughed. I did not point out that once Frank went to the bar, he would not need Jasper. But I thought it: Only one year and we would be free of him.

Frank said, "I think winning a case has gone to your head."

"Making money is a fine thing for a second son," Jasper said with a wink at me.

"Let's figure out what happened to the Lord of Beornmund," Frank said. "Then we shall see."

Chapter Fifteen

Jasper and Frank spent that evening reviewing and the next morning they argued a separate case. A bobbie witnessed a theft from the man whose solicitor hired them. They won in court and it was so easy I could not tell the matter required a barrister at all.

That afternoon winter's breath grew dreary and cold when we left to meet Miss Maria Keppel. Jasper hired a hackney, and chattered about how he preferred to be in Chancery Court someday, but the win at criminal court felt good.

Jasper coming at all made me wonder how much an Earl's portion was. Being the mistress of a powerful Lord clearly had grandeur attached to it. The house was in good part of Chelsea, with a park on one side and stables for hire to the rear. Jasper was impressed by the location and said, "It would seem Lord Beornmund settled close enough to Cadogan that he may subscribe to the gardens. They hold very exclusive concerts there."

"Unless it is a very expensive subscription, I doubt that is where his portion has gone," Frank said dryly.

"Yes, well, if we could hurry this up a little, I have some place to be," Jasper said, and the way he looked at me, I could see he did not mean to admit aloud where he wished to be. He rammed the knocker into the door as he reached it.

The door opened quickly. The butler held a silver tray of letters like he just collected the post. A medium-sized man, he wore a grey suit with white gloves. Jasper began stating our business but stopped when Frank bowed to the man, who seemed caught off guard by the action.

Frank moved too quickly through the door and knocked the tray out of his hand.

"Oh, excuse me," Frank said dropping to pick it up.

"Sir, please! I shall call a maid," he said glaring as Frank handed him up the tray.

I could not think what Frank was doing but I knew he was playing a game with the man.

"We have come to see Miss Keppel," Jasper said sternly, glaring at Frank, embarrassed by his antics. The man looked at us with distrust and showed us to a parlor.

"The lady of the house," Frank said twirling his hand at the butler, as if to hurry him up. The butler, seeing Frank's impatience, left us alone in the lavishly decorated room to get Miss Keppel.

"I think we have found his money," I said quietly.

"This is not an Earl's portion," Jasper said, unimpressed.

"I'll be back. Distract them," Frank said. He quickly left the room before the butler returned.

"What?" I asked to his back.

"Yes, we'll be back," Jasper said tiptoeing ridiculously after Frank.

Out of sorts, I more perched than sat on a settee. Panicking, I watched the door, trying to decide who would come first: A woman whose lifestyle I could not reconcile in my youth and innocence. Or my husband with his supposed master following him at every step. The door opened and I stood twisting my wedding band.

Miss Maria Keppel entered the room. She was thirty at most, barely older than Lord Beornmund's children. She was beautiful in a striking way. Her hair curled in creamy blonde locks and her blue eyes and red shapely lips gave her face an angelic, glowing quality. Yet I knew her to have an illegitimate child with a man almost twice her age who was married to someone else.

"Good day," I said. I could not look at her, and I was sure I hadn't enough nerve to question her.

"Excuse me, I do not remember being introduced to you," she said, politely, but confused.

"Oh, no we have not… I am Mrs Millie … my husband, Mr Frank Hadleigh, works with the Barrister, Mr Jasper Shaw…"

"A barrister?" she asked, and she looked around the room trying to understand.

"It is a long story," I said. "We are not working in the capacity of law arguing, but rather Mr Archer, Lady Beornmund's solicitor, hired my husband to investigate the disappearance of Lord Beornmund."

"And you are here to question me," she stammered, confused. I did not answer. Distracted, she indicated I should sit, and sat down herself, her hands clasped at her chest.

I sat back down trying to steel my nerves to stall for Frank, despite my burning face.

"I understand you are an actress by trade," I said.

"Yes," she said coldly.

"That must be a diverting thing to do," I said.

"I have not trod the boards for over six years," she said relaxing at the sight of me blushing like a child.

"Why not?" I asked. My voice sounded high pitched.

"I… My Lord did not like it. My daughter is almost five now," she hinted, her eyes almost laughing at me.

"Yes, what a lovely age," I said. Humiliated, my voice raised two more notches. "They are so adorable at that age." I looked toward the door willing Frank to come back.

"I suppose you dote on her," I said when he did not.

"She is a beautiful child," she said, also glancing at the door suspiciously. Her initial fear left and she started to grow distrustful.

"Did you…Were you glad for a girl child?" I asked rambling, unsure what to say. She paused and written on her theatrical face was a pain.

"I was. My Lord wished for a boy," she said.

"Why he has two already, the child cannot inherit …" I stammered and stopped. Her child's future support was not a subject she wished to chat about. But then I had no idea what one talked about with the mistress of a Lord.

"I do not know," she said. "He … perhaps he feels he is the only real man left in the world and he alone should re-populate England."

She gave a bitter, sardonic laugh, and her anger so near the surface startled me.

"He does not sound like a desirable companion," I said wondering how she had come to love him enough to put herself into such a precarious position.

"I … do you know what it means to be on the arm of an earl?" she asked, affronted.

"No," I said, "but I would prefer my husband's companionable arm to that of a disagreeable man. No matter who he is."

She laughed. It was not a humorous laugh, but the sound of a wounded animal, that somehow came out as derisive.

"You are naive," she said. "I did not choose Lord Beornmund. He chose me. Do you think I could say no to such a man?"

"I…" I stopped. I suddenly realized this woman was me. This was my life if Mr Williams had lived. He would have married Clara, and if he didn't leave me to starve, he would have set up me up in a house close by. He would have come around when he needed what Clara wouldn't or couldn't give him. I would have been his mistress. Again, I hoped I would have been strong enough to starve to death.

I felt the tears on my face before I could wipe them away.

"Are you…" she looked at me deeply concerned.

"I am sorry for you," I whispered. She searched me as if she could not believe I would pity her. But how could I not?

Frank came through the door and his look was curious. I should have averted my gaze as I could not keep the tears from my cheeks. Frank forgot everything and came to squat in front of me taking my hand. Jasper followed him at every step.

"Millie?" Frank questioned. I could not respond. Miss Keppel recovered sooner, standing outraged.

"Where have you been? I did not give you leave to wander about my home," she said to Jasper as Frank slid up to sit next to me and put a warm arm around my shoulder.

"Ah yes," Jasper moved toward her quickly. With an authority bordering on rudeness he said, "We mean to find out what has happened to Lord Beornmund by any means necessary."

It surprised me how condescending Jasper sounded.

"Millie, are you quite all right?" Frank whispered in my ear while they argued.

"Yes, I am just very lucky. We can talk later," I said quietly. I leaned in to wipe my tears on his coat. He nodded and kissed my temple. I smiled for him and leaned away so he could get back to work. Frank then looked up at Miss Keppel trying to decide how to get her to talk to us as she snapped something at Jasper I did not hear.

"What have you been doing in my house?" Miss Keppel asked again, glaring at me this time so I could hear her. The sight of Frank and I seemed to frustrate her. Frank took his arm from around me and stood up. Before he could speak, Jasper stepped in.

"We were hired by Lady Beornmund, and whilst her Lord is missing, she and the Viscount may take whatever liberties they like as you are here on their generosity," Jasper said. Miss Keppel's eyes went wide, and she leaned away from Jasper, perturbed.

"Come now, we need not be uncivil. There is no need to fear us. I was confirming a suspicion," Frank said. His voice sounded kinder, trying to make up for Jasper's rudeness.

"What is that?" she asked. She fixated on the place where Frank had sat next to me focused with adoration.

"You are moving out of this house," Frank said.

"I was…I suppose I must, but I do not know… before My Lord disappeared in July last, he wished to move to the country. He prefers the country. I was supposed to prepare… I had the house packed up. Now I am… I do not know what I am to do," she said. Her tale was believable to a point. She could deliver a line with reasonable honesty. Still, something about the way she moved behind the settee so it was between her and us, or perhaps the way her fingers ran along the wooden rim as she went, belied her words.

"He had not informed his other household such. They hoped to remove to the country in May last but were told not to expect it due to finances," Frank said. Keeping his movements slow and his face kind he maneuvered toward her. I'd seen him do it several times. He was coaxing information from her.

"I… do not know what he says to them," she said.

"Would he have taken you to the country without them?" I asked delicately.

"I...I do not know what he would do anymore," she said flustered, glaring at Jasper who stepped in as if that would force the truth out of her.

"May I ask who decorated this home?" Frank asked brushing Jasper aside.

"Yes, who was your decorator?" Jasper repeated sternly like she may not have answered Frank but she would answer him.

"Excuse me," she said squinting from one man to the other.

"It is not a custom decorating style," Frank said.

"No, the study is ghastly, and the dining room does not leave one with an appetite," Jasper said critically.

I looked around. The sitting room, papered in an elaborate dark blue swirling pattern, set off the cream-painted wood panels and carpets, ornate dark wood outlined all the navy and cream decorative furniture. Though slightly masculine, it seemed the right level of audacious for the Quality. I could not tell it was anything different than fine furnishings.

"Lord Beornmund made every decision to do with this home. His lady would not allow him any of the paintings he preferred. She could not bear the scandal if they were seen," she said quietly.

"What paintings?" I asked looking at Frank. The windows and fireplace limited the decoration on the walls, but the few paintings of fruit bowls and flowers couldn't be construed as offensive.

"May I show her?" Frank asked politely.

"Very well," she said.

We walked down a passageway to a closed door. She nodded to the footman to stay, and we followed her into the study closed to the servants. She stepped out of my way, and my mouth dropped. The room opened to huge frames lining the walls where bookshelves had been removed. The paintings were like three windows on each wall, but windows that showed into a fantasy world.

"If this were a gallery it may be acceptable, but the clumping of artwork is not the thing," Jasper said to Miss Keppel.

"I did not do this," Miss Keppel said, exasperated with Jasper.

Enamored with the room, I stepped in. Despite Jasper insisting it a faux pas to squeeze in such enormous paintings, I liked it. He pointed out one painting extended over a window frame to make it fit. The paintings were realistic in technique, but dreamlike in subject.

The largest painting behind the desk portrayed a man astride a black horse roping a glossy calf. His image took most of the canvas, with a sunny field in the background. The man's face was handsome though past his prime. The picture somehow insisted that, despite the subject's age, a deep well of vitality was still available for him to draw from.

The next largest painting, on the opposite wall over the fireplace, pictured an unearthly huge u-shaped waterfall that threw a mist over aborigines, who stood with their backs to us looking at the view. Another landscape featured a double rainbow over an enormous body of water with an island jutting out in the distance. The next was a mountain so tall it broke into the clouds. The whole room depicted fables, but I couldn't place them.

"Is this someone's dream?" I asked of the waterfall.

"No," Miss Keppel said. "It is a place in the Colonies…ur, the United States. There is a school of art there. Lord Beornmund supports it and they send him these."

"That must be where his money has gone," I said.

"Oh no," she said. "These cost more to ship than they are worth. Student artists painted them."

"The rest of the house has been packed up, but not these," Frank said.

"He meant to have them crated," she said absent-mindedly looking at one of the pictures.

"Not covered for his return, but crated," Frank noted quickly before she could withdraw her choice of words. She stopped breathing and turned a little red before turning back to Frank. She looked him straight in the face and finally said:

"Yes, crated."

"Lord Beornmund meant to move you across the ocean to this place," Frank said nodding to the picture, "and not back to his country home near Birmingham?"

She took a long look at Frank.

"Yes," she finally said.

"What?" Jasper asked astounded. He had not seen past the abysmal decorating to the heart of the thing.

"He lost faith in England. Oh, how he ranted so," she said putting a hand on her stomach as if it made her ill to think about.

"What were his complaints?" Frank asked.

"The House of Lords is no longer anything special but more like children who stay out all hours gambling and drinking. His political society in Birmingham is losing members. They could not ensure who was sent to represent them in the House of Commons. Those insisting on free trade will force his tenant farmers to compete with foreigners. Over the last few years his colliery is under scrutiny, though the children must be ten to go down into his mines. Some of the Ironmongers have refused to use his Iron Ore. They say it takes too long to work due to all the impurities, even with all the new methods of cleaning it."

"Was he losing profits?" Frank asked.

"No, he…well he owns the colliery. If they want his coal, they must take his iron," she snapped.

"His father and grandfather have been fighting the same fight; it cannot be new," Frank said.

"Yes, but underneath it all, his ancestors would be ashamed how the family lands have been mined and stripped of their treasures so his son could buy carriages, fobs, and I don't know what else. His son, his heir, is at the heart of it all, drinking and gambling away his fortune. In his mind, his country no longer exists and his family name doomed," she said.

"But would not retiring to the country have kept him from witnessing the Viscount's behavior he did not like?" Jasper stated as if everyone knew that is the way to take care of bad seed. "It is the only way to keep his son away from the temptations in London."

"His son found plenty of trouble in Birmingham. The radical preacher traps any man with a few pounds to donate to his cause. Social reform is a term used freely there," Miss Keppel said.

"As I told My Lord many times, at least in London he associates with the Quality! At the clubs here, instead of filling the Viscount full of ridiculousness, he gambles with men of standing and is seen drinking the finest port. Is that not to be preferred?"

Jasper begrudgingly agreed with her. I stopped myself from commenting.

"Before this year, you went with Lord Beornmund to his country estate," Frank said refocusing her ranting.

"Yes," she answered.

"Near the family home," he observed.

"Not so close, though he stays with them when in the country. He bought a lovely little house, surrounded by a beautiful garden five years ago. I think he meant for it to be mine when he…I…it is where I think of as home."

I could see she meant for us to ask, on her behalf, that the house be given to her. She overestimated our position with the family.

"Why did he not stay with you?" I asked.

"He did not like to be parted from me. I have that effect on men," she snapped like I meant to insult her. "The only time he spent away from me was three years ago. He was thrown from his horse and spent six months recovering. He came back stronger than ever in the last year."

"I simply thought it curious he did not stay with you there as he does here," I clarified.

"It is…different there. Birmingham is where his business is conducted. He must keep up appearances."

"He doesn't like it there?" Frank asked.

"The city is a filthy place. The Irish coming in for work, people everywhere. Redditch, which is south of my little place, has a needle maker that is becoming well known and attracting those in search of work. Lord Beornmund feels people creeping over him, until he… Until he must get away and find a new place where he may be Lord of the Manor."

"To here?" Jasper asked pointing to the paintings with his head tilted like he could not understand.

"Interesting, he wanted his way so badly it drove him to fake his death, put the peelers to the trouble of an

The Basra Pearls

investigation, and all for what? To be the one dictating how people live," Frank taunted.

"He is Earl of Beornmund. The nobility has been dictating to people for generations. Do you believe that as peer in Her Majesty's realm, he has no right to dream so?" Miss Keppel asked Frank.

"Can you, of all people, think he should be dictator to us?" Frank asked curiously.

"I live his strict ideals; I would not recommend it. He does not allow for amusement. He must always be correct. Even when he is not, I must pretend he is. At times I have rearranged engagements when he mistook the day. Everyone, they... they overvalue the title and the man until he cannot help but do the same," she said.

"That does not make it right of him," Frank said. Miss Keppel smiled at Frank, as though he unburdened her somehow.

I did not like the way Miss Keppel looked at my husband. Feeling Frank's respect, she stood a little taller. He smiled congenially, fueling her adoration instead of repelling it.

Instinctively I knew she needed a man to be respectful to her; I just didn't want it to be my man. Part of me also knew Frank was giving her what she needed so she would cooperate with him, but I did not like it at all. Finally, Frank said kindly, "You do not know where Lord Beornmund is. You believe he has left you to go to the colonies by himself?"

She looked at him a long time. Finally, she said:

"It would appear so."

"That wasn't the plan, though," Frank said.

"No," she said. "He talked so often of taking me and the child there."

She pointed to the painting of the waterfall.

"That dream is what he spent his money on?" Frank asked.

"My Lord kept his personal money with a very discrete solicitor over the past several years. He's going to buy a huge estate in the America. He's going to ride his horse all day long wrestling cows. He gloried in the idea of living the life of a dead man."

I stared at her.

"Would you have liked that?" I asked.

"I… I am feared here. People believe I have the ear of one of the most powerful men in the country. But I never have, not really. His wife would… fight him on matters and he… he preferred me. I treated him as he deserved," she said, but she looked tired.

"But you could not sway him as Lady Beornmund did," I said.

"No, nor should I."

"Who thought you could?" I asked.

"A year ago, in September, the Viscount married. We all moved back to London in February; he brought his bride with him. In the bloom of March, the Viscountess came to me in the guise of touring the botanical gardens where I have a subscription. I endured her for My Lord's sake, but oh, I had shooting head pains every time that ridiculous woman left me. She thought I could influence My Lord to give his son more allowance. She soon found I could not. In her spite for me, she spread rumors that I fell out of favor with Lord Beornmund, and he was ready to move on. An unplanned circumstance that it would appear My Lord has taken advantage of. He slipped away and now I will probably be hung for his murder, and he's not even dead."

"You will not be hung," Frank said. "Even Lady Beornmund's solicitor, who would heap the blame on anyone to have the matter resolved, does not believe you had anything to do with it. You would lose everything."

"Yes, I suppose being destitute has its advantages," she said sardonically. None of us could answer this awkward statement.

"How did you discover he is not dead?" Miss Keppel asked.

"Due to other circumstances, I suspected before we even came. It was confirmed when I found the butler who let us in is missing his left little finger," he said. "The glove folded strangely on his tray. I bumped hands with him to be sure it was gone."

"Yes, you are clever," she said, and her eyes welled with tears. Frank passed her a handkerchief. She wiped her tears. I crossed my arms and looked up at the picture of the man roping the calf. I tried to tell myself Frank was just being kind to her so she would answer his questions, but I was extremely uncomfortable with the compassion he showed the pretty woman. When she regained control over her emotion, Frank asked: "To be clear, his family believes he is dead, but you do not. How is that possible?"

"They could never believe he would part with his signet ring, his symbol of power, unless it was cut from his corpse," she said.

"That is why he sent his ring down the privy with a finger attached? So, it may be found? The ring belongs to the estate and must go to his son, anyway," Frank nodded.

"The Viscount does not deserve it. He cannot sire an heir," she said snidely glancing at Jasper, knowing instinctively he could start a rumor among the Quality. She did it to return the favor to the Viscountess.

"What does that mean?" Jasper asked, intrigued, taking the bait.

"I do not know exactly, some accident in his youth left him…unable. My Lord was very discouraged with his son and said his earldom would likely go extinct when the Viscount could not produce an heir."

"He has a second son," I reminded.

"Hugh…rather, Captain Beornmund, Lord Beornmund's second son, was greatly disappointed two years ago, and will never leave the sea long enough to have an heir now," she said. "Neither of his sons had the gumption to keep the family line going."

I blushed, unsure how to feel about this candid statement. I looked to Frank. He watched her. His previous suspicions against her swept away and it bothered me. His focus left me feeling vulnerable. Jasper must have noticed because he came in close putting his shoulder to mine as if I needed him to console me for losing Frank to the actress.

"It is surprising such a bauble as the Lord's ring made it to the waterworks," Frank said, thinking.

"He had such low ideas of the poor. He supposed they would stand outside the place waiting to sift through our filth."

"He could not ensure it would be found," Frank said, and his look said he was not really talking to anyone but himself. Miss Keppel answered anyway.

"My Lord realized his mistake. He went looking for the ring. A few days after he sent it down, he followed the flow himself. When he could not find it, he put on disguises and went to the auction houses and pawnshops to see if it had been sold. The family crest was recognizable enough. He thought perhaps it wasn't reported to the authorities, and meant to search it out, then send an anonymous note alerting the bobbies where to find it."

"Because the ring was not found you sent the note by way of the pad groom alerting the family he was gone," Frank said.

"I...Lord Beornmund told me what to write. He made me sound like... like a scorned woman who'd been left. It was after that Lady Beornmund alerted her solicitor so he might inquire after him."

"What did he do?" Frank asked. He was curious if Mr Archer made any effort at all in the last four months to find Lord Beornmund.

"He sent a message to the country inquiring after him."

"When did the police start an investigation?" Frank asked, confused.

"It was not until...oh, the third week in July, perhaps. Mr Archer sent the message to the country when My Lord was meant to collect his portion and did not. Only after that Mr Archer believed it serious enough to involve the police. It was a few more weeks before the ring was finally found. By then Mr Archer didn't know what to think. He had nothing but the dated note I sent as a clue."

"Did Lord Beornmund know when his ring was found?"

"That is when my Lord really disappeared."

"When did you see him last?" Frank asked looking up.

"It was in the last few days of July."

"The ring was not pawned until the seventh of August," Frank said.

"It was around then," she said shrugging. It had been so many months; she could not be sure about anything.

"This is important. When did you see him last?"

She took a deep breath and closed her eyes. Frank watched her, seriously intent on an exact answer.

"The messenger returned from the country house with no news of him. It was that last week in July the police were investigating. They talked to the butler briefly, then moved on," Miss Keppel said leaning toward Frank.

"The police are meant to discourage crime," Frank said. "They are not trained to investigate. It is the burden of the Beornmund family to bring forth witnesses they wish to have interviewed. And again, you seemingly had nothing to gain from his disappearance."

"I suppose," she said.

"What was Lord Beornmund's behavior like the last time you saw him? You must remember the last time," Frank insisted.

She closed her eyes.

"It had been weeks since he sent his ring down. He was peculiar at the end. He started to look less like himself. He dressed like a middlish man, never grand like before. He was amused with himself at first. His enjoyment ran out. By the end he was... he seemed... different. It was not August yet. The last time I saw him he drank. He did not often drink much except an after-dinner port now and then. He opened his Vinho da Roda, an expensive Madeira wine he'd been saving for the America. He said something sympathetic toward his miners as a toast," she said.

"Was it like him to think about his miners?" I asked.

"No, never. He had not been to the country for so long. It was peculiar," she said.

"Perhaps he thought of them because he had to experience their hardships in play-acting," I said. She frowned at me.

"Or likely he feared for them under his son's guardianship," she snapped.

"You saw him the last days of July then," Frank interrupted, "Can you tell me how he got away with coming here after he sent his ring down the privy?"

Frank opened the top desk drawer and rummaged through it looking at a few letters that were still sealed while she answered:

"After he sent his ring, he only came after dark. Often, at first. He used the servant's entrance and wore ..." she glanced up and down at me and Frank. She looked away and said, "working man's clothes. By the end, he came twice in one week, possibly less. He brought several sets of what he called his Sunday best to pawn as a decoy, but he left most of them here. He did not wish to be seen with many sets of clothing. He needed them that he might go into the shops without being noticed. He did not replenish them when he ran out. That was when he disappeared for real."

"And now you are afraid he left you here to be blamed for his disappearance," Frank said cutting off her rambles, nodding to himself.

"After all the rumors that he lost interest in me, it must have been so easy for him to slip away… but in all he did… it is hard to explain… He did not mean to be cruel, just… he just held to his views of life so rigidly. He truly believed he was right in this action," she said.

"Did he think so highly of his views he would sacrifice you for them?" I asked.

"He was not an overly affectionate man, but I thought he valued me. At the end he seemed irritated. He did not like all that went wrong. Surely, he would not wish his death blamed on me," she said looking to Frank.

"No, he did not. He spread rumors that he had nothing, therefore you had nothing. He did it to keep you safe," Frank said leaning across the desk emphatically.

She disregarded his assurance and stood. She moved to him behind the desk as she continued with her desperation.

"Whatever he felt for me, he grew attached to the child. He wished for another child, but had to recover for some time after his accident. Could he be so cruel as to send my beautiful little one to adorn the cells of Newgate?" she asked, genuinely trying to discern what happened. Her tears came again.

I was reminded of the terrifying scream echoing through the halls of Newgate. This time Frank patted her shoulder. I gritted my teeth. Why would he touch her? She was like a wounded animal looking for a protector, and he encouraged her to let him be it. Frank took a deep breath. He glanced at me, and I saw a bit of an apology in his eyes. He turned back to her, his hand still on her shoulder. He said kindly:

"He did not leave you. He is dead. And I promise you will not be blamed."

Her mouth opened in surprise. I also looked at Frank in surprise.

"You've just convinced us he isn't dead. Is he dead, or he isn't?" I asked.

"He is dead, but he did not die when he first went missing."

Miss Keppel forgot her hatred of me and shrank back. Jasper just squinted. He thought Frank was trying to trick him.

Chapter Sixteen

"How...how can you know that he is dead?" Miss Keppel asked. She moved, trembling, to sit so she did not fall down.

"Firstly, he did not take his paintings," Frank said still standing behind the desk with the picture of the horseman looking heroically off in the distance over him.

"I believe he could not take them without arousing suspicion," Miss Keppel said.

"Which means he had a plan to get them to the colonies with you. I believe he thought everything would happen much swifter. He thought an investigation would take place within days of his disappearance," Frank said.

"Yes, that is true," Miss Keppel said.

I mused: "What a letdown it must have been to him. No one noticed his absence. No one started an investigation for weeks. To find his own estimated importance was not in line with everyone else's must have been distressing."

"Nothing of the sort. It was the solicitor's incompetence, not Lord Beornmund's insignificance," Miss Keppel snapped at me, irritated.

Frank ticked his head at me to stop. I did not continue with my musings, but folded my arms and fumed. Frank needed Miss Keppel to be soft dough, easy to work. He approached her where she had sat in the huge leather chair, leaning against the corner of the desk.

"Lord Beornmund thought you would be kicked out of this house by his heir when he was declared dead," he said.

"The servants would scatter and you would have no choice but leave. The house was packed and ready for your departure months ago. Someone would be sent to crate and move the paintings. The furnishings that he chose would be put on wagons and all would be moved with you."

"I was not removed from the house," she said.

"No. Something went very wrong. Here you are. You have been here months with no sign of Lord Beornmund. More peculiar is that you have not heard from a bill collector," Frank said moving back to the desk drawer and pulling out a few of the letters.

"His solicitor must be paying the bills," she said, "but I cannot see it will last much longer. I wait for them to come take the house, but…"

She looked at Frank. Waiting for him to reassure her again.

"I have no doubt as soon as Lord Beornmund gave the word the solicitor has strict instructions to have this room crated and moved with you. It was meant to happen in great haste. I would wager he meant to make it appear as if you've been thrown out of the place," Frank said waving the stack of letters, which must have been important.

"Why did he not warn me of such?" she asked.

"You… he probably wished for you to cry and look the part of terrified," Frank said apologetically.

"How would he have found me if I left here?" she asked. "We had not arranged to meet anywhere."

"Your butler would arrange it all. Lord Beornmund would never have lost sight of you. You would likely have picked up an extra servant to care for your furnishings and the crates. Your new servant would look vaguely like Lord Beornmund, but dressed as a hired servant, a hat and a thick growth on his face would likely be disguise enough. Your passage on a ship would have been secured and you would have been gone, along with the mystery of what happened to the Earl of Beornmund."

Miss Keppel turned her head and made her eyes big and innocent.

"How can you know all this?" she asked.

"It is supposition based on facts. I can be very sure he would not leave you, though. The account the secret solicitor works out of is in your name," Frank said handing her one of the letters from the stack he held.

"What?" she asked, startled. She stood to take the sealed post from Frank. I glanced as she took it. It was addressed to her.

"I...this was not delivered to me," she said.

"No, your butler knows they are your Lord's. He just received another by this evening's post; it was on the tray I dropped. It was a risky move, but Lord Beornmund must have put everything in your name to keep his son from reclaiming it," Frank said. "If the solicitor is an honest man, you will likely be very wealthy as Lord Beornmund spent little of his allotments, and whatever is in the account is in your name. If he has been saving to buy land it must be significant. This money was his share and is not entailed back to the estate; it is yours."

"I do not know what sort of man the solicitor is," she said stepping closer to Frank. She completely ignored Jasper who came in close, taking an interest in her now that she had money.

Miss Keppel gave Frank a look of true vulnerability, knowing he was a good man and could help her.

She explained how Lord Beornmund had her sign papers when she started to increase with child. He was furious when she had a girl. Lord Beornmund meant to have another child, but his accident prevented it for a time. Then she asked if perhaps when she did not increase again, he left her.

Frank explained again Lord Beornmund needed her to gain access to his wealth. He did not leave her. Inside the drawer letters were neatly stacked, many bound together, probably by the butler who also assumed his master would call for their retreat at some point. Finally, when she would not be convinced, Frank took a letter opener and asked, "May I?"

She did not answer but focused on opening the letter in her hand.

"This is just a confirmation of bill payment. It is only signed with initials," she said.

"Yes. I am hoping to find a ledger," Frank said twisting the letter opener into a locked drawer and prying it open.

"You best hope he's dead because if he comes back and finds you've marred that desk..." she said, pretending to be playful with Frank, but also still afraid Lord Beornmund would be angry about the broken lock.

Frank had soothed her into trusting him implicitly. She did not seem inclined to call a servant nor raise an alarm of any kind at his rifling through Lord Beornmund's personal papers.

Frank pulled things out and handed them to me. We both examined the papers for a quarter of an hour. Jasper did not bother looking over the financials but tried to gain some trust with Miss Keppel now that she was an heiress. He wasn't having much luck.

It was clear Lord Beornmund's plan was in its last stages. He had everything thought of.

"He has purchased two lots of land totaling 640 acres in Massachusetts. There is a grand estate already built," Frank said. "If he were alive, he would never have left this deed behind, nor you, since it is all in your name."

"How?" she asked and sat back down in her large chair near the fireplace that swamped her small body.

"You are unmarried, so it is your property. He likely would never have told you as much. Once in America, he would marry you under some false name. Then it would revert into his property."

"Is that the law there?" I asked.

"I do not know, but I would assume," Frank admitted.

"He did all this?" Miss Keppel asked, astounded.

"He has been preparing for a few years at least," Frank said.

"He happened upon a radical rally. Men there, even titled men, believe that every man should vote. His family's land had been mined of coal and iron ore, and he is expected to give his workers equal consideration to himself."

"He thought London was being poisoned," I summed up, so she did not start ranting again, but as an afterthought, I said, "Do not all the men in the United States vote?"

"Only land-owning men, same as here. My Lord was clear on that," Miss Keppel glared at me.

"The steward left months ago. He is there managing the land. It looks like Lord Beornmund also sent his valet ahead of him; he paid for his passage," Frank said pointing to the ledger. "That explains what happened to him."

"As soon as the family learns of this, it will be taken back," Miss Keppel lamented.

"They have no jurisdiction in the United Colonies," Frank said, absent minded.

"I think they prefer to be called the United States," I said. "Besides, we are not being paid to tell Lady Beornmund nor her solicitor what happened to the man's funds, but the man himself. I would imagine your butler is quite trusted and has prepared for the journey. You should just pretend you can no longer afford this place and go," I said wishing her very far away.

"She cannot just leave now. If any word of this gets out, which it may, she will be suspected. It turns out she had much to gain from Lord Beornmund's death. She must stay until after the trial," Frank said, thinking.

"Who do you intend to put on trial?" she asked, frightened.

"Clearly not you," Frank said forcing himself to stay patient. Even Jasper could see the woman would do nothing for herself, even with all the money in the world. She required…protection. I couldn't help thinking she and Jasper were very similar in that way. Neither seemed to think they should have to do things for themselves, but instead found someone capable to attach themselves to.

"Must anyone be put on trial?" Miss Keppel asked.

"He is no longer with us. I am sure of that," Frank said. "Whoever killed him will have to answer for it. As long as you are here and bewildered as to his whereabouts, we can find the culprit. If you leave, you will be a murderer on the run, and that will follow you wherever you go."

"I will be able to keep the estate if I stay through this investigation?" she asked.

"His man is looking after it. I doubt he knows anything is amiss," Frank said.

"The Viscount will find a way to take it all from me," she said.

"They haven't a right to it. It was his money to do with as he pleased. In the weeks before his man disappeared, Lord Beornmund bought gold bars. He must have sent them over in crates with his valet. I do think you will lose those if you wait longer than the new year to go over," Frank said honestly.

"Gold bars! Really," Jasper said, his excitement bursting from him.

"Yes, they don't take the same currency there. It looks like Lord Beornmund traded a majority of his secret account for them," Frank said putting his finger on the ledger again.

"The family cannot take the gold?" she asked. Astounded, she sat in the chair again, trying to appear calm, but she shook with anticipation. Frank bent down before her.

"I do not think so but it is best not mentioned unless it becomes unavoidable," Frank said glancing up at Jasper.

"No, no need for that," Jasper soothed, but it was forced. None of us doubted he meant to get his hands on some of her gold.

"The money is out of everyone's reach now," I snapped, agitated. Frank looked up at me. I glared down upon him bowed in front of the beautiful actress. He flinched and his face changed. He stammered looking up at me, confusion creasing his brows.

I crossed my arms indignantly. Frank stood but looked at me like he missed his step. He glanced at me trying to catch my eye, I looked up at the picture of the man on his horse to ignore him. To his credit, Frank stepped away from the actress and back toward the desk.

"If we tell Mr Archer about the little finger, and the butler, but not the American dream," Jasper said thinking out loud.

"We will have to tell of the man's plot," Frank said, clearly put out with Jasper. "How he was alive until the end of July. We must search out the shop that pawned his clothes. Someone killed the man, of that I am sure."

"His trail of pawn shops was written in the ledger," I said. "Strange he left that in his desk to be found."

"Likely he did not dare leave it where he was staying, but meant to have it crated up with his paintings," Frank said moving closer to me. I scooted away.

"This implicates me... he meant to implicate me," Miss Keppel fretted, trying to force Frank to focus on her.

Frank, annoyed he had to keep assuaging her, said: "Lord Beornmund led everyone to believe he had no money. In such a case the first payment missed on this house, Miss Keppel, you would have been asked to leave. He must have believed he could control the timing. He made sure you appeared to have no benefit and everything to lose from his death. Down to the very detail of the note you sent that indicated you believed he left you. He meant to make it appear as if you were kicked out within days of his supposed death. You would appear to have found a wealthy American to offer you his protection, and no one would have questioned anything. He did not implicate you."

"Yes, and we will not tell anyone of the gold. You will be safe with us," Jasper said.

Jasper tried putting a hand on Miss Keppel's arm. She pulled it away and turned to Frank, wanting his assurances.

As Frank explained again, Jasper squinted like he was trying to get it all straight so he might be the one to retell it, or at least skew it to his benefit if he could. I was thankful Frank took the twenty-pound note, because it may be all the money Jasper let slip through his hands. By the end, Frank was talking more to himself. Both Jasper and Miss Keppel looked out the window.

"Lord Beornmund must have died sometime between this last pawn noted in his ledger, July 28, but before the seventh of August when Cecil was forced to pawn the ring…unless Lord Beornmund found his ring and meant for Mrs Ellis to…"

"That would implicate Cecil was in league with them, which I cannot believe," I pointed out.

"Yes, you are right. Miss Keppel, can you say if Mrs Ellis and Lord Beornmund were ever friendly?" Frank asked to be sure the conspiracy didn't reach the young man's door.

"No, certainly not. He thought her one of the silliest women of his acquaintance, second only to his son's wife," she said.

"Are you certain?"

Miss Keppel explained how four years ago, Mr Ellis could not pay a debt of honor he owed. Mrs Ellis cried and cried that they would lose their standing at Almac's. Lord Beornmund paid the debt, but swore it was the last time, and she was never to come to them again. He even tried to send her husband to distinguish himself in the West Indies, just to get rid of her.

Lady Beornmund meddled on her cousin's behalf, she continued. It may be regretted since Lady Beornmund has given out of her own pocket to assist Mrs Ellis a few times. The Lady's maid reports it to Lord Beornmund's man every time it happens. Lady Beornmund would not sink so low to ask him to again save her cousin from ruin.

Miss Keppel finished by saying, "If you are looking for someone who wished My Lord gone to his rewards, it was Mrs Ellis. The moment My Lord is proclaimed dead, Mrs Ellis will look to her cousin for support again, I can assure you."

"I suppose that does explain Mrs Ellis' actions," Frank said. He continued, "Where was Lord Beornmund staying after he left here?"

"He did not tell me. He spent a few hours in this study when he came, then sneaked out the servant's entrance," she said.

"Is that he?" Frank asked nodding at a picture behind the desk I had been examining. I suspected he was the muscled man upon a bucking horse represented close to his true age, but extremely fit in his riding coat and tight breeches.

"It is. He sent a likeness to the school of art, and they sent this back," she said.

"Is it very like him?" I asked. I thought he would be heavier as these pampered men often were.

"He sent them his exact measurements. He believed a man should keep himself in a certain shape. He prided himself on his figure at such an age. He rode often and did not indulge, nor enjoy his wealth as his counterparts in the House of Lords," she said. She stood and walked toward Frank, who had retreated behind the desk.

"That is wise," Frank said, his head in the desk, as if he could take back his overly friendly behavior.

"Yes, I've kept my figure, even after having the child," she said giving him a flirtatious smile.

"You are fetching," Jasper said when Frank didn't answer.

Frank pulled a letter out from the bottom drawer. "This is addressed to… to Lady Beornmund."

"Do you think he meant to confess all to his wife?" I asked, sure to add the word wife louder than the rest.

"I cannot say," Frank said holding the letter to the window as if he might read some of the words.

"May I deliver this?" Frank said looking at the letter.

"I am also an avid horsewoman," Miss Keppel was saying to Jasper and didn't answer.

"May I borrow this?" Frank asked louder, tucking the letter into the Lord's ledger.

"I suppose if it helps you end this charade as soon as possible. I must go see about my land and gold," she said moving around Jasper and giving Frank her hand. He shook it briefly, but quickly let go, putting the ledger in the satchel he always wore slung about his body. Frank turned to me. I glared at him, balling a fist at my waist. He stopped. He examined my face and grinned at me, of all things. He turned to Miss Keppel and said sternly:

"You must hold your tongue until I can look into this matter. Mr Archer would hang you to have the matter done with. I would wager only your butler can be trusted. Come, Millie, we have much to do."

He took my arm just above the elbow, as the hand he usually held was balled in said fist at my waist.

"Wait. Who killed him?" Miss Keppel asked. We all stopped to look at Frank.

"I have no idea. Isn't this an adventure?" Frank asked, grinning at me.

"I'm no judge, clearly," I said glaring, pulling my arm away. He let go, but I felt his hand on the small of my back, nudging me forward to the door. Jasper followed us bowing and using his best manners on Miss Keppel now that she owned crates full of gold bars somewhere. I glanced back to see Jasper hand her a card that she tossed aside carelessly. She waved again to Frank with not an ounce of shame though I stood next to him.

The wind whipped relentlessly against my skirts.

Chapter Seventeen

"That was very productive," Jasper said, sounding more like himself, "I am invited to tea at… a very good friend's house now. And then there is a little dance tonight."

He walked toward his waiting hackney and finished, "Nothing so grand as a ball – it is not the season you know, but still I will not be in early tomorrow. You do not mind, do you, Old Boy?"

"You do not mean to blab this about?" Frank asked.

"I would be a fool to say anything… I am a gentleman after all," Jasper said winking, but we both knew opportunistic was more apt a description. At least it would keep him quiet.

"Isn't this working out well – our arrangement? We will both take the morning off," Jasper said.

"Yes, I shall get Millie a new pair of boots. Hers are worn and she begins to limp with all the walking we do."

"Oh, well that cannot be ignored. A new pair of boots will be just the thing to go with her new dresses," Jasper said. He ignored Frank's hint and waved to us as he climbed into the hackney and left.

Frank and I stood on the relatively quiet street with no way to get back to Middle Temple except walk against the frigid gusts that cut through my cloak and stung my eyes and cheeks. The icy air felt thickest between Frank and me.

While we walked, I thought about moving home to live with my mother and aunt in the country. The pain that seethed through me at the sight of Frank bowing before the pretty actress hurt me even more intensely than anything

Mother did. I wanted to hit Frank, or maybe bite him. I couldn't put a finger on the strange hurt building into rage pulsing through me.

"Millie," Frank started. I could feel his flimsy excuse in the way he looked at me.

"Are you so positive Lord Beornmund is dead or were you just flattering his pretty mistress?" I snapped. I whipped my cloak about me tighter.

"I do believe he is dead," Frank said. I raised my hand in exasperation losing my cloak to the wind. He grabbed it and kissed it happily. I pulled away astounded he dared be so flirtatious with me.

"You cannot be sure of anything," I said. I resituated my cloak in my folded arms and stormed forward.

"It is a pretty good guess," Frank said following me. "If he lived, he would have had his room crated and that drawer emptied long before a formal investigation started. In fact, if Mr Archer were interested in protecting his clients more than ensuring the transference of the trust, he could likely have found the Lord before he died. Or perhaps, if the investigation had not been entirely focused on forcing Cecil to be guilty, they would have learned all of this by now when memories were fresher."

" So Mrs Ellis did need to keep herself in the latest fashions after all."

"Her efforts obscured anyone from learning when the Lord's death took place."

"Which implicates her," I said unable to disagree. I dropped the folds of my cloak and put my hands to my ears that felt numb.

"Yes," he said sounding too chipper to be speaking of death while we walked among icy gusts. He stopped me. I crossed my arms tightly across my chest and glared up at a fine carriage passing.

He waited for something, but I could not be sure what. We stood by the side of the street, the world raging wildly around us, lifting, and blowing my skirts, but he did not move. He watched me. Thinking he wished me to keep his chain of thought moving I said:

"Do you truly have no idea who killed him then?"

"I must suppose it is someone who wanted him dead and found out he wasn't," Frank said trying to catch my eye.

"His mistress had every reason to kill him. Everything was in her name," I said turning and walking down the street again, moving quickly to warm myself.

"But she did not know until just now he was dead," he said. "She did not have anything to do with it."

I knew he was right, but I wanted her to be guilty. He held tightly to my arm, I did not pull away, my feet were sore and blistered with all the new distances that had to be walked. The dusk was cold and the wintry wind cut through me. His warmth helped me not to shake.

"We have Lord Beornmund's wife and her cousin, his mistress, his heir, his heir's wife, his son in the navy, his daughter, his daughter's beau, not to mention all those whom we do not know about, but held a grudge," I said.

"And such a man as Lord Beornmund is likely to have made enemies along the way," Frank said. "We cannot forget he was disguised with no way to prove his identity. It could have been someone who wanted his finery. I would suspect his counterfeit clothes were too fine to pawn, not to mention that women are mostly sent to pawn clothes. He wouldn't have known how to make himself look authentic; someone would have noticed him."

"So, we go to the pawn shops he noted, with his likeness, asking about finery that is too fine. Or we look into the deaths of unknown persons during your dates. The latter would indeed be the easier way to find him, would it not?" I asked.

"Any unknown person found dead under suspicion months ago would already be buried in a pauper's grave. There will be descriptions kept in coroner's court if the death was suspicious," Frank considered. "What an excellent way to start. You are a clever lady."

I looked up at him and found him watching me again.

"Why are you buttering me up, just as greasy as you did Miss Keppel?" I asked. I stopped and yanked my arm away from him.

"I buttered her up so she would let me take the ledger, which I thought you knew, and would not mind so much as you do. As your husband, it is my duty to keep you buttered up," he said. "Butter on bacon."

I glared at him. He put an arm around me and turned into a doorway along the row of buildings that we may get out of the wind and warm for a moment. Putting his hands on my shoulders, he coaxed me to look up at him.

"Why are you vexed with me?" he teased.

"Why would I be vexed with you?" I replied, refusing to play his game.

"I did not mean to be overly attentive to Miss Keppel. Only I saw if she thought me charmed, she would continue to be open with me and give me the ledger," he said watching me again. I could feel my face on fire.

"Yes. Well your mother would not have liked it."

"You did not like it," he said.

"Nor should I," I growled, shoving his shoulder.

"No, I suppose not. I am sorry Millie. I will try not to behave in such a way that will hurt your feelings," Frank said lifting a hand to my cold face and pushing back the hair curling over my forehead. I looked up at my oldest friend in the world. He did not look apologetic. He looked... I could not place the look on his face.

I examined him. He had the same big blue eyes and crooked smile. The one piece of hair that often fell to his forehead was there, but I found it...I think I found him attractive and infuriating. He seemed older, someone to be reckoned with, safe. I blushed, then stammered, but couldn't say anything.

"Come, let us find something to feed you," he said grinning and taking my hand.

It took us almost two hours to walk the five miles back to Middle Temple against the frigid wind. I was frozen through. Frank started a fire, and I made tea, but I could not wait for it to steep and drank the hot water.

After a quick meal, Frank got into the bed with me, and wrapped us in our blanket. I fell asleep to the sound of his voice telling me a fable. As he held me, trying to get me warm enough, I slowly believed he still loved me and only meant to flatter Miss Keppel.

Chapter Eighteen

The next morning, Frank and I went to the shops. Frank bought me padded boots and a lovely dark blue cloak. I pointed out his jacket was not likely to keep him warm enough and he bought a rather dashing wool coat that cut in tightly with four buttons. He had of late allowed me to comb his hair back neatly. Together with his new coat he looked quite dashing.

Midmorning, we went to Jasper's chambers. Only Mr Clarkson was there.

"Can you get me an appointment with the coroner?" Frank asked. "I need access to the inquests from late July and early August of this year, please".

"Yes Sir," Mr Clarkson said. Frank opened a book to catch up on his studies. I went to find us tea and biscuits. Mr Clarkson had not returned when I came back with a woman rolling the tea trolley. We sat at the little desk to the side and ate. We drained our cups, and I was thinking about getting another when Mr Clarkson finally returned.

"You may go in this afternoon. His clerk will be back and show you to the inquests," Mr Clarkson said.

"Thank you," Frank said.

Frank researched a few hours. He looked mostly at inheritance law and evidence presented in a similar case of murder. I straightened the desk and kept the fire stoked. Jasper finally came in. He appeared out of sorts and sent Mr Clarkson for tea.

"We have an appointment to meet with the coroner's clerk to look for suspicious deaths in our time frame," Frank said.

"You made an appointment without my permission," Jasper snapped. "You realize you use my name every time you move, do you not?"

"I believe since I arrived, I have only increased the value of you your name," Frank said sternly.

"Well, if you had consulted me, you would know the coroner inquests will do you no good. That is where I started. I have read all the coroner's reports on unexplained deaths since the first of July," Jasper said, "I did not pay much attention to the end of the month, as I thought him murdered sooner. Still, if he were there, I think I should have found the man."

"Yes, but if it were me, I'd be looking for a finger to be missing on his left hand," Frank pointed out, more kindly than Jasper deserved.

"Yes, that is true," Jasper admitted, relaxing, and I could see he was starting to feel pressured by Frank's brilliance. It was almost like Frank's master was a child to be soothed. Checking his pocket watch, Jasper said, "I have a meeting with a new client. While you research, I will take Millie. She can take notes, so we do not have to send so many notes for clarification."

"I cannot spare her. She has a very good memory for details, and examined the painting of Lord Beornmund longer than I did," Frank said looking at me. Trying to lighten the mood, I said: "I found something remarkably interesting in the cut of his jaw. I thought he would be more like the pictures in the papers of politicians, or the wealthy who look like toads, or a lizard with a small face, and a puffed-up neck."

Jasper laughed. Frank looked at me in a way that reminded me he adored me. It used to trouble me, but now it reassured me.

"I never saw a likeness of Lord Beornmund," Jasper admitted. I couldn't help thinking he was not very thorough, and I wouldn't want him defending me. Frank said as if he coaxed a child, "It was never your job to investigate. Not to mention you would have thought he'd have the identifying mark of a missing finger."

"It is all I looked for but be warned, the coroner does not appreciate sloppy work, as he calls it."

Neither of us pointed out that Jasper was extremely messy. Frank nodded and dug into what he was reading. I sat beside him, trying to make some sense of all the notes I'd taken by writing out a timeline. Jasper came up behind me and looked over my shoulder.

"What do you think happened to Lord Beornmund?" Jasper asked putting a hand on my shoulder to look at what I wrote. Frank looked up at him and glared. Jasper removed the hand.

"I cannot say what happened to the man except that his plan did not go accordingly," Frank said piercing his friend with a stare.

"No, that is clear," Jasper said ducking his head and moving away to the desk where he worked. After a short time, Frank stood. I took this as a signal we were leaving and scurried to clean up my space.

"Let's not be late, Millie," Frank said giving me his hand. I scooped up all my papers and then took his hand allowing him to pull me up. I followed Frank before Jasper told me to stay.

"Jasper wants something from me. He is trying to endear me to himself," I said.

"He finds you beautiful," Frank said.

"I think he wishes me to be his assistant, even after you go to the bar so I can do the work he does not care for," I said.

"I do not know what he is planning with regards to you, but I would appreciate it if you were very modest in your behavior to him."

"Oh, you mean like patting his shoulder in compassion, and giving him my handkerchief in his distress," I teased.

"I am sorry, I will not be so warm to Miss Keppel in the future if you will try not to encourage Jasper," he said.

"Very well, but Jasper does not seem to need encouragement. He thinks I must be violently in love with him and will do whatever he asks. I find him boorish and cannot understand his attentions to me."

Frank said nothing because we passed the Fleet Street debtor prison. He always tried to give a few coins to the beggars. It was hard to walk by those in such need and not feel low. I did think perhaps Mr Bethell was right, and it would be more effective to allow them to work instead of chaining them up in great disgrace and making them beg.

When we were clear of the prison, Frank met a barrister he knew from his school years at Middle Temple.

"Frank, Old Boy. What are you doing with Jasper Shaw as master?" The short stocky fellow asked.

"Mr Bethell arranged it," Frank said.

"Yes, to keep Jasper from disgracing us all. Everyone around Middle Temple knows it is a sham for you to train Jasper and not the other way around."

"It is better than groveling over a bencher for a year," Frank shrugged.

"You only have to pupil for a year?" he asked, impressed.

"That is what I was told," Frank said.

"Well, apparently, Mr Bethell is serious about enacting some kind of reform for learning and practicing in the law."

"It is high time," Frank said.

"Yes, I suppose. Well, here we are, good day to you Sir," he said, and they shook hands.

They parted at the doors of Old Bailey, and we walked over to the staircase.

"Do you suppose Jasper has been confronted by the knowledge that you are meant to help him and not the other way around?" I asked.

"It might explain his foul mood today," Frank said.

We said little else as we climbed the stairs. I had to take my cloak and bonnet off as we climbed so as not to overheat. We climbed so high my head grew light and I thought I may pass out. When we reached the top floor, I stopped to catch my breath. I often looked up at buildings, but never did I enter the height of them and look down.

Far below, a coach teemed down the muddy street, while carts were pulled out of the way. It felt a desperate thing to see. No matter how fast the horses flew, they could not move with the stamina of steam engines. It was telling how the carts were all shoved back into place, life adjusting to the change of steam engines as if it had always been that way.

"I can see all of London," I said reaching out. My hand searched the air for Franks. Instead of taking my hand he stepped into my shoulder so I might rest against his chest He and he put his arms about me while I caught my breath. I relaxed back into him and sighed.

"This is beautiful, Frank. Do you suppose this is how a bird feels flying free in the sky?" I asked.

"Not so different than standing atop a mountain," Frank said.

"I've never stood atop a mountain. I've been to the top of a few of the higher hills near home, cliffs over the sound, but never with so much life scurrying beneath it," I reminded him.

"Yes, I suppose not," he said. We watched people bustle below, each with lives pushing forward, apparently not even noticing time passing and everything changing. With such a high perspective, our lives felt a little clearer and our feelings a little sharper.

"Come, I have caught my breath and we do not wish to keep the clerk waiting," I said finally.

"He does not mind, I think," Frank said resting his chin to my temple. I closed my eyes and relaxed further into him. Frank tensed. His grasp on me tightened, strong. I turned to him.

"Everything all right Frank?" I asked. To my surprise he leaned in, and for just a heartbeat I thought he would kiss me. I thought perhaps I wanted him to kiss me. Before I could collide with him, fear struck me from a place I could not name.

"Come along Frank," I said quickly pulling away and grabbing his hand.

Chapter Nineteen

We walked into the musty storage area of a barrister whose sole job it was to investigate suspicious deaths. His clerk showed us to a room where all the records of his inquests were kept. We set up at a small desk in this room. Frank lit the lamp and requested the clerk get us the inquests from the middle of July to the middle of August. There were twelve suspicious deaths in the period – at least twelve deaths that made it to the coroner's inquests. I heard the door close indicating the clerk left, and felt myself relax but did not bother to look back. Frank watched me instead of getting to work.

"What?" I asked.

"Would you rather have gone with Jasper today?"

"No, he is… I don't know… uncomfortable. I have promised not to encourage him," I said picking up a bundle of papers.

"He is a very attractive fellow. He never had a hard time attracting the fairer sex," Frank said. I examined him. He was playing with me. Trying to get me to say or do something, but I did not know what and was rather focused on trying to find Lord Beornmund.

"I could see that about him," I said turning to the next inquest, as the first clearly wasn't Lord Beornmund in disguise. I untied this one to investigate further but quickly saw the deceased was under thirty years.

"But not you," Frank said watching me again. I looked at him now. He was so focused on me I stopped and said, "He loves himself too far. He is not sincere. I doubt he has ever kept the interest of a woman after the initial banter he offers begins to dull."

"Many ladies would have married him if he asked," Frank said.

"I am starting to find the men who are best at courting are not the sort you would wish to be stuck with as husband," I said with a little laugh.

"I ... I just sometimes wonder if you regret running into our situation so quickly," Frank said. I stopped and returned his gaze.

"You think there is anyone I'd rather be married to? Surely you cannot suspect me of harboring affection for Mr Shaw?" I asked, surprised.

"I don't know," he said, "I…it is hard for me to see inside you. I…" he turned red and I smiled at his uncertainty. He knew everything, just at a sight; it was sweet and a bit strange that I alone baffled him. I leaned in and kissed his cheek. I hesitated, my mouth near his face. I felt warm unnaturally this time. His hand came to my waist. Like a bolt of lightning, a sharp pang of fear hit my chest. I pulled away embarrassed, saying "I very much prefer you to him."

"Thank you, Millie," he said removing his hand. Picking up mine, he kissed it. I could not look at him but squeezed his hand before I let go of it. Turning back, I quickly shuffled through the bundles of papers in front of me. Remembering I had already decided the inquest was not the lord's, I bundled it up again.

I quickly untied another one. When I could tell it was not the inquest of Lord Beornmund, I sorted the papers neatly back in order and tied them again. It took Frank a little longer, but he nodded and turned back to our purpose. I dug through three more inquests, really studying the sketches, but found nothing promising. Finally, after I rifled half the stack, I found him.

"It is not so gallant as his picture in the library, but this may be him," I said looking at the sketch of a bearded face, "It is labeled unknown clerk in his late forties, though."

"Lord Beornmund is fifty-six, but never having been in hard labor would be young in appearance," Frank said taking some of the other pages of the inquest, "His body was examined at Westminster Charitable Hospital by a student studying to be a surgeon. His findings were inconclusive, and no jury was convened. The only reason the record was saved was to justify the cost of a coroner and medical examination."

"It is lucky there is at least this," I said spreading out the few pages.

"Yes, another bit of luck is the student did a full exam. A practicing surgeon would not have taken so much time for an unknown clerk with no family to push the issue and only on coroner's pay. The sketch shows a long distinctive scar on his stomach. This, coupled with his level of physical strength, led the the student to suppose he was a soldier at some time. Also noted was a birthmark on his lower back. Those together will be key in identifying him since his body is buried in a pauper's grave, but the plot is noted."

"How did he die?" I asked.

"It says he was stabbed, but that did not cause his death," Frank said. He examined his page and said, "The child who reported the death said the clerk fell down and then was stabbed. With no family to ask for witnesses, no further questioning took place. The inquest was made by the coroner because of the stabbing, but it is not the official cause of death."

"What killed him then?" I asked, setting down the likeness.

"The stomach was examined but arsenic was not present. The cause of death was inconclusive, and it could not be determined whether foul play was involved at all."

"A healthy man dies with no explanation. Then after he is dead, he is stabbed?"

"The student surgeon left it at inconclusive. The coroner, with little medical training, concluded the clerk looked as if he succumbed to a long illness," Frank said.

"Why would someone stab him after he was already dead?" I asked.

"I suppose so his death looked violent enough for an inquest," Frank guessed.

"Oh, yes! That is clever, Frank. Perhaps someone wanted his death found out. Wouldn't he have been identified faster if they cut off the little finger on his left hand as an identifier?" I asked.

"The inquest closed August the fifth. The finger had not been dug up yet. The killer did not know to cut it off as an identifier," Frank said.

"You are right. The killer made the killing violent supposing the body would be identified. Discovery of the ring only two days later automatically disqualified anyone killed with all their fingers," I said.

"Yes, he missed his escape by days," Frank agreed.

"I can't believe he just fell down and died, and some well-meaning person stabbed him so he might be found," I said.

"They took a sample of his blood and tested his stomach for arsenic, which means the surgeon suspected poison. They even checked his stomach for any other poisons, but found nothing. The skin was chalky and he looked sickly. The coroner says here," Frank said putting his finger on a spot, "the stabbing must have been ritualistic from some heathen culture."

"Yes, the heathen are known as the Quality in London, England," I said feeling something angry build in my chest. "They think they are entitled to do whatever they like, ruining lives with no consideration. They don't have to play by anyone's rules but their own. No one is watching them, regulating their cheating, and lying or even murders."

"We will get the murderer, Millie," Frank said putting down the papers to look at me.

"Why? Lord Beornmund deserved his fate. Perhaps if he had treated the people around him with more respect than he would vermin, he would not be dead," I said. He made me so angry with his two families and his faking his death. His taking whatever he wanted with no respect for anyone else.

"It is not for us to judge, Millie; it is our job to gather the facts. In court, all will be known. That is where the judges are meant to be. If every man went around exacting justice as he saw fit, society would be in chaos," said Frank. He put a hand on mine.

I pulled away and nodded looking down at a rendering of the man, trying not to cry. Trying not to remember the way it felt to be claimed as a slave to a rich man. I could remember Mr Williams' eyes when he told me I was his. The way he drove recklessly through the groves of trees, taking me as far from safety as he could manage on his tight schedule.

I hated the people nicknamed the Quality. Those who believed everyone else was beneath them. The Quality my mother would give anything to be a part of, even the life of her daughter. I hated them.

Frank must have felt the hot anger raging like fire from me. He watched my shaking hands sort the papers, putting them neatly back in order. I do not know how it happened exactly, but his arms came about me, pulling me onto his chair with him, and I fell into his neck. He let me have my cry out. Not once did he tell me to grow up or to stop being silly as my mother had in the days after Mr Williams took me. Frank held me until the wave of emotion withdrew.

"Lord Beornmund is not Mr Williams. Mr Williams died as a consequence of his own actions," Frank said quietly into the top of my head.

"Did not Lord Beornmund as well?" I asked. I pulled away and looked at Frank. His face was so close to mine, and his eyes were so full of compassion.

"I do not know. It is what we must learn. We must give him his own chance. Not blame him for another's fault," Frank said.

"Yes, I…I see what you mean, I will try to give him his chance," I said moving back to my own seat and tying the stacked papers of the inquest back together. After I finished, I moved quickly to the door as shame crawled over me for acting like such a child.

"Oh, my sweet Millie," Frank said standing and following me. He put a hand on my arm. "I would, if I could, take the memory of Mr Williams from your mind," he said. "Oh, how I would."

I turned to look at him.

"I will overcome his memory, Frank," I said. "I believe it is a part of me now, never to be forgotten, but I will not let it taint my views on mankind. I will give Lord Beornmund his own unique moment in time."

"You are just the sort of woman to do so," Frank said with pride, and he leaned in to kiss my temple. I felt something in my stomach lurch as I turned my head to accommodate his kiss. With Mr Williams so fresh in my head, I could not understand my own mind or feelings.

"Very well. Come Frank, let us go find this man's truth," I said raising the inquest bundle and taking my husband's hand.

No, I did not wish to be married to anyone but Frank, not ever. Trust meant more than romance. The former was warmth cocooning me in hope for the future. The latter tasted bitter and bloody and made my heart thump too fast and tears spring to my eyes.

Chapter Twenty

We took the inquest back to Jasper's chambers to show him. He was just getting ready to leave for the evening, and begrudgingly put his hat back upon the rack to look.

"Are you sure it is Lord Beornmund? It would be a jolt to our new investigative firm to go to the family and it really be a middle-class... clerk," Jasper said, spreading the papers across his desk and reading the assumption made based on an unnamed child's witness.

"That is the ruse. I would like to approach the family in indecision, and have them verify the features of his body. There is a promising scar that ought to do. Less distinguishing is a birthmark, but I doubt it will be necessary," Frank said.

"Yes, then it is not directly our fault if it is not correct, but their own misinformation. That is...wait... Why would you need a ruse? They only hired us to find the body," Jasper said.

"I think one of them may have been involved in the death."

"Well, if it is the old woman, I doubt she'll pay us for finding her out for murder," Jasper said, exasperated as he knocked a paper to the floor.

"I doubt she would have hired us in the first place if she'd murdered her husband and wished for it to stay a secret," Frank said, picking up the straying page.

"She needs a dead husband so she can gain access to her jointure," I said.

"Perhaps, but I saw something noble in her. I do not think she did it," Frank said kinder to me.

I watched Frank as he deliberated in his head. The way his eyes moved one way or another I felt sure he was trying to force himself to do the right thing. The push between just giving them a body to collect a king's ransom, or going a little further to find Lord Beornmund's killer.

"I do not know if they had anything to do with it. I would like to meet them and find the truth, even if we do not get paid," Frank finally said.

"I will be paid, and you may do as you like," Jasper said holding his hand out.

"You will write to Mr Archer and make the request to interview the family."

"Of course. We must have the body proved no matter what ruse you will play," Jasper said wiggling the fingers on his outstretched hand. Frank rolled his eyes and took out the twenty pound note he had folded in his pocket, but had not yet taken to the bank. He handed it back to Jasper, and collected the rest of the inquest. Frank sat next to me at our desk, and together we put them back in order and bound them after Jasper's hasty perusal.

"How will you know the culprit?" Jasper asked as he finished scrawling the note.

"I have a body, fingers intact. I have a family who wishes to identify said body. Anyone innocent would assume the finger missing is the Lord's. The killer alone will be the only one to know the body is not missing a finger. In his or her desperation to cover up the mistake, I suspect the murderer will have an explanation ready for why this body of Lord Beornmund has all of his fingers intact, when he should not."

"We know why the body has all his fingers," Jasper said.

"Yes, but they do not. They are desperate to identify the body. Someone will likely give me a reason why his body has ten fingers," Frank said. Standing, he put the neatly bound inquest in his satchel hung by the door.

"At the very least, the killer will know the finger is not cut off," Jasper said.

"Yes, but they will not admit it outright. I will wait for someone to offer an explanation as to how a dead man restored his finger. I am willing to bet the killer has spent many hours coming up with a reasonable explanation after they realized their misstep of not taking a finger," Frank said.

"Very well. Mr Clarkson, you will be so good as to get this to Mr Archer to schedule a visit," Jasper said handing the note over. Jasper then sat in Frank's chair next to me and leaned into my space like he wished to chat.

"We shall depart for the evening," Frank said.

I stood quickly, and Frank took my arm almost shoving me out the door. We had supper at the Hall and then quickly went to our rooms to avoid the chill and to rest our feet.

The next morning, we went to Jasper's chambers. Jasper came in by half past nine, which was early for him.

"The family will see you at the Beornmund estate in Mayfair at noon. You know where it is," Jasper said.

"We have seen the stables in the rear," Frank said sardonically.

"Well, they must be desperate. To meet at such an early hour. I know they will likely be entertaining callers later. Mrs Nicolas has just come back to town on a shopping trip," Jasper said.

"Are you coming?" Frank asked before Jasper started gossiping.

"No, I have much to do this morning," Jasper said. Frank nodded with a little bow, and took a book off the shelf, to study. I suspected Jasper. The way he had recoiled from accusing Lady Beornmund set me on my guard. If things went wrong, Jasper meant to put the blame on us. He saw us as disposable. That is likely why he did not come. His cowardly heart could not be more obvious. I sat and opened my notebook to review what was said on occasion about the family. Despite his self-proclaimed workload, Jasper pulled a chair in by me.

"Millie, I am glad you look so pretty today. What are you reading?" he asked.

"I am reviewing all we have learned of the family members," I said.

"If you feel nervous around the great folks just remember the Viscount's favorite story to tell is that of how his family helped rid Mayfair of the actual fair when it had become a nuisance. I know for a fact they did nothing of the sort."

"I do not know what you are speaking of," I said confused as I had no intention of being cowed by these people.

"Over a century ago, showmen, jugglers, bare knuckle fighting, and many other activities that… bring in the wrong sort of crowd were allowed at the May Fair near Hyde Park. It became such a nuisance, the annual festival had to be banned," Jasper said. "It was done to keep the neighborhood exclusive, and you will find the very name of Mayfair now means there is no place more elegant.

"With iron mines, the Earl of Beornmund seems to have bought gold," Jasper said, laughing at his own clever statement certain he had bested Frank. In his triumph he thought to move his chair closer to me.

"Come now, Millie, let us leave so we may have a ride through the mall and gape at Buckingham Palace before it gets busy," Frank said taking my arm. I followed him quickly because Jasper seemed determined to breathe my air.

Chapter Twenty-one

  The omnibus did not go to the part of Westminster where the Beornmunds' resided. Frank hired a hackney and we drove along the palace. The Beornmund house itself was in the highest situation a building could be, aside from the queen's castle. Located off Piccadilly to the east of Hyde Park in an exclusive Mayfair neighborhood, mansions grew taller than the trees, and the lovely views were vast.

  Frank knocked on the door, and we waited. Their solicitor stood at attention behind the butler who opened the door. Mr Archer motioned us into the place. Piano music echoed through a large glittering rotunda. Long golden mirrors and chandeliers hung suspended in rows down a great hallway between two huge staircases. Draped in white stone, Grecian statues stood in niches up the stairs. This house was so far from my home parish I could not imagine how one ever sat, or lay down in such a place. Only standing at attention made sense.

  Mr Archer accompanied us between the staircases as though a guard escorted prisoners. We walked toward the sound of a march played upon an instrument in such a melodramatic way, I felt myself in an elaborate pantomime. We were shown to an extravagant drawing room where the music from the pianoforte bounced off every wall. Mr Archer looked toward the piano with fervor. He did not interrupt Lady Charlotte's playing. We stood quietly waiting.

  The room was done in gold trims and cornflower blue furnishings. A massive crystal chandelier vibrated in clusters overhead. The enormous room had a fireplace at one side with velvet-covered benches near it. Here sat a pair who must be the Viscount and his lady. They were the picture of a lovely young married couple. Well-dressed did not fully describe their appearance. The maid had called them butter on bacon. Their clothes were ostentatious, she in lace, he in silk, each dripped, she in jewels, he in fobs; seeing their excess, I understood her term.

The Viscount was a handsome man. Especially in the face he looked like his father, but was petite in frame more like his mother. He sat slumped forward, and turned toward us, looking impatient, almost as if he couldn't place us or the reason for our presence. If any man were to stab another man with little force, it would be him.

His wife, the Viscountess, was a pretty, robust woman. Her features were all even, and of good proportion to her face. Her skin was almost unnaturally creamy white against her dark hair and eyes. It enhanced her rosy lips that looked…wrong somehow. She had a fine figure even sitting, and in height she must have been almost as tall as her husband.

On the other side of a huge ornate rug, Lady Charlotte played the pianoforte. Lovely as ever, her hair hung down her back in waves, and the look of concentration on her face, and the intensity with which she played indicated she was not aware of anything else, even of the man who turned pages for her. Her beau stood over her like a mother hawk, his plump lips pursed, his nose stubby, and eyes squinted in attention as he followed her notes.

Near the front of the pianoforte, Lady Beornmund sat at what must have been an uncomfortably close distance. Perhaps she wished to feel the music and not just hear it. I feared for her small frame; she might literally be moved by the strident notes. The elderly Lady Beornmund had been young with Lord Beornmund and I thought him cruel for replacing her as soon as the silver streaked her wavy locks tucked into an elegant twist. Her drawn face with a thin nose, and thin mouth looked weary. I could, as Frank had said, see she was noble, not just in birth, but in ideals. Perhaps being born in such a high position came with as much trouble as those who pawned every week for their supper.

Behind the piano, plants grew in huge pots that could, with some effort, be moved to make space for enough couples to dance the quadrille. Behind them, life-sized renaissance images hung on the wall. On the other side, large windows looked out to the sparse dying landscape of a courtyard with a little mossy pond and bare trees, taunted by the indoor boxes flourishing with such lovely exotic plants as I had never seen.

Standing in such a place, waiting to be acknowledged, made me sink inside. The discomfort intensified when the Viscountess glanced at us snidely and whispered to her husband. He nodded at her as if to placate her. She turned to clap when the piano music died. She faked a smile at the end of her sister's piano solo, one side of the bottom lip did not rise with the corners of her mouth, but stayed under her teeth.

"Ah Sir, you have news for us already," Lady Beornmund said finally turning to us.

"I may have, but it is a delicate situation. It must be approached with great prudence," Frank said moving toward her seriously. He glanced back at Mr Archer, still preoccupied with the daughter at the piano. He didn't notice Frank glance at him again, showing his discomfort at speaking.

"You may leave us," Lady Beornmund said addressing Mr Archer who flinched, confused he was being addressed. He stammered, but she raised her brows at him. He bowed and left. Perhaps it would teach him to use some restraint when ogling young women.

"First," Frank said, pulling the letter addressed to her from his satchel, "I found this among Lord Beornmund's things in Chelsea, and hoped it might be a clue as to his state of mind, or perhaps even a confession he meant to make. I ask you to read it, and if it contains any pertinent information to our case, I must hope you will trust me to read it."

"You infer Claude…knew he was in danger?" Lady Beornmund put a hand to her chest in surprise.

"I cannot be sure, only it is a curious thing he did not send it," Frank answered. Lady Charlotte left the instrument and sat by her mother. Her beau, never far behind the young beauty, took a seat next to her. The Viscount got up and moved to stand on the other side of his mother, the very picture of the dutiful son. He broke the picture when he read over her shoulder. The Viscountess, in a light silk and lace gown, stayed seated by the fire slightly apart from the family.

As she read, Lady Beornmund swiped away a few tears running down her face.

"He thanks me for being such a good partner to him. He makes the same apologies he has given me in the past, and wishes to work together for the betterment of our family name. I cannot say when it was written; it has no date, likely he is referring to…" She paused glancing at her daughter's beau. She continued more carefully, "He implied a few times he needed to stay in London over this summer to recoup some expenses. He knew I did not like it."

"He simply wished to apologize?" Frank asked. He sat on the settee across from Lady Beornmund, his eyes so kind no one noticed they did not invite him to sit. I took out my pad of paper and the sharpened pencil to take notes, but stayed back standing so I could observe the group unimpeded.

"I cannot imagine it had anything to do with his death," she said looking away.

"Very well, I need to ask you some very personal questions," Frank asked. "Do you think you can manage that?"

"What is personal these days?" the Viscountess said from across the rug. She snickered at the back of her throat. The way she laughed sounded inane and idiotic. The others did not turn to her, but instinctively the whole group, including her husband, tensed and leaned away from her as she made the noise. She must have been very wealthy to marry into this family.

"We shall do our best," the lady said. She took her daughter's hand.

"I have found a body among the coroner's inquest that seems to match his lordship, only I have some questions concerning it – "

"Yes, I am sure we can verify if it is him," Viscount Beornmund said sliding in to sit next to his mother.

"Very well. Did Lord Beornmund have a long scar along the bottom of his abdomen?"

I saw her flinch, a quick jerk out of my peripheral vision that caught my attention. I turned to see a flash of recognition. Not from Lady Beornmund, but from the Viscountess, her son's wife.

How would she know of the scar?

"I do not recall," Lady Beornmund said, flushing with embarrassment.

"I believe, Mother, if you will remember, he was thrown from his horse three years ago," the Viscount said quickly. "He was laid up for some time over Christmas. When it was just Hugh and I with him, his man changed the bindings along his midsection."

"Oh yes, of course. He had a great number of stitches upon his belly, and could not ride to his…about the country as he usually did. I remember now."

The Viscountess watched Frank, and did not notice me standing in the background watching her. Frank thought her husband, the Viscount, more interesting, and obviously hungry, and he was. He wanted his inheritance. Frank meant to move on to force his hand, but I needed to know something else.

"Just for the sake of identification, do you have any idea the shape of the scar?" I asked poised with my pencil and paper.

"I never looked closely. If Hugh were here, he would know. He often assisted," the Viscount said wistfully glancing out the window. He valued his brother. Perhaps, like Jasper, he needed someone capable to take care of the hard things so he might not be bothered.

I glanced over at the figure isolated from the rest of them. The Viscountess looked to the ground. She wasn't embarrassed like Lady Beornmund. She wasn't desperate like her husband, she was… I couldn't place the look. It was something more than her idiotic exterior should be capable of. She was…thinking, intelligently. Finally, when no one else could answer she looked up at Frank and said, "I do remember his saying once he… Oh what was it, Darling?" she asked, laughing with her inane laugh again looking to her husband.

"I do not recall," the Viscount said looking back to her hopefully.

"Oh, it was something about looking like a pirate because he had a hook," she said drawing a perfect rendering in the air while pretending she had to think extremely hard to

The Basra Pearls

know the truth of it, then ending with her laugh that grated every last nerve in the room.

"That is consistent with the scar," Frank said pretending to be encouraged. Frank watched the Viscount. The son was all excitement at the idea of finally having a corpse, despite it being his father's. Frank did not spare his knowing eye for anyone else. He watched only the husband.

I wanted him to see the wife.

"It is a hook shape. You are right," I said kindly turning to the Viscountess. "You have an abnormally good memory." Hoping Frank would turn to look at her because he would certainly see the intelligence behind the mask of absurdity she wore.

"Not so. You may ask anyone; my mind is dismal," she said. She looked up and made her eyes wide and her mouth pouty, intensified by the dead spot on half her bottom lip that did not move. "I do remember because I was not yet married. I was pinning a pillow and I meant for my line to go straight, but then his lordship spoke of stiches and a hook, and my stitching went askew," she said then gave that terrible laugh. When she looked down as if embarrassed, she did not blush. She did it to divert attention away from herself. She was immediately disregarded. I felt she was an exceptionally good liar.

"Well, that is one point of identification. I think under the circumstances we need another," I said, looking again at Frank. He gave me his little smile and read me perfectly. Knowing I wanted him to keep the dialogue up, and the family desperate, before he went in for his trap, he said, "Yes, there was also mention of a birthmark in the coroner's report."

"Ah yes, on his back," Lady Beornmund said, and I saw the Viscountess relax. She thought she would not have to help the situation along, but I was not ready to let her off that easily.

"The shape of it?" I asked, again my pencil at the ready.

"It was... I," Lady Beornmund closed her eyes, like she'd blocked it out and had to pull it up from some memory deep inside her. The Viscountess looked to her spot on the ground, thinking. I could see she knew the answer and it was killing her that she could not just say it.

I glanced at Frank. This time he watched me, trying to understand what game I played. I gently nodded at the Viscountess. He glanced at her confused, but he trusted me, and watched her as Lady Beornmund said, "Ah yes, it was almost the shape of a kidney bean on his..."

As she stammered to place the birthmark putting her hand to one side of her back then the other, the Viscountess watched her, subconsciously putting her left hand to her hip, almost willing her the answer.

"I believe it was on the right side just above his buttocks," she said. The Viscountess winced, but as I bent over to write her answer the Viscountess said, "What more could be left?"

As if I may be confused and put the word left and not right in my note, I wrote down her efforts to misdirect us instead. The Viscountess glanced at Frank. He squinted, taking her in. She grew uncomfortable under his gaze. Did she realize she overplayed her hand and was not in fact the smartest person in the room?

"I do believe this must be the report on Lord Beornmund, however this brings us to my concern. The body is not missing a finger on his left hand."

We were all quiet for a moment.

"But if the finger is not missing, it cannot be him, can it?" young Lady Charlotte asked, innocently taking herself out of Frank's pool of suspicion. Frank nodded, feigning agreement.

"It must be him, with his scar and birthmark," Viscount Beornmund argued.

"Sir, consider how his family signet ring ended up on an entirely different man's severed finger. It is quite a trick," Frank said.

"But his... you know his," the Viscountess held up her finger looking ridiculously innocent, like a grown woman playing a child on stage, "Didn't you suppose the other evening, my love, that the finger could have belonged to the thief? Perhaps someone stole the ring from your father, and then killed him, but with such an expensive ring, pure gold, surely it could have traded hands several times before it was cut off someone."

"Yes, it could have, couldn't it," the Viscount jumped on this too quickly, implicating himself. "That must be why there is not a finger missing on this body. Someone killed my father, stole the ring, then had it cut from their finger by someone else. Then he realized it was a family signet ring, and since they were not as foolhardy as that boy, they sent it down the water closet."

I glanced at Frank. He examined the two politely and nodded.

"I suppose that may be something. Millie, do you wish to write that down?" Frank said.

"Is that likely?" I said. I made it sound ridiculous.

"You cannot know how we are hounded by the impoverished," the Viscount said with great passion.

"Very well." I turned to the Viscountess. "Your ladyship, will you please state the supposition again?"

The Viscountess looked at me. Something flickered behind her eyes, something dangerous and intelligent, and very annoyed. Then it was gone, and she said, "Well, you are a bit presumptuous to address me instead of your master. Are you recently come from the country?"

"I am. Excuse me, My Lady," I said, noticing how she changed the subject. Frank did not notice, but grew offended at her slight of me. Lady Beornmund and her daughter looked embarrassed.

I grinned, and matching her ridiculous simper, addressed the Viscountess again, feigning I had not understood she wanted me to address Frank, and that Frank may address her. Instead, in exaggerated politeness, I said:

"My Lady." Then I nodded at her politely but making her theory sound even more ridiculous said, "what was your theory about a robber and another robber and the finger?"

"I do not have such notions," she said with a little bit of her laugh. Pulling back, trying harder to appear innocent, she turned to her husband, "My darling, what... are you saying about a thief?"

"I…" the Viscount squinted and since his wife hadn't just told him the theory, he struggled to remember what he'd said before, "Yes. What if a robber cut off his finger… or rather killed my father, and then had his own finger cut off for his troubles." The Viscount's tone sounded more like he asked a question more than gave his opinion.

I nodded, but did not write anything down, and I could see from the corner of my eye the Viscountess glared at me. Lady Charlotte cracked a smile that she tried to suppress, and drew the ire of the Viscountess to herself. There was something tense between the two young women.

"I recall you informed us his man is no longer with you, so there is no one to examine the severed finger to be sure," Frank observed.

"No. His valet went on extended holiday and has not been heard from since," Lady Beornmund said.

"Sarah would know," Lady Charlotte said. "She's a little rough but her heart is good. Father couldn't prove—"

"Your maid will not know his lordship's finger any better than the rest of us," the Viscountess interrupted. "A servant, Charlotte! You are soon going to be as bad as this countrified maiden over here," the Viscountess said, pointing to me. Lady Charlotte glared.

She meant to distract Frank away from the maid. What reason could the Viscountess have to keep us from speaking to Sarah? I would have to look over my notes of that conversation, which to her detriment, had already occurred, and was lengthy.

As for Frank, I could see at a glance that her tactic of distracting him worked. He looked annoyed with the Viscountess for insulting me. I often wondered why Frank loved me in the first place. Especially since women like Miss Keppel, and even Lady Charlotte, looked to him with such reverence. Even the smart, pretending-to-be-simple Viscountess found him interesting. Whatever the reason, he did love me, and the Viscountess made a grave error distracting Frank by pushing me down. Frank did not like that, and from then on, he did not like her.

Chapter Twenty-two

Lady Beornmund showed such a conflict about our news. Her tears fell as she called him poor Claude, but twice convinced herself, and her children, it was better that we found him than to be always wondering. Lady Charlotte was comforted by her mother's words and tried to be brave. The Viscount only looked at the floor, and I could not tell how he felt, except perhaps, that he did not know either.

"I will speak to the coroner in the effort to reopen the inquest that his body might be exhumed and re-examined so it may be proved to be Lord Beornmund," Frank said. "This will soon be over, My Lady. If I may take my leave, I will go back to Middle Temple and arrange everything."

Lady Beornmund dismissed us with a charge to get back to her by the end of the day with news. We left the lady only to find Mr Archer's large form pacing in front of the door. At some point he must have realized he should not have left the room.

"I am sure she wishes to speak to you. There is much to be done," Frank said. Mr Archer did not see us out, but entered the room behind us, and Frank took his big steps toward the door. I ran a little to keep up.

"Come, Millie we must disappear before Mr Archer takes the inquest and hushes the whole thing up," Frank whispered to me as we opened the door for ourselves and did not wait for a servant.

Sadly, we had not yet learned to hold the hackney like Jasper did, and it was gone. Instead, we hurried along our way. We rushed north a few streets turning at every corner to obscure our route so Mr Archer could not find us. My legs burned by the time we made it to Oxford Road where plebians were again plentiful. We caught a hackney back to our part of the city, and I could not catch my breath. We entered the temple gates, and though my heavy skirts weighed me down, we did not stop moving until at Jasper's chambers.

"How did it go?" Jasper asked as I sat in my chair wheezing.

"Where is Mr Bethell? At Court of Chancery?" Frank asked.

"No, the Vice Chancellor is out of town for the next month. He is likely at his chambers here," Mr Clarkson said.

"Good. We need him immediately; can you fetch him please," Frank said seeing my exhaustion.

"Why?" Jasper asked.

"Because Mr Archer is coming. I can promise you that," Frank nodded to Mr Clarkson, who did not wait for Jasper to tell him, but moved out the door.

"What is happening?" Jasper asked.

"We must get the law involved before the solicitor takes this," Frank said holding up the inquest, "and proclaims the Lord dead to hush up the murder entirely. He can do it. The student surgeon could not prove poison, so the coroner, upon his investigation, found the Lord died of natural causes after a long illness. It is enough to close the case. I never said what the subject of the inquest died of. I kept them trying to prove it was him. It was the Viscount who said his father was murdered," he said.

"For the ring, which we know is not correct," I said.

"No. Even before, he did not hesitate to infer his father was killed," Frank said. "I just did not contradict him.

Mr Archer will not be so distracted. We cannot let him get his hands on the inquest."

"Why not? If he takes it, we get paid and this is all over," Jasper said.

"Mr Archer will put an end to the matter and someone may get away with murder," Frank said. "I am leaning toward the Viscount. I suspect Millie thinks it was his wife. We both may be right. They may have done it together."

Astonished, Jasper replied:

"Millie, am I to understand you would blame the Viscountess Beornmund? Do you know who she is? Before she married, she outranked Lady Beornmund. Her brother is Duke Leicester."

"I cannot see how that would make her less likely…" I drifted off. Frank glanced at me, and with just a look he quieted my words. He did not wish for me to discuss the matter with Jasper, so I stopped. Jasper continued to argue the point with himself for some time. Finally, when Mr Bethell did not come, and the space of time for Mr Archer to be upon us passed Frank pulled me up and said apologetically, "We must go to him, I'm sorry. Are you recovered Millie?"

"Yes, of course," I said standing, the burning in my legs coming upon me much more quickly this time.

"I will come with you," Jasper said, not wanting to face Lady Beornmund's Goliath alone.

We shuffled down a lane toward the Hall near Mr Bethell's chambers when we heard someone call to us. We pretended not to hear and shuffled faster.

"Give me the inquest," the breathy voice of the solicitor demanded. Frank turned. Jasper and I followed suit.

"It is locked away," Frank said. "We are about to sup; would you join us?"

"I will wait here whilst you get the inquest."

"It is not so simple. It is not ours to hand over…"

"I will wait here whilst you get the inquest," he said louder.

"What is this?" Mr Bethell asked, coming upon us with Mr Clarkson. The perceptive clerk kept walking as if he had only met the bencher by chance.

"I believe we have found – "

"Not out here," Mr Archer snapped looking around to be sure no one heard.

"No. Of course. Come to my chambers," Mr Bethell said turning back in the direction he'd come from.

Mr Bethell's chambers were larger than Jasper's, and very nicely furnished in leather. The windows behind the desk let in ample light. The rest of the walls were papered in shelves and books. A table with several chairs stood to one side of the room and two large armchairs near a fire on the other. Mr Bethell settled himself near the fire where he only glanced at a half-eaten plate of food on a side table and asked, "What is this all about?"

"They have found Lord Beornmund, but instead of giving me the inquest so I might have the man properly buried, they have hidden it away," roared Mr Archer.

"Is this true?" Mr Bethell asked surprised.

"The corpse was identified by two distinctions," Mr Archer snapped, "It is unlikely that a body found so close to the time Lord Beornmund went missing, with his scar and birthmark, can be anyone else. Finger missing or no."

"Has the man been identified by the family?" Mr Bethell asked turning to Frank, as if he would only believe it from his mouth.

"It would seem so," Frank said.

"How did the Lord die?" Mr Bethell asked looking at it from a lawman's perspective.

"A student surgeon found it inconclusive. He thought it poison but could not prove it. The coroner then concluded it must have been an unknown illness."

"You do not think he was sick?" Mr Bethell asked.

"No, Sir. He was healthy from all I have learned. He rode vigorously to Camden Town, even raced his pad groom back the last time he was seen by that man just two days before he was reported missing."

Frank did not mention the month that passed between that time and the death.

"It is suspicious," Frank said.

"Yes, but not proven," Mr Archer said looking almost cheerful at this news. "The coroner claimed it illness. If there is not a malicious cause of death, this is a family matter,"

"The body was stabbed after he died. I believe it was done that it might draw an inquest," Frank said taking a deep breath.

"Which would indicate someone, who knew it was Lord Beornmund, wished for the body to be found and likely identified," Mr Bethell said.

"That does not indicate he was killed," Mr Archer said.

"Mr Hadleigh, you believe he was?" Mr Bethell asked.

"I do. It would have to be a poison, but not arsenic," Frank answered.

"Very well. You have yet to be wrong. I will trust you," Mr Bethell said.

"Sir," Mr Archer questioned, though with much more respect for the bencher.

"Consider Sir, Mr Hadleigh has learned in two days what no one else could in four months. His observations cannot be set aside when you have not even heard them," Mr Bethell said.

"Observations are not proof," Mr Archer said.

"No, but it cannot hurt to investigate," said Mr Bethell. "I am charged by Her Majesty to keep the law. I did take an oath when I joined the Queen's Counsel. We will give Mr Hadleigh until next week to look into the matter. It will take me that long to reopen the inquest. If he can prove there was foul play, then we will hand over the inquest to officers of the law. If it is nothing but an unfortunate illness, we will give it to you so the family might have him buried and in peace."

"The family has lived since July not knowing," Mr Archer said. "Is it not fair to give them the peace of putting this all to rest?"

"The very idea of being sure all is done correctly should bring peace. Certainly, we cannot have a repeat of the fiasco with Mr Chapman going on for months. We cannot forget it is that circumstance, Sir, which delayed a real investigation and left the family in such a precarious position. This way will be speedier, more efficient, and legal," Mr Bethell said with just enough power in his voice for the solicitor to know he was being threatened.

"I...the boy had the Lord's ring..." Mr Archer stammered.

"It is no matter now. I will personally start the process of reconvening the inquest court on this matter. In the time it will take to get the body exhumed, Mr Hadleigh will investigate. That is fair, is it not?"

"Very well, Sir, but I would like to see the inquest," Mr Archer said.

"As would I," Mr Bethell said. "Frank, my boy, can you please get it for us."

Mr Archer looked a little startled at such a familiar address. Frank stood, and I took this to mean I should come as well. Jasper as always was on my heels. As we walked out, I heard the solicitor ask:

"How do you know the investigator, Mr Hadleigh?"

"He is not an investigator. He is doing his pupillage; he is one of the most talented students I have ever mentored at the dinners here. He had to take a…"

Frank's story drifted off as we left the chambers. Frank took my hand and we walked slowly down the lane to Jasper's chambers. I could see he was thinking and he needed time so I didn't speak nor rush him. My legs were jelly and I could not have moved any faster if I wanted to. Jasper talked on and on that he should have been asked to get the inquest, not Frank, but neither of us heard him.

When we entered Jasper's chambers, Mr Clarkson looked up from his work, ready for any request we might make.

"Is there something I am needed for here?" Jasper asked.

Mr Clarkson glanced at Frank who nodded and without a beat he said,

"You have had a message, Sir."

"Oh yes, I must see to this," Jasper said reaching out for the letter without even looking at it.

"I will see to Mr Archer then," Frank said.

"Ah, very good," Jasper said. Almost as a threat, he finished, "I suppose we will not mention Miss Keppel's fortune, nor that the inquest was in your satchel all along."

"Very well," Frank said.

"Leave Millie," Jasper commanded.

"I need her notes," Frank snapped, taking my hand. We left – quickly.

"Millie, you think it the Viscountess?" Frank asked as we walked.

"I cannot be sure of anything," I stammered.

"Let us track Lord Beornmund's movements, and see where it leads us. Mr Bethell is correct. Mrs Ellis was very quick to put up a pawn, that unbeknownst obscured the investigation. The Viscount may just be eager for this to end. Miss Keppel does have so much to gain from his death after all. And I must admit the Lord did put himself in a position that could have made him ill, exposing himself to hardships he was not accustomed to," Frank said.

"Yes, and I suppose we haven't even looked at a robbery after he put himself lower," I said.

"Let us track Lord Beornmund's ledger and see where it leads us," Frank said.

"I will say this, and please do not think me indelicate, but the Viscountess knew Lord Beornmund's body better and more recently than his wife."

"That does not indicate she murdered him. When a young woman joins certain families, the Lord of the house – some of the more old-fashioned Earls – think they have whatever… rights they like. Especially when his heir is involved," Frank said.

"I suppose that would give her reason enough to have killed him," I said.

Frank took my hand, as appalled as myself. We said little else on the walk back to Mr Bethell's chambers.

Mr Archer sat at the table and spread out the inquest, Mr Bethell drew near.

"This is Lord Beornmund, not a clerk."

"Since it never went to jury, it is very incomplete," Frank said.

"Complete enough," Mr Archer said, "He died a month after he went missing. Come now, he must have been injured when he was robbed of his ring and died in some charitable institution after a long illness."

"In such a time he did not manage to contact you or his family?" I asked in the same tone I used to discredit the Viscountess.

"The case was closed. It was proclaimed he died of natural causes." Mr Archer ignored me.

"By the barrister who acted as coroner, not the surgeon who examined him – he favored poison," Frank said.

"This is enough for the trustees to transfer the estate to his son," Mr Archer said, looking at the sketch of the bewhiskered man.

"When you hired me to sort this out, Sir, you said something untoward happened and I must learn what," Frank shot back.

"Gentlemen please. I will reopen the inquest, and, in the meantime, Mr Hadleigh will look into the matter," Mr Bethell said.

"Just as a precaution, I would be very leery of what you eat or drink at the Beornmund estate," Frank said.

"I would not be so dramatic," Mr Archer said.

"Please, Sir. Take this seriously. I am comfortable Lady Beornmund is innocent," Frank said, "and I find I like her. Watch her for any signs she is being poisoned. Taking ill, being confined to her bed. If it was poison it will be a plant-based variety that cannot be detected. Coming into possession of her jointure, money being drawn lessening the percentage of the estate will make her a target if this all stems from greed."

"I will see to the family. Find out what you will, but Lord Beornmund will be put to rest as soon as it can be arranged," Mr Archer said looking at Frank like he had a thought. Instead of saying it out loud, he put his hat on his head, and moved toward the door. He left in a hurry, and I wondered what he thought of.

"Be very gentle with this, Frank. They can ruin your career before it is even started," Mr Bethell said.

"I cannot let a murderer go free, can I, Sir?"

"No, of course not. I would never ask you to. Just don't poke the hive if you do not need to," he said.

"I will be discreet," Frank promised.

We went back to Jasper's chambers only after we supped. The rest of the day Jasper tried to convince Frank illness made more sense than anything else, a result of Lord Beornmund putting himself lower. When Jasper slipped out to take a meal, Frank and Mr Clarkson left to sign some papers. Jasper returned before them. Finding me alone, he sat too close to me and lectured me all about the Viscountess, her family, and their importance. His gossip about the Viscountess only made me more suspicious of her.

Frank was livid to find us alone together when he returned, and Jasper unwisely began to lecture Frank on how the constitution of a person who is used to one lifestyle cannot endure a lower standard without falling down ill. He may as well have asked Frank not to breathe as to let the thing go at that point. He would hunt down Lord Beornmund's killer simply to prove Jasper wrong.

Jasper's persistence only made sense after he left. Mr Clarkson pulled Frank away earlier to inform him Mr Archer stopped by. Apparently learning Frank was Jasper's pupil, he meant to strong-arm him into letting the inquest stand. Jasper asked for more money, and Mr Archer said he would have to go to the trustees. Frank was outraged. For myself, I simply wondered if anyone would warn Lady Beornmund she may be in danger.

Chapter Twenty-three

The next day, while Mr Bethell worked to reopen the inquest, Frank and I started our day with another quick visit to the mistress. Frank eased his way back into Lord Beornmund's study, and, as before, Miss Keppel did not allow the footman to follow.

"How did Lord Beornmund appear in the last week of July?" Frank asked as he rummaged the drawers of Lord Beornmund's desk looking for pawn tickets.

"After he should have taken up his quarterly stipend, he rarely came, and never before the house was dark," she said.

"He had no horse, so he must have walked from where he stayed," Frank said.

"I suppose. At first, he brought flowers often. He must have gotten them on his way here," she said. She looked out the window like she could not understand what happened to him, or more likely, her flowers.

"You said by the end he seemed different, ill perhaps?" Frank asked.

"His hands grew rough, he… I often advised him he should not stay so long among the sad folks. The way they are content to live in filth and squalor was catching. I think his mind was addled."

"Was his body sick?" Frank asked growing impatient.

"No, he was stronger than ever, walking great distances with little fatigue. No, it was his mind that addled," she said matching Frank's impatience.

"Why do you say so?" Frank asked kindly to smooth her over.

"The last few times I saw him, he had little patience for me but took a new interest in Rosanna, of all things. He read to her and let her tell him all about her days. It was...odd. Before he only took notice of her on occasion. I do... I must think his mind is addled. Perhaps he is still alive, and does not even know himself." She turned, blinking her softest eyes and putting a hand on Frank's arm. "You must find him. His grandfatherly tendencies must have caught up with him. He is not young and clever like you."

Frank blushed and stepped back. He was a little unsure how to plug her for information and not get plugged for affection in return. She worked her charms ridiculously hard.

"Whatever the cause of his disappearance, I believe he is dead. You may believe as you feel, but you must not volunteer any information to Mr Archer. He is looking for anyone to bury so that this might go away," Frank said.

"I promise I will not say a word to that man," she said, emphatically tilting her head like she was doing Frank a favor instead of keeping her own neck from the noose. Frank quickly looked again through the desk, but found no pawn tickets, nor any ideas about where Lord Beornmund was lodging.

I stood aloof looking at the paintings. I wore my shabbiest dress, as Frank meant to visit the pawn shops and did not wish for me to be a target in my fancy new clothes. I hated the way I felt lesser than this woman fawning over my husband. I was angry and frustrated by the time we left.

"Can you be so certain she had nothing to do with his death?" I asked.

"She genuinely thinks him alive; she still doubts my word he is dead. You can see as plainly as myself she is not the murderer," Frank said glancing at me with an amused smile.

"I notice you did not show her the rendering in the inquest, that she might identify the body, which she could do with ease," I said.

"I wish her to remain in doubt. If it becomes necessary, she can witness that Lord Beornmund is in America, or wandering the streets addled and not dead. It will serve her well to testify such if she must prove her innocence."

"I suppose, but if anyone innocent must take the fall, let it be her," I said.

"Millie!" he said glancing at me.

"I do not like the way she behaves as if you are hers and only on loan to me for now," I retorted.

"She is frightened and desperate. We must pity her, but you need not ever fear her."

"Very well, Frank," I said taking the hand that reached for me.

"I wonder if Lord Beornmund was starting to see a littleness in Miss Keppel. Trying to convince him the poor enjoy their filth, whilst he was living among them," Frank said. He silently considered and we climbed into the waiting hackney.

We retraced Lord Beornmund's steps through the pawnshops. Thankfully, it was Friday. Being in the city for almost a month, I'd watched the women with their bundles moving back and forth to pawn like it was a usual part of life. I could only hope our business would not take us into Saturday when we would be squished in among the women thronging the Uncle and his associates to pay off their Sunday best for the next day. They must have them for the Sabbath. The only worse day to come into the pawnshops would be

Monday when they would bring their clothes back in to be pledged for another week's food.

Being a member of the farming community all my life, I thought the corn laws were a protection for us and all of England from foreigners coming to import their grains. Watching the scurrying, and what the humble women endured to keep their families fed, I understood why many started to oppose the law.

A few prominent Whigs swore free trade would make food more affordable and available for the impoverished. If any of the land-rich gentry in our area saw these women pledging every week for the sad scraps of grain they obtained for food would they not be Christian enough to give to them off their own table? And if that be the case, couldn't they afford to flood the streets of London with food?

Lord Beornmund took every farthing of his quarterly stipend and squirreled it away. He who protected his profits, and massive wealth: what did he think when he came into these shops?

Did he scoff at the insignificant advance given?

Didn't Miss Keppel say he seemed softer at the end of his life?

Was he capable of feeling shame, contrition?

With these thoughts running through my head, I tried to imagine him as he lived the charade. I also searched every shop for the items Sarah told us were stolen from Lady Charlotte. An idea was forming in my head, which felt too ridiculous to mention to Frank without any proof. Shortly put, what if Lord Beornmund ran into something in the shops he recognized as coming from his own house?

Of all the places Lord Beornmund went, all were in Westminster, and most were on the cusp of poverty, between middlish and the working man. We ended up in just one area

The Basra Pearls

of true squalor; its nearness to Buckingham Palace was startling. The last pawnshop in Lord Beornmund's ledger, with its three golden balls above the door, resided on a dirty, pungent street. I held a finger to my nose against the stench of human waste enhanced by the smell of illness like rotten eggs. Men hacked their cough, some were maimed, and struggled to stay upright. Makeshift shelters lined the street. I saw few women and no children.

Frank held tightly to my arm as we entered the men's space. Their perilous circumstances made them desperate. They looked at us with malice.

"His visiting this shop does not make sense. It is too far up the drains from Chelsea," Frank whispered not taking his eyes off the men staring. He sounded nervous.

"Perhaps he realized real scavengers would not have gone to the shops he felt more comfortable approaching," I said glancing around, a little afraid to look away as some of the slum dwellers shifted like they may come toward us. I could not blame them for feeling such malevolence; their situation was dire. But I also did not wish to be harmed by their desperation. I would never come into such a place wearing even my finest clothing from home let alone anything Mr Chapman sent me.

We entered the shop. Few other customers waited in the background. We started toward the counter. The pawnbroker, a man of middle age with a pointed growth upon his chin, eyed us. He wore a waistcoat, but tied on an apron over it to protect himself from the grime and dust. His associates scurried about helping the few other customers. But he stood with his arms folded waiting for us to approach the counter.

"I am looking into the whereabouts of a man who disappeared after he entered this shop," Frank said to the pawnbroker.

"Do you have a ticket?" the Uncle asked.

"No Sir. I was hoping you could look at a rendering of the man," Frank said.

"Do you have a magistrate's order?" the uncle asked.

"No, Sir," Frank said.

"Unless you have business to conduct, we have nothing to say to each other. Good day to you, Sir."

I looked at Frank, who stared at the man. He took his measure and knew we would get nothing from him. Perturbed, Frank bowed and we left.

"This shop is not like the others," I said.

"No, it would a be a strange place to come unless he heard a rumor of the ring being here," Frank said. We walked quickly away from the shop toward a main road where we could find an omnibus.

"Before this shop, Lord Beornmund was careful not to go so near Mayfair," I said.

"Likely so he did not run into his kin," Frank said. He moved me quickly up the street watching to be sure no one followed us.

"Perhaps he was murdered for money. It is just the sort of place where desperate people are," I said quietly.

"The inquest did not list the exact neighborhood, but I think we can assume this is not it. He would have met a much more violent end here," Frank said.

"You are right. The coroner stated he died of a lingering illness because there was no sign of a fight upon his body," I said.

"Yes, let us go to the hospital and see if we can find the surgeon who signed his name and learn where the body was found. It must be near where he was staying. If we can find someone helpful, we may get lucky."

"It has been months," I pointed out.

"Yes, and the inquest was dismissed before going to jury. I do not hold out much hope, but perhaps," he said.

Chapter Twenty-four

A massive brick charitable hospital with three arched entryways stood on Broad Street. The building was only a few years old, but upon entering it we smelled decay mixed with a sweet chemical so strong my eyes stung and I could taste it. I felt dizzy and had to take Frank's arm.

After asking many of the attendants, we learned the student surgeon we sought was still in hospital, just a few weeks away from finishing his one-year clinical practice. After he finished an amputation, he came to a parlor where we sat. The man was Frank's age, no more, but had a great hairy growth atop his lip that made my nose itch. He wore an apron over his waistcoat. It was covered in red-brown stains, and he smelled like oysters a week after they were cooked. His sleeves rolled up past his elbows, his arms, though washed, were tinged with blood.

Frank introduced himself and explained we found additional information concerning an inquest he'd performed the examination for at the start of August. The surgeon could not remember much about the case, but kept his own records of the incident.

Thankfully, he carefully documented his procedures when likely to testify as a witness at an inquest hearing. Though this case didn't go to a jury, he kept his findings. He'd been paid by the coroner's officer, even though the examination had been inconclusive. Many of his counterparts had a fight to be paid in such cases. We learned the case never reached the coroner himself. The police officer assigned to the coroner closed the case in favor of illness when no family nor concerned party came forward.

The student surgeon read his notes to us, and then remembered the details of the strange case of the man stabbed after he died.

"It says here," Frank pointed, "his nasal passage and throat were burned."

"Yes, red welts all down his throat," The surgeon remembered.

"Isn't that a sign of poisoning?" Frank asked looking through the notes that had been greatly condensed on the inquest.

"I thought so, especially at first, but I found no sign of it in his stomach. There are plant poisons I have no way of detecting that could kill a man. But, if it were a poison available through an apothecary, I would have had a sign of it," he said reading his own notes, shaking his head like it still bothered him.

"Do you know where the body was found?" Frank asked.

"Yes. The officers let students practice surgery on unclaimed bodies if we retrieve them before a crowd can gather. I usually keep the map of where they send me if an inquest is involved," he said rifling through the bundle and pulling one out. "Ah, here it is."

"May I take all your notes? I will be very careful," Frank said.

"If you reopen the inquest, I will need them back," he said shrugging.

"Thank you," Frank said. The man nodded and, checking his pocket watch, excused himself and went back to his work.

Frank, with a new hope we may solve the mystery of Lord Beornmund after all, followed the map to a bustling middlish neighborhood where omnibuses passed often. Shops or public houses were on every corner. Plaques of dentists or doctors were upon many of the doors we passed. The map ended in a tightly woven alleyway between brick buildings with a long series of doors and windows. At the end of the ally was a wooden gate, which likely held the shared privy.

It was not by any means a slum, or even an impoverished alley, and yet, it was classes away from Hyde Park corner where Lord Beornmund could have lay in a bed of downy and silk. A few women hunkered at door stoops, mending and watching children disappear dressed in their finished work. I supposed a seamstress in the neighborhood let work out.

"I believe this must be where he stayed while he pretended to be dead," Frank said. "It is comfortable, and safe, but tucked away so he may be sure he was not seen. Someone here must rent out rooms."

I could not put a finger on why the alleyway bothered me. I took a deep breath, trying to push away the feeling, like something bad happened here.

"There are many who must have witnessed a stabbing, even after death. I am surprised the investigation yielded so little," I said.

"They took scant effort as no family could be found to push the issue."

"Had they known the body was Lord Beornmund's they may have made more effort," I said.

"The Prime Minister himself would have gotten involved," Frank agreed.

'I suppose, but that will not help us now," I said. I turned him back toward the bustling street we stood on.

The Basra Pearls

"These women will talk to me, but not if you're here, I told him. "It would be easier if you went to find us some dinner and met me back here in an hour," I said.

"Millie... I...," he looked at me worried.

"I will be safe. I will not wander about anywhere but this respectable alleyway," I promised.

"Remember those littles have fast hands," he said kissing my cheek.

"It is a clean and cheery sort of place. I will be perfectly fine," I said.

I waved and he walked away. I walked down the alleyway until a woman nodded to me. I stopped and glanced around confused.

"Looking for something?" she asked. In her early thirties, she dressed respectably in clean clothes, though not grand. She hunched in a doorway sewing a beautiful flower pattern onto a skirt with quick, worn fingers. She barely looked up.

"Yes Ma'am. I am Mrs Millie Hadleigh. I had it that they let rooms here somewhere," I said.

"Nice to meet you, I am Mrs Alicia Clarke," she said returning the nicety, then more bluntly said, "Mare in seven has one left, but if you want it, you have to get a number. Also, you must know to settle in a place as fine as this it will cost you. She has three offers, just like you. Country folks coming in droves, and nowhere to put you all. Best go back and try home again."

"There isn't nothin' left for me 'an my Frank," I said in my best country accent. "

We have to try our luck here."

"It'll take a bit a luck," Alicia said.

"Is she the only one with rooms?" I asked looking for the seven.

"Abigail in number three does. She's alone with her little ones and has to let out most of the house. She won't take you, though. She has two rooms freed up; but her cousin just sent word of a large family looking for a place."

"Why won't she take us? We're here and clean," I said.

"She swore after so much trouble with the clerk, she was only taking people in on recommend. She has been unmovable on the matter, and cannot be blamed one bit," Alicia said, and I could hear a warning in her voice like she meant to put me on my guard, or at the least open my eyes to the cold realities of the city.

"What happened with the clerk? Did he run away with the widow's daughter?" I asked, sitting and picking up bedding. It looked like the woman was in the middle of darning her sheets when she needed a break from the intricate skirt she embroidered. This woman would talk all day with an audience, so I put on a fearful face, just as I should, being from the country. She threaded me a needle and handed it over while saying,

"Abigail's babies are all under ten years. No, it wasn't anything like that. In the summer last, Abigail was boasting of a respectable, middling sort of clerk from the country staying at her place. Only the professional sort can afford to pay around here, but we could all see he was too high class for this place even. He didn't sleep there every night at first. Then wouldn't you know it, after a month his mistress came to stay. Poor Abigail alone with her littles and here comes this clerk with his kept lady," she said.

"What is a clerk doing with a mistress?" I asked not having to feign shock.

"They think their kings now-a-day. The ordinary man thinking he can take on extras when his babies are home with

The Basra Pearls

the wife, and he's pawning every day to keep the mistress satisfied, from what I heard," she said angrily.

"If Frank ever tried that, I would give him another thought on the matter," I said, feeling bright red and minding my perfect stitches.

"Well, the mistress did it for the wife," Alicia said leaning forward, her hands pausing for the first time.

"What?" I asked laughing. "She gave his head the rolling pin?"

"I have no idea what she did, but one afternoon he came out into the street wobbling like a drunk man. He comes toward me mumbling something, his body shaking. I can't hear a word he's saying. Then he falls down dead."

"He drank his self to death?" I asked.

"Nah, he was never drinking that I saw," she said. Then she whispered, "I don't know what she did, but she did something. One day the clerk come home whistling, nodding his head to my husband and me like we were best of chums, then a few days later he falls down, shaking like he's possessed, and then he's dead."

"Did the mistress call the apothecary?" I asked.

"No, his moaning stopped a few moments after he fell, his breaths stopped before I could even reach him. This is the strange part. The mistress knew he was a goner before she came out to even check."

"How?" I asked.

"Don't know, but she brings all his earthly possessions with her, preparing to go to the Uncles with his things. But that's not even the strangest part! She took Abigail's big knife."

"She took the widow's knife?"

"Likely been helping herself to Abigail's bread while Abigail went for a doctor. Abigail made an extra loaf that day just for the mistress she ate so liberally."

"But why would she steal the widow's knife?" I asked, forcing her to focus on what I needed to know.

"She didn't steal it. The Mistress yelled at the clerk a few times to get up. I tried to tell her he had no breath. She shook him in a way that would wake the dead. Only it didn't, he was dead as dead can be.

"She screams 'What did you do this to me for?' and stabs him straight through the heart with the knife. I pulled my boy away so she did not turn it on us next."

"Did she try?" I asked wide-eyed, still surprised, though I knew it was coming.

"No. She grabs up her bundles – his clothes she dropped to stab him – rewraps up her fine tea pot she brought with her – Abigail's wasn't fine enough – and runs away."

"Did the constable come?" I asked wide-eyed and astounded.

"In London we call 'em bobbies, but they don't do much. I sent my boy for them, and they eventually came, but we all closed up. If you know what's good for you, you don't tell them anything, or you'll find them accusing you of the murder of a man who just up and died, and got stabbed for it."

We both laughed.

"Well Missy, that is good work," Alicia said in a way that told she had young children and didn't mind lumping me in with them though she couldn't have been more than ten years my senior. She handed me another piece from her darning bundle.

We were quiet for a minute. I repeated all the details in my head, chanting so I didn't forget anything. I repeated the part about the Earl being healthy before the mistress and then falling over dead. I thought perhaps Frank started to yield to the idea Lord Beornmund may have gotten sick after he left his comforts for this alleyway. Finally, I asked:

"Was the mistress...was she pretty or very fine? There are many pretty ladies in London."

"Oh, child, she was nothing to you. You are very pretty and young."

"Was she fair? A girl from my parish married a banker's son for being fair-haired with perfect bluebell eyes," I said.

"No, nothing like that. She was nothing out of the ordinary, just desperate. You and your Frank hold tight to each other and you'll be just fine," Alicia said.

"I suppose," I said sewing up the piece neatly. "Do you think I could talk to number three... if her cousin's family isn't in town yet..."

"I suppose you could ask. Won't come too much... She took the clerk's death mighty hard," she said. "You can tell her I said you have a neat stitch and would make for a good helping hand."

"Thank you," I said. I stood and handed her back her work. I bobbed respectfully so she wouldn't hand me another piece. I turned to go but she called me back.

"You are a sweet thing. Go home. This city is too dirty for you. You are too pretty for the masters," she said.

"I must try. For my Frank, I must try," I said entirely serious. City living was not as comfortable as living in the country, but this is where Frank would prosper.

"Yes, I suppose you must. But don't go too far east in the city looking for housing if you can help it. And cover that pretty hair of yours wherever you end up. Never look a master in the eye with those huge just-baked-bread eyes," Alicia said waving me off like she hated to see me go, but had to let me.

"Thank you," I said bowing to her again despite the action mortifying her. She deserved respect, treating a stranger with such kindness and a warning. It hurt her to let me go and I wondered if she mourned someone lost.

Thankfully, I'd found my luck already with Frank. How naive I was believing I could have found a place and made my own way in this city. London would have swallowed me and I'd be lost.

I turned and walked quickly back toward the mouth of the alley to number three. I knocked and an angelic little girl of five or six opened the door.

"Is the Mrs here?" I asked.

"Yes um," she said pointing me into a makeshift sitting room, and yelled, "MUM!"

"I haven't time to be…" a woman yelled back, but came to a stop when she found me at her hearth.

She took one look at my straw bonnet and said, "I let all my rooms already."

"I am here about papa," I said. "He went missing in the summer months of this year. He is matched to a man who died near here. He is a clerk by trade."

"That clerk has given me no end of trouble," said the woman I knew only as Abigail. She took a moment to exhale, and snapped at her daughter to go back to the kitchen and watch the pot. I looked her over. She was younger than I had expected, perhaps the age of Miss Keppel, no older. Despite her lack of finery, there was something about her that was very pretty. I couldn't help thinking a man like Lord Beornmund would choose her as landlady. Her figure indicated she worked from morning until eve, her light hair curled naturally, and chocolate brown eyes were painfully emersed in reality. Unlike my mother, when this woman lost her husband, she stayed awake and went to work.

"My Papa wasn't always such a heartache," I said playing the role of Lady Charlotte who often looked conflicted about him.

"No, not so. When he first came... he paid in advance, kept to hisself. I had the perfect tenant."

"He did not interact with you?" I fished.

"After about a week he came out of his room. Ate with us. Helped around the place... often found great joy in the evenings drinking tea and conversing with the other tenant family. After a time, he even laughed a great deal," she said. She gazed at a lone chair near the far wall that must have been his.

"Is the other family here?" I asked.

"They've just found their own place, but I've already filled their rooms so no point in harassing me over it," she said.

"No...I mean... perhaps they could tell me... Papa just left us. What was he about?" I asked.

"He was very private... I cannot say, but he was very kind to my son," she said.

"Yes, he was always kind to my brothers. It is often said he was too kind to my oldest brother who followed into the ease of his profession," I said quietly to keep her talking.

"Mr Beorma hated I had to send Matty every day to tend the factory machines. Since my husband passed, I have to... My husband was a bookkeeper at the bank and his father before him, but Matty was too young when he passed... Your Papa, he talked of apprenticing my Matty. It gave us hope... made it easier for a time. Then he went and... well he up an went to his rewards," she said, and I thought she may cry. I could see signs that the house had once been kept in a better way, but this woman was slipping from the lifestyle to which she'd once been accustomed.

"He… we hadn't been a proper family for a time. He must have enjoyed the evenings he got to…" I stopped before I said pretend. This woman's time with Lord Beornmund meant something to her. He must have been kind to the widow and fatherless. When she said no more, I asked, "I hate to mention it, but…there were some items that went missing, a family heirloom…"

"It isn't here. Your papa was in something with the Uncles. She looked me over. And said, "Since the bobbies never came for it, I suppose you can have his papers. It'll cost you a fortune to buy the clothes back, if they aren't already on their way to auction."

She went to another room and brought back a worn leather hat box. This sort that held a clerk's hat twenty years earlier. I couldn't Imagine Lord Beornmund had brought a top hat with him so I took it.

"This is everything they … he left," she said and growing gruff said: "He paid in advance the month of August, but I spent it on enough lye to clean up the mess he left. I rented him his bedding and everything. Anything that were his is in that box. He kept it locked in the pantry, or the misses he brought with him took it."

"What misses?" I asked. "My mother has not left our parish."

"It isn't my business," she said. I watched her clench her jaw, and glare. The mistress hurt her. Lord Beornmund bringing such things to her door hurt her. She did not want to admit what my faux papa had been doing, but she was angry, and I knew I could get it out of her.

"It is how he destroyed our family," I said sympathetically, "He cannot seem to … was she…was she fair, with bluebell eyes?"

"No, she was dark hair and eyes darker than yours," she snapped.

"He must have met her here, then," I said.

"He was here a month alone; she only stayed the last four days with him."

"Was he drinking? He was never known for it, but it seems like he up an' went to the devil," I said sadly.

"I never saw him drink. He ate at the public houses the first week, but after that ate here. He never took a drink here; this is no brothel. He did like to... he took a great deal of...."

She didn't know what it was and put her finger to nose in the action of taking snuff.

"Ah yes, it is a way of taking tobacco without smoking it and getting the smell everywhere. Mamma loathed the pipe," I said. I did not mention that very few besides the nobles did it that way.

"Before the other lady came, Mr Beorma mentioned your mother a few times. He spoke of her as a very good lady. He had great respect for her."

"Thank you," I said. This woman was kind, giving me compassion, despite her anger. I waited a moment as if affected then said, "Do you know what he died of? He was always in good health."

"I...I don't mean to tell tales, but that mistress was a witch. He started feeling ill the third day after she came. I never saw someone fail so quickly. I asked to get the doctor, but she said no. She cooked in her own fancy tea pot like she was serving the queen. Brought all sorts of herbs, like she was a regular apothecary," she said.

"She would not send for the doctor?" I asked.

"No, she was certain she could cure him. I finally... I thought her wrong and went to see about a doctor, but didn't get back in time. He passed in the morning hours of the fourth day after she came, and she left the place before I returned," Abigail said.

"She took all but this… all he had?" I asked.

"Yes, she collected everything of his before she left. I don't know why, but she… she took up my knife and stabbed his dead body when she left. Do you think she…maybe she's a witch?"

"Oh dear," I said. "She hasn't… have you seen her since?"

"Thankfully she never came back."

"Yes ma'am," I said feigning fear. Just then a clatter came from the front door followed by a lovely nine-year-old boy with buttercream curls and soft brown eyes, very like his mother, bursting into the room. Quickly Abigail hissed, "My boy, he liked your Papa. Please don't… he thought the woman was the clerk's wife who finally came to stay… please don't…"

I nodded my understanding as the boy finished taking off his coat and hung it by the fire to dry.

"This is Miss Beorma, the clerk's daughter," she said to her son.

"Charlotte, must be. Rosanna is younger than me. He gave me her stories," he said.

"Oh yes, I forgot," the woman said blushing in a way that told she hadn't entirely forgotten but instead couldn't force herself to remember.

"Did you know my Papa?" I asked after she left the room.

"He learned me…ur he taught me to read, and where to find the best meat pies here about," he said.

"Oh, I like meat pies," I said, surprised I could have anything in common with the man.

"Yes. He said I was just as smart as both your brothers, maybe even smarter than the oldest."

"Did this surprise him? He sometimes... well, he at times felt himself superior," I said as Abigail came back in with a beautiful children's copy of Aesop's Fables.

"At first, but after a time, they got on well," she snapped like she could not bear to relive it. I wondered if she had loved Lord Beornmund a bit. Like my mother had loved Mr Williams, not for himself, but for filling a role in a story in her head that gave her hope for a time. She handed me the book and I opened it. One of the first pages illustrated with cherubs showed it had been printed in Birmingham. He must have brought it from the country.

"I need you to go now. The child is exhausted from working all day and we have much to do tonight before we can take our rest," she said, unable to look at me, and I knew I was taking something tangible from her very soul.

"Yes, of course," I said, hesitating. I knew Frank would wish me to collect everything, but I loathed the idea of taking the boy's treasure. I convinced myself I had no real right to take the gift.

"Thank you for letting me see it. It is beautiful. Take very good care of it," I said handing the book back to the boy.

Abigail pulled the child and book into her chest and whispered, "Matty makes such progress in it...when Edward passed, I had to sell... I had not the resources to teach him... Thank you."

I smiled down at the fellow. "Your progress would have pleased my father."

"I liked your papa very much. I am sorry for you," the boy said following me.

"Thank you," I said.

"He would read me the words, until I could read them. Now I read them to Mary Eliza. She picks out the smaller ones."

"Which story was Papa's favorite?" I asked.

"He liked the story of the body. The one where the limbs thought they did all the work, so they starved the stomach until they realized how weak they had grown. He said society was a lot like that, and when we all worked together everyone could... um... tt.. th... um... be happy."

"That is interesting. He once thought some parts of society were more important than others," I said.

"That is something he often discussed with Mr Hornblower," Abigail said. "My other tenant. He is a scholar and has taken a position with the new University – not the church one, but he was very pleased to have it. He went back and forth for hours with your father."

I did not know how to respond to this, so I just chanted the name Hornblower a few times in my head.

"What about you? What is your favorite story?" I asked bending down to Matty.

"I like the one about the fox and swallow," he said.

"I do not remember that one," I said.

"The fox is stuck in some tangles and he's trying to untangle himself. The flies are sucking his blood. A swallow tells the fox he will shoo the flies away. The fox says it is better to leave the flies who are full than shoo them away and get new hungry flies in their place," he said.

"That sounds smart," I said.

"Yes, I thought the fox very clever, but your Papa didn't like that one so much. He said he knew of hungry flies and couldn't help that they would take his place," the boy said. He looked quizzically at me and his mother as if he didn't understand.

"Yes," I said. I glanced at Abigail who looked upon her extremely bright son with sad eyes. I had only known the child for minutes and wondered if Frank couldn't do something for him. I couldn't imagine how helpless Lord Beornmund felt. Every resource at his fingertips was taken from him by his own foolishness.

"Thank you for giving me back a part of Papa," I said patting Matty's head. Abigail hardened herself to defend her house. Her form went rigid, and she said quickly:

"I don't have any heirlooms. You can see all he pawned from the tickets. Don't come back here with the bobbies. It'll do you no good."

"I have no intention of doing so," I said trying not to cringe. She would likely have many visitors in the next few weeks.

"I have nothing else. I spent everything I made on a new knife, and then to wash the street so the rats would leave it alone," she said. I could hear the fear in her voice. To be so alone with little mouths to feed would terrify me. I did not fake the shudder that ran through my body.

"I wish you luck, and may God bless this house," I said bowing to her.

I kept the top hat box in front of me, and walked slumped from the house so the helpful woman down the street would see I had no success – and not look at what I carried. I walked to the mouth of the alleyway and spotted Frank across the road. He came to me quickly.

"I notice you have nothing for us to eat," I said.

"You are smart and careful. I just… I pictured you alone on these streets once… let us be together going about," Frank said.

"Very well," I said, knowing he was not being paranoid. A person, even a middlish person from the country, could be killed in an alleyway with little investigation into what happened.

"Come, let us retrench to Middle Temple," he said, eyeing the top hat box.

"Let us," I said.

Chapter Twenty-five

Once alone in our rooms I told Frank everything I learned.

"There was a second mistress?" he asked as I cleared our meal from the table, and he started to disembowel the hat box.

"It cannot have been Miss Keppel. I asked if she was pretty and the woman compared her to me, saying I was prettier. The landlady said she was darker featured than me. I do not think anyone who saw Miss Keppel would forget her beauty," I said.

"You are prettier than she," Frank said absentmindedly spreading out the tickets he found in the hat box.

"As my husband, you are obligated to say so, but I do not think either lady would have said as much if they had seen Miss Keppel," I said. Exhausted, I almost collapsed in the chair next to him.

"I do not like her coloring, nor her simpering manners, the way she expects me to grovel over her. That makes her unattractive to me. However, I do not think she would have dressed down. If such a finely dressed woman had entered the street, all would have noticed her."

"I believe you are correct, but it means he could not go a month without taking a new mistress. While he seemed to value the widow where he lodged, he so disrespected her household by bringing in a mistress. From all she said, it seemed he had grown aware of his pride, but in the end he...

his actions hurt and dismayed Abigail. I do not understand his character at all."

"No," Frank agreed, laying out the tickets, obsessed with his puzzle.

"The mistress tried to collect everything he had. The only reason she didn't get the hat box is because Lord Beornmund asked Abigail to lock them in the pantry. She was fetching a doctor when Lord Beornmund died, or the mistress may have asked her if there was anything else," I said.

"I do not think these tickets are the same as the others," Frank answered, laying out three tickets of the same brownish color about the size of a playing card.

"Yes, all the others have the name of shops in Chelsea. So those three must have come from the shop in the slums," I said, separating the three from the others like I'd found my hand of cards from the deck.

"This one is filled in entirely. A waistcoat was pawned," he said pulling one of the three tickets toward him. "I think we can safely guess it was by Lord Beornmund. He filled it out using the name Beorma."

"That is the name he gave his landlady," I said.

"The date matches the last entry in his ledger. Thankfully, he noted the name of the shop and its street as the ticket is not printed," he said.

"These two tickets match this final ticket in shape and size. But Lord Beornmund did not fill them out. He was meticulous in all his records," I said leaning into Frank to look at the illegible scribbles meant as details of the pawn on the other two tickets.

"These two brought a pound each, and the waistcoat only brought shillings," Frank said, fiddling with the other two brownish tickets that matched each other.

"The number is legible, but why wouldn't they make better notes?" I asked.

"The lack of details indicates neither the pledger nor the Uncle expected the items to be claimed," Frank said. He examined the two tickets in turn.

I knew Frank was more in his head than listening to me so I tried out my theory on him. "The items may have been stolen," I said.

Frank, looking up to consider, said, "The items would be sold by the pledger at a discount so the Uncle would make a profit. Each item was paid out at a pound. The uncle would have to get double that at auction to make such high payouts worth his while. The pledger would have to be content with half of what the items were worth, and still they are paid out at a pound." Frank squinted to read the ticket, and said, "Something silver would likely be worth more than a pound. You may be right, Millie."

Frank studied the tickets as if they could answer his questions.

"Thankfully the number is telling enough."

"Yes, and for such a price, let us hope someone remembers who sold them," Frank said.

"Frank, I can't help supposing these higher-priced items were stolen from Lady Charlotte Beornmund. It would explain why Lord Beornmund was so close to their estate. I think he somehow found out who was stealing from him."

"It is an interesting supposition," Frank said. "Let us approach the Uncle looking for stolen goods. Let us only present the two higher-priced tickets. He will be more likely to help us to keep the bobbies away."

"What else is in the box?" I asked, pleased Frank hadn't just disregarded my idea.

"A wooden dressing case. It's never been used. He must have thought he should shave himself," he said.

"It would not be unheard of for a clerk to go for a shave," I said.

"Clearly he did not know as much," Frank said opening it to be sure there was nothing else inside, and then placing it on the table next to the tickets. He sat thinking.

"Was she after the money from pawning, or more concerned with wiping away every trace of her identity?" Frank wondered, looking at the tickets. I could see he was starting to suppose what I'd already come to.

"Shall we visit the Uncle and see where it leads us?" I asked, weary to the bone, but picking up the three tickets.

"I suppose we must go back," Frank said, standing up. Both of us were exhausted with no desire to leave our rooms again. I struggled to force myself up.

"If we go this evening, we may catch him closing up shop," Frank said. "If not, we will have to wait until next Tuesday as we will get no answers over the rush of Saturday or Monday. I doubt Mr Bethell can keep Mr Archer from the body much longer."

"I know it is so," I said giving him my hand to pull me up.

Frank splurged and hired us a hackney. He instructed the uncomfortable driver to wait for us in the dimly lit street in front of the rundown pawn shop. The muck of the street and the grungy pawnshop were even more intimidating at dusk. The counter emptied for the evening as the Uncle and his associates closed up.

"I have two tickets this time," Frank said addressing the man with the pointed growth upon his chin.

"Is they your tickets?" the uncle asked suspiciously.

"Does it matter?" Frank asked.

"What do you claim?" he asked, taking the tickets from Frank. He examined them and then squinted at Frank. He stepped away and pulled a book from a shelf. He opened it on the counter before us and looked at something, then looked back at Frank. Finally, he said: "What game are you playing at?"

Frank and I both saw the slight fear playing behind his eyes which darted quickly between the two of us. Frank dove on it like a bird of prey.

"I am employed by a very noble lady who has missed several little items, combs, silver cases," Frank said. The man's eyes grew wider. When he said, "a set of pearls," the man flinched.

"I don't want no trouble," he said.

"I believe you, and My Lady, she does not wish the bobbies interfering. She certainly doesn't need the papers learning she has a thief in her house," Frank said.

"It ain't my business to ask where she got 'em from," the uncle said.

"I want them back. I will take them quietly, with a description of the thief, or I can alert the authorities. My Lady is angry, and will testify if it comes down to it. She would rather not," Frank said.

"I am charging you the penny per ticket," he said, frustrated.

"I would expect nothing less."

The man brought out a round silver vase with flowers etched into it, worth at least five pounds, and a sewing box inlaid with ivory, worth more. Trinkets at the Beornmund house, yet months of food to Abigail's little ones, were set upon the counter.

"I want the pearls," Frank said.

"They is gone. A man already came and bought 'em back; they'd be to auction by now if he hadn't."

"When did he come?" Frank asked.

The man looked at his logbook. The page he examined did not have a name on top, but instead listed the items.

"The hair combs," I said quickly. "Do you still have them?"

"Get it all," Frank said.

The Uncle glared at me. He looked at the number and walked back into another room behind the counter. Frank put his finger on the ledger. It noted the pearls, pawned 10 October 1839, and claimed 29 July 1840.

I made a note of the dates and Frank pulled away from the book as the Uncle returned with a burlap bag. One of his associates returned with a few bundles and they set them in front of us.

"That is all she pawned, twenty pounds for the lot," he said looking at Frank.

"I can see you never paid out more than a pound for each item, no matter their value," Frank snapped tapping his ledger, "and shillings for the final bundle. No, Sir, you are not in any position to haggle, taking in stolen goods."

"Very well," he said. This time, actually looking at the ledger, he counted and then said, "Thirteen pounds and five shillings, plus thirteen pennies for the tickets."

"I will have a receipt for all these items with dates of when they were pawned and the cost," Frank said, and took time for him to make a copy out the entire page of his ledger in detail.

I could not stop myself. I reached in the bag until I pricked my finger on the sharp comb. I pulled out a butterfly with an opal in the center.

"Them's bad luck anyway," the Uncle said.

"They are – for the thief," I said. I looked at Frank to appreciate my joke, but he cringed as he raised a bundle to examine what looked like blood.

When the Uncle finished with our copy of the ledger, Frank said, "You will wish to keep that to prove your business was done legal and without knowledge, if it comes to it."

The man nodded with a scowl.

Pulling his coin pouch out of a pocket sewn into his satchel, Frank counted out a round, golden stack of thirteen sovereigns and change. Money he'd brought with us from the country. He replaced his pouch, now considerably lighter. It made me sick to see him use our own money to smoke out the murderer of a man whom I could not reconcile vindicating, now that he was on mistress number two, and she brought into a widow's house with young children.

Without hesitating the uncle recounted the coins that would pay the wages of a housemaid for a year. Since I had not yet found anyone to take on that role, I told myself it was no matter, but felt a lump in my throat.

"And the thief?" Frank asked sternly.

"A woman," the Uncle said. He didn't like Frank. I wondered if I could ask, and he would answer. The Uncle leaned toward me, looking to me for assurance when he spoke. I couldn't tell why, but he seemed more comfortable with me than Frank. I bolstered my courage, and decided the maid Sarah Smith would be just this man's sort.

"Please, Sir," I said moving away from Frank and the bloody bundle on the long, worn, wooden counter. I began imitating Sarah's mannerisms: "My young lady is tryin' to marry. We must have this matter cleared up before her beau gets any idea of it. Was it the old lady's maid?"

"I don't know about that," he said moving to me with the bag between us, and, as I suspected, he would gossip. "She had dark hair, dark eyes, very red lips but the bottom one had a dead spot. Her skin were too white for an outdoor servant. She dressed down, but I thought her gentry in disguise. I get more of the fancy sort in here than you'd suppose. They get into a tight spot and here I is," he said, grinning, his yellow-brown eyes leering down on me. His eyes and teeth were the same color, and his pointed chin beard made him appear wolfish.

"Yes, the lady's maid isn't so trustworthy. My Lady has never trusted her," I said. He flinched at my mention of a titled lady.

"I were thinking she must a been at least a lady's maid. She didn't act lower or middlish. She was a medium-sized woman, but all her curves were just right," the uncle said winking at me. I held my face without letting it appear disgusted.

"Can you remember who claimed the pearls? It weren't a younger fella – plump lips, small nose, I suppose?" I asked pursing out my lips.

"No miss, it were an older man, likely a working man. Not clean under the nails like her. He were very fit, maybe a soldier. He were of such an age – at the time I thought it was likely her father. Looking back, with what I know now, mind you, I can see if she were the old lady's maid, her papa would try to stop her from pledging the family's goods. He would suffer somethin' awful from the loss of her wages if she were dismissed. Or perhaps he were in on it, and she cut him out of the pearls. I dunno, but I thought he may a beat her right there in front of me."

"He was angry then."

"He came upon her in the private box after I wrote those two tickets," he said pointing to the vase. "He didn't care for the items she had. All he wanted was them pearls. I thought he was going to try and steal 'em from me. I paid twelve pounds for um."

"They're worth over a hundred," Frank said.

"She was very pleased to get so much. If she don't know her business she shouldn't come in," he glowered. I rolled my eyes pretending to be annoyed with Frank and waved him away. Then I asked:

"But... but he paid the pledge. He didn't steal them?"

"Didn't make no sense because he took out the money in pounds and paid off the pearls easy as can be, except he just traded my associate a waistcoat for shillings the day before. I can't say what he was playing at."

"He came in one day, pledges a waistcoat," I said pausing to let the man fill in the rest.

"Says he saw a catalog with lovely pearls, ready to go to auction. My associate shows him, and he says nothing. Next day the pledger comes in doing her business from the side door, same man barges in, and pounces on her. She's scared of him once she sees his face."

"Like she saw a ghost?" I asked.

"I suppose," he said.

"But he calmed down... they left together?" I asked.

"First, she tried to give him the money. She had more than just the two pounds she'd gotten, but he didn't want her money. When she couldn't be persuaded to take the money, she kept promising she'd recover the price of the pearls. She'd give him what he wanted," he said.

"What did that mean?" I asked.

The Basra Pearls

"Dunno, but the only time she came back was with that," he said pointing to the bundle with blood on it. "Haven't seen her since. It's been months."

"That is very strange about the pearls," I shrugged unconcerned but said clearly so he'd know, "He'll never be able to sell um. Steps have been taken by the trustees; they'll never make it to auction."

"The trustees, you say?" he asked.

"Yes, Sir. I think you will be glad not to get into that scrape," I said.

The man nodded to me, resigned. I looked to Frank and finished, "I am in no doubt who the thief is. And you, Sir?"

"There is very little doubt," Frank said, clearing his throat.

The Uncle glared at Frank and said, "We are closing, time to take you off."

"Thank you, sir,' I said with a curtsy, and he smiled at me again. I couldn't think his teeth would be long in his wolfish mouth.

"Come, let us take these and think about this," Frank said. We picked up the bundles. Considering we carried a fortune, my stomach turned as we walked out the door. Every hungry eye on the street watched us, some even stood like they may move toward us. Thankfully, the hackney waited. My weariness was wiped away in fright. I quickly climbed into the hackney. As we left the shop I wondered if the driver would take payment in combs and vases.

Altogether, it only took us a little over an hour from the time we left our rooms to the time we came back. In that time, we spent a year's savings. It felt out of proportion.

Chapter Twenty-six

"I am sorry I squandered your maid away on these trifles," Frank said as he laid out the treasure on the table. All the trinkets Sarah was dismissed for stealing.

"As we have everything done for us, I cannot think it a burden," I said fingering the little oval moonstones set in silver, the bracelet that Lady Charlotte had liked so much.

"Still, I will make it up to you, Millie," he said.

"It is no matter. I suppose we can continue as we are since you do not seem to mind," I said.

Frank looked up at me and grinned. "I do not mind."

His look made me laugh and I sat next to him helping him place the items in order from the time when the items were pawned.

"If the pearls had not been reclaimed, they would have been at auction by now, likely recovered by the Beornmund estate," I said.

"When received by the broker, they would have been appraised, found to be genuine, identified through the picture of Lady Beornmund, and returned to the Beornmund house," Frank agreed.

"The estate would have paid more than the price pawned to reclaim them?" I asked.

Frank said more to himself than out loud: "Likely the hundred pounds would have been paid simply to hush up the matter. I wonder if the maid would have been blamed, or if it would have been traced back to Viscountess Beornmund."

"Lord Beornmund risked his scheme to get the pearls when all would have been righted. He must have been concerned about her being implicated," I said.

"Why would the Viscountess pawn a family heirloom – pearls that could be identified in the first place?" Frank asked.

"It was foolish," I agreed.

"She married into the family at the end of September last year. She pawned them October 10 of last year," Frank said, "Perhaps the Viscount had her do it and she did not know any better?"

"She may have found them in Lady Charlotte's rooms. Because they were not with the family jewels, she did not think them overly valuable," I said.

"Or perhaps after they married, the Viscount desperately needed money for something," Frank said.

"You just cannot believe she would do this of her own volition, can you?" I asked.

"It does not seem possible," he said.

"Just as I cannot possibly be wise enough to help you in your work and ought, as it has been suggested to me several times, stay home and manage the place."

"Oh, no Millie. You ought to be with me. I would never have learned so much from the Uncle if you were not there. I would never even have known the Viscountess was involved if you hadn't noticed her."

He stopped and looked at me. He thought it through. Then he said, "Yes, you are right. The Viscount would not have his wife pawn such a treasure that was likely to get them caught. She thought they were the young lady's trinket, glass ornaments gifted to her," he said gesturing to the table full of finery meant as gifts to Lady Charlotte. Nothing else was recognizable, or overly valuable.

"All the pawned items are worth between three and five pounds, but paid out at one pound. Perhaps you are right, the Viscount would not have taken so little," Frank said.

"I don't know if that is truth, but thank you for letting it be a possibility," I said taking his hand. He raised our clasped fists and kissed mine. I leaned over and, feeling the pressure of his kiss against my hand, I kissed his. He pulled away, surprised at the action. His charming blue eyes became confused. I explained, "I just… I need my opinion to matter. I do not know why; it just needs to be so."

"It is so," Frank said watching me intensely. "Where I fall short, you thrive. I love you, Millie."

I had to blink not to cry. I could not look at him.

"I cherish that love, Frank," I said closing my eyes and pulling his hand toward me. I kissed it again. I felt something surge through me and I was embarrassed to feel it. My face burned and I did not know where to look. I let go of Frank's hand and began straightening the pawned items, though they were already neatly in order of when they were taken. Frank watched me, but I could not look at him with my face on fire.

"Very well," Frank finally said. "Let us know Viscountess Beornmund. I researched the family to learn what I could yesterday. I certainly did not dismiss your claims."

I glanced up from the table to see if he teased me and he grinned. I rolled my eyes and laughed.

The Viscountess was born into a very wealthy family. Her father was the ninth Duke of Leicester, a title that encompassed the Earldom of Warwick at one time, but was dissolved and recreated for a relation along the line. It is rumored the first Duke was very important to Queen Elizabeth. Yet, his son Leicester was one of the major leaders of the parliament in the civil war, and he picked up much land in the Midlands at the time.

Frank's information comprised of facts that could be learned in histories. Jasper was quick to slather gossip on me after I accused the Viscountess. Which I related to Frank. Lady Beornmund and the Duchess of Leicester were very close friends. They spent holidays together in the country. During the season in London, the women were inseparable. They became leaders of society, just a word from either lady, and a voucher to Almack's was issued.

After the Duchess Leicester died ten years hitherto, Lady Beornmund mourned greatly and withdrew from society. Even now she only goes out and about on occasion with her daughter.

The Viscountess often spent holidays with Lady Beornmund in the country before and even after her mother's death. She only came to London with her father after her mother died. When she reached an age to have been presented, she was not, nor was she thrown into the marriage mart. Without her ever having a season, she was consented to her marriage to the eldest son of his late wife's dear friend by Duke Leicester. Many think it was due to his own failing health.

Some speculated the Leicester-Beornmund marriage was arranged by their mothers at birth so there was no purpose to sending the Viscountess for a season. After the Viscountess made her debut on society, at twenty-five years of age, it was supposed her father did not send her because she was a nincompoop.

"I saw intelligence in her, though, I swear it, Frank," I said at last.

"Yes. I saw it too," Frank agreed. "I do trust you Millie, but I cannot lose suspicion against the Viscount. He has not the proper remorse for his father's death."

I looked up at Frank. Ever since the accident that killed both our fathers, he had mourned. He could not understand a young man not mourning his father.

Giving his idea credence since he did the same for me, I said: "I suppose the Viscountess could have introduced her husband to the idea of fencing his sister's property. How would she know the pawn shops? How would she navigate her way in the first place?"

"I cannot say. Considering she only got twelve pounds for the pearls, I would not say she was good at bargaining. That vase is pure silver, and worth five pounds. She could have gotten at least three. The Uncle lost at least forty-five pounds in gains this evening. That does not include the pearls," Frank said.

"Is it a thrill for her to simply enter the shop? She looked very much like she enjoyed the game she was playing the other day," I said.

"Let's find Lord Beornmund's pearls," Frank said. "They are the proof we will need. They were last seen with Lord Beornmund five days before his death. They were not found on the body nor in his things. What are your thoughts?"

I looked at him. He wanted me to say it, so he did not have to.

"He would be unwise to leave them anywhere the Viscountess could get at them," Frank hinted.

"Which only leaves Miss Keppel. She must have them," I finally said.

"Yes," Frank said looking at me and cringing.

"I do not understand Lord Beornmund. If he let the pearls go to auction, they could be reclaimed by his family.

Lady Beornmund would be forced to at least suspect the Viscountess if they were traced back," I said.

"He must have worried it would have gotten out and marred his family name," Frank said.

"Or he meant to take them with him," I said. "The maid said they meant something to him."

"He wanted them. As one reminder of his old life," Frank said. I could see he was caught up in this new idea.

"He must have left them with the Mistress then," I said knowing all roads led back to Miss Keppel.

"I suppose so. Do you mind terribly if we go question her tomorrow? We will have the hackney wait for us," Frank said.

I shrugged trying to look as if I didn't care, but it wasn't my favorite idea for the evening.

"One thing is for certain," I said, standing up to prepare for bed.

"What Millie?"

"The Viscountess made it very easy for him to take the pearls to America, but in the same turn, Lord Beornmund set himself up to be murdered and never found."

Chapter Twenty-seven

The next morning, we were shown into the drawing room in Chelsea by the nine-fingered butler.

"Ah Mr Hadleigh, it is so good to see you," Miss Keppel said reaching her hand to him. She ignored me, after taking in my appearance and grimacing. I grinned with confidence. I wore my fine day gown and spent long upon my grooming ready to beat her at her game.

Frank asked, "Have you stayed very quiet about Lord Beornmund's scheme?"

"I have seen his solicitor and told him nothing. I fear him. I think he would like me to confess to killing Lord Beornmund just to have someone to blame so he may move on."

"It is best not to see him if you can manage it. I have come to ask you about a set of pearls," Frank said moving on quickly as she meant to slow him into flirtation.

"Yes, My Lord was very angry about them. They were his mother's. I cannot believe someone would be fool enough to steal them. They have been painted into her picture."

"You do not know where they are then?" I asked.

"How would I know?" she snapped at me. "I did not take them. Nobody has seen them in months."

"Lord Beornmund found them just before he died. It is important we find them. They were not at the room he rented. He kept as little as possible there," Frank said.

"You found his rooms?" she asked. "You are very clever."

I did not respond. I felt certain she would snap at me again. She wished to come between me and Frank. She needed another cow-boy to take her to America where her fortune and house awaited her. Did she think Frank the man for the job?

"Why do you think I have them?" Miss Keppel asked when Frank suggested they may be hidden.

"He could not have taken them back to the mansion. They all thought him dead," Frank said.

"Well, I assure you Sir, they are not here. You checked his desk through. He did not go anywhere else in the house but this room when he came. Our butler brought whatever he asked into this room," she said.

"Can I meet your daughter?" I asked, struck by a thought.

"I…the child is a clever little miss, but I do not think she can work this out for you," Miss Keppel said condescendingly.

"I think you are wrong," I said.

She shook her head and had the footman call her daughter. Likely so she could prove me wrong in front of Frank. Lord Beornmund had seen the child in his last days by Miss Keppel's own admission. He had loved Lady Charlotte enough to entrust her with his pearls. Perhaps he felt the same for his illegitimate daughter. After all, the landlady's son added her name to his other children.

The young miss came skipping in. She was her half-sister's likeness in miniature form. Her hair, the light brown of the Beornmund's, went straight down her back, instead of waving. It was the only difference. Her face smiled beautifully, and her fingers curled delicately as she pulled her skirt to curtsy.

"Rosanna, this is Mr Frank Hadleigh," she said introducing Frank to her little daughter.

"Hello," he said shaking hands with her. "Rosanna was your grandmother's name; did you know that?"

"Yes, papa often told me stories about her. I did not know her, but I look very much like her."

Rosanna turned to me next. Her mother was then obligated to say, "This is Mrs Frank Hadleigh."

"How do you do," she said. Her nurse must have been of her father's choosing. The child was very polite and did not seem inclined to favor Frank just because her mother did.

"Can I ask you a question about your papa?" I asked.

"He died," the young girl said, but a little smile crossed her beautiful features belying her words.

"Yes, I am sorry," I said.

She nodded.

"Before he died, he came to see you I believe," I said.

"He always came to see me," she said.

"But this last time did he give you a secret present?" I asked.

She didn't say anything but looked at her mother confused.

"Did he give you something, my love?" Miss Keppel asked. Her daughter's face was easily read.

She said nothing.

"It is a secret," I said.

She nodded.

"But your papa died, and now you must share all secrets with your mama," I said.

"Oh, I did not know it could be so," she said looking relieved.

"Can you please go get the pearls," I said.

"They are hidden under my bed things in my trunk. When we go on our long boat ride, I am to take them with me," she said.

"I am sorry love, but I have to take them. They will help us. Can you please bring them here?" Frank said kindly. When the child still hesitated Miss Keppel fumed.

"Go get them."

The child dipped and left with the footman.

"How did you know he gave them to her?" she asked me.

"He gave them to his other daughter, but went to fetch them a few days before his ruse began. I believe he always meant to take them to the Americas with you. No one would think to look in your daughter's trunk for an heirloom. No one would question her."

"No, perhaps not," she said.

"It also helps us establish a timeline," Frank said.

"How so?" she asked.

"We know Lord Beornmund came back into this house after he found the pearls, but his body was not found until at least four or five days later," Frank said looking up at the ceiling as if he was thinking.

The butler came back in with Rosanna, and looked very displeased. In both hands the child held a beautiful rosewood box with an inlay of dark ebony flounces and swirling purple and green mother of pearl flourishes made for the purpose of holding the treasure. We all moved in

The Basra Pearls

as her mother took the box and opened the latch on the front.

The sheen of pearls reflected light from overhead. I held my breath not to gasp. The headdress, a comb decorated in pearl flowers attached to strands of pearls on silk to be woven through the hair, was strapped into the top of the velvet-lined box. Both the necklace and bracelet were three strands clipped with a golden clasp and drop earrings, all fitted into the bottom. The pearls' luster made them iridescent, and looking upon them felt euphoric, like watching the sunset, or sitting in a field of flowers listening to the birds sing. I had never been so close to such finery. The artistry in the headdress, and the beauty of the pearls caught me unprepared for the sight.

"The child was meant to have this parure as a gift," the butler said, taking the box from Miss Keppel. As he tried to close it, a pledge ticket caught. The butler shoved the ticket into the box, and latched it up.

"Rosanna, can you go look at a picture book for a few minutes while we speak," Frank suggested. She nodded and skipped to the corner, distracting herself.

"Your master is dead, and those pearls are imperative in proving how he was murdered," Frank said. The butler nodded, but clearly believed his master was in America.

"We have found his body," Frank said. "Lady Beornmund will testify that the corpse containing a hook-like wound at the bottom of his abdomen, and a rather large bean shaped birthmark above his left buttock, is him."

"What?" Miss Keppel whispered, this being the first she heard of his identifying attributes, tears formed in her eyes. The butler stood before us aghast. I supposed he took the place of Lord Beornmund's valet and knew the features of the corpses were true to his Lordship's body.

"You believed he would contact you soon," Frank said.

"Those are his... those identify him, but... he was meant to be in the New England by now," he said.

"He is not. I have found where he was lodging under the name Beorma. His landlady and another woman saw him die. I am sorry, but his plan to go to America failed."

The butler nodded, struggling to compose himself.

Frank waited for the butler to regain his composure. Then he asked, "When did you see him last?"

"When he gave the child the pearls. He made certain I knew she had them so I might ensure their safety on the trip. He... he meant for her to have his mother's pearls," the butler said.

"Though legally they will go back to the estate," Frank said.

"These," he said lifting the lid like he opened a box to the moon's glow, the light shone off the glossy white pearls in iridescence, "were harvested off the coast of Persia. The finest Basra pearls in shape and size. They once belonged to the Nizams of Hyderabad, taken as a prize by the East India Trading Company and given as a priceless gift to the family for their support seventy-five years ago. Priceless gems, and they were sold in the slums for pennies. If that household cannot hold on to their treasures, they deserve to lose them," he said.

We were quiet. I wondered how Lord Beornmund had come to find a person so loyal to him that he would defend him even now after he'd given a finger to his botched plan.

The Basra Pearls

"You are quite certain he is gone," the butler said.

"Yes. I am sorry to say so, Sir," Frank said.

"Very well, I will see the misses and his kin to their new home," he said.

"If she disappears, she will be implicated in his murder by Mr Archer," Frank said.

"Do you believe it was murder?" the butler asked Frank.

"Unless he had dizzy spells, or slept late due to a bad heart. Had he endured a long illness when you saw him last?" Frank asked.

"No, he was the picture of health. Swore he'd live to ninety," the butler said, dropping his head and tearing up. His shoulders began to shake in grief.

"I must take these, I am afraid," Frank said walking toward the butler and reaching out for the box holding the pearls. "They are key to establishing a timeline with a jury. You must know if I take them, they will end with the estate."

The butler grimaced, holding the pearls more tightly.

"What's more, if we ever find the murderer, you may be called upon to witness when the pearls were given to the girl."

The butler said nothing, still struggling with his emotions, and I could only suppose the idea did not sit well with him.

"There is an alternative," Frank said. "You may take the child and pearls to New England now. If that be the case, I have no proof and we all must pretend Lord Beornmund was not murdered.

"In two days, Mr Archer will leave the matter saying he died of illness," Frank continued.

"He was not sick," The butler said. "Yes, but if I make the effort to prove it was murder, and Mr Archer even suspects Miss Keppel's American fortune…"

"She will hang," the butler, said, seeing the gravity of the situation.

"However, in two days, after Lord Beornmund's body is in the family tomb, we can say nothing. We can allow him to have died of illness. You are then free to leave with Miss Keppel and her child and the pearls.

"But then Lord Beornmund's murderer also goes free," Frank taunted.

"No," he said, outraged. "You must find his murderer. He was the last of a dying breed. The world is a sadder place with his loss."

Frank said nothing, but put his hand out for the pearls. The butler relented and handed them to him.

"It is your statement then that after he redeemed those pearls from the shop, on Wednesday, the twenty-ninth of July, he brought them here and entrusted him with Miss Rosanna Keppel?" Frank asked. I wrote as quickly as I could to get his statement.

"No, it was Thursday in the morning hours. I had been to the wine merchant; I go every Thursday for Miss Keppel's weekly dinner party. Master met me in the servant's doorway. He was dressed low; I carried the bottle of red I'd procured. I asked the master if he would not rather I kept the pearls in my pantry. He insisted the child should guard them; they were to be hers."

"How did Lord Beornmund seem?" I asked, my curiosity into his character getting the better of me.

"He was fit as any man could be, not ill," the butler snapped surprised I would address him. I did not care.

"His temperament though... I have been told he was whistling before he died," I said.

"Yes, in fact he did seem very... satisfied... not chipper especially, but he seemed to find himself. It was not his way of late. He'd been restless and frustrated, but when I saw him the last week or two, he was at peace. Like everything righted itself," the butler said.

"Any idea why?" Frank asked.

"He did not speak concisely. He indicated his heir may have finally done something that pleased My Lord. Something about the family name may be saved," the butler said.

Frank looked at me. I could not say what I thought in front of the butler.

Miss Keppel came to Frank and more desperately she grabbed his arm. She now believed Lord Beornmund dead. She said, "That does put me in mind. I am having a supper party Thursday next. You and Mr Shaw will wish to attend. I am having several men with whom it would be very valuable for you to be acquainted."

"I am not sure that is a good idea. It would look very bad to be employed by Lady Beornmund and dining with... you," Frank said delicately.

"I suppose you are right. I am determined to find a way to help you. I can, you know," she said holding Frank's arm to stop him from retreating. She ignored the butler's look of contempt and said: "If you could give me Mr Shaw's card. I misplaced it. I would like very much to be able to get in touch with you."

"Yes, of course," Frank said pulling a card out of his case. Miss Keppel took his whole hand in both of hers to take the card. Frank turned from the butler to Miss Keppel.

"Remember, do not speak to Mr Archer."

"No, of course not," she answered, the gravity of the situation finally hitting her. She took Frank's arm again and gripped even tighter, more desperately. "Thank you for all you are doing for us."

"You are innocent. It is only fair to punish the guilty," Frank pointed out, pulling away and bowing to her.

"You are kind and modest. I have never met your equal," Miss Keppel said groping for where his arm had been, suppressing a sob. I saw her fear. I felt sorry for her.

"Take courage," I said as kindly as possible, "Lord Beornmund has planned for you, taken care of you. All will right itself. Your butler will care for you."

She looked hard at me and called to her daughter.

"Rosanna, my love, our company is leaving."

"Come Millie, we must take these to Mr Bethell. They prove that Lord Beornmund was alive Thursday the twenty-ninth of July," Frank said carefully putting the pearls in his satchel. I nodded, but stopped to put away my notepad. It grew tattered with use, and I had to bind it to keep it together.

"Good day to you," Frank said seriously to the butler.

"I will keep the wolves away, Sir," the butler said, and Frank bowed to him.

As Frank went to leave, Miss Keppel finally brought her daughter to attention.

"Good day, Mr Hadleigh, come again," the sweet little girl chirped happily. Frank grinned and waved to the little miss, while Miss Keppel began speaking to him, drawing him into conversation using her daughter.

I turned and walked away from it all. It would not be long before the child snubbed the women who came to visit, and adored her mother's conquests. Then one day, when Rosanna was barely a woman, those conquests would also be her own. Perhaps she would wonder why men treated her so badly, and why she had no true female friends. It made me sad for the beautiful, innocent creature.

Perhaps Lord Beornmund did not like his wife so much because she did not fawn over him the way his actress did. But if he had lived, would he prefer his confident, capable adult daughter over this poor child who would be passed about, bowing and charming every man who came her way?

I jumped a little when Frank took my folded arm into his large hand.

"Sorry, Millie. I'm sorry about that," he said when we were both seated in the hackney.

"You are manipulating her, just like every other man has," I said. "Is it any wonder she must charm you into protecting her? She has no security. How is that fair?"

"I am proud you would defend her, Millie. You are right; it is not fair, but she has gotten herself into this mess. She made her own choices," Frank said.

"You do not choose a Lord; he chooses you," I said, quoting her. I felt the rhythm of the horse's hooves vibrate through the carriage. This is the pace of our life until Frank's money pouch runs out and we are condemned to walk again.

"Whatever she may say, she has charms and uses them to get what she wants. At some point she wanted the arm of Lord Beornmund," Frank said after my breathing eased up.

"Perhaps, but what other choice did she have?" I asked.

"I do not know. I am sorry for her. I am sorry you must see me manipulate her, but I cannot appeal to her sense; she buries it to manipulate me. The alternative is much crueler. If Mr Archer gets a hint she had reason to wish Lord Beornmund dead, he will pounce on her and she will be hung as a murderer simply to protect the estate," Frank said.

"I know," I said. "But think of the ease of just leaving it. Letting it be that Lord Beornmund died of illness."

"Millie," Frank chided as the carriage jerked to a stop at a crossroad.

"If Lord Beornmund were really a clerk, he would have gotten three hours of the coroner officer's time, not even the coroner himself. That is all, not even enough to learn his identity, or what he really died of. Why must you make all this effort for a man who played such a game as this?" I asked.

He took my chin forcing me to look him in the eyes.

"It is who I am," he said forcefully. "If the puzzle of a clerk were handed to me, I would solve his murder just as tirelessly as I do for the Lord. It is the very core of who I am, Millie. I am justice."

"No, you are Frank. You have kind eyes and a playful side you do not bring out enough. You have a way of seeing the world that is fair and true. Yet, you delve into the abyss of the dark secrets of hollow, soulless men to right their wrongs. That is who you are. I am proud to be your wife, Frank," I said.

"I am proud to be your husband, Millie," he answered.

"I am not looking for you to reciprocate. I just want you to know I…"

"Millie, I am, though," he said rubbing my cheek with his thumb as the carriage lurched into motion again.

"Why, why…I do nothing for you," I said, tears forming as I pulled away.

"You do everything for me," he said. He scooted over the seat and pulled me into his arms.

"I love you, Millie."

"I can't see why, Frank," I said resting my head on his chest.

"One day you will," Frank said kissing my head. "One day, I promise."

I couldn't say anything. Fear crushed my heart painfully, immobilizing me. He would grow sick of me as my mother did. One day he would realize what Miss Keppel would do for him that I could not. I hated her. I hated her desperation that drove her to my husband. I certainly would rather Miss Keppel go find Rick Bolton and stay away from my husband.

Did I love Frank after all?

The fast beating of my heart tied my tongue. I said nothing.

Frank reassured me: "Our part is almost over, Millie. We know Lord Beornmund died at the end of July. With pawn tickets we can account for the weeks between when he was presumed dead and the the date he actually died. We can prove he was alive July the twenty-ninth. This is something."

"Yes, it is," I said taking a deep breath to slow my heartbeat, but it would not with Frank running his fingers over my face, pushing back my hair in comfort.

What is love?

Chapter Twenty-eight

All observed Sunday in the temple. We did not get back onto the trail until Monday morning. We were early, sure to be in chambers long before Jasper would come in. Frank wrapped the pearls in parchment, and sent them to Mr Bethell, by way of Mr Clarkson just in time. Jasper was at his desk by ten.

"Have you proved how the Lord Beornmund died?" Jasper asked settling into his desk I'd just put back in order.

"I am starting to believe it may have been a long illness after all," Frank said not looking up from the law book he studied.

"Yes. Well, it makes more sense than a Duchess doing the deed," he said with a laugh, but he glanced at Frank with distrust and annoyance when he realized his pupil wasn't listening to him. When Mr Clarkson returned, he looked a little abashed to find Jasper in chambers so early.

"Where have you been?" Jasper snapped.

"Mr Bethell asked for my help." Mr Clarkson turned to me. "He sent a note around to your rooms, Mr Hadleigh, but when he did not find Mrs Hadleigh, he asked me to."

"Me?" I asked surprised.

"Indeed, I believe you have an illustrious visitor in his chambers."

"Me?" I asked again, confused and looking over at Frank. He stood and asked, "May I come with you, Millie?"

"I would like that very much," I said. Jasper stood. He walked to the hat rack. Apparently, he meant to come, too. I put on my cloak and bonnet. I took the hand Frank offered me and turned my back on Jasper. He caught up to us and walked near my side anyway. Like a little boy afraid of missing out on a treat, he would not be left behind.

We followed Mr Clarkson through the lanes and courtyard toward the Hall. A cold wind cut through even my new cloak as we walked the cobblestone past the skeletal remains of trees and bushes emptied of every last leaf. When we entered the warm, well-lit chambers of Mr Bethell, the large room was filled with people. The most prominent in my vision was Miss Myra Bolton, of all people.

"Miss Bolton," I said, rushing to give her my hands. Anyone from home was such a pleasure to see and I hadn't realized it would be so until she grasped both my hands in hers.

"Lady Grey Hull, now that I am married," she said showing me a beautiful band woven with diamonds encrusted in it. "Call me Myra as we are near kin."

"How is Clara, has she… is she recovered?" I asked quietly.

"Mr Williams did not have any measure of her heart and she does… well. She is slow to trust, but I suspect that will fade," she said. I flushed. I did not wish for my new friends to know about Mr Titus Williams.

"Millie, may I introduce my husband, My Lord Lawrence Grey Hull, Marquess of Dorset," she said, gesturing to the man who'd been in church the day the rector forgot to read our banns. The Marquess of Dorset stood on the other side of the table near the impressively large desk by the window. When addressed he started and turned from looking out over the grounds where he whispered to Mr Bethell. He came to his wife when she looked for him.

"How do you do," I said bowing to the impressive looking man in his forties who appeared with no fobs beside his watch. His chestnut hair curled, and his eyes of the same color were bright. He smiled at me, and I found him charming. Then Myra introduced a young, extremely handsome man who stepped from his place at the table on the other side of the large chambers. This is Lieutenant Reginald White, a regular in the 95th Regiment of Her Majesty's Foot Rifle Brigade."

I felt Frank flinch by my side. I could not look from Myra I was so confused.

"How do you do," I said bobbing my head. Lt White had a penetrating look in his eyes as he bowed to me. I felt strangely vulnerable in his presence. Turning to Frank, I said, "This is my husband, Mr Frank Hadleigh, and his associate, Mr Jasper Shaw."

"I am in fact Mr Hadleigh's learned master," Jasper corrected as he moved forward and handed Lord Grey Hull his card, which distracted me.

"I suppose you have been introduced to everyone else," I finished, looking to Lord Grey Hull, who politely took Jasper's card.

"I met Frank some time ago when he came to the scene of Mr William's demise," Lord Grey Hull said gesturing for Jasper to go sit at the table, out of the way.

"Titus Williams," Jasper asked, not budging. "The banker's son who died?"

"Perhaps…there are a few things we need to say to Millie in private," Myra said looking to Mr Bethell.

"Yes, My Lady. I would be honored if you would use my private sitting room," he said opening a door that led back into a cave-like library of sorts.

"Lt. White," she said. He walked around the table and through the door. After he disappeared Myra motioned to me to follow. I could not understand what any of this had to do with me, but I went, giving Frank a curious look. He shrugged while Myra took my arm as we went through the door. Frank watched us, waiting to be asked. Myra did not invite him. Instead, she closed the door behind us. When we were all three settled into comfortable reading chairs, the soldier asked, "Do you know who I am?"

"No. I am sorry Sir. I am new to London and do not know the to-do," I said.

"I am not from London. I am the man who challenged Mr Titus Williams to a duel. I sent him running, and he… I am the reason he took you away," he said hanging his head with immense guilt. He was a beautiful man. My chest raced and I could say nothing. My heart did not race because he was attractive, though.

I could see what he was carrying on his shoulders and it made me sad. I felt for him because it was not his burden to carry. I saw beyond his perfect exterior. I smiled a little. I was no longer a child.

"I ask for your pardon now," he said, and before I could stop him, he was at my feet bowed before my chair. He looked up at me with blue-green eyes, vowing to protect me in the future.

"Please Sir, I do not blame any man, except the one who acted," I said. "You were very brave for trying to stop his madness."

"I should have sought him out. I should have dragged him from his house before he could hurt you," he said.

"No!" I snapped, angrily bending over, pulling at the man to get up. He looked at me confused as I had his sleeve clutched in my hand forcing him to stand with me. When we were eye-to-eye, I nearly begged, "He is not to have any power left over me, or you. It is time to stop letting that deranged man hurt you. He is dead. Do not let him keep you captive."

"Does he keep you captive?" Myra asked, watching my passion with pity. Lt. White looked at me in concern. I let go of his sleeve.

Looking away embarrassed, I said, "Sometimes, but I am trying to leave him behind. I certainly would not blame a person such as yourself who tried to stop his madness. The wealthy must be responsible for their own actions as anyone should. My only wish is that you would not blame yourself."

"I... how?" Lt. White asked pacing away from me.

"I find purpose. I help. I have Frank," I said quietly. Suddenly, remembering back to the day Mr Williams ran away with me, I realized who this man was.

"The girl Mr Williams took, the one who died. She was your lover?"

"Miss Marigold Black was my... I loved her. She was taken by Mr Williams. He took what he wanted from her, and then left her to die at an inn," he stammered. I stared at him.

"That is not what happened," I said, certain now that I allowed myself to recollect that day in my head.

I sat him down so I could see him and said, "Marigold did not place herself under Mr William's protection. If she had, she would not have died. She must have loved you; it must have been an epic love for her to starve to death in order to stay true to you."

"Do you really believe that?" he asked taking both my hands in his, almost pulling me over the arm of my chair, begging me to tell him her story, which only I could because I lived it.

"She would not give in, and died for it. I believe you had a romance worthy of the poets," I said.

"But... I would rather she lived," he said releasing me and standing so he could pace the room again.

"She would have betrayed you to do so," I said standing to follow him. He turned. Grabbing my shoulders, he pulled me to his face.

"Is it betrayal to do whatever it takes to live? Is that betrayal?"

My mouth opened, but I had no words. I could only see the sincerity in his eyes and nothing else.

"I am a soldier. I have taken lives in order to save my own. Would it have been so different if she had done whatever it took to live until I found her?" he asked.

"I… I do not know. Would you still have loved her?" I asked.

"If she had lived, if she had done what it took to live, then I would have found her. I would be loving her still. She could never be lost to me except to take her last breath. I never would have blamed her for giving in to live," he said letting me go. He looked into the distance.

"If only I could hold her still," he said.

"You…you wouldn't have cast her off?" I asked, my cheeks hot.

"No, not my Mari … never my Marigold," he said.

"Your Frank, it would seem, has done the same for you," Myra said.

I looked at her. Did he?

"He…he was very angry at first," I said sitting and looking at a shelf trying to remember.

"At you or Mr Williams?" Myra asked.

"I… I do not know. Perhaps both," I said.

"He was very scared for you when I saw him," Myra said.

Myra told me about Frank. He was told where to find me. He left in the middle of the investigation into Titus William's death. He let the man who shot the illustrious banker's son go without even collecting his name or where he could be found. Frank did not care for anything but finding me. Myra didn't know Frank or the way he obsessed over his puzzles. And she could never know how much comfort her words gave me. I would always come before his need to solve, even before justice. He loved me as much as Lt. White loved Marigold.

I looked up at the handsome soldier, his light hair and eyes, his strong arms that would hold me tight. Despite how ridiculously handsome he was, I felt nothing for him. I had no vision of him sweeping me away or giving me a dream life.

I did not feel anything for Rick Bolton, either. He was a child's infatuation. I was devoted to Frank. Should not time and loyalty, dignity and friendship be something too? What was love? Frank was my best friend. He saved me. He continued to save me. My devotion to him made me realize I wanted this life I lived with Frank. There was no better life for me, not even in fantasy.

"I came to London worried you had been cast out. Put to work in the mills or worse," Lt. White said when I did not speak again.

"You meant to help me?" I asked.

"I meant to marry you. I meant to take care of you since I could not care for my Marigold, but I see you have a love match of your own," he said, bowing to me.

"I do," I said startling myself. "But thank you for your chivalry. It gives me faith in mankind. Just now, I need that."

"Well, Sir, are you satisfied?" Myra asked Lt. White.

"I am and I will gladly go back to my regiment," he said taking my hand and kissing it.

"Good day, Sir," I said standing and watching him go. Before Myra could follow, I held her arm and whispered:

"Myra what …"

"He would have deserted looking for you if Lawrence hadn't interfered. He is too tender for the army. Lawrence is in the process of buying him out. He means to hire him as his nearest guard as he is so loyal a young man," Myra said.

"I am glad to hear it," I said. Myra took my arm, and we went out into the chambers again.

Lt. White spoke quietly to Lord Grey Hull, then finally bowed to Myra. He gave me one last look, and left.

The chambers grew quiet at Lt. White's departure. Jasper broke the silence talking to Lord Grey Hull. Frank gave me a look; he looked... jealous. His eyebrows lifted in question. His face was so endearing as it ranged from irritation to anger. I smiled. I do not know what I looked like imbued with endearment, but he went from jealous to confused. I loved my husband deeply, and hoped he saw it on my face.

I started to think maybe I had always loved Frank. Rick Bolton was not my love story; he was a fantasy I used to avoid the messy, scary, vulnerable place where my feelings for Frank resided.

Frank stammered. He looked ready to ask me a question. I gave a shake my head in the negative grinning at him. He relaxed. I wouldn't tell him now, not like this. I would admit my love for him when I could kiss his mouth. Just the idea of that moment sent a thrill through me.

Chapter Twenty-nine

"We have been discussing the case of the missing Lord Beornmund. I met him a few times," Lord Grey Hull said, interrupting Jasper to address Myra who stepped to him, taking his arm. I stood aloof, leaning against the door I'd just come through, trying to understand what was happening inside me.

"I read of his disappearance, I believe," Myra said deciphering her new husband's interest. She sat in a large armchair near the fire, slightly apart from the table where the men sat. She settled in so her husband might feel at leisure to hear the particulars. From where I stood, I could see the others in the room turn toward her and scoot in.

"It has been hushed up then?" Myra asked. Jasper was quick to move into the chair across from her, without invitation.

"No, it is just unknown," Jasper said. "A rather curious case, My Lady. It all started with a finger..."

Frank did not notice Jasper stealing his work. He used Jasper's storytelling to whisper with Mr Bethell behind the table. I could see why Frank hid the pearls before Jasper could see them, and pretended to be convinced Lord Beornmund died of illness. Listening to Jasper, I applauded Frank in being tight-lipped.

"And when the body was found at last, it turns out he died of an illness, but who can wonder when he put himself into such a lower situation – isn't that so, Frank?" Jasper finished.

He turned, insistent his pupil agree, and for the first time realized Frank had not been attending. Instead, Jasper found Frank whispering to Mr Bethell. Jasper's eyes got small, and he turned red in irritation. Mr Bethell, who faced him, noticed.

"Mr Shaw." Mr Bethell interrupted Frank's steady flow of words, and moved around the table.

"Yes, Sir," he answered.

"I meant to speak to Lord Grey Hull about the matter. Can you, and Mr Clarkson, return to your office. I believe Mr and Mrs Hadleigh would like to enjoy their company," Mr Bethell said.

"I will need my pupil if I am to get anything done today," Jasper snapped seeing himself extracted from the room. He sounded very petty when saying, "Come, Frank."

I watched him wide-eyed. Frank looked to Mr Bethell. He could not argue the point, Jasper was his master. Frank began walking around the table toward the door. I turned to follow.

"Actually, I mean for Millie to come stay for a few days with me," Myra said, reaching an arm to me as I passed her. "It is a whim of mine to keep my parishioners close."

Jasper looked like he had enough audacity to refuse her my company as if he had any right. He opened his mouth, but Myra reared back, her expression daring him to interfere. His words stopped before they could leave his pouty mouth.

I stood next to her chair holding her warm hand. "Mr Hadleigh," she said forcefully using his name, "We are in London to prepare for our wedding trip to a place in India called Bombay. It will be at least a year until we meet again. Mr Hadleigh, you will not begrudge me your wife's company for a few days whilst I am in town?"

"No, of course not, My Lady." Frank bowed with a grin. Coming to me he said, "Millie, would you like to have a little holiday, enjoy the company?"

"Yes, thank you," I said, reaching my free hand to him. He took my hand, but I could not think of what I should say to him. When he came near, I felt alive and nervous. Leaning in further Frank put his cheek to mine and whispered, "Tell Myra all. We will need their help if this is ever to go to court."

Then he kissed my cheek. As he pulled away, I put my forehead to his and he paused. I hated that everyone watched us. It would have been so easy to kiss his mouth as he whispered, "Are you quite all right, dearest?"

"I...thank you, Frank," I whispered. He drew away examining me, and I could not think of a reason to keep him near, except I wished for him there.

"I will be fine, I just... thank you for being so good to me," I whispered forcing myself to nod and smile so Frank could be comfortable and follow Jasper who sighed loudly his impatience at the sight of us, husband, and wife, close together.

"We will send a note around for the hour on Thursday when you might escort Mrs Hadleigh home," Lord Grey Hull said to Frank as he moved toward the door.

"Thank you, My Lord," Frank said bowing. Jasper looked to Lord Grey Hull, impatiently awaiting his invitation. His lordship did not notice.

"We must start if we are to finish in time," Jasper snapped as if he had to be anywhere but a tea at the house of the miss he courted, and according to Mr Clarkson, her mother wished him away. He stomped fuming from the chambers. Frank smiled at me again. He looked uncertain about leaving me, but finally followed.

"I did mean to speak to you about that case My Lord," Mr Bethell said after the door closed, "but Frank has all the particulars. He was trying to explain just now, but I'm afraid I haven't grasped it. We will need help bringing charges if the Viscount is involved."

"I would wager Millie knows it all – may I call you Millie? You are just of my daughter's age," Lord Grey Hull said.

"Yes, My Lord," I said.

"Can you explain what happened, Millie?" Mr Bethell said, surprised. I hesitated, a little afraid of such powerful men, apparently both taking on a fatherly role using my Christian name.

"I can," I stammered. "Frank does not confide in Mr Shaw. He has not told him any evidence he amassed."

"With good reason. Mr Shaw has been in contact with Mr Archer. The Beornmund's solicitor wrote me a note, letting me know the young barrister is now trying to extort the family to hush it all up. He wishes to be paid handsomely for his efforts," Mr Bethell said.

"Jasper would…" I stammered.

"He would, and Mr Archer assures me the Viscount will pay double the agreed upon amount to have the whole thing over with."

"But…. Does he not wish to know?" I stammered.

"I hate to admit it, but the Viscount implicates himself simply in his desperation to have the thing over with," Mr Bethell said.

"Come, Millie, I wish to know all," Myra said pulling me next to her into the large chair. We fit comfortably, and it gave me courage.

"Lord Grey Hull, are you able to see inside people, like Frank?" I asked as we all settled in around the fire.

"No, he is spectacularly observant," he answered. "I watched him do it once. I use deductive reasoning. Frank left, brooking no refusal at Mr Shaw's unreasonable request, trusting you could give us all the particulars. And so you shall, I suppose," Lord Grey Hull encouraged.

"Yes, my Lord. Mr Shaw told you about proving Cecil Chapman innocent, but it had little to do with Lord Beornmund's death, except if they hadn't been looking for a scapegoat, all may have been discovered much sooner."

I told them about Lord Beornmund wishing to immigrate to America and continued my narrative:

He claimed the city is spilling into his space. Frank even confirmed Birmingham is becoming just as populated as London. Lord Beornmund made his very loyal butler cut off his finger whilst he wore the Beornmund family signet ring. Then he sent it down the privy. He believed it would be found quickly and be enough to proclaim him dead.

"He realized his mistake when it was not found. It was sent down the first of July. He was not looked for until after he did not withdraw his money in the middle of July. His solicitor, Mr Archer, did not send the bobbies in until the end of the month. By the fourth of August, Lord Beornmund was really dead.

"A student surgeon examined him. He thought it poison, but could not prove it conclusively. With no family to further the investigation, the coroner's officer reviewed the student surgeon's examination, and closed the inquest without taking it before the coroner, or a jury, ruling it a death of illness. The case was closed on the fifth of August."

Lord Grey Hull asked, "The Viscount is willing to pay young Mr Shaw to keep the cause of death illness, instead of investigating the claim of poison. Which makes us suppose the young man killed his father?" Lord Grey Hull asked.

"Frank and I disagree. Not to mention the findings of the inquest. I will tell you the facts. You may decide for yourself."

"Very nicely done, young lady. Frank has taught you the importance of unbiased evidence without bending to hearsay," Mr Bethell said smiling. I nodded with a little laugh and said, "Over the last year before his disappearance, the Beornmund household was being robbed in small increments. The first missing items coincide with the Viscountess' marriage into the family."

"She sent a servant to pawn for her?" Mr Bethell asked, surprised.

"No, she went herself. The Uncle who runs the pawnshop has identified her. She has a dead spot on her bottom lip. It was certainly the Viscountess who pledged them," I said.

"She was pawning her husband's family's goods – herself?" Myra asked. She leaned away from me so she could see if I were serious. Mr Bethell only stammered in disbelief.

"I think she enjoys dressing up and moving about the city undetected. Her mother died when she was young. She spent much time in London with her father after that. I can only suppose it is something she learned after her mother died and she had not a constant companion," I said.

"She knows how to barter then?" Lord Grey Hull asked.

"Oh, no. She does terrible. She does not get the worth out of anything," I said. "Her biggest mistake happened when she was first married. She pawned a set of pearls. They were a set of rare, natural pearls that belonged to the estate's treasury. The Viscountess only received twelve pounds for them, though they are worth more than a hundred."

"Terrible indeed," Myra said.

"How did she get to them?" Mr Bethell asked.

"Lord Beornmund lent them to his daughter. They were among Lady Charlotte's things."

"Not with the other family treasures?" Lord Grey Hull asked.

"That is the case, My Lord. The Viscountess was not wise in her first plunder. After that she only took gifts that she witnessed Lady Charlotte receive from her many admirers so as to not make the same mistake. Over the span of ten months, she pawned many items worth four or five pounds and only ever received one pound from the Uncle."

"Was she trying to recover the twelve pounds to buy back the pearls?" Myra asked.

"Oh," I said. "Perhaps. She could have recovered them after her last pawn. She would have finally collected enough. She may have been trying to get them back before they went to auction. She was in great danger of being found out as a thief if the auction house found them to be stolen."

"Do the pearls mean anything?" Mr Bethell asked, thinking I rambled a bit.

"Yes. While looking for his ring, Lord Beornmund found his pearls. In front of the Uncle, Lord Beornmund confronted the Viscountess Beornmund. This was long after he had disappeared and was presumed dead."

"How did he find them?" Myra asked.

I explained the Uncle, feeling he was free to do so, published the pearls in a catalog in preparation to go to auction. On the twenty-eighth day of July, Lord Beornmund pawned a waistcoat at the shop that held the pearls. Thankfully, he did not think he could enter the shop unless he meant to pledge. Lord Beornmund kept impeccable records in a very neat ledger. The shop tickets are not printed, and have not a formal name upon them, only the Uncle's signature. Even after the tickets turned up, it would have been impossible to find the shop without Lord Beornmund's mistake. He asked to see the pearls from a junior associate, who took them out for him. He asked many questions about them. The next day on the twenty ninth day of July he...

I stopped explaining struck by a thought.

"What is it?" Myra asked.

"I do not know how he insured the Viscountess would come," I said realizing it very peculiar.

"Excuse me?" Myra said.

"The Viscountess came the very next day to pledge. He must have lured her somehow," I said thinking this odd. Mr Bethell cleared his throat.

"Yes, well," I continued. "He waited outside the shop until she entered the side door. He burst into the box she used for privacy, and scared her something fierce."

"She thought him dead?" Mr Bethell asked.

"I believe so. The Uncle said she looked like she'd seen a ghost," I said.

"She must have been startled," Myra said with an amused chuckle.

"He got the pearls back then?" Mr Bethell asked.

"Lord Beornmund bought the pearls back from the Uncle. The Viscountess swore to him that she would repay the price. He did not want the money she collected. She said she would somehow give him what he wanted for the pearls."

"What could she give if she had to pledge stolen items for ready cash?" Mr Bethell asked. I looked to the ground and burned bright red. It was a hard thing to say. I stated it as delicately as possible.

"When we found his lodgings, the landlady said his mistress came the last four days before his death."

"You believe the Viscountess became his mistress?" Mr Bethell said, shocked.

"It fits the timeline. The woman the landlady described was very like Viscountess Beornmund."

"It cannot be proved emphatically?" Mr Bethell asked hopefully.

"We recovered all her pledges, items stolen from the Beornmund house, and there are witnesses enough who saw her. The landlady would have noticed the dead spot in her lip," I said.

"The landlady will not be believed over the Viscountess, though," Mr Bethell said. I opened my mouth, but closed it. The woman who kindly warned me against the masters would not be believed over the simpering woman who stole from her family and clearly could not manage her finances, though she had so much.

"I wish it were not so, Millie, but it is," Lord Grey Hull said kindly when I did not continue.

"I suppose," I said.

"Because of the pearls you can prove without a doubt the Viscountess knew Lord Beornmund was alive," Lord Grey Hull reminded.

"Yes, I..." I realized why Frank needed them now. A courtroom full of men would believe the irrefutable path of a family heirloom before a woman from a middlish neighborhood when contradicted by a viscountess. Considering the word slander to a middlish woman who could not defend herself would likely deter any testimony at all.

"Please continue on with your timeline," Lord Grey Hull said encouraging me with a kind smile. I glanced at Mr Bethell. He tapped his naturally red face with a handkerchief thinking. I could not tell if he even believed me. Were all of mankind just dreamers, living their lives, skewing things to see what they wanted? Like my mother, who made herself comfortable by stomping over the facts that were in her way. Or was it I who refused to see what was before me? The

Quality lived chosen lives, and we, the plebians, were only put on the earth to serve them?

I shook. I could not stop myself. Myra shifted giving me more space on the chair. I used my hands when I told a story. I must have been squishing her. I slid to the back corner of the chair, allowing it to cocoon me.

"Let us start from the recovery of the pearls," Myra helped me. I closed my eyes and continued.

I told how, after the pearls were reclaimed, they were given to Miss Rosanna Keppel, Lord Beornmund's illegitimate daughter, by the Lord himself.

"Wait. Where are they now?" Mr Bethell asked, recovering.

"Frank sent them to you by way of Mr Clarkson this very morning," I said.

"Oh," Mr Bethell said, the edges of his red face turning white. He stood with some effort and shuffled to his desk, opened a drawer, and took out a package wrapped and tied up just the size of the pearl box.

"Perhaps I will lock these up," he said taking the package into the back sitting room. When he returned, Mr Bethell asked, "Lord Beornmund could not have been with the… his new mistress the thirtieth of July then?" I could see he was trying the case in his head already.

"Not in the morning hours when the butler would procure wine. The mistress stayed with him at his lodging, so if it were the Viscountess, she must have taken some time to get her affairs in order. Lady Beornmund would know if she was absent at the time," I said.

"I suppose we could prove the Viscountess the mistress, but through circumstances only…" Mr Bethell said quietly. It disturbed him he had to concede the Viscountess was the mistress.

"She may very well have gone home and told the whole family he was alive," Lord Grey Hull said.

"Yes. The Viscount must have concocted a plan to finish off his father so that he might inherit. Even Mr Archer may have had a hand in what came next," Mr Bethell said, nodding to himself.

"I do not know about Mr Archer. It would seem unlikely since he honestly told you Mr Shaw and Viscount Beornmund were trying to stop the investigation," I said glancing at Mr Bethell.

"That is so, but the man is most concerned with the money being extorted," Mr Bethell said, and he looked almost confused glancing at me twice so I could think through the problem as well as himself.

"Frank thinks Viscount Beornmund involved," I said.

"You do not," Myra said looking at me.

"I do not see any evidence of it."

"How could the husband not have noticed his wife's absence, even accounted for it to his mother and sister?" Mr Bethell asked, growing slightly aggressive toward me, like he needed to be smarter than myself.

"Yes, that is true," I admitted, taken back.

"Why else would the Viscount wish to hush the matter up?" Mr Bethell said forcefully.

"I do not know, unless Mr Shaw has convinced him it was in fact an illness. The Viscount is very ready to be master," I said quickly before Mr Bethell could rebut.

"It is no secret there has been bad blood between the father and son for many years. Which rather proves if Lord Beornmund was poisoned that his son is responsible," Mr Bethell said, and I could see he was much more comfortable accusing the Viscount than his wife, and would never yield to my opinion.

"Whatever else, we cannot ignore it was likely the Viscountess who actually poisoned him," I said.

"She could have given him something upon the instructions from her husband. She may not even have known she was being used as a pawn, poor dear," Mr Bethell said.

I opened my mouth then closed it. This was no use. Finally, I said, "The landlady said she was like a regular apothecary. She steeped many things in a very fine teapot she brought with her, and would not let him drink from the house tea pot. Especially after he started ailing. The woman in the street witnessed him die Monday, August the third."

"There was an actual witness to his demise," Lord Grey Hull said.

"Not the cause but at the final moments," I said.

"How did he die?" he asked.

"Lord Beornmund came out of his lodgings like he hailed the woman in the street. He made it…thirty steps or so, down the alley. Alicia, the witness, ran to him. Before he could speak, he fell down shaking like he was possessed and then died. Alicia checked, but he did not draw breath. The mistress came out behind him with all his belongings, but those hidden in a cupboard."

"She took his belongings," Mr Bethell said, cringing because this denoted she knew to clear up any evidence.

"She wrapped the teapot, and whatever else she had to get rid of, inside a bundle of a coat, nightshirt and such. We have the bundle, but have not found the teapot. If it were poison, she likely got rid of it," I said.

"She pawned his things," Mr Bethell said.

"Yes, she must have believed the pawnshop would never be found with Lord Beornmund gone. It was obscure. She did not know Lord Beornmund pledged there himself and the last note in his ledger was the name and location of the place."

"Still, that was very bold of her," Mr Bethell said, faltering.

"Yes, considering his coat has his blood on it."

"Was there blood if he just fell down in the street?" Lord Grey Hull asked.

"She stabbed him," Mr Bethell said, astounded but also having read the inquest he knew it happened.

"What?" Lord Grey Hull asked.

"The mistress entered the alleyway after he fell. She took the time to drop her bundles. She kicked him a few times to be sure he was dead. The witness assured her he drew no breath. The mistress yelled, 'How could you do this to me?' and she stabbed him with a large kitchen knife," I said.

"She could not be sure he was dead?" Mr Bethell said astounded.

"The student surgeon did not think the knife wound could have killed him. It was not deep," I said.

"Yes, that does make more sense," Mr Bethell said relieved, wiping his brow again.

"She did it to draw an inquest. She wished for the body to be found and identified," Lord Grey Hull said.

"Frank believes it so," I said.

"Her husband would then inherit," Mr Bethell said.

Seeing Mr Bethell's opinion matched Frank's, I wavered in my own. The Viscount did not like his father, and had the most to gain from his death.

"Was his death reported to the police?" Myra asked.

"The witness had a child run for the bobbies, telling them the clerk died – they thought that his profession. The coroner's inquest opened August the fourth, and closed the fifth. It found no crime but illness. Though the people who saw him last testify he was not ill until the mistress came," I said.

"He was not identified," Lord Grey Hull clarified.

I explained how the arrest of Cecil Chapman obscured the truth. Since he was arrested after Lord Beornmund died, the murderer didn't know a cut-off finger would identify him most quickly.

"If she could barely stab him, I doubt she could have cut off his finger," Mr Bethell said.

"Perhaps not," I said.

"All would have righted itself for the murderer if Mr Chapman had been hung," Lord Grey Hull said with sarcasm.

"Yes, and if not for Frank it would have ended there," I said. "Mr Archer, and even Mr Shaw, looked for a man dead the beginning of July, because that is when Mrs Ellis claims Cecil buried the finger and that is when Lord Beornmund disappeared."

"Silly woman. This is what happens when women interfere in men's work," Mr Bethell said, and glanced at me pointedly.

"It wasn't until we uncovered his ruse that anyone looked for Lord Beornmund's death at the start of August with all his fingers intact," I said, unable to look at the bencher.

"It is alarming. Frank is the only one who thought to follow Lord Beornmund's trail," Lord Grey Hull said quickly to distract me from saying something that would offend. We both knew Mr Bethell could make or destroy Frank's career. Sobered, I stunted my opinions to match Mr Bethell's. I spoke on a subject that he was comfortable with.

"Mr Archer tried, but he is obtuse and intimidating. It is not always the way to find information," I said. "Frank is just the sort to learn all these things."

"It is a wonder any cases move through Old Bailey at all," Mr Bethell said.

"Yes, with everything proved against the Viscountess and her husband, Frank is still not certain it will go to trial," I said discouraged.

"If I am being candid, with so much evidence amassed against anyone else, the husband and wife would both be hung," Mr Bethell said.

My mouth dropped open, but I could say nothing.

"Whatever happens from here, it was very cleverly proved," Lord Grey Hull said, and I heard the same tone of apology in his voice. I realized neither the Viscount nor his wife would be prosecuted.

"It is all Frank. He is the clever one. Mr Shaw will take credit for it, though, since Frank is his pupil," I said feeling very low.

"Not with me, Millie," Mr Bethell said kindly now that I had found my place as a supportive wife.

"I have seen Mr Shaw's like," Lord Grey Hull said. "Those who borrow other's light burn out quickly, while true brightness will always shine through. Do not fear, young one. It does not seem so, but you have many years to live and much time to thrive. You and Frank will keep the course, while those who burn out will curl and blow away as ash with the passage of time. Keep heart, young one."

I nodded, strangely comforted. I could see Lord Grey Hull and Myra took care of people. Frank and I had just joined those they meant to keep an eye on. It was a touch condescending, like we could not do for ourselves, but also comforting. I liked Myra's husband.

"What happens now?" Myra asked.

"The coroner is reviewing the first examination. No foul play could be proved. The coroner is outraged he was never given a look at it. He claims he would have known it was Lord Beornmund, and I would not be shocked if his officer is relieved of his position," Mr Bethell said. I did not voice my thought: the working man could be punished, while the exalted murders would go free.

"If he reopens the inquest, will Frank's evidence be heard at least?" I asked.

"Much of this depends on the family's wishes. Likely, the body will be exhumed, and entombed in one grand gesture. The Lord will be officially proclaimed dead, his son officially inheriting the trust," Mr Bethell said.

"How long until the body is exhumed?" I asked.

"Two days," Mr Bethell said.

"And the Viscount would stay married to a murderer?" I asked.

"Millie, the Viscount arranged the whole thing, including… giving his wife to his father when she was found out. The Viscountess Beornmund is… considered simple. It is unlikely she acted alone," Mr Bethell said.

"Frank thinks so, too," I admitted.

"Why do you hesitate?" Myra asked me.

"I suppose the Viscount must have been involved to wish to hush the thing up, but he would not have pawned the pearls in the first place, let alone for twelve pounds. He knew how much they were worth," I said.

"Yes, that I believe," Mr Bethell agreed. "She must have pawned them on her own. Selling a family heirloom is the act of someone simple. Perhaps the Viscount sent her out after he found she knew how to get him money. His father cut him off in recent years. The Viscount could have caught her months ago. He likely used her to fund his exploits."

"I cannot say. We have found no evidence to support that, but it may be so," I said.

"Consider, what reason could the Viscountess have for killing the Earl? Acting alone? It would not have changed her situation in the slightest. Even in pin money she may not have improved. The Viscount has borrowed against his expectations. It will be some time before he is clear of debt and she will get nothing out of him," Mr Bethell said.

"I did not know that," I said. I looked to Myra then Lord Grey Hull who looked unsure what to think. I admitted, "Frank believes if the Viscountess knew Earl Beornmund wished to take the pearls to America, it was in her best interest to let him go. By letting him leave with the pearls, unbeknown to the family, she would not have been implicated for stealing them. They would never have been found. She had more of a reason to keep his secret than to kill him."

"It is hard to find a reason if she acted alone," Lord Grey Hull said.

"Yes, the Viscount, who has not recently been on friendly terms with his father, is now assured of his inheritance," Mr Bethell said. Watching the fire, he spoke more to comfort himself.

"If you will excuse me, I must contradict you on one point," I said truthfully. "The Viscountess is smart. Much smarter than she pretends to be."

"Millie, if something you have observed favors the guilt of the Viscountess, and not the Viscount, you ought not discount your impression of the situation. You were there and we were not," Myra said, watching me.

"Come now My Lady," Mr Bethell said, "The Viscountess could not do such a thing alone. None of this is in the nature of a woman, especially not a noble woman who comes from such a line as hers. She is Duke Leicester's sister. I am not entirely convinced she was the mistress at all. The viscount could have sent another woman in her place when she refused."

This opinion astounded me. She pawned his bloody clothes for heaven's sake. I stopped myself. I could not blame Mr Bethell for having an opinion.

Perhaps, like my tendency to favor beauty as a noble quality, he was unable to accuse a woman of a crime. He was limited in his sphere of knowledge, blinded by his upbringing. I did not stop liking him. None of this made him bad or cruel, just limited, like me.

"What happened to the bloody bundles?" Myra asked more to remind Mr Bethell of the evidence amassed against Viscountess Beornmund.

"Frank has them. We have all the rest of the pawned items in our possession. Frank redeemed it all," I said.

"That must have cost him dearly," Lord Grey Hull said.

"He needs justice more than I need a maid," I said with a laugh, wondering why I said it, except it all felt so ridiculous.

"I will send my clerk to collect it. I am certain the Beornmund's will pay the tickets back," Mr Bethell said growing even rosier. If Jasper was to be believed, Mr Bethell's position at Court of Chancery afforded him a very healthy salary, especially after being made Queen's Counsel. He looked embarrassed that Frank and I had borne the cost of the investigation. I did not think he should. His success only gave me hope that a middlish man, the son of a physician, could make a good living, competing with the Quality.

We were quiet in awkwardness for a time.

"I would like to see these people," Lord Grey Hull said, and I felt like crying because he trusted me. Strangely this made me understand why Miss Keppel felt such relief to have man's respect after being patronized and underestimated.

"I can contact their solicitor," Mr Bethell said furrowing his brow.

"No, I would like to observe them in public," Lord Grey Hull said.

"That is an interesting whim, My Lord," Mr Bethell said, analyzing him with distrust.

"I will not mention this matter, just observe them. There is not much happening in town. It cannot be so hard predicting where they will be," Lord Grey Hull said.

"The younger brother, Captain Hugh Beornmund, is finally home. He was in the West Indies when his father disappeared and is just now returned to London. He is very fond of music, and my man has it from a maid they will attend a concert in the Assembly Rooms at Hanover Square. It is only a small concert of locals," Mr Bethell said. I realized with relief he had taken Frank seriously, and was keeping track of the family despite his blind spot for the Viscountess.

"I am just in the mood for a musical," said Lord Grey Hull, turning to his wife. "And you, my dear?"

"Of course," Myra said standing, "I would like Mrs Hadleigh to accompany us as my special guest."

"I have a very nice dress in my rooms, even nicer than this," I said, also standing and looking down at my pretty new day dress. They focused on the subject of my clothing as intently as they had on murder.

"You are about my daughter's size," Lord Grey Hull said politely and apologetically at the same time.

"My dear, there is a blue gown Eva was supposed to wear it to a ball, but her aunt thought it too dark a color for a young unmarried lady. We can have it done up, and it will do very well for you. There are wardrobes full of finery at My Lord's home," Myra said.

"I am honored, Sir," I said realizing even my pretty things were too middlish to go about among the Quality. "May I tell Frank what we are doing? He worries when I am in London by myself. He does not think the city the place for me."

"I think it best if you do not write Frank," Mr Bethell said.

I jerked in surprise. "Why not?"

"Frank does not expect you until Thursday. If you write, Mr Shaw may suspect something. I have advised Frank to keep Mr Shaw from everything we find from this point on. He has contacted the Viscount a few times, and may tell him you are going to the concert to observe them. It is not the best way to be noticed by the heir apparent just now," Mr Bethell said.

"You will not warn them?" I asked.

"Millie, I favor you observing them in public," Mr Bethell explained. "I would like you to see how the Viscountess is, without any interference. I can see you are an… an exceptionally intelligent woman. Frank would seek out such a partner. Most of your…counterparts cannot problem-solve as you do. It is hard, being smarter than most, to understand that the majority of your gender is not as capable as yourself. If you are at the top of the ladder, the Viscountess is on the bottom rung."

Lord Grey Hull only nodded to me slightly and I knew I was not to contradict the man who had taken such good care of my Frank.

"Very well. I will try to be fair," I said, but could promise nothing else. I stood and allowed myself to be led from the room.

Chapter Thirty

I left with Myra and her husband, trusting eventually they would get me back to Frank. Outside, Myra's lady strolled about the grounds waiting for her. She saw us, and walked quickly over.

"Why did your lady not come in?" I asked.

"She is my housekeeper," Myra said.

"What?" I asked confused.

"My brother sends her as my protector. It started as his idea of a joke. I do not think he knew how vigilant she would be even after my marriage," Myra said.

This made me laugh, for I knew Mr Bolton and his playful personality. My smile fell. The woman walked briskly toward us looking about her, alert. I did not think the queen's guard looked so serious. I feared her a little.

"You need not be disappointed in a maid, Millie. I'll pay her wages if you will take her," Myra whispered nodding her head to her housekeeper.

"No, thank you," I said watching the austere woman coming toward us. Myra laughed.

"Come Millie, I promise I will keep you safe," Myra teased. "We cannot have you falling off your ladder." We both laughed, and I was glad she did not take offense at Mr Bethell.

It was hard to leave the temple grounds without Frank. The discomfort of our situation soon found another avenue to traverse. Myra took me to shops and bought me all kinds of sweets and fine things for my hair and feet for the evening. I tried to refuse, but she would not hear of it.

Finally, we settled into a beautiful house in Westminster, not so grand as the Beornmund's mansion, but more intended to put one at ease. Servants scurried about us, while Myra's lady, who may have been the housekeeper after all, snapped instructions at anyone who stood still. A bath was drawn, and I soaked for a long time until the warm water released all the grime the city put upon me.

When the time came, I dressed in layers of indigo satin. The sleeves, adorned with slightly darker lace, cut into my shoulders, and sloped deeply across my chest. I could not keep my hand from tugging my sleeves upward. I felt so exposed. The bodice wrapped over my corset tightly and cinched in my waist while the skirts floated about me. I did not recognize myself. Myra herself did my hair in beautiful layers of twists. Inside the twists she tucked silk irises, that shifted from the indigo of my dress to deep purples, as though they grew from my hair.

"I wish Frank could see me," I said, thinking all the effort wasted since he could not admire me.

"I will do it again when he comes for supper," Myra said smiling down at me.

"Thank you, Myra. I do appreciate this," I said standing, as she helped me into a warm paletot that matched the dress. I wondered if I would have to surrender it when we arrived at the concert.

"I meant to come and meddle in your life until I fixed all Mr Williams did to you," she said buttoning up the paletot. "Instead, you have fixed it yourself. You prosper. All I can do is buy you trinkets and style your coiffure. I am proud of you, Millie."

I blushed.

"It is Frank who is flourishing. He just brought me along," I said.

"That is not so. You must learn to take off Mr Bethell's opinions as you would a cloak. Every woman of sense that I know, and I know many, have at some point to learn not everyone will value you as you deserve. Some women, confronted with opinions that are harsh and belittling, allow these underestimations of their worth to seep inside them and then sink under the weight of it. Others learn, as I have and you must, that we think differently than men, but that does not make our thoughts less important or even less intelligent. When taking your worth, the Mr Bethell's of the world must be disregarded. From your own mouth, you found witnesses. Those who would not see the bobbies talked to you. You are just as important in this investigation as Frank."

"It was I who noticed the Viscountess first. I saw her intelligence when even Frank did not," I said, surprising myself.

"You are lucky to have Frank, but he is just as lucky to have you," Myra said.

"Thank you," I said. I thought about all she said as we finished up. When we started down the steps, Lord Grey Hull, who must have heard us coming, strode out from the sitting room.

We rode to a building dedicated to music and balls. I felt intimidated as we entered a vast, long room with tall windows and beautifully painted frescos on the ceiling. The chandeliers hung in rows, like clusters of crystal grapes along a vine. The stage at the front of the room stood before long padded benches, most facing forward, but a couple of rows sat against the wall as if the audience should be the real show. Since the crowd was not expected to be as numerous as during the season, booths lined the back of the room, decorated in holly and other evergreens. Sheet music was set out for purchase in these booths. It amazed me how beautiful the nobility kept their surroundings.

Music already filled the room, and Lord Grey Hull's entrance made an audible disruption. He was thronged by people who wanted to know him, or use him. He stayed back near the booths.

"Company is thin. Most of the Quality are at Christmas parties in the country by the beginning of December, and those stuck in the city are desperate for anyone to admire," Myra said in feigned distress that made me laugh as we walked up the wide aisle toward the stage.

The concert was well attended, but I thought perhaps many of the seats had been filled by the friends of the performers because when the string quartet finished a knot of people in the front center seats clapped more loudly than the others. Myra and I choose a sideways facing bench so we might have a view of the whole room instead of just the stage. After a piano soloist started to play, I whispered, "This music is new."

"It has come over the channel from Paris; a composer name Chopin. He does not perform much himself, but his piano solos are greatly admired. This performer will give us a selection of his works," she whispered back, showing me her program. I closed my eyes to decide if I liked the feeling of the notes that floated over me like my warm bath. The chords of the music glided as if the night spoke.

Just as the first stanza was played, Viscount Beornmund entered the room with his sister on his arm. She wore cream trimmed in fur, and blue lace. She was the sound of Mr Chopin's notes. Her delicate, but purposeful movement caused the musical trills to run the scale, and somehow reminded me of the stars appearing at night.

They were a handsome pair, and clearly considered the highest of the Quality in attendance. Lord Grey Hull did not spend his days cultivating his value to the Le Bon Ton. If a person could be invited into Lady Charlotte's drawing room, they would be considered well placed for the season to come.

An eldest brother, Viscount Beornmund soaked up the attention, even from afar, that was intended for his sister. Full of pomp he dressed in shiny boots, and tight black and yellow plaid breeches. His bright yellow waistcoat was framed by a tight black coat buttoned low on his waist and an extravagantly tied black cravat. He looked like a bee buzzing from group to group, leaving his sister to her beau who had been waiting near the door for her.

The Viscount either greeted or made a point to snub everyone who came toward him. He only graced the best flowers with his presence. He did not bother to notice how people actually viewed him, but rather, he imagined himself reigning over the assembly, all in a receiving line to meet him as if he were a blushing bride. He did not see the few who made the effort to avoid him.

For some reason, he reminded me very much of his father's picture upon the stallion. Each lived in a version of life that was real only to them. Lord Beornmund inflated what he deserved, but it was a fantasy dreamed up, so he did not have to face a world that increasingly diminished his importance. This life, lived inside a lie, did not discriminate between an earl, his heir, or a country widow, but instead seemed to link them. Each found a way to ignore the hardships of life but instead embraced what they deemed life should be.

I started to think everyone did it to some extent. My holding so tightly to a fantasy love for Rick Bolton was done on pretense and fear. It kept me from facing Frank, who was my reality. The reality I knew my mother would not accept until she had no other option. She made it known Frank had no chance with me. From a very young age, I knew Rick Bolton was an acceptable choice to her. Titus Williams – that was a man to make my mother proud.

I could not love Frank when my mother was near because I felt disappointment oozing from her until I breathed it in, and such feelings drenched me in shame. She had such strange ideals about love. And in the end, I did not live up to those ideals. She turned her back on me the day I married Frank. Some part of me always knew she would, which is why I learned to love Rick Bolton in the first place.

But then, my mother danced around a room with a duster so she did not have to be lonely. Her picture of love never made her happy. No matter how my father tripped over himself to satisfy her, she never was. I would not make her same mistake. I would be happy.

If everyone had to have a dream, or perhaps it was simply hope, then Frank would be mine. Frank and I would be happy, and one day, when we visited home, my mother would have to see what true happiness and devotion looked like. I would be proud to be with Frank. She would see love had nothing to do with wealth, or intrigue, flowery words, or gifts; for me, it was the companionship of a husband I adored.

Satisfied with my life, even with myself, I sat among the Quality – my mother's ideal – trying to determine if the Viscount killed his father by way of his wife. Did the two men's fantasies collide, and she, forced to be the playwright, simply preserve her husband's fantasy?

The younger brother, the newcomer, Captain Beornmund, came into the room handing a plate of some refreshment over to a servant near the door. I only knew it was him because he wore his uniform and was immediately

The Basra Pearls

invited to his sister's side. He stood at attention, observant and strong. His looks did not favor his mother or father. If one stirred the parent's features into one, that would be him. His hair waved, his nose pointed, he stood well above his brother.

A very fine-looking man, he was not perhaps as fine as his father or brother, but handsome enough to be of great interest to many young women in attendance. Such as the Miss Chapmans of the city, the wealthy sort who did better for themselves with second sons before the influx of the season brought in the eligible daughters. Miss Keppel's opinion of the young man, when she stated Captain Beornmund had been disappointed in love, and was unlikely to leave the sea long enough to have an heir, did not hold true. He was not shy nor burdened when speaking to the women present.

I liked the younger brother. He appeared annoyed with his older brother's need for pomp, and did not snub anyone. He even went to booths after his brother threw sheet music about and bought the ruffled bent pages. Captain Beornmund then took the pages to his beautiful sister, who searched the booths of sheet music with more care. He bought her whatever she seemed inclined towards. Within little time, she had an armful of music. Many women followed her about and bought whatever she did. Her beau also stayed near, but could not keep her attention when her brother wished to tell her something, or show her a sheet that caught his interest.

I thought at first the three Beornmund siblings would be the only ones to enter. After a time, Lady Beornmund and the Viscountess came in, detained in measures by Mrs Elliot, who was on a much larger scale in height than Lady Beornmund, and blocked her way. She tried to engage her cousin's interests, but Lady Beornmund responded coldly, and would not remove a barrier she put up between them.

Lady Beornmund finally hissed something at the woman, the Viscountess laughed, and Mrs Elliot colored. She retreated to a nearby booth to look over music while Lady Beornmund, by look, warned the Viscountess. With a set jaw Lady Beornmund went to the part of the hall where her children were. The Viscountess trailed behind her pouting.

The Viscountess did not join her husband spreading his pollen around the Hall, but instead stayed near Lady Beornmund. Neither lady browsed the booths, but stood behind where the siblings would come to join their mother every so often.

Even the Viscount tried to improve his mother's mood, giving her a sweet to suck on. Any effort by her children made the mother smile. They were her world and had been all the years Lord Beornmund chased his fantasy.

Captain Beornmund's interactions with the Viscountess proved most interesting. He spoke to his mother, but the Viscountess often answered him. Captain Beornmund looked almost perplexed when she did. Lady Beornmund grew annoyed again, and I could not say if it were at the Viscountess for speaking over her, or Mrs Ellis, who scooted about the room eyeing her cousin as if she may take another try at tearing down her barrier.

I soon decided Lady Beornmund's foul mood more to do with the Viscountess. Her eldest son's wife smiled flirtatiously at his brother. The Viscountess was a changed woman. Spring bloomed on her face. She responded happily to the navy Captain as if everything he said was meant for her. She looked like a lovely young woman should. Only she never remembered her husband.

"I think she has a little crush on the brother of her husband," Myra said quietly to me. That broke the melodrama I watched to Mr Chopin's dreamy notes.

"Perhaps she does," I said as the Viscountess brought the glass of punch she held to her lips. Her eyes, like a frog, watched the captain over the rim as she sipped.

"Do you suppose the young lady married, but regretted it shortly after?" Myra asked.

"I cannot say. Her mother and Lady Beornmund were great friends. She must have known the family her whole life. He must know her," I said. I watched, hoping the Viscountess Beornmund would look upon someone with a friendly eye and a confiding tongue, but she did not. She simply waited for her turn to say something to Captain Beornmund.

Shortly after the family mingled with the crowd, Myra herself was called away by a friend. I assured her I would sit in my seat and listen to the music. I felt very chilly in my new dress and looked to see if any of the other women looked cold. If they did, they hid it well.

I grew distracted listening to a commanding, fast moving part of the piano solo when I felt eyes staring down upon me. Just from the shadow cast over me, and the way the piano moved through a stanza, I knew it was not Myra and her warmth. I stood when I saw who loomed near.

"They dress you up, but they may as well have put that finery on a beast of burden," Viscountess Beornmund said. "You cannot hide your very poor manners. It is clear you do not belong among your superiors."

I could see she meant to sink me, to force me to cow to her in this setting.

"There is a pawn shop in the slums surprisingly near the palace that is rumored to have the grandest of patrons," I replied. "They learned to respect me there. Why not here?"

She did not say anything for a time. She pretended to listen to the music, but her breathing was shallow, her jaw clenched.

"Join me for a turn through the tea room, won't you?" she asked.

"I suppose," I said scooting from the bench and moving in time with her.

"What have you found?" she asked leaning toward me, but continued to look about the room. Presumably so no one could sneak up and overhear our conversation.

"Many things," I answered. "Beautiful treasures."

"The most precious treasure could not be found, no doubt," she said, casting a net.

"Certainly not at the pawn shop. I understand the real treasure was reclaimed before either of us could get to it. It must have been disappointing, being so close. Especially after you worked so hard… scraping together the money to reclaim your ticket. The Uncle said a dead man came to call and easily paid the price of them. Now that is an impressive trick."

"Where are the pearls?" she snapped, glancing over her shoulder as if a booth we passed caught her eye, but really she looked to see where her family was.

"Stolen, a family heirloom, easily identified and yet, taken. Unwise on the thief's part," I said.

"They have not been proven stolen," she fished. "They may still be found among Lord Beornmund things. Once he is officially pronounced dead a certain actress of his will be searched. It is very comforting to know they are likely safely awaiting me there."

"The actress does not have them," I said.

"You haven't any idea where they are," she snapped.

"He gave them to his illegitimate daughter," I said.

"He had no right to do that. They are mine," she snapped, but quickly poised her face to be bored while she glanced about again to be sure no one overheard us.

She walked a little faster toward the the tea room. It was in a pretty corner of the building, more windows than walls, though even a touch chillier than the main room. The tearoom had a few small round wooden tables, each with more chairs than fit comfortably. We paused as the Viscountess scouted the room. She led me to a quiet corner, furthest from the heat of the fire, where we could sit while she monitored who came upon us. The tea lady brought her cart and bowed to the Viscountess.

The cream tea offerings were like works of art – the flakey pastry, swirling clotted cream, and just a hint of the jeweled jam that awaited inside. The Viscount handed over a mostly full punch cup she'd been holding and took up a teacup instead, clearly meaning to keep her mind sharp. I reluctantly passed on the pastries, as the rich food served me over the day I'd spent with Myra began to take its toll. Instead, I chose a cup of plain black tea.

When the woman left with her cart the Viscountess said, "You did not leave the pearls with the child, I assume."

"No. Does it bring you comfort to know they are perfectly safe, entered as evidence along with the tickets used to pawn, then reclaim, them," I said.

She said nothing for time. Finally, she leaned forward. Her eyes glared.

"No matter," she said, extending the glower to the tea lady who looked like she might come upon us with more offerings, but turned away at just a glance. "It complicates things, but I will get them back. They are the estate's, after all."

"If you want them so badly, why did you pawn them in the first place?" I asked as we were speaking so bluntly.

She could not answer right away. She took a deep breath and let it out. She knew I could prove all.

"I thought them glass. They were perfectly white... so shiny with a silver tint. I did not know about the gleam upon Basra Pearls. Pearls have pink or gold in them; they are duller. These almost glowed. They were all of perfect shape, and the eardrops were too big for real pearls."

"They are beautiful. And have the look of great expense upon them," I argued.

"I have known Lady Charlotte a long while. She wears moonstones, and garnets. She has never cared for the finest gems; I thought the box with mother of pearl was the true treasure. For her to have personal possession of the family's jewels... it is absurd. I do not expect you to understand," she said.

"I do not. The sheen of the pearls mesmerized me," I said.

"They were the finest of jewels, or glass. They could be nothing in between," she agreed.

"I suppose," I said, "but it did not hurt that you wished them to be glass so you could have ready money, just as I wished them to be the pearls so Frank could solve his mystery. Yet, the density of the pearls did not change with either of our wishes."

I sipped the hot amber liquid, allowing the earthy strong flavor to warm me and the herbs to settle my stomach.

"I do wish to know two points that have piqued my curiosity," I said setting my cup down.

"You may ask; I may not answer," she said.

"Very well, when did you realize they were the famed, genuine pearls?" I asked.

"Auntie Lily asked Charlotte if I could borrow them when I was presented. I, of course, opted to wear my mother's diamonds so she would not go search them out," she said.

"Very wise," I said.

"And?" she asked.

"How did Lord Beornmund know you would be at the pawn shop the day he confronted you?"

She looked at me with one piercing glare, then went back to glancing about the room. To an onlooker, she would appear embarrassed by her low company. I did not mind her need to keep up an appearance. My mother often did so. I was good at waiting her out as well. Finally, the Viscountess, her creamy, almost unnaturally white face, leaned toward me while watching the doorway.

"He...he sent an ivory sewing box to Charlotte under the guise of a secret admirer the day before. She prefers drawing and never stitches anything. We both knew it would mean nothing to her and be disregarded. I...I asked her for it, and she gave it to me. I already had something..."

"The vase," I said. She flinched meeting my eyes again. I realized I was probably the closest thing she had to a confidante in all of London. I almost felt sorry for her, but just then a man and two women passed close. She forced out that grating sound she used as a laugh.

"You will refrain from that titter if you wish to speak to me," I said. "It is insulting to you and me and all women to pretend this way."

"I have been overlooked my whole life. There were three brothers and me. Even if I were the smartest among them, I would never have been given their opportunities. But in the end, I received my mother's jewels. Diamonds – those are gems to be proud of," she said showing me her wrist that held an intricate glittering bracelet. "Women must take whatever opportunity, no matter how it comes. Heaven knows, men do. I could teach you to use your intelligence to better your situation."

"I do not wish to be covered in diamonds," I said.

"It is not the jewels, but what they represent. I bested every man in my life. This is my proof," she said leaning toward me so the table across from us would not hear, but before she started again, I snapped:

"And now the pearls are proof you bested the Earl of Beornmund. He drew you out, tricked you into exposing yourself. How did you best him?" I asked breathing heavily, watching her, willing her to admit she killed him.

She smiled. She knew I could prove her involvement in the pearls and pawning. There was no point in lying. She clearly was not going to admit further. She folded her arms and shut her mouth, which curved into a smile, all except the half on the lower lip that did not move.

I set my teacup down.

She looked so smug.

That is when I realized she bested me.

She provoked me into telling her what evidence was found against her. I might have ruined all of Frank's case. She could now defend herself based on what we could prove and be astounded by what we could not. I stood up leaving the last dregs of my tea on the table. I did not trust myself alone with her. I started to walk away and she followed me. As we walked back into the music hall near the vendors, I said angrily, but barely heard above the rushed notes running along the piano, "I refuse to conform to the idea that I must be insipid, and hide my intelligence to thrive in the eyes of men. I would rather change the way men – and even other women – think," I spoke into the space where our conversation sat between only us.

"Until you do, I will stick with my laugh," she said tittering loudly in my ear. She made the noise just as the music went quiet, so it sounded as if she were meant to play the last note.

In that small instant I pulled away, Captain Beornmund also flinched and glanced in our direction from all the way across the room. She noticed him flinch and she faltered, only slightly, but her mask came askew with the drop of shame in her eyes. The room was then filled with applause for the piano solo. People stood and clapped, and it felt like they applauded this woman who tricked me. The smattering like rain on the rooftop fueled my anger. I wanted her to falter, to admit more then she wished to. In a hushed voice I said, "That terrible noise bothers the younger Beornmund as well. He is a captain, I think."

"He is not the youngest ever made captain, but close... he is an old friend. He knew me before I laughed so much," she said, and we walked slowly in his direction.

"Ah yes. One cannot settle for a second son even if he has made captain when there is a first son to inherit," I taunted.

"If Providence is kind, he will not always be," she snapped, proving her attachment.

"Oh, I see," I said. I had taunted her into being reckless, and meant to keep her there. She stopped and turned to face me.

"What do you see, Mrs Hadleigh?" she hissed. "If you continue to interfere in my affairs, I will sink your husband. His career will never be."

"No," I whispered angrily, "I see that a person doesn't just have a plant-based poison lying about in wait, just in case their husband's father is brought back to life and must be disposed of. One has such a thing for one's husband."

Her eyes widened and she looked at me in shock. Suddenly I was very afraid for her husband. The lingering expression on her face told too much.

Everything shifted. I was no longer concerned about proving anything. Instead, I reasoned in favor of her husband's safety:

"Now that his father has died under such suspicious circumstances, certainly you cannot suppose your husband's death would be overlooked?"

"I cannot be blamed for his ill health. He keeps such hours and is so reckless; such a frail man," she snapped glancing at her husband. He spoke to his mother with big arms and facial expressions, while she smiled indulgently upon him. Did he know his wife favored his brother? He had not come near her all evening.

"It would be better to abandon such a scheme all together, and learn to love the Viscount. The captain is just the age for marrying, and appears to have come home ready to be charmed."

She cleared her face, but could not control her sporadic breathing that proved her insides fumed. She clutched her fan to her stomach and watched Captain Beornmund interacting with a few lovely young women as he walked in our direction.

"I suppose there is every chance you will get away with murdering your husband's father," I warned. "If only you will leave it at that. I cannot see how you will do away with your husband and escape suspicion."

I saw a clench in her jaw as a very pretty woman touched the arm of her captain, swaying her more than I ever could. Standing so close to her, I noticed something else. She wore her bodice high, so the point of her dress wasn't so tight or so low. The rector's wife had done the same so she did not have to go into confinement so early.

"You carry a child," I whispered out loud simply to confirm my suspicion.

"I have produced an heir. I have done my duty. The Beornmund line will continue as long as I am safe. As you can see, you cannot come near me with your accusations," she said, but she looked away and swallowed hard.

"Perhaps it is so, but no matter how you twist the facts you paid a price for the pearls; you did not best anyone."

"Lord Beornmund died," she hissed, just a statement, but so close to admitting guilt. It did not matter anymore.

"The child cannot be the captain's – not ever. You would do well to give your husband an heir and live out life as a Lady, covered in jewels," I repeated.

"I will choose my own fate, not you. I will ruin you, your husband and anyone else who gets in my way," she hissed while smiling and waving in her childish way to Lady Charlotte who came toward us.

I could not reason with her. I would have to find someone who might believe me, over her, and warn the Viscount. But then throughout the investigation, it was made painfully clear there were few people in such a position.

"I suppose we will see if I can put you in Newgate before you can hurt your husband?"

She balked and looked at me in surprise. I laughed in her face, and then waved to Myra who came to find me. She showed an extremely worried look on her face.

"I could put you forward," the Viscountess hissed quickly under her breath. "I could make you and your Frank successful. So much so it would raise you into the Quality. If he will but collect his reward for finding Lord Beornmund and move on, letting the findings of the first inquest stand."

"Frank can make himself and I've had enough of your Quality to last a lifetime," I said as her Captain and his sister made it to us.

Chapter Thirty-one

"Constance, you have not introduced us to your lovely friend," Captain Beornmund said sounding strange in a normal volume not bothering to hush his voice as the applause for the piano soloist finally died down.

"Your sister could do the job," she snapped curtly. "This is Mrs Frank Hadleigh. She is the wife of the man investigating your father's death."

"Oh, Mrs Hadleigh. I did not recognize you; you look so lovely," Lady Charlotte said. Subconsciously I put a hand to my sleeve, and pulled up. The Viscountess smirked.

"Thank you. May I introduce you to Lady Myra Grey Hull?" I asked as Myra reached us.

"Oh, you are all anyone speaks of these days, your ladyship," Lady Charlotte said with a curtsy. "Congratulations on your recent marriage to the Marquess of Dorset, Lord Grey Hull."

"Thank you," Myra said demurely. Lady Charlotte introduced her brother, the captain. As she did the Viscountess turned and with just that motion stood nearer him and away from me.

"How do you know Mrs Hadleigh? I would have thought this company to be above her," Viscountess Beornmund asked Myra, feigning innocence.

The captain cleared his throat and looked at her.

"Oh, excuse me, My Lady," she said, acting chagrined for him.

"Millie and I grew up in the same parish. We are very fond of her at my brother's home. She and my niece are the very best of friends," Myra said.

"How fortunate that you have such friends, Mrs Hadleigh," Viscountess Beornmund said, her eyebrows contracted only slightly at the lie.

"Yes, I treasure them," I said grinning.

"We are the fortunate ones. Millie is witty and I always value my conversation with her," Myra said.

"I can imagine. You were a governess for a time where you not?" Viscountess Beornmund asked with her laugh. Lady Charlotte's eyes got wide and she looked like she would throttle the Viscountess.

"I was companion to a motherless girl," Myra said. She didn't look offended. She crossed her arms, cocked her head, and dared the Viscountess to continue as if she did not know any better.

"I understand you were awarded a baroness for services rendered, arranged through letters of patent by the Duke of Surry," said Lady Charlotte. She emphasized the man's title to the Viscountess.

"Yes," Myra said. She watched the Viscountess but said nothing more.

Lord Grey Hull came over shortly after this exchange. It was apparent he loved his wife very much and though unfashionable, made no effort to hide it. A man, following Lord Grey Hull, engaged him in a discussion on politics and a question arose about the lawfulness of constables in rural parishes. Many had hoped with the police force, constables would be dissolved so something would be done about local magistrate corruption in the country.

Thomas, Frank's brother, was a prime example of why parish constables could not always be trusted. I thought their indignation at local injustices was rather one-sided considering there was a murderer standing among us who

The Basra Pearls

could not be touched because of her inclusion among them. Then I worried for Viscount Beornmund all over again.

Lord Grey Hull said: "I am not certain of the particulars of the law. There is a young man in London who will answer for us. Mrs Hadleigh's husband has been trained as a barrister, but for a time was a constable. I value his opinion greatly."

"I have interacted with the young man. He is not so bright. Certainly, he can do little more than tell us the crop rotation of the local farmers," Viscountess Beornmund said with her titter.

"No, he is very well versed in the law, be it answering complaints among the locals, or arguing Her Majesty's common law in the courtroom. I have heard my husband mention the very matter you speak of. You would do well to consult him," I defended.

"Oh please," the Viscountess tittered to Lady Charlotte. "If it is left to Mr Frank Hadleigh, he will have the Lord Mayor caught up in poaching concerns next."

"Constance!" said Lady Beornmund, who had just walked up behind the Viscountess. "I quite depend on that young man."

"No," I said in my most condescending voice, "My Lady, it is quite all right. We must make allowances for her," then I turned to Viscountess Beornmund and talking slowly as I would to the child she pretended to be, "I know it is probably hard for you to understand, dear. That's fine, nobody expects you to keep up with conversations about the law. Perhaps you ought to concern yourself with the music. We cannot have you straining yourself, surely."

She glared.

Captain Beornmund barely contained his laugh. I could see he knew of her farce and did not approve of it. Lord

The Basra Pearls

Grey Hull turned to the Viscountess, and I could hear just a hint of warning in his voice as he said, "Yes, let us give her leave to listen to the music. I do not wish her to… over-extend herself into matters she should not."

The Viscountess examined him, and glanced at me as she bowed and moved to Lady Beornmund's side.

"As I was saying," Lord Grey Hull finished, "Frank is a near genius. His wife is clearly very sharp-witted. I'm sure he'll be able to answer all our questions for us."

When all eyes were focused on Lord Grey Hull, I chanced a glance at the Viscountess. She had her jaw set, and I wondered if she wished she had played a touch less of a simpleton, so her opinion in serious matters might mean something.

I also wondered what she would take if she bested me. I had nothing to give but my wedding band; she would have to cut that from my dead finger. Certainly, the look in her eye told she meant to best me. Myra must have read something in her eyes as well, because as a soloist set up to perform, she said, "Millie, will you come sit with me and enjoy the music. I have come to hear this next soloist in particular."

"May I join you, My Lady, I am a musical enthusiast," Captain Beornmund asked offering his arm.

"Please do," Myra said and took the arm he offered.

"I would enjoy the music as well," the Viscountess said. He looked surprised, but did not stop from leading us to the benches. Just before we reached them, the Viscount Beornmund walked in our direction. With the music quieted, he jingled as he walked, and I could see it was all the baubles hanging from his chain to his pocket. Captain Beornmund heard his brother approaching and stopped our progression.

Viscount Beornmund looked about as if he had to be sure he'd spoken to all he meant to. Like a child in need of constant entertainment, he approached his wife, carefree. He meant to be on to the next thing. He smiled at his friend's conversation as he walked toward us, his handsome face alight in amusement. Had I overreacted? Perhaps the Viscountess had no designs against him. He reached us. Addressing his wife, he said:

"My Lady, I suppose you will not mind if I leave you to the care of my brother that I might be off to another venue. I have it that there will be a fight of fisticuffs," he said. In a lower voice he admitted, "I may try to get a little blood on my boots. It will make a fine story to tell during the season since I have not been hunting. You will not miss me too terribly if I leave?"

"No, certainly not, but do make haste before the next performer begins," the Viscountess said, shooing him away.

"Very good, very good. I swear I will try not to drink so much, and be sick on your night things again," he said turning, the last more as a joke to benefit two of his riotous friends. As he turned, his laugh fell short. He leaned forward and wheezed a little to catch his breath. His eyes sunk and his expression gave just a hint of weariness when he looked back at us. Something was hidden in his expression, but he turned and was away before I could see what. Surely, he was not already on his father's heels? I watched him to see any sign of poison, but with his back to me, I could find nothing.

We found seats and listened to a few songs. The woman performing sang homey, country songs. Songs I'd grown up hearing, but presented them with a clear beautiful voice and new artistry. It surprised me such songs would be performed in such a place. After a time, Captain Beornmund leaned over and asked in a hushed voice as we sat near the musician:

"Do you know if your husband has made much progress on what happened to my father?"

"Frank has traced his movements to his last day," I said.

"Mr Shaw will not allow me to speak with Mr Hadleigh, whom my mother insists is the only trustworthy of the lot. Mr Archer is fairly certain father died of illness," Captain Beornmund said.

"I think it naive to say so," I said. "His death was shrouded in suspicious circumstances."

"Like he lost his ring that turned up on a finger that was not his?" Captain Beornmund asked.

"That was an interesting happenstance, but has little to do with how he really died," I whispered.

"Please, I cannot hear," Viscountess Beornmund hissed.

"Oh yes, sorry Constance. I know how much you love music," he whispered back. I examined the Viscountess. She was aggravated, pretending to listen to the music. She did not wish for me to tell the particulars to Captain Beornmund. Her fear showed in the shaking hands she clutched together against her growing abdomen. The carefully constructed world she lived in was crumbling around her. Captain Beornmund did not suspect her. He spoke to her with respect. He was a good man. She loved him and knew he would not approve what she had done.

"I can have Frank stop by to give a report if you like," I whispered when the song ended.

Captain Beornmund nodded without saying a word so he might not aggravate the Viscountess further. The soloist ended her set with *Blow Away the Morning Dew*. I had not heard the little ditty since I was a child. The song tells of when the maiden locks the knight out of her father's house so he might not take advantage of her, I almost cheered. I had a new respect for the maiden, but then the musician added a proverb to the ballad I'd never heard. She admonished the knight to take the maiden defenseless when he could, despite her protests, or he did not deserve her. My heart sank and I could not believe another woman would sing such a thing so beautifully as if legitimate advice to young, entitled men.

The Viscountess and I glanced at each other. She lifted her brows to me, as if she proved her point. I could not dismiss her assertions right away. To chastise the maiden for getting herself out of a desperate situation felt so wrong. Had not I been carried away in the very style of the Sabine women? If I could have killed Mr Williams to save myself, would I have? Should I have? The Viscountess looked away, so I did not see her vulnerability. Tears filled my eyes, and I could feel the desperate, hopeless scream from Newgate Prison heavy upon my chest again.

I stood after the woman stopped pouring her heart into the ballad. Myra took one look at me, and in the truest beauty of womanhood showed me her compassion bowing slightly to the others.

One look from Myra at her husband and he abandoned his conversation to call the carriage. I glanced back at the Viscountess who craned her neck to watch us. We started out the same, both of us stuck. What must a woman do to get out of a desperate situation? Or rather, why must women be put into such desperate situations?

Chapter Thirty-two

"What did you say to her that made her lose her pretense?" Lord Grey Hull asked, once in the carriage.

"I'm sorry," I asked confused by his abrupt manner, and still deep in thought.

"When you spoke to just Viscountess Beornmund, you said something that made her eyes light up with intelligence, and fear, I think. What did you say as Captain Beornmund approached with his sister?"

I squinted. That's right, she meant to harm her husband, simply to get him out of the way. Planned out long before the pearls, or her husband's father came upon her. She could have come forward about the pearls: her mistake. She was not taken captive. She stumbled deeper and deeper along her own path until she killed a man.

"Millie," Myra asked looking at me.

"Yes, sorry," I said shaking my head. "I asked her who she meant to kill since one does not just have plant-based poisons lying about. I believe she loves Captain Beornmund and means to do away with her husband if she can manage it. He must be warned."

They stared at me.

"I will see to it," Lord Grey Hull finally assured.

"That would be highly suspicious," Myra said.

"I did point that out to her but I believe she is with child and growing desperate to be done with her husband."

"Because she cannot be certain who the child's father is?" Lord Grey Hull asked.

"Miss Keppel, Lord Beornmund's mistress, indicated the Viscount could not sire an heir. Some accident in his youth," I said.

"If her husband knew nothing of his father's resurrection, nor his wife's infidelity, it may cause her much trouble to be with child," Myra said.

"And she cannot confess to him the child is his father's without telling him all. It may cause her to be reckless," I said.

We were all quiet.

"I believe she killed Lord Beornmund," Lord Grey Hull said. "I watched her talk to you. She went in and out of a character. Her husband is unaware of her, dismissive even."

"He married her for wealth, but her portion went into the family estate. He was greatly disappointed," I said.

"Yes, but I mention it because, if the Viscount had plotted his father's murder with her, he would watch her more closely. At the very least, he would notice she is speaking to the wife of the man investigating it all. He does not notice anything. Simply by his neglect of her, his not caring who she talks to, his complete lack of paranoia, leads me to doubt he had a part in it."

"No, he is so far from suspecting his wife it leaves me concerned for his safety," I fretted. "If only we could bring charges for Lord Beornmund's murder to simply get her out of her husband's house."

"How? Unless the coroner can be convinced by Mr Bethell and Frank…" Lord Grey Hull said.

"Captain Beornmund perhaps? He indicated Jasper will not let him see Frank. He is a man of action who would push the investigation if he knew half of it," I said closing my eyes wondering if, by taunting the Viscountess, I made a bad situation much worse."

Be very careful how you speak with the Viscountess," Lord Grey Hull said trying to sound matter of fact, but he didn't. Lord Grey Hull sounded afraid for me.

"She has resources you cannot understand. It would be best not to interact with her again."

The Viscountess got away with killing her husband's father, an earl. What would stop her from killing her husband or even me?

Chapter Thirty-three

Despite Lord Grey Hull's warning, I could not help accompanying Myra the next afternoon when she went calling. She had received an invitation from Lady Charlotte to call. I promised Myra I would avoid all tete-a-tete with the Viscountess, but I meant to ask Lady Charlotte how her eldest brother did, even contrive to see him if I could. Perhaps some warning, a hint from my own lips may put him on his guard. The butler ushered us into the beautiful Beornmund drawing room.

"Please be seated," Lady Charlotte said in an elegant gesture she pointed to a sofa near the fire. I sat near two other finely dressed women.

"I see Viscountess Beornmund is not here," I said looking around, waiting for her to jump out at me.

"She begged Mother to take her to a hot house in the Kew Gardens. They've just taken in some rare exotic plant she had to see," she said. "Can I pour you a cup?"

"No thank you," I said politely. Despite Viscountess Beornmund's absence I still did not feel comfortable taking the tea offered us.

"I am so curious," I said, knowing I was not being polite, but I didn't care. "What are you growing?"

"They are Constance's boxes," Lady Charlotte said standing and walking over to them. I felt she wished to separate me from the group, so I walked over with her while Myra engaged her friends in conversation. She stood near rectangular ceramic pots at the height of the window on lovely wrought iron stands.

"She is quite skilled," I said. "The hyacinth grows as if it is spring, and her jasmine is so fragrant." A round stone pot set back exploded with golden orange, and dark blue flowers.

"What is this?"

"Marigolds, and the tall ones are monkshood. It is mother's favorite. It has gotten so big mother insisted she move it from the conservatory for our guests to see," she answered.

"I did not know that you could grow monkshood indoors," I said.

"Not me, Constance. These are nothing to what she has managed over the summer in the conservatory and the garden itself. She transplanted the monkshood to the pot so she might have some for over the winter. She swears it does wonders as a cream for the face and sore muscles."

"We never kept it in our garden for fear of the animals," I said.

"She knows everything about her plants and how to use them." Lady Charlotte paused, looked me straight in the eyes and said, "Especially in her snuffs. My father especially loved her snuff."

I watched Lady Charlotte carefully while remembering the student surgeon said Lord Beornmund's nose had been burned.

It was the snuff.

"Does your brother take snuff?" I asked, hoping she could read the fear in my eyes.

"Hugh?" she asked confused. She clearly suspected the Viscountess of her father's death, but had not realized her brother was in danger.

"Her husband," I said. "Does the Viscountess give snuff to her husband?"

While Lady Charlotte suddenly realized what I was saying, her friend called:

"Oh, that puts me in mind, can you get Lady Constance to spare some snuff for my father. He has asked me several times to get him some."

"I shall ask her when she returns," Lady Charlotte said, but her eyes did not move from mine.

"I have heard the marriage of your eldest brother to the Leicester line was planned in their infancy, your mother and hers being such good friends," I said.

"No, it was all arranged rather suddenly only two years ago."

"Was it?" I asked, and she, latching onto my fear, said, "Constance and Hugh, my second brother, were always together in our youth. Even more than us. He was her age. He went to the Royal Naval Academy when he was twelve, and already, they claimed to be in love even so young. Constance always… well she loved Hugh. She loved Hugh and her father."

"Why did she marry your older brother then?" I asked.

"Her father would not accept Hugh until he distinguished himself. Constance had little choice in the matter. Her father preferred her to marry Augustus. When Hugh learned of their engagement, he volunteered on a ship and sailed to the West Indies. He has not been home until now," she said.

"And he's been made. That must be rather vexing for the Viscountess," I said.

"Hugh was made Captain of the ship when the captain died of illness en route. He was made a month before Augustus and Constance married."

"She could not have waited?" I asked.

"No, her father ailed and insisted she be settled before he passed. He died a month after she married."

"I cannot imagine Lady Constance settling for a second son anyway," one of the other women said.

Just then the door opened, and Captain Beornmund came in. We had just been speaking of him; everyone went awkwardly quiet.

"Excuse me for interrupting. I was told there is some tea in here," he said grinning at his sister.

"Actually, we must go," I said nodding to Myra. Myra looked at me astounded as she barely sat down.

"Please excuse us, My Lady," Myra said standing and glancing at me confused.

"Do ask after your eldest brother for me," I said quietly to Lady Charlotte. She nodded. Then I walked straight toward the captain who walked toward the tea things.

He noticed me charge him. He stopped short.

I felt my eyes water with humiliation. The women glared at me for approaching him in such a manner. I stopped before him unsure what to say. I glanced back at Lady Charlotte. She cleared her throat. Her brother looked from her to me, trying to understand my abrupt movements.

"May I escort you ladies out," Captain Beornmund finally asked, catching on.

"Please," Myra said, taking the arm he offered. I turned back and nodded to Lady Charlotte. She looked very much like she wished she could come with us, but her friends, who had exclaimed several times there was no one else to visit, did not seem inclined to leave.

We walked to the street and as none of the passersby were of the Quality, he felt comfortable to say, "I stopped by the office of Mr Jasper Shaw to speak of my father's case. I feel I have been stonewalled by that gentleman. He assures me it was all in the inquest, and that I need not concern myself as the investigation has yielded nothing."

I looked to Myra. She nodded and said: "Tell him. He must see the truth of it."

"Jasper is extorting your eldest brother to stop the investigation and let the inquest stand. Your mother has made it clear she wishes for Frank to finish his investigation. In the next day, your father's body will be exhumed. His lordship will be declared dead, and your brother will be in control of all the family assets," I said.

"Was my father…was he murdered?" he asked.

"I can lay forth the facts for you. I am no judge," I said knowing it is what would honor Frank the most.

"Come, let us go somewhere we can speak freely," he said. I looked at Myra, who ushered us toward her carriage. We moved too slowly. I wished I could simply tell the captain my concern for his brother, but he would likely think me mad to speak so of his family, especially of a woman he had loved his whole life.

Myra's lovely carriage took us a few blocks to Dover Street where a beautiful new hotel had been built. Captain Beornmund asked for a private parlor often used for the wealthy to entertain. It was a snug room with a roaring fire. This room had a sizeable round table with only a few highbacked armchairs, upholstered in a color between yellow and green. The tea lady brought in all sorts of pastries and my stomach turned, my nerves on edge for the story I must tell this man about his father. Captain Beornmund ordered tea. Both Myra and I passed on the pastries.

With very little interruption, I quickly told of everything relevant that happened. His father meaning to leave his title behind. The pearls, the mistress, the tea pot, the burned nose, and snuff, all the way to the stabbing. He sat with his mouth slightly agape in disbelief. He was very quiet. When he finally spoke, he said, "I have been coming to find I did not ever really know her heart, but for Constance to do this!"

He nodded to himself, and I thought he probably could believe it.

"Is she capable of altering snuff so?" I asked trying to force him to be ready for what I must tell him.

"She has knowledge enough of plants and the effects of snuff if it came down to it. Her father liked it very strong," he admitted.

"Your father put her in a difficult position, what with his own plans and hers conflicting. I do not think she started out to hurt him. She just pledged the pearls and from there it would seem she has tumbled down a hill of sorts until she ended up… I believe she is with child and grows desperate," I said.

"It cannot be Augustus's child," Captain Beornmund said.

"That has been hinted many times," I said. "How can you be sure?"

"When he was five, Augustus had…a stone blocking his urine. He was in a lot of pain and bleeding. My father was old fashioned. He did not respect surgeons to be any different from barbers. He went to his man to be let of blood, and cupped several times. He did not hesitate to take Augustus to his barber to… cut the stone out."

"Oh dear," I said. I had no idea what he was talking about, but it sounded bad.

"It took the man over an hour to get the thing out. With his blade he destroyed Augustus's future expectations. My mother was very angry when she saw how he mutilated her boy. I was a small child and my sister a baby at the time.

My father was never allowed the care of us again. I think it… their marriage ended that day, I believe," he said.

"Could they do nothing for him?" I asked, appalled.

"My mother took him to surgeons. Most agreed something was severed, and though it would eventually heal, a connection was broken. It would be unlikely for Augustus to have children."

"Is your brother angry?" I asked.

"Not as he once was. Augustus is content. He and Constance have…consummated their relationship. He is a married man. He wrote me so… so I would let her go. The surgeons said he would likely be capable of limited…"

I turned bright red, and Myra glanced at him in pity. He caught us and smiled.

"I am sorry. I spend my days on a ship and speak too freely."

"I am sorry for you and your heartache," Myra said kindly.

"I am recovered, and have even found it liberating to be free of an engagement made when I was too young to know myself."

"Does your brother know that?" I asked.

"I do wonder…Augustus leaves me alone often with Constance. At times I do wonder if he thinks… With our father as example, I do not know what he thinks. He does wish for an heir. He may think I will take care of it," he said with a clenched jaw.

"He does not know she is with child?" I asked.

"No, I do not believe so," he said.

"She must find a way to explain her child then," I said delicately, "but the way she is growing, it is likely your father's."

"Or she will claim it a miracle. That is what one surgeon said it would take," he said. Growing angry he continued, "My father was at her baptism as a baby. How could he delve so far from decency to do this to her?"

"I cannot say," I said looking to Myra who shrugged. I could see he needed time to digest all this information, but I was quite concerned for his brother and wished to get to my point at last.

"You believe she did this then?" I asked.

"I… I can believe she pawned the pearls. All she ever wanted was jewels and clothes, carriages, and pin money. I can believe my father… He was desperate to have an heir. He would have seen impregnating her as his duty. I can see Augustus…" he paused, and I interrupted impatiently.

"This is what I hoped for. You must be convinced so on some level you will believe what I say next."

"What is it?" he asked.

"I believe your brother in danger… I do not think the Viscountess has stopped loving you."

Captain Beornmund stared at me, taken aback.

"Is he well?" I asked. I wished to shake the stupor out of him.

"I have only been in London a couple of days. We are not as we once were. It is the first time I have seen him in two years… but now that you say…"

"What is it?" I asked.

"Augustus does seem ill," Captain Beornmund said his eyes rising from his tea to my face, written in fear.

"What do you mean?" I asked, but I knew.

"I thought him drinking too much. He has vomited and …he is not well," he said looking at me, horrified.

"We warned your mother's solicitor, Mr Archer, to watch your mother. Instead he bribed Mr Shaw to pretend all was right. It never occurred to me until last night, when I saw her look at you that she might try to hurt your brother," I said quickly.

"I must go," Captain Beornmund said, standing, "I have not seen Augustus yet today."

"Go," I said. He stood up pulling out his coin pouch.

"I will settle this. Go," Myra said.

He tore out of the room frantic to get to his brother.

"Is everything all right?" the serving lady asked coming in after he ran out.

"I will settle this now," Myra said.

Chapter Thirty-four

Myra paid and we hurried to find Lord Grey Hull. We told him all. He went immediately to look in after Viscount Beornmund. It was a long afternoon of waiting. When he finally came back, he brought Lady Charlotte with him. She trembled, her eyes rimmed in red, and she looked extremely pale.

"Are you well?" I asked.

"Augustus is very ill. He was vomiting, and could not stop. I sent a footman to his room after you left, just as you said, to check on him. He returned immediately to fetch me. I found him…" she closed her eyes not to see it all.

"Did you get a doctor?"

"I sent the footman for the doctor, and Hugh came rushing in. He stayed with Augustus."

"The Viscountess – she must be kept away from him," I said.

"She came home with my mother," said Lady Charlotte. "Hugh locked her in her room. I thought it impossible, but whatever you said to him, he believed," she cried.

"Thank you for believing me. No one ever does when I tell them she is terrible and veery intelligent. All they see is the fool."

"I see her. I see her for who she is," I said. Lady Charlotte, who was not a small person, buried her head on my shoulder putting all her weight on me.

"Is…is Augustus still with us?" Myra asked taking her by the shoulders and moving her to a chair near the fire.

"His heart beats, but he will not wake," she said sobbing. "Before she went out with mother, Constance... fetched him his tea and snuff saying he drank himself silly and not to bother him. She sent his man away. I said nothing, because she insists. She is right no matter what I say. But I saw him come home early last night. He did not stay for the entire round of fisticuffs. He said he had been feeling ill for the last few weeks so he did not wish to be out late. He kissed my forehead and told me he loved me. He gave me his winnings," she said showing us a few pounds clutched in her fist.

I began crying with her. Something I could not control grew inside me. This was my fault. I pushed her.

"She is with child," I said. "Your brother is the only one who can say it is not his."

"Oh," she said, closing her eyes. "Yes, she has been sick. Then when Augustus wasn't feeling well, she decided what she had was catching."

"I taunted her last night. I told her she could not poison her husband or everyone would know. Do you suppose she took it as a challenge?" I asked, appalled.

"No dearest. He has been failing for weeks," Myra pointed out, "likely since word Captain Beornmund was coming home. Do you know what is expected of a second son when the heir dies with a young bride who is having his child?"

"Oh," I said, the hysteria dying down.

"She will get Hugh after all. She gets whatever she wants," Lady Charlotte sobbed. I put an arm around her. I felt so helpless. It was all so terrible.

It was hours before any word reached us. We all sat pretending to be occupied, but really we just waited. Finally, Lord Grey Hull came home, somber.

"How does Augustus?" Lady Charlotte asked rushing to him.

"They do not think he will make it through the night," Lord Grey Hull said. "I am so sorry."

She sobbed. I had to know.

"Have you seen Frank?" I whispered so as not to disturb Lady Charlotte's pain, but aching to hold my husband.

"Frank is looking into the matter, Millie. Lady Beornmund is keeping him very close to her. She trusts him far more than her solicitor. She does not wish to believe the girl she thinks of as almost a daughter could do this. I do not think anyone can doubt what happened."

"Is Mr Bethell helping to… put her before a magistrate?"

"Mr Bethell is very angry. He feels if Mr Shaw had not been working against him, they may have noticed earlier the man he extorted was being poisoned. He does not know what to do. He cannot think the Viscount involved anymore."

"Augustus is…he is silly, but not so unprincipled to hurt anyone. He is a gentle soul. My father's betrayal a few years ago, cutting him off, hurt him. My father showed his affection by buying us things, Augustus especially," Lady Charlotte said defending her brother.

"I am sorry," I said wishing I had listened to my own voice, which insisted the Viscount innocent. It would not have made a difference, no one heard me. Only I felt guilty for suspecting him now that he ailed.

"What will happen now?" Lady Charlotte asked.

"I do not know, but you may trust us. We are your true friends," Myra said turning her toward the door. "Come let us get you a bed and some warm chocolate to help you rest."

I followed. I did not wish to cry in front of a marquess.

Viscount Beornmund died during the night. A coroner's inquest was opened the next morning. Many doctors were called to examine his stomach, but no arsenic could be found. Nothing could be detected in his system. His throat was swollen, and his nasal passage excessively burned, but since he had vomited the burn could not be explained conclusively.

Frank sent a note asking me to stay with Myra a little longer. He did not wish to scare me, but our rooms had been ransacked. Thankfully the pearls, along with all the other evidence, were locked in Mr Bethell's chambers.

He swore he would come for me when he cleared this all up but his situation with Jasper was a little tricky. I wrote back telling him I understood and I was proud to be his wife. I wished dearly to sign my note with love, but I doubted he would believe it was from me.

Over the next two days Frank joined efforts with Lady Beornmund's Barrister, Mr Bell, in presenting the facts to the coroner's jury. The Viscountess, supposedly still locked in her room, must have had someone helping her. She found a way to write her brother, the Duke of Leicester. He came to London three days after the Viscount died. That is when everything dissolved.

Witnesses recanted, evidence was lost. In short, everything changed. Still, because they had a body, the inquest jury found there was enough evidence to charge the Viscountess for the murder of Lord Beornmund and his son Viscount Beornmund. It was a short-lived victory. The inquest was found, but hushed up. No man was to speak of the case outside the proceedings or he would find himself in Newgate.

They would not keep the Viscountess company there. Instead of awaiting a trial in Newgate, the Viscountess stayed with his grace, the Duke of Leicester, at his townhouse.

Frank came to dinner the day after the inquest jury approved going to trial. He looked very down and when he entered the sitting room, I rushed to him. Despite Lady Charlotte and Myra looking on, he wrapped me in his arms.

"I have missed you, dearest," Frank said in my ear.

"And I you," I said feeling a sob in my throat, "I do not sleep when you are not on my back."

Frank kissed my forehead and reluctantly let go as the master of the house entered the room.

"Ah Frank! What news have you?" Lord Grey Hull asked.

"It is grim," Frank said. He took my hand and allowed me lead him to a seat.

"The law is on your side," I said.

"It is complicated. Her brother kept the coroner's inquest confidential. He means to hush the whole thing up," Frank said.

"The coroner had to concede to keep it quiet under the appeal of the chief judge," Lord Grey Hull said.

"The papers are full of claims of corruption," Frank said. "I thought it exaggerated, but every judge Mr Bethell has appealed to will not go against the Duke of Leicester. Mr Bethell swears he is going to find reform if it is the last thing he does, but he does not believe it will be in this case."

"But if it goes to trial, they will not be able to keep the thing quiet," I said.

"It will not go to trial," Frank said looking to Lady Charlotte with pity.

"She killed my father, and brother. How is it possible she will not be trialed?" Lady Charlotte asked, the words foreign on her lips.

"The Duke of Leicester has claimed for his sister the rights of a peer, and asked that members of the House of Lords form a private committee to examine the evidence before any public trial be had. He has demanded the inquiry be confidential as the news has already printed stories that the chances a father and son died so close to each other cannot be an accident."

"Who will be among the peers?" Lord Grey Hull asked.

"I believe you could be among them if you go to the House of Lords on the morrow. There are not many in town, and Duke Leicester is writing his set to come to town for a few days to sit in judgment. He will appeal to his friends until the matter is cleared up. If you offer your services before they come… it will be our last chance to get justice for her deeds," Frank said.

"I will certainly go. I will at the least be sure you and Millie can give witness," he said.

"I don't understand. What is 'privileges of a peer'?" I asked.

"The peers, those with titles, are given special considerations to be judged among themselves in private," Frank said.

"No doctor will tell their benefactor it is murder for sure," Lady Charlotte complained.

"Yes, and the chance of a Lady being sent to trial when no murder can be proved is not likely," Lord Grey Hull said.

"The most we will prove is she stole the pearls," I said, more a question than a statement.

The Basra Pearls

"She grows monkshood, not to mention her exotic plants, deadly ones I am sure," Lady Charlotte insisted.

"I am so sorry, My Lady. It does not signify. She claims she does not know their potency. Apparently both men asked for her snuff, knowing they are untried," Frank said.

Lord Grey Hull and Myra began to console Lady Charlotte. Aside to Frank I said in a low voice, "I... I must confess what I did. The Viscountess goaded me, and I told her our evidence. I am sorry Frank. You have worked so hard."

"Oh, Millie! She knows exactly what she did. She has likely had her defense for months. Dearest, you cannot take her sins upon yourself."

"But...what if I had a way to kill Mr Williams, would I have?"

"He took you," said Frank. "You have the right to protect yourself in whatever way you can. Millie, the Viscountess chose. To save herself the embarrassment of admitting she pawned the pearls, she killed a man. She married her husband with the idea she would one day kill him so the man she loved could be Earl. You can relate to her. It is how you understand, but consider, Millie, she has plotted and killed two people. It is something you would never do."

Frank kissed my hand. I nodded and leaned against my Frank. I loved him. How hadn't I known it before?

Dinner was announced. While we ate, Myra insisted on speaking of happier topics as Lady Charlotte was growing very depressed in spirits. She grieved deeply her family's losses.

On top of everything, her beau had not visited her since it all began, though she sent him a note telling him where she was. She confided she felt him deserting. I could not understand these men who were supposed to be noble but showed themselves as cowards when it came down to it.

Lord Grey Hull went the next morning and fished around until he was admitted on the secret investigation of peers to assess the inquest.

The peers assembled, and the tribunal against the Viscountess began two days later. In the afternoon after the peers had been convened for some time, Mr Clarkson came to Lord Grey Hull's home to fetch me. I was summoned to the home of Duke Leicester where the committee heard testimony.

"It is not even in a judge's chambers?" I asked Mr Clarkson.

"No ma'am," he said.

"I suppose Mr Bethell is not pleased with this development?" I asked.

"He is calling it a gross abuse of stature, which is among the mildest of his sentiments that I might repeat in a lady's presence. He is crying reform; I can tell you I have not seen him so determined to get something done as he is now."

"Where is Mr Jasper Shaw in all this? I suppose he is giving his card out to anyone with a title," I said.

"No Ma'am. He developed a belly ache and has gone to his brother's in the country for the rest of December. He may stay until after the new year. I suspect it will last until he does not have to face the Duke of Leicester to indict his sister," Mr Clarkson said.

"Well, that is something," I said with a small laugh.

"Mr Bell has taken a liking to Mr Hadleigh though, and I think he will be sure he is well situated once he has been called to the bar," Mr Clarkson said.

"Well, thank goodness for that," I said as the hackney came to a stop and he helped me out. We were at an estate in Mayfair, not far from the Beornmund mansion. The Leicester mansion was perhaps a little older and less grand, but still a very impressive building with sculptured bushes that looked like the puffs of an old woman's poodle.

"Can this be effective?" I asked Mr Clarkson.

"Most bills are decided in the noble man's dining room, long before they ever see the House of Lords, or Commons, Ma'am," he answered.

"Very well," I said and allowed him to lead me through the columns to the grand door laced in intricate rectangular windows.

Mr Clarkson bid me farewell and I alone stepped into a very spacious, nearly empty room.

Chapter Thirty-five

The hum of voices stopped when the door opened, and all looked toward me as my steps echoed through the quiet room.

A fresco, in imitation of a perfect blue sky with only a few puffy clouds, adorned the ceiling, enhanced by rays of actual late afternoon sun shining through huge arched windows on the far side of the room.

The winter sun did not give off enough heat to make the room warm.

The main area of the floor, set up with two rows of six plush chairs, was nothing like the wooden benches in the jury box at Old Bailey. The picture of Cecil came to me, standing on the dock while men snarled down at him in riotous anger. He had only found a ring.

Viscountess Beornmund sat on the front row nearest the door, and watched me come near her. This woman, with so much evidence against her, sipped tea among her victims, while a footman offered her berries and clotted cream. She wore a loose smock, so her belly showed its size. Now that her husband was gone, she was using the child in her womb to garner sympathy. I suppose if one was going to murder her husband, one ought to be born a lady among the Quality.

On the other side of the room, near a raised platform where musicians would play, a settee comfortably accommodated Lady Beornmund and Captain Beornmund. Behind them was a long table. One side spread out with refreshments; the other side with all the items we recovered from the pawnshop. Standing over the table I found the face I'd been looking for, though I almost didn't recognize him.

The Basra Pearls

Frank listened nodding to Mr Bell, Lady Beornmund's barrister, but he glanced at me, trying to hide his impatience. Frank wore a dark coat and crisp white shirt I'd never seen. His serious look only hinted at the boy he once was. I longed to make him smile.

Frank nodded with finality to Mr Bell, and then turned toward me. His face was everything to me. He was freshly shaved, and every hair stayed in place as he navigated his way swiftly to me. I loved the way his body, lithe and strong, moved. It almost overwhelmed me that he was mine and I could love him my whole life.

He reached for me even before he was in my space. I gave him my hand and he kissed it. It hurt me, but I pulled away quickly so we would not be discredited by affection.

"Try not to mind them too much, Millie. This has turned into nothing but a… a witch hunt. We are the ones on trial. This is all done to discredit us. I wish Mr Bethell had left you out of it, dearest," he whispered clutching my hand in his, offering me the little shelter he was allowed.

"If it is other worldly they want, I will give it to them my dear friend," I said lifting my brows to him flirtatiously. He laughed a little, and my heart spasmed at his handsome face with a smile upon it.

"What part will you play today?" he asked looking down upon me with adoration.

"Myself, considerably outraged for my husband and his hard work," I whispered. He squeezed my hand and turned. I could hear the pride in his voice as he said:

"This is my wife, Mrs Millie Hadleigh, who knows the particulars of this case and was with me throughout much of the investigation."

"Sit," said a demanding, impeccably dressed dark-haired man with dull eyes and the dead spot in the movement of his bottom lip. He stood next to the Viscountess pulling a chair toward me. I saw the Viscountess smirk as I felt Frank tense indignantly. I would not cower. I looked up at Frank and grinned my mischievous grin, pretending to be braver than I was.

"I will be with you in a moment, Sir. It is respectful for me to receive my friends at the moment," I said stepping toward the only two I knew, who stood at my entrance.

"It is respectful for you to address me as your grace," Duke Leicester said, startled.

"Oh, excuse me. I am to intimate you are the Duke of Leicester then? You must excuse me, Your gGace, as I could not be expected to know your title. I am from the country, where we are accustomed to introductions. Your sister may tell you all about my poor manners… Your Grace," I said. As I bowed, I gave a slight smirk at the Viscountess, whom I was glad to see did not look so smug. I patted Frank's arm and pulled away from him, so I did not look like a child afraid of moving about the room by myself.

I walked a few spots down the row to shake hands with Mr Bethell who received me. He shook my hand too long and whispered too loudly for the men clustered around him not to hear, "Stay brave, dear girl, do not fret. If you cannot remember clearly, it is quite understood. Also, if you must stop and take a rest at some point, please do."

I would have been offended if I didn't know his propensity to underestimate females in general, and, I suppose, I did tremble a little. I grinned at him and gave a quick curtsy. I moved down the line to the end of the row where Lord Grey Hull reached his hand for mine. His Lordships eyes twinkled. He knew I lingered simply to be insolent.

"May I offer you a seat," Lord Grey Hull said pulling his chair from the row. He sat much closer to Lady and Captain Beornmund.

"I do not wish to offend her ladyship by putting my back to her," I said politely.

"Under the circumstance I do understand. Thank you for your consideration," Lady Beornmund said dropping her head to me.

With such impeccable manners, I chose to sit.

Lord Grey Hull walked back toward the entrance of the room, taking up the seat nearest Duke Leicester whose condemnation meant to intimidate me out of testifying. Frank, who followed me from a distance, came to me, and put a hand on my shoulder.

"Millie, this is Duke Leicester's Barrister, Mr Athill. He is going to ask you a few questions. Please answer to the best of your ability," Frank said caressing my shoulder, then he stepped back toward the Beornmund's with great gravity at seeing me so vulnerable.

Mr Athill, a man whose large nose took up his face making slits of his eyes, raised his heavy eyebrows in condemnation. Something in me raged instead of feared this man as he stood at the front of the room for all to see, like he might open a ball.

"Mrs Hadleigh, I understand that on November 20 of this year you went to a pawn shop and retrieved a set of pearls," he said quickly like he could get me to say something wrong.

"No, Sir. On November 20 we met with a pawn shop owner who informed us a man matching the honorable Lord Claude Beornmund's description came and confronted a woman matching The Viscountess, Lady Constance Beornmund's description, on 29 of July this year about her

The Basra Pearls

pawning pearls that belonged to the Beornmund estate. At that time, Lord Beornmund took possession of the pearls."

"You cannot be certain it was The Viscountess the shop keeper spoke of. You will not identify her, since you only heard second hand," he said.

"The shopkeeper is available to identify her, I am sure. I believe he did so in the inquest, did he not?" I said feigning confusion.

"He has withdrawn his statement. We are only looking for yours at this time," he snapped.

"Well, then it is my testimony that the women described looked like the Viscountess. She has a dreadfully telling dead spot in her bottom lip," I said calmly, but felt the fire grow inside me. I was not to be bullied by these men who could not keep themselves to one home, and believed they owned all the world, people included. Well, if the Uncle would not testify, I would testify for him.

"You spoke to a woman on the street in the neighborhood of Pimlico, and she described to you how Lord Beornmund died," the barrister asked.

"Yes, the clerk, who was identified as Lord Beornmund in my presence by certain bodily markers, fell in the street--"

"Was anyone near him when he fell?" he asked.

"A woman doing her work in a door stoop. His mistress was not present. The very women described and identified as the Viscountess, Lady Constance Beornmund by the shop keeper--"

"You will refrain from identifying her. It is not your testimony to give," he snapped. I nodded and taking a deep breath, I continued:

"The woman on the street in Pimlico said the mistress of the clerk--"

"There is no proof of adultery. The lady was not caught in criminal conversation."

I looked at him astounded. The Viscountess was with child. Was that not proof criminal conversation occurred?

"You asked me what the woman on the street said. She called the woman his mistress," I said.

"The woman who found Lord Beornmund ill and tried to nurse him back to health cannot be identified as a mistress," he insisted.

"You asked me what the woman on the street said. She identified the woman as his mistress," I said sternly. "She also said the woman stayed four nights under Lord Beornmund's protection in the same room. It is a mouthful, but I can describe her thus?"

"No," he stammered.

"Very well, the mistress came out of number three with a knife. After she was certain Lord Beornmund was dead, the mistress then stabbed him. The mistress picked up the bundles with Lord Beornmund's blood on them, and took them to the shopkeeper. We later found the very bundles with the blood still upon them. They had been pledged, identifying the mistress to be the same woman who pawned the set of pearls."

"I did not ask you to identify the mistress... ur the other woman," the barrister said as a few of the men grew uncomfortable under my precise information.

"No, again that would be easy work for the shopkeeper," I said. I glanced at Duke Leicester as the barrister consulted his notes. His Grace looked furious and the Viscountess blinked innocently. She knew she had nothing to fear. The peers – the men meant to act as her jury – looked uncomfortable, not because they would convict her, but because they meant to ignore all this information and claim the case not found.

If they meant to act against her, they would look outraged. They did not want to face this situation but get it over with. Almost as if they had to, as though the Duke of Leicester held something over them. The only reason Mr Bethell called me in was so they would be more uncomfortable dismissing it. But why? Mr Bethell did not look like a man who still fought for justice.

Watching Duke Leicester digesting my words while growing in irritation gave Mr Bethell such a look of satisfaction. I could not help thinking Mr Bethell wished the man to know he was doing him a favor dismissing his sister, and at some time in the future it would have to be repaid. Is that how things really worked, this for that, favor for favor? Did justice live in Frank's breast alone?

"Did you speak to the woman who rented a room to Lord Beornmund, under his guise of a clerk?" the barrister finally asked. I could see his purpose was to cast blame on Lord Beornmund himself.

"Yes, Sir," I said.

"Did she give reason for Lord Beornmund putting himself into such filthy conditions?" he asked. The faux jury looked at me with curiosity. Very well. If the Duke of Leicester wanted an exhibition that these men had to dismiss as a favor to him, it would not be one that made me look ridiculous.

"His reasoning is quite simple to see. His landlady had no idea of his real name, but she revealed Lord Beornmund was rather obsessed with pawn shops," I continued. "His ruse began three days after he learned his pearls had been stolen. Will you not conclude he was looking for his family heirloom? The pearls were very important to him, worth a substantial amount of money and he condemned thievery in his own home."

A few of the gentlemen looked down uncomfortably. If they truly believed the only sin the Viscountess committed was pawning the pearls, then I would suppose Lord Beornmund put himself lower to find them. When he got cholera because of it, did she not still kill him in a way?

"I did not ask your opinion, madam," Mr Athill said trying to recover, while glancing to the side of him where Duke Leicester sat glaring at me across the room. I was thankful not to be directly in front of him, breathing his hot breath. He gave one quick nod to the barrister and Mr Athill said, "I am done questioning this woman."

Mr Bell took over.

"Did the landlady admit Lord Beornmund, who put himself in such low conditions, had grown ill because of it?"

"She did not. He was fine one day and gone the next. She said he was the picture of health until his mistress came." I tried not to smile. I swallowed it down and said, "She feared the mistress. She thought her…a… a harpy. The mistress brewed all sorts of concoctions for Lord Beornmund. The landlady did not understand snuff, and found Lord Beornmund's need for it a strange part of the mistress's…heathen ritual," I said the last two words emphatically hoping Mr Athill had read the inquest through.

Likely all these men had partaken Viscountess Beornmund's snuff. A few, the most superstitious, shifted away from her. The Viscountess looked at me confused. Certainly, she hadn't thought I may ruin her reputation among the Ton, but then if she cared, she would not act such the fool.

"He was not ill until the – do you prefer we use the term 'mistress' or 'harpy'," Mr Bell asked Mr Athill, his lip twitching.

"His constitution cannot be used to living in squalor. No one can think Lord Beornmund murdered," Mr Athill snapped, concerned by the way the men suddenly listened to me.

"He lived in the same manner for a month before growing ill," I said. "The woman on the street said Lord Beornmund whistled the last time she saw him before the mistress came. After the Viscountess…"

"You cannot say it was her for certain. We are only here to prove a murder occurred. It did not," Mr Athill snapped at me.

"After the mistress came to stay, he grew sick. In his final moments, he fell down in the street, shaking violently," said Mr Bell. "The woman thought he may have been cursed. He only stopped shaking after he died."

"Clearly, he was sick, violently so," Mr Athill said.

"The stabbing must also have been violent. Whilst the mistress, or harpy, plunged a knife into Lord Beornmund's chest, the woman on the street pulled her child away, affeered the lunatic woman would turn the knife on them," I retorted.

"Clearly a blowse making her story more interesting over chatter broth," Mr Athill quickly stammered showing his frustration with me.

"Really, Sir!" Mr Bell snapped.

"Excuse me, My Lady," he said bowing to Lady Beornmund.

Mr Athill turned from me, muttering something. Mr Bell then questioned me in detail. Mr Athill looked from Mr Bell to me while we spoke. I was shining a light on the Viscountess he did not like. Some of the gentlemen were growing uncomfortable listening to me. Surely none of them would harass the Viscountess for her snuff again.

The most uncomfortable looking man had plump lips, a button nose, and large eyes. He looked like an older version of Lady Charlotte's beau. Duke Leicester must have held something over him by the way he sweated and glanced behind me at Lady Beornmund.

Mr Athill must have decided he could not get me to slip up, nor did he wish for Mr Bell to continue to question me about the dried blood on the bundle that apparently disappeared. When Mr Bell drew breath, Mr Athill turned to Lady Beornmund, and with far more respect said:

"My Lady, Viscountess Beornmund already admitted she took the pearls, mistaking them for a trinket. Pawning was something she and her father did for sport when he brought her to the city. He had just died, and she was in mourning… lonely for him. It was an honest mistake. She did not know what to do so she tried to recover the price and buy them back. Has she not been punished enough? She is delicate. Look at her weeping before you," he said pointing to the Viscountess who did her best to look affected.

"My Lady, before this committee decides the fate of this young woman, can it not at least be acknowledged that she is your goddaughter. Can you not consider her?" the barrister asked.

"We are here about my son, not only my husband," Lady Beornmund said, "I do not care about the pearls, or what she chose to do instead of admitting her guilt. She has taken my son from me. Is not a son more to a woman than a goddaughter? Perhaps she should have considered her godmother before she poisoned him."

"Nothing of the kind has been proven. Your son, even by your own admission, was living in a… reckless way. There is no sign of purposeful poisoning, My Lady," he said.

"The snuff she left in my son's room killed two animals in the investigation," she said.

"We have already submitted the Viscountess did experiment with some of her snuff choices, Some of the exotic plants your son brought her may have, unbeknownst to her, done further harm to her husband, but nothing more than he did to himself. How was she supposed to know? It was the burden of Captain Beornmund to know if the plants could cause harm before he gave them to her."

"Careful where you take this line of questioning, Sir" Mr Bell bellowed. "The young man could not have known she would powder the plants and add them to her snuff."

"We are in no way saying that Captain Beornmund knew the plants could cause harm, or gave them to the Viscountess knowing she regularly made snuff. But as heir apparent now, he certainly has more to gain from the death of his father and brother than the Viscountess," he said quickly, eyeing the noble jury to be sure they agreed with him. Many looked skeptical of this theory, especially after they were expected to ignore mine that was supported by actual witnesses.

Mr Athill cut off, and did not pursue accusing a highly decorated officer in Her Majesty's navy, who was out of the country protecting the Kingdom when his father died. Turning to his faux jury, Mr Athill said, "To go to the trouble and expense of a trial is pointless as Lady Constance can easily plead her belly. She is with child, the heir of the Beornmund line. She will be acquitted of all charges. The only purpose a trial would serve is to drag the illustrious names of two noble families through the news: the names Beornmund and Leicester will be salacious gossip on the filthy lips of the lowest commoners. But I suppose all that is left is to take a vote."

The Beornmund barrister took another turn at restating the evidence amassed against the Viscountess, starting with the father's death, and ending with the son's, but I could see in the eyes of these nobleman she did not seem capable of the acts she was being accused of. After all, there was not aggression, nor willful force in her feminine nature. She was not capable of such an act as double murder. Especially not in the most delicate act of becoming a mother.

The vote was taken. Only one of the seven peers present voted to send it to trial, Lord Grey Hull. Instead of keeping the results of his inquest, Mr Bethell charged the coroner to destroy all record of the accusations.

After the proceedings ended, the noble jury donned their hats and cloaks and left that they may not miss teatime. The nobleman with plump lips approached Lady Beornmund and said, "Leon is returned to London. He insists he will not leave for Christmas until your lovely daughter is allowed to come to us."

"Really, Sir, we will be in mourning. You chose your side. You may tell your son whatever you must, but he will not be admitted to my drawing room again," she said angrily and moved away from him.

"Perhaps we will speak again when you have a chance to…" his voice drifted off when it was clear she would not turn back to him.

Chapter Thirty-six

Lady Beornmund came to me and I stepped away from my chair to take the shaky hand she offered.

"Thank you for defending them, Mrs Hadleigh," she whispered.

"I am sorry my truth could not be heard," I said squeezing her hand. Duke Leicester came quickly to us as if I were trying to convince Lady Beornmund of something. I could see he thought me the slanderous villain in his poor sister's story. When he reached us, he tried to dismiss me with a head nod, as he would a servant, but Lady Beornmund held tightly to my hand. I could see she wished me to stay. I did not budge.

In the strangest, familiar way, he said, "Auntie Lily, now that this is all cleared up, we must decide what to do with Constance."

"You know what I want," the Viscountess said, joining our little group with a simper.

"You will please not use that girlish act here and now," Captain Beornmund snapped. "We all know you are play acting."

The Viscountess jolted a little but said, "Play acting, for years, years of the simpleton so my father would not notice I was grown and send me to have a season where I might find a noble man to marry. Is that the act to which you are referring?"

Captain Beornmund balked and went quiet. Lady Beornmund, clearly more accustomed to this sudden intelligence in the Viscountess, turned to the duke and asked:

"What can you expect from us, Philip?"

"The inquest has been overturned. In good faith we must all move forward. Constance wishes to retire to the country house. Since she carries your heir, it would be in everyone's interest if she and Hugh married," Duke Leicester said in a calm manner. "It will show a measure of goodwill for our families to come together and overcome this unpleasantness."

I realized whom the Hugh his grace spoke of when I looked over at Captain Beornmund and his mouth hung open, but no words came out.

"It is unfortunate you have forgotten, Phillip, that Augustus had surgery when he was five, it left him very unlikely to produce an heir. Though your barrister danced around the matter, we all know Constance is just far enough along that it could only be Claude's child," Lady Beornmund said fuming.

"Auntie Lily, the child is in your daughter's womb. In this manner it will be your heir," he said sternly.

"Phillip, I was not aware that my husband's bastard children were able to inherit. There are a few in front of your sister's if it be the case."

Duke Leicester was left speechless. The Viscountess sat hard in my chair, shocked. This idea had never occurred to her.

"Sadly, Claude died before he could provide for the child or legitimize it," Lady Beornmund said crossing her arms, and setting her angry jaw defiantly.

"If the child is seen as Augustus's, all will be righted," Duke Leicester said.

"All will be quieted you mean! This is not right. You cannot expect me to take her into my home as if nothing has happened," Lady Beornmund said.

"She and Hugh have always gotten on well. If they marry it will hush all this up. I will give her the property my father offered them so long ago as another dowery," he said, flustered.

"I could never marry her," Captain Beornmund said.

The Viscountess stood.

"You could not... you... This is all because of you," said the Viscountess. "If you had just married me in the first place, we could even now be on our own estate with children and wealth from the ample number of tenants my father's unentailed land provides. Or when that did not suffice for you, a year later he offered to place you in the government that you might receive wages far above what a captain can make. You would not take it. Why couldn't you just have done the right thing and married me back then?" she raged.

"I asked. You refused."

"I refused to run away," she snapped.

"You refused me. I only refused to be your father's lacky," he said.

"My father would have seen to us, and your father, who is a horrible, stingy man, would never have any say over our living," she said angrily. Holding her belly, she began to cry.

"Let us be clear. I did that," Lady Beornmund said.

"What?" The Viscountess croaked, and stopped crying immediately.

"My Lord lavished upon Augustus everything to the point of ridiculous excess over guilt from the past, from his medical incident. It disgusted him Augustus wanted so much, and yet he still gave. When he was hurt, and at home laid up among us, he saw Augustus for the first time in years. My Lord witnessed Augustus's behavior, his desperate struggle to be content, his unhappiness even, so I finally convinced him to cut Augustus off. Claude gave him only the essentials so he might grow up. When Augustus married you, I convinced My Lord to put all of your doweries into the estate that it might be saved for you in your later life and not dwindled away in a year's time. I hoped you might learn all the money in the world would not make you happy. It is all your mother ever wished for you – your happiness."

"You did this to me!" she whispered in disbelief.

"No child. You did this to yourself. You always act in a superior way with your diamonds and titles. It keeps you from friendships and love. Yet those are where joy lives."

"My happiness has always been with Hugh," she retorted. She showed she was not capable of understanding what Lady Beornmund explained. Rather, she shifted the subject so she might not have to admit she made a mistake and killed the wrong parent.

"Constance, did you truly believe… did you think I could marry the woman who killed my father and brother?" Captain Beornmund asked.

"Do not say such things," she said angrily. "This is all your fault, and you don't take any responsibility. I love you. I have always loved you. And now when everything is righted. Your family can grow straight again. How can you turn your back on me?"

"That is the problem, Constance. I could never turn my back on you, not without fear you would plunge a knife into it," he said.

"Come, Hugh! That is not fair. She stabbed a dead man so he would be identified. She did not kill him," Duke of Leicester said.

"Phillip," Captain Beornmund said. "If you truly believe that Constance has done nothing wrong, you take her into your house, but be warned, do not use her snuff, especially if you have displeased her in any way."

The duke's face contorted for just an instant in concern. He spent the last few days ensuring no one would find out his sister was suspected while controlling the outcome of the committee. He had not stopped to consider his sister might actually be guilty.

"Very well. Constance will retire from society in the country with her plants. She is so careful with life," he said more to comfort himself.

"Yes, but only after a good pruning can the parts of the plant she deems worthy thrive," I said. "Being told her whole life of her superiority, she deemed herself the master gardener."

Ignoring me, Duke Leicester said, "What shall we do with the child?"

"Give it to a nice country family to raise. You must be sure it has an education when the time comes if it is male," Lady Beornmund said, stone-faced. "I believe that is the case with these things."

"Auntie," Duke Leicester pleaded.

"She took my family. We were not perfect, but they were what I had. She took them," she said.

Chapter Thirty-seven

"This will not do," the Viscountess said imploringly to Captain Beornmund, "If I had run away with you, if I had displeased Papa, and run away with you, where would we be even now?"

"Married I suppose, or perhaps I would be the corpse instead of my brother," he said.

"Don't be dramatic," she said.

I'm sure my mouth dropped open. Certainly, his assertion had merit since he would not have had any jewels to give her.

"Thankfully, we did not run away," he said. "You love the games you play, the bending others to your will as you would a vine, or topiary. It will be best for you to give the child to a family so you do not twist it all up."

"We could raise the child together, and I would be... I would give it everything it ever wanted. I could give you everything you wanted," she begged.

"You tried once. The only thing that has changed since then is I no longer want you as a wife," he snapped.

"Who would you want besides me?" She laughed in her aggravating way.

"That is who I want," he said. Startled I looked up to find his hand drawn toward me.

"Excuse me," I said my face burned hot as I looked to Frank who still spoke quietly to Lord Grey Hull and Mr Bell.

"You are loyal, and clever – unabashedly clever. I have seen the way you look at your husband. I wish to be looked at like that by a clever woman. I honor you," Captain Beornmund said bowing to me.

"Thank you," I said thinking I may shrivel up from embarrassment.

"She looks like a child whose been overexposed to the sun. How can that be your ideal?" the Viscountess lashed out.

"She is, to the very core of her, good. You killed my father and brother to give me a title I did not want. I was content with my lot. I love the sea. You could never accept me as I am."

"This isn't about you. Together we are meant to raise the Lord of the Beornmund from the dirt in rebirth."

"No, Constance, no. You must let go of the idea. I will never be your husband."

"After all your father did to restore the line, and this is how it is to be resolved," the Viscountess said in disbelief.

"Restore the line, or destroy our honor. He's known you since you were a child. He watched you grow," Lady Beornmund said, her anger and grief overwhelming her. Thankfully I still held her hand so I could catch her as she sagged.

"He did not wish to," the Viscountess comforted. "He apologized many times, but swore it was the only way to restore the family line. Augustus couldn't do it."

She proved her attachment to Lady Beornmund real, perhaps the only real attachment she had.

"We did not know that for certain," Lady Beornmund said, hesisitating.

"We do, Aunty," said the Viscountess. "He didn't even notice me at the end, obsessed with his trinkets."

"That is rather rich coming from you," I said looking at her as Captain Beornmund sat his mother in my seat.

"I earned everything I have," she said and the diamond bracelet she always wore slid down her wrist.

"In the end," I said, "Lord Beornmund had to be sure he gave the Viscount the title and an heir. I suppose in his strange, unorthodox way he was trying to fix his mistake, not his family line."

"He mentioned it several times," the Viscountess agreed.

"Why couldn't you just let him go then?" Lady Beornmund asked, looking up at the Viscountess. "Why not let him move away and live his...." She looked up to gather some kind of inner strength, and said, "... his American dream. We would have assumed the child was a miracle. There would never be a body to find."

The Viscountess glanced over at Frank and Mr Bell. She would not answer.

Why didn't she just let Lord Beornmund leave?

Did she, like the landlady, learn to love him? No, her fixation with Captain Beornmund left no room. She did not hesitate to give him the tainted snuff even though he showed sorrow for... he was sorry for bringing her into the widow's home... I stopped mid-thought. He meant to make the widow's son an apprentice; he couldn't do that from America.

"He decided not to leave after all?" I asked more as a question, with a little laugh.

Viscountess Beornmund flinched, her eyes went wide, and she gave me the most genuine look of surprise.

"I am not communing with the dead," I said. "Miss Keppel said he changed. His landlady said he had long debates in the evenings with the other tenant, a scholar. She used the term 'at first,' to describe him, and then moved to 'after a time,' indicating he changed." I watched the Viscountess, who still looked shocked.

"He often tried to be a better man," Lady Beornmund said.

"He played at living the life of a middlish man, and found he was content with chores, splitting wood for the widow's fire, getting dirt under his fingernails," I surmised.

Everyone stopped talking and listened with rapt attention. So I continued:

"The Uncle said his hands were those of a working man. The lord whistled, content. The widow was sinking into poverty, her son losing his chances at education because he must work.

"Lord Beornmund taught the boy to read," I related to them. "The boy cleans the machines for the factories. His mother prays over him all day that he still has his limbs when he comes home. What, if at some point, the mother mentioned being thankful that at least she did not have to send him into the most dangerous places of all, a nobleman's mines," I said.

The silence continued as everyone listened.

"I have found more purpose working on a ship than I thought possible," Captain Beornmund agreed.

"We found a letter to your mother. He apologized. He asked if they could start anew and make the name Beornmund mean something. She thought it the same old promises, but what if it was something new, the words of a changed man?" I asked.

"He…the tone of the note could not be read for sincerity since the last time I saw him he was terribly angry about the loss of his pearls. It is all I could remember," Lady Beornmund said.

"Could he have meant it when he said he would be a force of change in England?"

We all were quiet. We looked to the Viscountess. She shook her head and closed her eyes in annoyance. She wanted to tell us of his folly. Finally, she decided it was not admitting guilt as we already knew she saw Lord Beornmund last.

"He said England may be saved from the bottom up. Can you imagine? He said there were still those who worked and tried for each other—those in the slums," she said.

"He happened upon a generous situation," I said.

"He would not give me or Augustus a farthing more, his own kin, but meant to change other people's lives, as he called it. And you would call that generous? He spoke like the squalor deserved his money. He meant to find his ring. Then go back to his mines, and bring up worthy lowers, as if there is such a thing. To search out worthiness in the lowers – like a nut from a tree – and put them into positions of overseers that everyone might earn together. He said he would never have another child work in his mines again. What are the urchins to do if not searching out the mines?" She leaned back content she had done the right thing.

"They could go to school," Captain Beornmund said.

"If he meant to strive for redemption why not give you back the pearls?" I asked, knowing she still saw them as her prize for some reason.

"To be cruel. He kept the claim ticket and promised to keep my secret as long as I... he meant to have an heir."

"You could not escape him," I said.

"He was heartsore over what he did to Augustus, but to... Couldn't he see Hugh would likely produce...to be so backwards in his efforts," Lady Beornmund stammered, turning red.

"He thought, as I did, that Hugh loved me, and would never get over that love to have an heir with another," the Viscountess concluded, glaring at the captain.

I would not hear her rant about her love again. Captain Beornmund grew uncomfortable and his guilt over her deeds did not need to be helped along.

"If he meant to stay in England, why did he give the pearls to his illegitimate daughter?"

"So, I could not have them," she hissed. "He was going to send her and Miss Keppel away. Miss Keppel would never be satisfied living in diminished circumstances. He meant to submit the entire family to Augustus. But not the actress. She would be allowed to escape, and if you are to be believed, he would have let his brat take my pearls with her."

"He gave them to her that she may always know," Lady Beornmund said closing her eyes and a tear fell out. "That is why he gave them to Charlotte on her fourteenth birthday. After he moved out of our house, he gave her the pearls so she would know her papa loved her, and she was a noblewoman."

"Father had his moments of generosity," Captain Beornmund said.

"Augustus also had moments of true kindness," said Lady Beornmund. "If you had not entered my family, what could we have become?"

"I saved you," the Viscountess stammered in disbelief. Defending herself, she said, "He meant to use his own money to pay miners. His ideas about not needing so much was… he would have destroyed your family name, your… he would have destroyed you."

For the first time, perhaps in many years, tears fell down the Viscountess's face.

"Oh, Constance, to go to such lengths," Captain Beornmund said with pity for her.

"Clearly I have always loved you, more than you loved me," she said with a sob. Her tears fell real and beyond control.

"Does anyone really wish to be loved so far beyond ration?" Captain Beornmund asked. He glanced at me to answer, since the Viscountess folded her arms in silent anger.

"In a dream perhaps, but it seems quite overwhelming in reality. I am no romantic, so I cannot say," I answered.

Chapter Thirty-eight

Duke Leicester, seeing the women crying, stepped back from speaking with his barrister across the room.

"Ah, look now. You have your cry out and reconcile. All will be made right in time," he said.

Lady Beornmund stood and said bravely, "The best I can do for her is to hush up the matter. I will...I will take the child."

"Mother!" Captain Beornmund said.

"I must do this," she said brushing him aside. "I will come for the child. Pray for a girl, because it will not be heir, you understand. Hugh will have his own heir. I think it best if the child has nothing to do with its mother. She has wreaked such havoc on my family. All I can do is pray your departed mother will see my efforts with the child and acquit me the promise I made to look out for Constance. Clearly her will was set so firm by your father I could do nothing for her," Lady Beornmund said quietly.

I watched all this, captivated, and flinched when Frank came up behind me taking my arm, indicating his business complete.

"Your Grace," I said before moving away. He looked down upon me impatiently. I almost stopped myself, but knew in my heart I must warn him, acquit myself of his life if he died like the Viscount Beornmund.

"I understand your father would not let Constance marry Captain Beornmund until he was made?" I asked.

"Yes," he said.

"He preferred Viscount Beornmund to his brother for her?" I asked.

"He wished for the heir."

"How long after your sister was set to marry the Viscount did your father get sick?"

"Excuse me?" he said affronted.

"He died shortly after her marriage. That's what I was told. Was your father a sickly man, or did he take to his bed all at once just after your sister agreed to marry the wrong man?"

Duke Leicester looked at me and I could read the fear in his eyes.

"It is a lovely bracelet she wears; it was your mother's I believe," I said.

"Yes," he said in a hoarse whisper, stricken by my implication. I could see in his wild eyes, searching mine, some understanding. His father's illness must have been unforeseen and swift. Duke Leicester would have been sent to school when his sister was just a child, but perhaps some whispers of her reached him, because the fear in his eyes creased his brow into concern.

"When your father died, the estate fell to you, but your mother's personal jewels went to your sister?" I asked. He said nothing but looked at his sister, who looked daggers at me.

"I have done my duty by you, and now be it upon your own head to protect your family from her pruning," I bowed and finished, "Your Grace."

Turning to the Viscountess, I said, "I suppose you will not go to Newgate, but my husband will be made. Between us a draw, which is better because I have no jewels to give you, and you cannot be without the ones you have."

I bowed.

"I hate you," she hissed.

"I understand. I see the world as it is, and cannot always be liked by romantics determined not to. I will say I did not think it possible to wake such a person as you from your dream state. Clearly you are not capable of opening your eyes, but Lord Beornmund changed. At the end he woke. That is something I will think on. Goodbye to you, Lady Constance," I said.

Lord Grey Hull moved into our space, unaware of what was being said. "Frank, I believe you are expected for dinner at my house," he said. "Lady Beornmund, I would be honored if you and your son can make a small family dinner tonight. I believe Lady Charlotte may need your presence. She is brought very low."

"I shall send her flowers. She has always been such a pretty young thing," Duke Leicester said looking between me and his sister, unsure what to think. With sincerity he said, "I truly hope your family recovers."

"Thank you, Phillip," Lady Beornmund took the hand he offered and said, "I shall pray for the safety of yours. I can see the rest will be for God to sort."

Frank led me from the room with Captain Beornmund and his mother.

"My Lady," I said as we waited for the carriage to be brought.

"Yes, dear," she answered.

"Would it be very impertinent of me to ask if Miss Sarah Smith be returned to her post as your daughter's lady maid? She is devoted to Lady Charlotte and I believe may help her in the coming months."

She smiled at me. "That is a very considerate thought. I will see to it. Thank you," she said dipping her head to me.

"Also," I said blushing, "I believe you should read the note Lord Beornmund left you with sincerity. The landlady mentioned he spoke several times about his wife and partner being a strong, good lady. He respected you greatly."

"I will. Thank you," Lady Beornmund smiled and took my arm. Captain Beornmund glanced at me with admiration. I smiled, but looked to the ground embarrassed. Frank squinted and took my hand to lead me to the carriage as it approached so Captain Beornmund could care for his mother.

The drawing room was a very somber that evening. Lady Charlotte declared she could not go back to the mansion and asked if she could stay with me and Myra while the preparations were made by Captain Beornmund to go back to their country estate.

Frank could not deny the girl our company, but seemed a little forlorn I would not go home with him. I feared going home with him. Watching him across the table over dinner made me hunger for him in a way that scared me.

Chapter Thirty-nine

The next day Jasper miraculously recovered from his illness and came with Frank to call at Lord Grey Hull's home. I could see he meant to take over Frank's pupillage. The very sight of him made me ill.

"With the family moving back to the country, Miss Keppel is ready to make her move to the colonies," Jasper said. "She has requested our company before she forfeits her house."

"Mine as well?" I asked surprised.

"You will be needed," Jasper said putting a hand to my shoulder in strange tenderness.

"Can you be spared, Millie?" Frank asked, scowling at Jasper. I quickly moved away to Myra.

"I know it is time you go home, but Charlotte depends on you so," Myra said smiling. "Go now, but if you will come back one more night, I will have your things sent to your rooms on the temple grounds tomorrow."

"Thank you," I said kissing her hand.

"I mean to be home by next Christmas. I expect a large party at Grey Manor for the holiday. I wish you and Millie to be a part of it, Frank," Myra said.

"We will commit to it," Frank said bowing from behind me.

"I do not think you can be spared," Jasper interjected. We all looked at him.

"It is a year away," Frank said. "I will likely have gone to the bar by then."

"That is very presumptuous," Jasper said. I thought him sour because Myra did not extend the invitation to him.

"I think you must find a way," Myra said in a manner that felt like a threat. Jasper said nothing, but bowed to her, taking his leave.

I kissed Myra and caught up to Frank, twisting my arm in his and taking his hand again so we might not be separated.

He helped me into a carriage. We rode to Miss Keppel's house in silence, which was odd for Jasper. He looked nervous, or guilty. I couldn't be sure which. When we were let into the place, it really looked like Miss Keppel was leaving. Before, it almost appeared like the signs of moving were a scene on the stage and not real. Now trunks were loaded, and everything was in upheaval. We stepped into the sitting room, but there was nowhere to sit.

"I see you have crated the pictures," Frank said as they lined the main hallway. "You will take them with you, then."

"My butler insists," she said. "It is clear he has more instruction than I do."

"It seems you have things well in hand," Frank said, indicating he did not see why we were here. Neither of us felt inclined to tell the woman Lord Beornmund meant to leave her after he gave Rosanna a parting gift.

"Yes, well, there is a proposition I must make you," she said.

"What is that?" Frank asked.

"If you will take me over to America, establish me in my house, with my gold, I will give you and Mr Shaw ten thousand pounds each," she said.

I said nothing. I only looked at Frank. That was wealth he could not earn in years, possibly ever. He looked stunned.

"You would propose I leave my wife, my pupillage, and go across the ocean on a treasure hunt?" Frank asked.

"You could do it, Old Boy. I'll watch out for Millie," Jasper said, "She can run our investigative firm. I'll walk around with her, pretending she is just taking notes for me like you do."

"Why don't you go with Miss Keppel?" Frank asked.

"I am partial to you," she said, sidling up to Frank, taking his arm.

"I have much in London to keep me occupied. You have nothing," Jasper said as if our lives, not filled with teas and balls, were not as important as his.

"I do not like this," I stammered. I was weary of Jasper and weary of this woman flirting with my husband as if I were not even present.

"Come Millie, we will be happy together," Jasper said.

"What do you mean, together," Frank asked pushing away from Miss Keppel, who backed away, affronted.

"I wrote to your brother so he might give you character," Jasper said.

"When?" Frank asked.

"At the same time I wrote and offered you a job."

"You already knew my character," Frank said.

"My brother insisted, before he… before I sent you a train ticket. Anyhow, your brother told me all about your arrangement; the two of you are childhood friends forced into marriage. He painted a picture for me," Jasper said.

"He did so because he did not wish for me to leave the parish," Frank snapped.

"That was before you had even proposed to me," I said, realizing Frank never meant to leave me behind.

"I… I was plucking up my courage," said Frank. "I went to my brother as a support, but he could not be one for me. He feared he would lose the magistrate if I left," Frank said.

"I do remember how guilty he looked the day you offered for me," I said.

"You are a clever girl, Millie," Jasper said with admiration, "Frank, I need her. She keeps me organized and sees like you do. You can be free of her, and she can help me."

"Do you wish to be free of me," I asked looking up at Frank. He was livid. He looked down at me, and I realized he was not angry with me, but the fire in his blue eyes somehow tortured me because I had not kissed him on the mouth yet.

"What exactly did my brother say?" Frank asked, his teeth clenched.

"Millie ran away with a fellow, but it did not work out, and you had to patch the thing up. I do not mind her past. I will set her up in a nice situation, keep her company while you take Miss Keppel to find her fortune. Miss Keppel dotes on you and Millie does not actually love you," Jasper said.

"That is not true," I snapped. "I love him."

"What?" both Jasper and Frank said together.

"I love Frank very much. He is my husband and the only man I have ever loved," I said. It was the truth.

"Oh, Millie, poor girl. He cannot want you when he could have… he will be with Miss Keppel now."

"Maybe so, but you will never have me. You have been sadly misinformed making such assumptions about my character," I said, hurt.

"I know exactly what kind of girl you are," Jasper said right before Frank balled his fist and launched his whole-body weight into punching Jasper's face.

"Stay away from my wife," he yelled. Jasper fell almost into Miss Keppel, who could not move away fast enough. Jasper scrambled backward, unsure if Frank was going to follow up. Frank stood his ground.

"Fine, don't go make us a fortune, but don't bother coming back to my chamber's tomorrow. I will dismiss you and see to it no one else will work with you," Jasper said holding his bleeding face.

"You are a sham, and everyone knows it. I am not your pupil, Jasper. You are mine. You do not know the law any wit, and have never tried to earn your silks. I will go to Mr Bethell myself tomorrow to request our situation be dissolved. It will be your ruin, not mine," Frank said. Jasper let go of his nose to say something, but blood spurted everywhere. His face was no longer symmetrical. Jasper could say nothing, trying to stem the flow of his blood, while keeping it out of his mouth.

Miss Keppel stepped forward like she might speak to Frank, but I balled my fists. I would strike her if she tried. She backed up to find something for Jasper to stop the dark red mess falling to her bare floor.

"We are finished here, Frank," I said glaring at her.

"Yes, I believe we are, Millie," he said. Taking my hand, we left the room together.

"Millie, I have to get in front of this," Frank said after he lifted me into the carriage and climbed in after me.

"Are we going to make away with Jasper's carriage?" I asked.

"No, it is Lord Grey Hull's. I was always running from place to place, and he needed me quicker than I could go, hiring hackney's even. That is what he said at least. I think he did it to spare me the expense, but he has a curricle he and his wife prefer so I do not feel guilty."

"He is a good man, and does not seem to need his things so desperately as some noblemen do."

Frank smiled.

"I need to speak to Mr Bethell. I know him to be at Lincoln's Inn in Chancery Court and I may be able to catch him before he leaves. Will you go back to Myra, just for this night?"

"Of course," I said feeling my stomach lurch, and my heartbeat furiously. I had been so forward and he had not even acknowledged my declaration of love. Perhaps he did not believe it. I could not blame him.

"I will send a letter to Thomas when I finish with Mr Bethell. I mean to inform him we are no longer brothers," Frank said.

"No. Come now Frank, he will change. You could not expect him to send a note favorable to your leaving him?"

"But to tell a stranger--"

"Please. Wait a few days. Try to calm down before you write him. Think only of Captain Beornmund who has no brother left to reconcile with," I said.

"Millie... you know I don't wish for you to..."

I looked at him. He stammered, too afraid to tell me I didn't have to love him. How could I blame him for not believing my declaration? I had professed many times that I did not love him. Instead of plucking the courage to ask me if I'd been lying to Jasper, he said, "I do not prefer that woman."

"We are right for each other," I said, and I put my head on his shoulder, to hide from him. He put his arm around me.

"Is this a new jacket?" I asked. It smelled wrong.

"Mr Bell got it for me. He wanted me to look the gentleman to the committee of Lords. It did not help," he said.

"You look very nice, Sir," I said as the carriage stopped at Lord Grey Hull's house. Frank helped me down, but I knew he must hurry away. He would not leave until he saw me safely into the house so I rushed in. I'm sure it had nothing to do with my humiliation.

Chapter Forty

The next morning, I introduced Captain Beornmund to the young boy to whom his father had taken such a liking. He committed to helping him into a profession. The widow could hardly believe her luck, especially after she being harassed by the investigation, and then inquest of the lord her lodger turned out to be. Charlotte came with us, and by the end of the interview, the boy swore if she would wait to marry, he would do right by her.

While they explained to the widow what happened, I went down the alley way to the woman who'd been kind and given me warning.

"Well, you are a sneaky one," Alicia said, looking up at me, also having given witness at the inquest. She handed me the piece she darned, and moved back to sew a fine pattern upon silk.

"I am just from the country, and I do have to live in London for my Frank to thrive," I said grinning, sitting next to Alicia and minding my stiches.

"I still say you're a sneaky one," she said with half a smile. I sat helping her until the Beornmund's finished.

"I'll come by again sometime if you don't mind," I said when I stood. "I don't know many people in the city. I value the ones I can trust."

Alicia dipped her chin, but I bowed to her.

"Be off then, be off," she said waving me away, but she hummed a little as she worked her pile.

We all climbed back into the Beornmund carriage and Captain Beornmund said, "Thank you, Mrs Hadleigh."

"Yes of course," I said. "Now where are we off to?"

The Basra Pearls

"I need to settle with your husband," Captain Beornmund said. "May I see you back to Middle Temple?"

"Yes, please," I said hoping that meant I was finally going home. I did hate leaving my friends, but could not stand to be away from Frank any longer.

"Should not Mr Archer take care of the matter?" I asked.

"That man was warned twice my family was in danger. He did nothing. Not to mention he arranged for my mother to perjure herself, despite her asking him to find a better way. He will no longer be our solicitor. I am only sorry I cannot send him to be flogged. Some cannot learn their lessons any other way. I cannot work with a man I cannot trust," Captain Beornmund said, proving the estate would be run much like a ship in Her Majesty's navy.

Charlotte took my arm as was her custom when we walked near each other and said, "I am not sorry he is gone. He made me uncomfortable."

"He did stare at you in the most abysmal way. And you, Sir, will be a fine steward over the Beornmund estate," I said. I hoped he wouldn't take to flogging his servants. He bowed, but had a faraway look like he may be trying to find the Thames we could smell that would take him out to sea.

When we entered Middle Temple Grounds, I did not know exactly where to go. Jasper was no longer Frank's Master.

"Frank has been going through um… a transition," I said, "Perhaps if you will go to the Hall and take some tea, I will be able to find him. Mr Shaw, I suppose you know, is not the most reliable fellow, but his clerk is, and always knows the hubbub."

"Yes, of course," Captain Beornmund said. He and Charlotte went to the Hall. I could only think to visit Mr

Clarkson or go to my rooms. I was closer to Jasper's chambers, so I went quickly to find Mr Clarkson. I doubted Jasper would be there since his face was likely bruised and broken.

When I reached Jasper's chambers, I found Mr. Clarkson with a man who looked a bit like Jasper, but older.

"Excuse the interruption, Mr Clarkson," I said as he looked to be clearing Jasper's books.

"Mrs Hadleigh," he said bowing politely, and glancing at the other man. "May I present Mr James Shaw, Mr Jasper Shaw's eldest brother."

I bowed.

"Oh yes, I must speak to your husband," Mr Shaw said.

"I will go to our rooms and find him," I said looking to Mr Clarkson to find out if perhaps he had seen him. He gave me a slight shrug to indicate he had not, and I turned to leave.

"Ah, you are very pretty," Mr Shaw. He moved toward me ande took my arm to hold me back. Instantly uncomfortable, I pulled my arm from his grasp and backed away.

"I...uhm..." I looked at him wide-eyed. He examined me as if I were on display.

"Jasper said you were a beauty with a noble brow. It is a pity you were not born a few degrees higher."

"I am content with my level, Sir," I said and bowed. The door slammed open, and Frank ran in.

We all turned to stare at him.

"Is everything quite all, right?" I asked.

"I saw Captain Beornmund at the Hall and learned you were looking for me," Frank said out of breath, taking my hand and pulling me toward him.

Mr Clarkson, pointing to Mr James Shaw, introduced him to Frank.

"Is everything quite all right?" Frank asked, nervous, as it would be just like Jasper to make trouble over his nose.

"I am afraid I have rather unfortunate news. I received a letter this morning stating that my brother is eloping to America with Miss Maria Keppel, of all people. He has the idea of teaching the Brahmin Bostonians how high society is meant to be. New England indeed. Does one elope to America?"

"I suppose one can elope to America," I said, shrugging, and suddenly greatly relieved that those two were out of my life.

"I fear this must shock you, but he has given up practicing the law, and must give up being your master, though he said it was going so well."

"Very well, Sir," Frank said. He didn't bother to explain what really happened.

"I can repay the price of your pupillage," Mr Shaw said.

"I did not pay, but rather I investigated for his cases, therefor making it a mutually beneficial arrangement," Frank said.

"Oh, well that is a relief, though I am sorry you will have to find a new master."

"Thank you," Frank said bowing.

"I would give you all these books if you'll have them. I have no use for them," Mr Shaw said.

"That would be greatly appreciated. Thank you, Sir," Frank said. I smiled, remembering how he smelled them once.

"Very good. You can clear this place out and take whatever you like with you," Mr Shaw said happily, picking up his cane and hat, wishing to leave.

The Basra Pearls

"Yes, Sir, and if you like I will be sure it is in perfect order for the next tenant. You need not concern yourself with these details," Frank said grinning.

"Wonderful, mutually beneficial," Mr Shaw said. "You have until the day before Christmas when the lease is due." He put his hat on.

"Thank you, Sir," Frank said.

He opened the door and Captain Beornmund and his sister walked in.

"Is everything quite all right?" Captain Beornmund asked.

"Perfect," Frank said bowing again to Mr Shaw. Mr Shaw took the time to shake hands with Captain Beornmund, who was to inherit everything. I looked at the two men, who both admired me, but for different reasons.

"What happened here?" Charlotte asked quietly after Mr Shaw left.

Frank told her and Captain Beornmund all that happened. He told them of their father's American Dream, and the gold bars. How Jasper heard the term New England and thought he may as well go teach them how to be an English gentleman. Frank told it in such a diverting way we all laughed, including Mr Clarkson, whom I had not known could make such a delighted noise. When Frank finished, Captain Beornmund said, "Well, I believe this belonged to you anyway," pulling out a letter and handing it to Frank.

"What is this?" Frank asked.

"It is what Mr Archer promised you for finding out what happened to my father. It is Father's quarterly stipend from the estate, and once taken out, it cannot be given back if you wanted to."

"Sir, you give my character far too much valor. I thank you," Frank said putting the envelope into his satchel.

"I thank you. The letter Father wrote Mother before he died has taken on a whole new meaning. Old wounds seem to be healing in her. I bless the day you came to London," Captain Beornmund said bowing. Frank looked embarrassed, but bowed a little, thanking him again.

"What will you do now that Jasper has fled the country?" Charlotte asked to turn the subject.

"I went to Mr Bethell last night to explain what transpired with Jasper, and Mr Bell happened to be there. He said he would be happy to take me on as pupil."

"Oh, Frank! I am so glad for you," I said giving him both my hands.

"I knew you would be," he said kissing my forehead.

"The two of you have much to celebrate," Charlotte said, grinning at me, her eyes big. I blushed to the roots of my hair. I had forgotten in the rush of the moment I had professed my love for Frank, and he had not believed me. The humiliation of it was torture. I regretted telling Charlotte about it. She was too obvious in her removing of herself and her brother to leave us alone. Captain Beornmund was all confusion at her sudden need to visit a shop.

I waved and bowed, and was kissed by the lady who winked, of all things, and then left.

"Come, Mr Clarkson, let us take an early day, and tomorrow we will find you a new position," Frank said happily.

"Mr Bethell will see to me. He sent a note around this morning."

"Oh well, good luck to you, Sir. I will be sure you get your share of this," Frank said patting his satchel.

"Mr Shaw paid my wages through the end of December; I was never promised a percentage. I believe you earned that, Sir," Mr Clarkson said gathering his belongings

The Basra Pearls

in a carpet bag. "Tomorrow I will have these Chambers cleaned and send you anything of value."

"Thank you, Sir," Frank said.

"It is my pleasure; I hope you will consider me when the time for you to get your own clerk comes. I feel we could do much good together," he said.

"I would be honored," Frank said with a bow, and we walked out of the chambers so Mr Clarkson could finish his work and lock the door.

Down the hall a way, I asked, "Frank, I cannot stand it. Did we at least recover the thirteen pounds?"

He grinned at me and took the envelope out. Exaggerating the action, he broke the Beornmund seal. He unfolded the note, and stopped walking.

"What, what is it?' I asked thinking he still teased me.

He handed me the letter and tucked inside was a note written on the Bank of England for just under twelve thousand pounds.

"This! This is what they could not live on?" I asked astounded.

"This is only a quarter of the yearly 4% from the estate, I would suppose," Frank said looking at the letter.

"Thousands of men's wages in a quarter of a year, and they cannot manage on it?"

"We shall manage it splendidly," Frank said folding it up and securing it back in his satchel.

"Yes, Sir," I said happily.

"Would you like to move out of Middle Temple, find a snug place in the country? Live a quiet peaceful life together?"

"No, certainly not," I said surprised he would even suggest such a thing.

"Town is so cumbersome at times," Frank said confused.

"I… perhaps it is, but I feel with a quarter's allotment from Lord Beornmund you must go to the bar, set up your chambers and become the great man you were meant to be."

"I… you wish to stay in the city?" Frank said, surprised.

"Frank, even if your name was never upon it, as a boy you changed one law. What can you do as a man? Lord Beornmund learned children must be taken from factories or mines and sent to school. You can push such a law. Wages must be made fair, so children need not work from morning until night to support their parents. Those willing to work hard and long should see more reward than barely enough to eat."

"With you around, my dear Frank, those living in squalor may elevate themselves to food and clothing, a decent situation. Mr Bethell – and Lord Beornmund – are right. It is time those who are qualified creep their way up the ranks until the Quality, so busy at their balls, do not quite know how we came upon them."

Grinning, Frank took my hand and kissed it.

"It is you who will change the world, I think, not me," Frank said simply.

"We will do it together," I said.

"You can help me keep my chambers when the time comes."

"I would like that. I do like to be of use," I teased.

"Come, shall we go home then?"

"Yes please," I said leaning against his arm.

Chapter Forty-one

We went to our little apartment where I felt more at home than I had in Lord Grey Hull's mansion. Frank sat looking at me while I prepared us a little meal. I felt shy and awkward toward him, which was an odd sensation as we were always comfortable together.

I wanted our partnership to be more than what Lord and Lady Beornmund had. I wanted him to love me. Not just in the way we were, but in the romantic way. As we ate, I noticed his hand was swollen. After everything was put away, I went to my trunk and took out some ointment Aunt gave me upon our marriage.

"May I tend to your hand, Frank?" I asked.

"Please," he said holding it out to me. I rubbed ointment on him feeling a fire grow inside me as our skin made slippery rubbed together. I watched his hand. I wanted to put it around my waist with an ache I did not know how to fulfill.

"What is it, Millie?" Frank asked. I floundered. I did not know what to do, how to get him to kiss me. I needed Frank. He was my dream, and I was his. Some dreams could be made, the ones dreamt by facing them and trying for them, instead of inventing them. I'd been brave enough to let go of my mother's romantic fancies, brave enough to see myself and what I really wanted. Could I be brave enough to push until my dream was just my life? Seeing how serious I was, his smile fell.

"Millie, you are worrying me," he said. I said nothing, but in the bravest moment of my life I slid from my seat and moved onto his lap. Surprised, he said nothing but wrapped his arms around me.

"I... I want you to be kissed, Frank," I said quietly looking down at his face.

"Millie, I told you, it's fine. I don't expect that—" I stopped him by smashing my mouth against his, just as Titus Williams had done to me. It hurt a little, but I still tasted Frank, and it was satisfying. Especially when Frank tensed and started to kiss me back. It only lasted a moment. With great effort he pulled away from me.

"Millie, I … I don't want you to… I mean I want to kiss you… I'm not going to…," Frank stammered putting his forehead to mine. I could see he was torn between kissing me and being a gentleman. I looked him in the eyes and rambled out all the words I'd been thinking for a week.

"I was in earnest when I said I have always loved you. I just didn't know what love was supposed to be. I don't think it's the attraction I once felt for another, but I do feel that attraction now for you. This isn't just polite infatuation. It is…it is like an eruption inside me."

"An eruption," he said.

"But more important," I said, refocusing him, "I think love is how when our fathers died, we spent days together. You did not mind crying with me. And it's when I saw you… when you walked through that door and rescued me from Mr Williams, I wasn't surprised because you always come for me, Frank."

I hugged him again.

"I wanted you to go to London and succeed, even though I knew I would never be fine without you. I think that is love. And this overwhelming knowledge that together we can change the world – I think that is also love, Frank. But I want it to be a full love. I want to kiss you. I want us to be everything to each other. I don't want you to… to need anyone but me," I stammered, flustered.

"On that day, in my brother's parlor, when you told me to leave, but I could see you did not wish me too. I… I thought you could grow to love me, one day," Frank said reaching up and playing with the curls on my forehead.

"Was that your game? When you tried to force me to admit I did not understand love," I asked with a laugh.

"Your mother … She filled your head full of strange romantic notions of love. I thought it best if we came here and left your mother behind us. I thought maybe then you could learn to love me," he said.

"I did already love you; I just could not admit it to myself for fear of my mother. She was very demanding and unrealistic in her dream for me," I said.

"She held such a…."

"I do not wish to speak of her. I wish for you to kiss me," I said putting my forehead to his again, exasperated. That's all I really wanted. I burned with want of it. The tears started in my eyes, and I said, "I swear I do love you, Frank."

"I am savoring this moment. I have always loved you, Millie," he said. Sliding his fingers behind my head, he softly pulled me toward him. Slowly, gently, he stroked his lips against mine. I felt the rhythm of his kiss, the pattern that was Frank, and I easily matched it as it grew intense. My passing thought was that my husband was much better at kissing than Titus Williams had been. Then I lost myself in it.

Perhaps I would never understand romance, but I felt complete enough and loved. It is all I ever really wanted.

Made in United States
North Haven, CT
24 September 2023

41927426R00248